THE DARK WEDDING

by the same author

★

SEVEN RED SUNDAYS

WAR IN SPAIN

A MAN'S PLACE

MR. WITT AMONG THE REBELS

PRO PATRIA

THE
DARK WEDDING

by

RAMÓN J. SENDER

translated from the Spanish by
ELEANOR CLARK

with an introduction by
ARTURO BAREA

THE GREY WALLS PRESS

First published in 1948
by the Falcon Press (London) Limited
7 *Crown Passage, Pall Mall, London S.W.*1
Printed in Great Britain
by the C.W.S. Printing Works
Longsight, Manchester

02352716

*This edition has been edited
for English readers by
Ilsa Barea*

863

for

JULIA

with the gratitude of

R. S.

Joy, sorrow, or simply our everyday dreams take us to God. Thinking to speak to Him of our true selves we speak only of the swine that sleeps in our hearts. And God listens and says: 'The reality of the swine or of the angel, like all reality, is for both you and Me only a pretext.' Yes, Lord, we accept this.

INTRODUCTION

It would be easy to produce catch-phrases about *Dark Wedding*, such as: a mixture of brutal naturalism and romantic idealism—prose poetry of our times—symbolist realism and realistic symbolism—a modern legend—and so forth. Each one of these labels would be true enough as far as it goes, and all of them would be too pat. Ramón Sender's work does not fit into neat literary compartments. It will be better not to subject him to an artificial classification, but to attempt a description of the writer and his writings against their own background.

Ramón J. Sender is not a 'new' author. Twenty years ago he already was established as the only great novelist among the young Spanish writers, through his novel *Imán*, in the English version entitled *Pro Patria*. He was a solitary rebel then and he is a solitary rebel now, despite his profound kinship with some modern novelists of other countries, such as Ignazio Silone. Although he is part of a living stream of thought, he does not belong to any group. He belongs to the host of dreamers and fighters who battled, each by himself, with an old Spain—and a superficially new Spain—that threatened to stifle them. Above all he belongs to his own country of Aragon with its dour peasantry and rocky uplands, the soil from which Goya came.

Sender is a writer of stories which are universally human even when the shape of the human problems and the 'local colour' are Spanish—and in *Dark Wedding* they are not even that. But the influence of the *patria chica*—the 'little country' as one's home region is tenderly called in Spanish, to distinguish it from the abstract 'fatherland'—is extremely strong in him. When he resumed his writing in exile, after the stunning shock of the Spanish War, his first novel was

9

about men of his Aragon, as though he wanted to escape into a life whose passions and hardships were comfortingly familiar to him. He conjured up the landscape and the air which enveloped his childhood—I am quoting from the English translation of *A Man's Place*, published in 1941 by Jonathan Cape:

'In the curtain of sandy rock formed by the cliffs, eagles and hawks nested. Their cries carried to my balcony, doubled by the echo which gave them a strange depth. In that echo I used to see the immensity of the night that was coming on. . . . In that grey, obscure wilderness one ran across occasional plantings of barley or rachitic wheat. The leaden green of the sparse brush was coated half the daytime with dust, and with frost the other half. In this way it took on the most delicate tones. The wind striking from Catalonia or from the Pyrenees froze it or covered it bush by bush. The upland was lost in the horizon without sign of any ending. . . .'

The immensity of the rolling tableland, the sting of the winds from distant mountains, the taciturn strength of men and women who were accustomed to fight for their right to 'a man's place' in life—these were the forces which had moulded young Sender, the son of Aragonese farmers, by the time he went to town for his studies at the university.

He was born in 1901, he came to Madrid in 1919. It was a turbulent Madrid, hectic with the gaiety of the wartime boom which was rapidly waning, shaken by the aftermath of the first big clashes between organised workers and the new employer class, stimulated by the many short-lived periodicals which sprang up to cater for a new, avid reading public. Behind the façade of elegance and luxury there was the rigidly hierarchical society of an older Spain, and there was the mass of poor clerks, small artisans and badly paid workers living in dark, crowded tenement houses, straining toward a better education and a greater social security, which their wage gains during the years of prosperity (the prosperity of a neutral country able to supply some of the belligerents' needs) seemed to put within their reach. Among the intellectuals there was a cleavage which became increasingly deep with the growth of the tension between the 'old' and the 'new', and more obvious the more social demands mingled with the purely cultural opposition against the obsolete standards of the old, semi-feudal regime. Already in 1913 the poet Antonio Machado had admonished the essayist Azorin, who was clutching at the traditions of the Castilian past:

> 'Listen, you, Azorin: Spain wants to rise,
> To surge, to flower, an entire Spain is dawning.
> Must we still freeze then in the Spain that dies?
> Must we be stifled in the Spain that's yawning?'

This urge for a new life drove Ramón Sender, who earned his living during his student days as an assistant in a chemist's shop and did not belong to the privileged intelligentsia, to political rebellion. As a biographical note says: 'He abandoned law and became entangled in revolutionary movements.' Being a minor, he was not imprisoned but was sent back to his parents, and there he stayed, editing a local paper until he was called up for military service. He served in Morocco, in the corrupt colonial army which fought the Riff War and in which he saw the lads from villages like his own slaughtered, crippled, or, at the very least, miserably uprooted for the sake of a frivolous policy of prestige, and through the ineptitude or greed of the military caste. When he came back to civilian life, he described what he had seen— the struggle of helpless soldiers—in his first novel, *Imán*. It was a revolutionary outcry, a work of art, and the first Spanish realistic novel which went beneath the surface, into the half-conscious life of the mind, and made the world of inarticulate people articulate through external symbols.

I read *Imán* while my own experiences of the disastrous Moroccan campaign were only too fresh in my mind, and it seemed to me that Sender had expressed all the misery, degradation, muddle, and resentment of any soldier who is an unwilling part of an ugly war machine. He had written a simple and crude story, in rough, popular language, the story of a village blacksmith who seems to attract misfortune, great and small, as a magnet attracts iron, so that his comrades in the Army give him the nickname *Imán*, 'magnet', when he continues to blunder into every possible mishap. I do not think that the novel is what one calls 'well constructed'. But it is far more than that, far more than a 'proletarian' novel, and far more than a literary accusation of the Spanish Army. The poor helpless 'Imán', clumsy brute as he is, grows into the symbol of a victimised people while never losing his narrow flesh-and-blood reality. There is one scene in which Viance, dragging himself along on the terrible retreat of Annual, hides from the persecuting Moors in the gaping belly of a disembowelled horse, and suddenly feels his own flesh, his own being, fused with the rotting carcass. Repulsive horror? Sender's humanity and his insight fill the apocalyptic vision with a dim but powerful glow:

'Can it be be—' this is what Viance feels vaguely and Sender expresses clearly for him—'that his life expands into the dead intestines and puts new life into them? He senses that his own matter is alike to that which encircles him, that there is only one kind of matter, and that all of it is animated by the same blind impulses, obedient to the same law. A vague tenderness mounts in him, a longing to do what is good and to find everything sweet and kind.'

This primitive human longing for the good, the kind and the beautiful, in the middle of cruelty and ugliness, is a misused and yet eternal force which Sender re-discovers in every one of his novels. It pervaded his famous novel *Seven Red Sundays*, in which he described an abortive Anarchist rising of the early-thirties. It is the 'message', if the word can be used without sounding too stilted and pompous, in *Dark Wedding*, the story of the convict settlement on a Central American island.

In the years between *Imán* and *Dark Wedding*, Ramón Sender went on searching, through his art and through his life as a social fighter, for the 'truth of living humanity', as he put it in a foreword to *Seven Red Sundays*. Compassion, that is to say, a capacity for sharing the pains and passions of others in his mind, together with an ardent wish to help, made him appreciate the high idealism of the best among the Spanish Anarcho-Syndicalists. Yet his acute observation and his tough sense of reality made him see that they are 'people too full of humanity's dream of freedom, of the good, of justice, giving these an emotional and individualistic significance. Carrying such a load, an individual can hope for the respect and loyalty of his relations and friends, but if he should hope to influence the general social structure, he nullifies himself in heroic and sterile rebellion.' (I am again quoting from the preface to *Seven Red Sundays*.)

Sender did not cease to fight against what he conceived as oppression. He was in prison for his activities against the—comparatively innocuous—dictatorship of General Primo de Rivera. Later he was attracted by the Communist movement; from it he expected that change of the 'general social structure' which the Anarcho-Syndicalists in his opinion could not attain, and which he knew to be necessary for the liberation of the individual. But when, as a soldier in the Republican front line during the Spanish War, he found that he would have to surrender his 'heretical' humanism, and his spiritual independence as an artist and man, if he wanted to remain within the fold, he renounced his last attempt at belonging to a political group and went into the wilderness, true to his stubborn self and true to his conception of a living humanity.

Sender's political and mental development is mirrored in the books he published between *Imán* and *Dark Wedding*. His second novel, *El Viento en la Moncloa* (*Wind in the Moncloa*), was born from his experiences in prison. *La Noche de las Cien Cabezas* (*The Night of the Hundred Skulls*) and *Seven Red Sundays* deal basically with the same problem, with violent action arising from ardent, confused dreams of human freedom. But the first of the two did not quite achieve the unity of emotional symbols and a objective description of social reality to the extent the more famous *Seven Red Sundays* achieved it. In 1935, when Sender had distanced himself from the Anarcho-Syndicalist movement, an historical novel won him the National Prize for Literature. This book, published in England under the title *Mr. Witt among the Rebels*, again took for its subject a local popular rising inspired by the dreams of Millennium. The stage setting—Cartagena in the 'seventies of the last century—and the social atmosphere of past struggles he had not shared, made the writer's approach more detached, his style more disp ssionate, his psychological plot more subtle, than his previous subject would have permitted. It marked a new stage in his develop-ment as an artist and indicated a change in his outlook. During the Spanish War, Sender wrote *Contraataque* (*The War in Spain*), which tries so hard to be the book of a politically disciplined soldier that it lacks the searching psychological realism he would otherwise have put into his description of outside events: it is nearer to a superficial 'realistic' reportage than any other of Sender's books.

Then came the two books of nostalgia for Aragon and the world of childhood, *A Man's Place* and *Chronicle of Dawn*, both filled with delicate lyrical descriptions which fit naturally into the sober, unvarnished picture of the harsh world Sender knew in his youth. At the end of *Chronicle of Dawn*, he undertakes a journey into the secret galleries of his mind and his dreams, and it is as though there he had recaptured his pristine faith in beauty and goodness. In *Dark Wedding*, he carries his search once again into the alien world of suffering and sinning people, at war within themselves and with each other. Once again, he achieves that which gives him his unique place in Spanish literature— and, so I believe, in the contemporary novel—a fusion of the elements of naturalism, symbolism, and idealistic faith.

If the violent action of his earlier novels created difficulties for the non-Spanish readers, who found themselves
remote from the passionate longings and outbursts of the
Spaniards Ramón Sender described at the time, the shock
of the hardly-past war must have changed the position, at
least for people who are not afraid to look into a magnifying
mirror. In *Dark Wedding*, Sender takes the degenerate,
vicious, and dangerous convicts herded together in a penal
settlement, with their hatreds, lusts, and hidden sentimentality, as a sample of mankind. Surely this is an exaggeration? His heroine is a beautiful, gay, untouched young girl
whose presence unleashes the sensual greed and the desire
for beauty and purity in those wretched people; he couples
her with a philosophising young school-teacher who sees her
as the symbol she embodies, and as the living, normal woman
she is; he makes both accept their work among the convicts
and reject their possible escape from all the hideous dangers,
for the sake of simple social comradeship and loving kindness.
Surely this is romanticism?

Yes, it is. And yet, it seems to me that the brutal realistic
'exaggeration' and the 'romantic' idealism are both true, in
the sense poor Viance's discovery of his wish for goodness
just when he was huddling in the belly of a putrefying horse
was true. But since he wrote his novel of the conscript
soldier, Sender has deepened and changed his artistic form.
He has clarified his human belief: '. . . life peopled by monsters,
but with a little path between the monsters. For everybody,
no matter whom, some little path.' This message of a modest
hope born from a ruthless recognition of the ugliness and
violence in our world makes Ramón Sender a writer for all
of us, because he can conceive this hope and clothe it with
the truth of his art so that we, too, can see it.

ARTURO BAREA

15

I

BLACK TRINIDAD WAS SLASHING HIS
boots with his whip as he climbed the stairs of the Department of Penal Settlements. They called him 'Black' Trinidad,
because his coppery skin had been darkened by sweat, sun,
and the smoke of the strong cigars he chewed incessantly.
He was a tall man with burly shoulders. On the island, he
felt at his ease, but here in the city a multitude of petty things
obsessed and irritated him. The people he passed in the
streets were aliens, not more than one in ten looked to him as
if he belonged to the country. Even though the others might
not be foreigners, they had an artificial way of smiling, walking,
and gesturing. Sometimes he seemed to discover a hint of
contempt in their eyes. It may not have been contempt, but
only indifference, the aggressive indifference of townspeople;
but whatever it was, it made him feel like lifting his hand and
hitting the stranger with his whip. Every time he overcame
the urge, he had to bite harder on his cigar. It had happened
to him a moment ago, when he was forced to stand aside for
two officials coming down the stairs. They had worn glossy
shoes, their moustaches were neatly trimmed, and one had
said to the other, showing a half-open parcel: 'Chillies they
are, the hot kind—most appetising. A present for the head
clerk.'

The staircase led to an interior gallery studded with the
doors and windows of office rooms. In a cage hanging in one
of the windows was a parrot. It was whistling the National
Anthem, and Trinidad stopped and listened. He slapped his
leg with the whip, turned away into another staircase and said
admiringly:

'The little so-and-so, I wonder who taught him!'

Another official was coming down the stairs, but this time Trinidad did not give him the right of way. 'Pimps and pansies, that's the city for you.' Still, the city was not the whole of the country. A good thing, too. What was the city, anyway? A warren of offices and shops. Two hundred thousand inhabitants, the statistics said. Naturally the biggest town of the country had to have a bit of everything. But all the same, there were too many of those people with fancy shoes. He longed to kick them in the teeth with his boot.

He had always avoided going to the capital. The girl he was about to marry lived there, but he had met her two years ago in a seaside village where he used to spend his leave. Since then they had been writing to each other. His letters told her that there were many big flies on the island, but that he would put wire screens over the windows; that his bodyguard had been slack on duty the other day—'I had to flog two sentries.' As if to counter this display of authority, he added that his kind heart had suffered. Sometimes he described the improvements in the 'residence', which he was having done in preparation for their married life. Finally he wrote: 'The cage is ready, nothing is lacking there but the little bird.' This, coming from Trinidad, was a notable flash of sentiment.

She used to answer him on scented paper. Black Trinidad would gently sniff the perfume and sigh. In the course of those years he had seen his betrothed three times, but not once in the capital. There had been nights on the distant island when he walked on the terrace, watched the moon-drenched sea, and sang to the sound of his guitar:

> 'By the sea I met her,
> By the sea I must make her mine,
> They shall lay us to rest by the sea.'

This time there was no escape, he had to come to the capital for their formal betrothal and the wedding, all of it to be done in a single week. His coming had been a wonderful surprise for his fiancée. She was so young—so tender, as he liked to put

18

it—that she was always surprised at everything. Trinidad thought of the smart city people and told himself: 'It's faces like that Niña Lucha's got to look at day after day!' The idea gave him an ugly feeling. He suppressed it by clenching the whip in his fist, and continued up the stairs. The staircase of the building, an old colonial palace, was under repair and the workmen were shuffling on frayed slippers between sacks of lime and slabs of concrete. Trinidad spat out the chewed tobacco shreds and said: 'They never finish repairing these stairs.'

He walked into the office, without taking off his hat, and told the typists that he wanted to see the chief. The ante-room smelt of tobacco smoke: all the girls were smoking. He sat down, rested one of his boots on his other knee and started flicking at it. One of the typists wasn't at all bad. He could imagine his marrying her for the same reasons for which he was going to marry his fiancée. But Niña Lucha was made of finer stuff. She struck you at once as a real lady. And no smoking for her. She never smoked.

He tried to frame the words he was going to say to his chief, but did not find it so easy. The chief was clever. Bland, silent, and shrewd as he was, he knew how not to commit himself. Trinidad felt it a humiliation to be kept waiting in the ante-room; obviously, that was the chief's intention. He got up to look at a map on the wall and ran his eyes along it until he spotted the island. It was a yellow blob bordered with green. There were some topographical markings, but he failed to identify a few black dots. Probing them with his finger nail, he found that they had nothing to do with geography but were fly specks. It tickled him to see the island so small, when it had taken him several days to cross it from north to south. The truth was that the island offered few attractions. Living there was a strenuous adventure for anyone. Malaria, and the difficulties in getting wine and spirits, made for a hard life. Yet somehow he felt homesick. He explained it to himself: 'I love the island the way one loves a bad woman.'

Another typist appeared in the doorway leading to the chief's room and invited him to go in. Trinidad felt awkward in the presence of this woman, who dressed like an opera singer and painted her face so that nothing of her skin was left visible. 'Made up as if it were a carnival,' he thought. Black Trinidad turned on his heel and walked in. He expected his superior to give him a great welcome, for they had been friends from childhood. But the chief continued with his instructions to his secretary, without even raising his eyes from the desk to look at Trinidad. He dictated two or three more letters and toyed with a pencil-holder. In the end he turned to him. But just when Trinidad believed he was going to shake hands, it turned out that the chief was only lifting his hand in a suave gesture of apology before picking up the telephone on the desk between them. Trinidad acknowledged the second hit scored against him—the first had been his wait in the ante-room—and thought: 'He's very good at this sort of thing.' He fixed a bilious look on a paper knife, a small gilt-handled dagger. The chief, so Trinidad noted, was correctly dressed, hair plastered down, face recently shaved: even he looked like a foreigner. But the first words, when they came, were friendly enough:

'I knew you were in town and I've been expecting you. There aren't many old friends like you left.'

The voice sounded in Trinidad's ears like a cracked bell. He rose, left his whip lying across the desk, pushed his hands deep into his breeches pockets and began to stride up and down the room.

'So you've been expecting me, eh?'

'Yes. I wanted to see if you'd changed in the last few years. But you're still the tough you were when I saw you last.'

The chief resumed his fiddling with the pencil-holder and added:

'I've some bad news for you. The Minister is not satisfied.'

This room, too, had a map. Black Trinidad examined it with studied interest. Without turning round, he retorted:

'And what's biting the Right Honourable?'

'I tell you, he doesn't like the way things are going.'

Black Trinidad shrugged:

'What decent person would? But I don't care what the Minister thinks'—he chuckled slily—'because you back me, don't you? You've got a lot of influence and you're going to back me.'

The Minister's notions were one thing and those of the Director of Penal Settlements another, Trinidad thought. Probably the chief was making it all up to show off. 'I know his sort of people inside out,' he assured himself. The Director went on in the same key:

'What a nasty brute you are!' But he, too, said it with a chuckle.

Trinidad continued to stare at the map, with his back to the chief. Then the other changed his tone:

'Come here. Even if you've nothing to say to me, I have something to say to you.'

Trinidad sauntered back to the desk, took up his whip and flicked with its thong at a speck of ash until it fell to the floor. Then he sat down and stared at his boss.

The Director of Penal Settlements began:

'You have entered this room as though we had parted yesterday. But it is years since we met last. Any poor yokel of an official from a district gaol would have put more cordiality into his greeting.'

'I'm not a poor yokel, and I am glad to see you again.'

The Director offered him a cigarette and told him to get rid of the foul cigar that stuck to his lips. Then he said:

'Take care, Trinidad. You rely on the fact that the island is too far away and has too many mosquitoes for our inspectors to go there.'

'Not just mosquitoes. Scorpions too.'

'And snakes, I imagine.'

21

'Plenty of them.'

'But though they won't go there, certain people are waiting for you to take a false step—and not exactly because they intend to give you a helping hand.' After a pause, the chief went on: 'Restrain yourself, Trinidad. That's my advice to you.'

'Restrain—with whom? With those b . . .' He swallowed the word out of respect for the secretary who was in and out of the room the whole time. 'Convicts who got a reprieve! Fellows who've cheated the hangman! What would you do in my place? Make noble speeches?'

'I'm telling you the plain truth. Up till now I've been warding off the blow. But if you go on as you do . . .'

'Why don't you go there yourself? Of course, you might get taken down a peg with your speech-making. Any one of the convicts is better at it than you. I've always found that drunks and morons share the craze of all politicians—to make speeches on street corners.'

The Director tried to be conciliatory:

'Granted, the Penal Colony consists of anti-social individuals. But we must do our best to save them as far as possible.'

'How?'

'Through education. Through moral influence.'

Was he by any chance referring to the teacher? Trinidad savoured the idea that the teacher should be able to redeem those people. At the same time he realised that the suspicion and mental reservation in the Director's talk sprang from quite another reason. A certain affair was in the chief's mind when he scolded him, but he would not even hint at it. He had not the shadow of proof. Nobody could have. This conviction gave Trinidad a feeling of security. He felt so confident that he dared to broach the matter himself:

'That business of the mail plane did me a lot of harm.'

The Director's silence expressed agreement; it amounted almost to an accusation.

'Yes, it did me a lot of harm. If only somebody had been left to make a statement . . .'

'It would have been good enough,' said the Director, 'if the mail bags had not been burnt.'

'So you, too, don't trust me?'

He knew very well that the Director had been the first to suspect him, but it did not suit his book to show this knowledge.

'That's all I needed to find out!'

It was difficult to explain the accident. The aircraft had not crashed in landing, but it had caught fire. The passengers had died, but not in the flames; some of them had had bullet holes in their skulls. So had the pilot. It was all very difficult to explain.

'I don't distrust anyone, but in a case of this kind nothing counts except the facts. The facts constitute either an accusation or a defence. It is not a matter of pull or friendship. It is just as that poster there says—' With an arrogant gesture he pointed at a conspicuous slogan on the wall, which read NEITHER FRIENDSHIP NOR BRIBERY. 'But I would be the last person to think badly of you.'

Trinidad beat an impatient tattoo on his leggings.

'It's always the same old story here in town. Distrust, suspicion, rumour-mongering. I'd like to be back home as soon as possible.'

'You're a barbarian, you've always been. And you like your island because you can let yourself go there.'

Trinidad gazed at him with a somewhat clownish expression of watchfulness:

'Is this all you wanted to tell me?'

'No, I haven't even started.'

At this point the door opened and a ragged, bare-footed man with a bootblack's outfit under his arm asked:

'A little shine, boss?'

The Director shook his head. The bootblack pointed at Trinidad's boots and said:

23

'Let me grease 'em for you, chief?'

Trinidad regarded him affectionately: the fellow had called the Director nothing but 'boss,' but him he called 'chief.' He sat there, knees apart, and nodded. The bootblack scurried over to him, squatted down and began to work in silence. The stiff brush scraped on the dry leather, and the Director showed that the noise made him nervous. This Trinidad took to be an indication of weakness. He hastened to launch his counter-attack:

'You won't ever start telling me, because there's nothing to blame me for. I know you. I know, all you want is to set me worrying so you can pretend I've got to be saved by you. You want to show off. But Black Trinidad doesn't need you. When we were both kids, you were the son of a good family and I was just a little tramp. But I got on in the world by myself, and I don't need anybody.'

The Director rose and walked over to the balcony.

'Anyway, you'll realise that you have only four days of your regulation leave left—when do you intend to go back?'

'Four days is two days more than I want. You can have them.'

'I see. You can't live outside your kingdom.'

'And you couldn't live in it. It's a place for men who're men.'

The bootblack grinned furtively, in fawning admiration. Trinidad swelled with pride. The Director put a hand on his shoulder, affecting cordiality. He knew how to dispel Trinidad's bad temper without having to take him seriously.

'I hear you're getting married.'

'Yes. I hope it won't be that false step of mine you mentioned . . .'

'I hope so for your sake. Who is she?'

'An orphan.'

'A Spanish girl?'

This casual interest seemed to Trinidad lacking in respect.

24

He puffed twice at his fag, stared at the ceiling, smoothed his moustache, and finally said:

'No. She isn't Spanish. She's living with an uncle and aunt of hers because her parents died when she was a little girl.'

Only two kinds of women could marry Trinidad, women so young that they were childlike in their trust, or so experienced and seasoned that nothing made any difference to them.

'Is she your age? Forty or so?'

'No, eighteen.'

The bootblack wanted to curry favour with Trinidad and winked a roguish eye. Trinidad burst into laughter, his lips moist. The Director turned to the letters waiting for his signature. Trinidad would have shown him a photograph, but he still felt that the Director was not displaying a proper respect in the way he talked. Also, in the photo his girl had dreamy eyes which seemed to look earnestly at whoever looked at her, and Trinidad did not wish the Director to get the benefit of all that. However, since he sensed himself on firmer ground, he began to put forward his claims. It was a matter of money. He wanted a compensation to the amount of the fares of all the leaves he had waived. In addition he proposed that the administration of food supplies for the penal colony should be handed over to him. The Director told him that this would be too arbitrary a step. On the other hand it might be possible to discuss an *ex gratia* payment, in general terms, although in view of recent events it would not prove easy to make the Minister favourably inclined towards him.

'The plane affair, is it? Still the plane affair?'

The Director knew that it was useless to argue with him, and fell back on the subject of his wedding. Trinidad invited him to the banquet. He paid the bootblack and repeated that everything would have to be settled within the next two days. Then he left after telling the Director time and place of the wedding dinner. By that time he had thrown the cigarette-end on the carpet and was again chewing a black cigar. The screen door of the secretary's room was swinging to and fro with a slight moaning sound. Nothing had been fixed. But the Director had not dared to confront him with the mail plane affair in so many words. Those men with plastered-down hair were easily intimidated, they let him alone. Besides, the Director would come to his wedding and this would increase his prestige with the bride's family.

He looked at his watch and made for a jeweller's shop to fetch the bridegroom's gift to the bride. He had already bought a dress for her. A show window made him stop; its naked dummies in pretty underwear attracted him. Every-thing about them was fragile, the fabrics were light as smoke, gentle as dreams. He looked at them and sighed. This was what Trinidad considered the 'prize of his life': silk, youth, intimacy. Silken slips, lots of silky little slips. Trinidad chewed his cigar and thought: 'My Lucha is even lovelier.' The dummies' underwear made red and blue sparks flicker in his eyes. 'My Lucha is even lovelier,' he repeated. He remembered mysterious cardboard boxes he had seen strewn around the bride's house, boxes with names of shops like this one, and he felt a soft ecstasy in imagining that Niña Lucha would have intimate clothes like these. He stared at the dummies and, seeing their nascent breasts, he smiled, his hand on his hip, slapping his back with the whip. One of the dummies eyed him coquettishly. She looked like Niña Lucha to him, and he lashed harder at his back. Where the silk folded over, it shimmered and yet it was transparent and you saw through it the faintly gilded flesh of the doll. This nakedness was like the dawn on the island with its rosy cloudlets, patches of clear sky, and a breeze from the sea. A scented little breeze from the sea. He lashed his back too hard, the tip of the whiplash flicked across his shoulders and stung his ear. His bride-to-be was as innocent as a small bird. Yet at this moment, in face of all this gauze, these silks, this thigh which swelled so sweetly above the knee, he realised the immense power of innocence. Little breeze from

26

the sea. But the sea, too, is a young girl at dawn; and it is immense, its power incalculable. Little breeze from the sea. He saw his face reflected in the glass and began to contemplate his moustache. His mouth looked twisted. And the dummy was clad only in panties and a dainty brassière. But for its silvered hair he would have said that it was Niña Lucha herself. He tugged fiercely at his moustache and tore himself away with an heroic effort. Again his lips shone with moisture, and in the left corner of his mouth he tasted saliva mingled with tobacco juice.

He walked with firm steps without seeing where he went. People coming from the opposite direction made way for him. When he became aware of it, Trinidad's smile broadened: 'That's what Niña Lucha needs, a man like me!' Around him he saw nothing but brittle, sleek little people with well-polished shoes.

'A real male,' he said, slapping his back with the whip.

He was staring straight in front of him, with a provocative look in his eyes. He would have liked somebody to jostle him, to challenge him in some way. Then Trinidad would have been able to show his mettle. On the whole, his interview with the chief had not turned out badly, although he would never get the money for all the journeys he had not undertaken in the last few years. He had to make up for the loss. Slowly he found his way to the little market of Santa Monica. There he scanned the stalls until he saw an old mulatto woman who sat there, vast and motionless, with a face as though carved in stone. She was calling her wares without raising her voice:

'Live ladies' hair! Leeches!'

Then she changed the cry:

'Nightdresses, silk and satin!'

She sold long plaits of hair, and leeches which stirred in their glass jars. There were piles of folded nightdresses made of cheap artificial silk. Trinidad saw in his mind the old woman, big and equine as she was, dressed up in a sky-blue nightdress that would reach down to her feet, dancing in the middle of the market square to the beat of the conga a loudspeaker was blaring forth. The vision sickened him. Every time the mulatto woman spun round, her nightdress would flash in the sun, and Trinidad felt sick.

But the mulatto was sitting motionless behind her stall. It gave her a start when she heard who her customer was.

'It's you who's getting stuff from the island,' Trinidad said, 'and now you're going to tell me the name of the gallows-bird who sends it.'

The old woman was sales agent for the marijuana which was smuggled out of the island. Trinidad showed himself very much concerned.

'I reckon it must be Gimpy, but I want to know it from you directly. Speak up, or I'll blow the gaff.'

The old woman disregarded the threat. Without changing her position, she dropped a fifty-peso bill at Trinidad's feet.

'I beg your pardon, chief,' she said. 'You lost something out of your pocket.'

Trinidad picked it up.

'I dropped two of them. Where's the other one?'

'Here it is,' and the old woman handed it over quickly. 'I must have picked it up from the ground without thinking.'

'The island isn't a free port. Don't forget it, Granny.'

He turned back the way he had come. Now he would go to the jeweller's and get the present. Behind him the old woman again called out her wares: 'Live ladies' hair! Leeches!'

By 'live hair' she meant that the hair had been taken, not from corpses, but from the heads of living women.

Trinidad kept thinking of the single diamond set in the platinum bracelet. At the same time he felt a sensuous pleasure in the handsome jewel case. Its velvet lining was very soft to the touch. He passed his finger tip along it and observed the metallic glints in the lines he drew on the pile. He was on the way to the house of his betrothed.

Niña Lucha lived with her uncle and aunt in a private

road, with two lamp-posts and a waterless stone fountain in its centre, where the children used to play. The squawk of many wireless sets came through the open windows. In Niña Lucha's house, which had two small balconies, there were always flower-pots. One of the plants was a passion-flower with two beautiful blossoms which had just opened. All the women of the neighbourhood exclaimed over it and discovered the religious symbols in the flower: the crown of thorns, the nails of the cross, and so on. Some of them would look at them and begin to recite, as though in prayer:

> '*By the nails of the hands,*
> *By the wounds of the side,*
> *By the sign of the Cross,*
> *Our Father, Jesus. Amen.*'

Trinidad smiled when he recalled it. The girl was pure as the cherry blossom.

In entering the courtyard, he felt a familiar atmosphere coming out to welcome him. As he walked upstairs, this feeling changed to the assurance of a man about to enter his possessions. Near the door he met a maid carrying a little cellophane box with flowers. He took it from her and glanced at the accompanying visiting card. When he came into the room, Niña Lucha's aunt took the flowers to be another of the groom's courteous offerings. Trinidad found this very right and proper and pocketed the card. The house was blazing with light. The aunt called out gaily:

'Niña Lucha!'

Lucha guessed by the tone of her aunt's voice that Trinidad had come, and called back:

'Just a second!'

Trinidad scented a faint smell of cinnamon. *By the sea I must make her mine* . . .

The girl was busy sewing a button on her uncle's shirt. There was little furniture in her room. The coloured picture

29

postcards which Trinidad had sent her were on the wall, set fanwise in a wire cardholder. Trinidad had selected them with great care in Eminencias' shop on the island. Those postcards with a flowering branch and a couple of doves, beak against beak, on the background of a sunset, had delighted the girl. Some of her friends had told her that they were in vulgar taste, but her aunt said the girls were only jealous.

Niña Lucha was an orphan living with her uncle and aunt. The fact that she was an orphan had taught her to be humble when she was very young, but it was a humility of the heart, which was never ostentatious. 'What a small thing is a girl who is an orphan and alone in the world', she used to think, perfectly content to be such a 'small thing'. Sometimes her aunt would look at her and wonder. She was humble without being in the least timid. The aunt would whistle nervously —this was a bad habit of hers—and shake her head. 'Maybe the girl has got some fixed idea of her own and doesn't talk about it to anybody.' Unlike other pretty women, Lucha had not a single enemy in the world. This fact, too, upset her aunt: 'My niece has her private ideas about how to avoid jealousy and ill will.' And yet there were occasions when she would have sworn that her niece was stupid. The family doctor was treating the aunt for a chronic illness and had taught the girl to give her injections. She did this well and was so proud of it that sometimes, when the aunt praised her dexterity to people who visited them, she would go up to perfect strangers and ask: 'Would you like me to give you a shot?' They all laughed, but the girl's expression never changed, and in the end no one could tell whether she was serious or not.

She hurried to finish sewing on the button. She heard her aunt laugh. The aunt was always laughing; when she did not laugh, her nervous condition caused her to emit short, sharp whistles, as if she were practising Morse code. The girl sometimes called her attention to this when she had distinguished company.

The aunt was saying to Trinidad that the whole house was upside down and that Lucha's happiness had infected the whole neighbourhood. Signs of the wedding were all over the room. There were newspaper patterns of blouses and shirts, also two boxes of shoes and a hatbox. The aunt, laughing and whistling, removed the patterns from the chair and invited Trinidad to sit down. She started for the hall, but just then Trinidad showed her the bracelet.

The old lady trilled like a songbird:

'A treasure from the Orient! How much did it cost?'

Trinidad threw out his chest:

'Three thousand pesos.'

It had cost eighteen hundred, but a little more or less ... The old lady went off with the sum ringing in her ears.

Some of the fabrics were like the dummy's in the window. Trinidad picked up a piece of pale green silk. He crumpled it until it was hidden in his hand; then he released it, noticing how the silk overflowed the side of his hand and fell slowly on the sofa. As it unfolded it assumed the shape of an intimate garment. Trinidad's hands trembled and felt heavy. He gave a deep sigh and looked around him.

The room had a large balcony. On the other side an open door led to the hallway. Beyond the door, deep shadow. In this frame appeared Niña Lucha, and stood still. She was very beautiful but thought it necessary to moisten her lips and push her breasts forward just a little. They looked at one another in silence, smiling.

At first sight of her Trinidad thought: 'Her eyes are wicked to-day.' In her eyes was a look of innocence asleep, but voluptuously asleep. Her naked arms reflected the light of the balcony window. What could he say of Niña Lucha to define her? One word only: virginity. In her eyes shone the privileges of virginity. Well-founded privileges of divine

31

origin. Trinidad watched her silently, and the refrain of a song flashed through his mind:

Of cinnamon smelt her flesh . . .

Slowly he took the jewel case from his pocket. The smell of the leather, too, was exciting. The girl came nearer, reached out, and Trinidad took the bracelet and put it on her arm. Then he gave her a gentle embrace, but when he tried to kiss her on the mouth she turned her head away and offered her cheek. Trinidad took no offence; after all, they were not yet really married. Niña Lucha ran to show the bracelet to her uncle, 'who was getting dressed'. Every time Lucha made allusions to her domestic life with other people Trinidad felt a tinge of jealousy. Her uncle getting dressed, the girl knowing that he was getting dressed, seemed an ugly business. He turned slowly and looked at his reflection in the glass of a print hanging on the wall. In the half-light of the room the colour of his face was somewhere between grey and copper. 'It's hot', he thought; but it was not hot. He unbuttoned his jacket and loosened his shirt. He smoothed his hair, put one hand on his hip, and lent against the doorframe of the balcony. A photograph on the wall showed Lucha on the day of her first Communion, with a white dress and a tulle veil like the one she would wear at the wedding. She was proudly holding up a little book with golden clasps. Trinidad thought he ought to buy one like it for the chapel on Faro Island; that is, when they would have a priest. At present there was none.

He opened an album of family photos and studied them while waiting for Lucha, who was taking her time. They told the story of the aunt, of the old Treasury official in his youth, the difficult years on a small ranch in the interior, and finally, the more peaceful life in the little property near the sea, where two years before he had first met Lucha. Then he came across a picture of her as a baby, which at first made him smile tenderly. It said at the bottom that she was ten

32

months old at the time. She was sitting naked on a sheepskin, facing the camera, with chubby little legs sticking out. Trinidad smiled with almost paternal emotion, then he grew livid, hesitated a second, and closed the album. When his colour had returned to normal he felt a little ashamed of himself and would have liked to open the album again, but he did not dare.

'Why do they take such stupid pictures?'

Lucha returned in her wedding dress. That was too much. Trinidad wanted to slap his boots with the whip, but he had left it on the sofa. He tried to laugh but produced only a queer guttural sound. He noticed in her expression a faint trace of surprise. 'It's only natural,' he thought. 'I'm not used to laughing.'

He stammered finally, conscious of the strain that had come between them:

'I ought to get dressed up too.'

But it irked him that the bridal couple should be made an object of curiosity. At the depth of his happiness lay something secret and sweet which the others were turning into an excuse for elaborate ceremonies. He was partly thankful, partly embarrassed.

'Pretty, the way the bracelet shines.'

The platinum gleamed softly on the white of her sleeve.

'Don't take too long getting ready,' he said in a grave voice which pleased his own ears. 'Remember that after dinner we have to take the plane.'

She wanted to go to the banquet in her bridal dress. Trinidad thought there would not be time to change afterward, but the girl had an inspiration. Couldn't she travel in white? Sometimes an absurd idea could sound very charming just because it came from Niña Lucha. Only once had Trinidad been shocked by something she had said, but it happened a long time ago and was quite another story. She was sixteen then; they had just met and were beginning to 'get together', as Trinidad put it. Lucha had spoken with

C   33

great enthusiasm of a handsome young film star, though her only specific praise was: 'In the love scenes, in the close-ups, his nostrils quiver.' It was then Trinidad forbade her to go to the pictures.

The aunt had gone to fetch some of the ladies of the neighbourhood to see her niece. With them came an old fellow with a bristling moustache, who had known the girl all her life and filled the house at once with his clumsy words of praise. Trinidad heard him say that he had held her on his knees, associated the old man with the picture in the album—that dreadful nakedness!—and took a violent dislike to him.

The old fellow was looking at the bride.

'That's what I call a fine female!'

The ladies were moving around, making a great fuss over everything. Trinidad retired to the balcony with an air of scorn. One of the women remarked:

'Don't worry, pretty soon she'll be all yours.'

Trinidad felt deflated and wrapped himself in silence. The girl laughed. He behaved so disagreeably that the visitors soon left. He turned to her in a huff.

'You're too—trusting,' he told his bride sternly.

'They're nice people.'

'You think everybody's nice, but life isn't like that.'

Niña Lucha failed to understand him:

'What's the matter with you? Has something happened?'

That she should take his normal character for a matter of dramatic incident made him furious, not at her, of course, but at life, at things in general, at everything he could not control.

'Life is not as you think. People are always watching for a chance to do harm. You shouldn't be so frank and easy.'

She didn't understand. Her uncle and aunt were 'saints'; the old neighbour was kind and harmless; the women of the neighbourhood, with their many babies and no money, were heroines. Some girls her own age made superhuman efforts to bring home a little money to take care of a drunken father.

34

'At least there's a drunkard in the bunch,' said Trinidad.

'But the poor man is desperate because he got an incurable disease when he was young.'

'Syphilis,' thought Trinidad, but in front of the girl the idea seemed a sacrilege. She went on:

'Don't make a mistake, Trinidad. At bottom they're good people.'

'All of them?'

'But you,' she said, 'you're the best of all.'

She was so sure of it! And she was right. At heart he was really good. Only it was hard for anyone to get to his heart; that was the trouble. But soon his mood changed. The women had passed the word along, and now the girls of the neighbourhood began to arrive. Some of them tried to sympathise with Lucha because she was going 'into the wilds', but Trinidad said with a note of emphasis:

'Don't pay attention. They're jealous. They're just jealous of you.'

The wedding was a brilliant affair. The aunt's chief concern had been to have good wine at the dinner, both red and white, and not beer. Trinidad, who had taken pains to find out what was done on such occasions, contributed a case of champagne. The best part of it was the popping of the corks. The aunt didn't like it because it tickled her nose. There was dancing until dark. The Director of Penal Settlements had the place of honour, beside the aunt, who wore herself to shreds thinking up courteous phrases and whistled nervously during any lull in the conversation. There were toasts. They wanted the groom to speak, and Trinidad raised his glass and drank to the health of the company. He would have liked to joke, but he saw that any step in that direction would incite the guests to dubious remarks about the bridal night. He became very serious and confined himself to congratulating the aunt on the dinner. She, in a burst of enthusiasm, dashed to the kitchen and dragged out the cooks, who received an ovation. Trinidad embraced the aunt, dropping cigar ash on her

35

shoulder. Lucha hugged her uncle and kissed him on both cheeks while Trinidad nervously stroked his moustache. The Director refused to make a speech, and Trinidad gave him a furious look. 'The party isn't good enough for him.' To make it worse, the chief rose as soon as possible and took his leave.

The guests danced until nightfall, but the bride and groom left a little after the banquet to catch the plane. She was still in her white dress. Settling down in the car, which had orange blossoms at the door handles and on the windscreen, Trinidad heaved a deep sigh, wiped his sweating hand on his trouser leg, and brought it down over the girl's. He looked into her eyes. She trembled and said:

'Now I'm your wife.'

People swarmed alongside the car and smiled fondly at the newlyweds. Trinidad clenched his teeth in rage. What were they laughing at? But he was soothed by the girl's voice calling him sweetheart.

They caused a sensation at the airport. The employees outdid themselves in congratulations. Trinidad thought of offering them cigars, but there was something which was not quite right. The other passengers—there were only two— thought the bride's presence a lucky omen. All laughed rather more than necessary, and Trinidad disliked the whole business. The bride climbed up the little movable staircase; her hips, which seemed almost childishly flexible, were on the level of Trinidad's eyes. But people went on taking his anxieties, his most hidden and intimate longings as the pretext for a public celebration. At every congratulation he clenched his teeth in fury. When the plane took off he had his first sense of being Lucha's lord and master. She, too, became serious for a moment and appeared on the verge of tears, but then she took her husband's arm, smiled, and called him sweetheart.

'Why do you make promises you can't keep? You promised me you would never say that to anybody but me.'

The girl looked at him in agitation. This was the first

36

emotional problem for her. What could have happened? Trinidad was very sure of himself. With a kind of stupid tenderness he added:

'You said it to the cat every time you picked him up.'

The girl blushed. She looked at the floor, at the ceiling, and at last, timidly, at Trinidad.

'Did Auntie tell you?'

Trinidad said he had heard her himself at the house. She said it to the cat. And the cat was such a wretched little beast that they called him Porky. Lucha was heartbroken.

'However could I call him the same thing I call you, when you're my whole life?'

Trinidad got out of that with a flourish:

'That's the way life is!'

He sighed. The girl felt that she had humiliated him. With the cat. With the cat! And without even knowing it. Oh dear; perhaps it was true that life was like that. She didn't dare look her husband in the face. They looked at the clouds and the green fields below.

She felt perfectly at home in the plane, though it was her first flight, whereas Trinidad, who had often travelled by air, got jumpy every time they hit a pocket. Black Trinidad began to think that the possession of the girl (who was much more his own than any of the things he had fought for so hard in recent years) was not an unqualified victory. Ahead of them lay three hours of flying in an atmosphere charged with electricity, over regions where a forced landing meant death. And there might perhaps be another case like that of the mail plane, which the Director hadn't dared to mention. With Lucha at his side he was conscious of a certain guilt, but he shrugged it off. It was just too bad. Thanks to that, he could face the future with calm. Calm? And why not? He was really not to blame. He had not conspired with the pilot. He didn't even know him. The pilot had no need to pass over the island. He had obviously chosen a safe and remote spot to fake an accident. The fact was that when Trinidad arrived on the scene the four passengers of the plane were dead. Their bodies were still inside the cabin, and the plane was beginning to burn, without, apparently, having suffered any damage. He came upon the pilot who was pulling out the mailbags in a great hurry. Trinidad did not understand how the four passengers of a plane could die in a normal landing, or how the machine could catch fire just like that. The pilot was a sullen and jaundiced-looking fellow. God knows that Trinidad's first reaction was honest and straightforward. He behaved like a conscientious policeman. He ordered the pilot to surrender and, seeing him reach for his pistol, he drew his own and fired. Trinidad had always prided himself on being quick on the trigger. Then he searched the pilot's body on the ground and found 120,000 pesos in a packet strung on red tape which was held together by the seal of a bank. He kept it, pushed the body under the plane, and waited until the fire had consumed everything. Should he hand over the money? Or keep quiet about it? He rode away on horseback, mulling it over, but at the thought of the girl he came to a quick decision. He stopped the horse, tore a strip from the tail of his shirt, wrapped up the bills, dug a hole in the ground at the foot of a tree, and hid the money there. After covering up the place and marking it with a stone he resumed his journey. When he arrived at headquarters he wrote out a report in a flowery hand, giving an account of the accident and saying that all had been found dead. The story was more convincing than the pilot would have liked, since he, too, was among the victims. Trinidad felt no remorse. 'I didn't steal,' he reflected. 'I only took over money that had already been stolen.'

Having acquired this fortune, he thought of getting married. The marriage would create a new situation; it would distract people's attention when they left the island a year later and moved to Nueva Alcalá, where he hoped to live in peace. A little villa, a garden—he would like a garden with a marble cherub spouting water from the usual place, like a little boy—with lovely little terraces facing west and a car in the garage. He had saved up 15,000 pesos of his own, and with 135,000 he would be a potentate, devoting his life to reading the paper and breeding canaries. He saw Lucha without looking at her, and her bright eyes, without the least hint of shadow, sent him farther into his dreams. He might be a savage, but his first impulses were honest. He deserved a girl like that. He put his arm under hers and gave a gentle squeeze. Lucha looked at him as if he were her father.

And she was going to the island, where there was one two-storey concrete building—the headquarters—a stone lighthouse, two bars—Eminencia's bar was the better one—and a lot of scattered huts. And there was one tree, one alone in miles of woods: the one at whose foot he had buried the money. But his happiness was still precarious, exposed to a thousand risks. Trinidad was glad that the arrangement of seats obliged him to sit beside Lucha, instead of opposite her, so that they were not face to face. In this temporary existence in the aeroplane, where everybody was feeling somehow linked in heroism, Trinidad kept himself all the more apart. The difference was that now the girl was with him in his isolation. 'Strange,' he thought, surprised at the discovery, 'husband and wife are not two. They are one.'

They would be on the island before dark. He remembered certain episodes of life among the convicts, and some of them carried with them the startling smell of gunpowder and the somewhat disagreeable sight of a man bleeding to death on the ground. But now it would all be different; besides, a year passes quickly. The air grew warmer as they came down nearer the sea. They opened the ventilators, but it was hot outside too. Trinidad felt a light moisture on his bride's arm. He ran his hand gently over her arm, trying to extend the caress up to the armpit, but took his hand away the moment she resisted, with an affectionate look at him. Trinidad thought he was going mad. The sun was setting, and on the other side of the horizon the green groves began to darken.

The pilot came out. He had his cap on backward, his shirt

unbuttoned. Trinidad started, remembering the other pilot who hadn't been quick enough on the trigger. But this one was a nice boy. He would have liked to have him for a nephew. He took out a fine cigar and offered it to him.

'Have one. They're from our wedding.'

From his way of taking it, Trinidad sensed a superior quality in the boy. The pilot made a gesture with his hand, smiled, and went on. He had left a hatchway open, and Trinidad heard hundreds of little valves of the engine open and shut, sounding strangely like ten frying-pans with oil sizzling over an intense fire.

Trinidad saw a village in the distance and smiled calmly. Lucha kept looking back, intrigued by the hum of the engines. The plane came down in wide spirals over the airport. Lucha was very excited at landing, and when the wheels touched the ground she announced the fact with delight. Trinidad began to give orders about the baggage. Lucha, finding herself in a car, was eager to ask questions, but Trinidad did not give her a chance.

'Now we're going to take a motorboat.'

They had to continue the journey in a launch. Half an hour, Trinidad had said, straightening the lapels of his jacket. It pleased him to think that his subordinates would see him so well dressed. The first of them was already waiting for him in the boat, but he had never seen Trinidad dressed in a solemn black suit, nor could he imagine him accompanied by a woman like that.

'What! Is that you?'

The engineer was a fat man with oily skin who bustled around the engine like a housewife.

Trinidad gave him a slap on the back.

'Here I am, and this is my wife.'

'Pleased to meet you,' said the engineer, holding out his hand.

The girl offered hers, but Trinidad pushed it gently aside. The engine began to hum, and Trinidad steadied the launch,

40

while the bride jumped in gaily. He started to take off his jacket for Niña Lucha to use as a cushion but thought better of it and asked the engineer for his. He said he was wearing a new one, too, in honour of the bride and groom, and offered instead a blanket which he folded carefully. Trinidad was going to shove off, when the engineer looked at his watch.

'There are two other passengers. A couple of fishermen who want to go to Virrey.'

This was a little islet halfway between the coast and Faro Island. Trinidad objected and ordered him to get going. The launch started, raising on each side a crystal wing of water. Moving at full speed, with those little crystal wings, Niña Lucha was radiant with joy. Trinidad now sat opposite and watched her. 'It is hard to talk to her,' he thought. 'It is hard to look her in the face. After the wedding night everything will be different, but now . . .' In Trinidad's torpid reactions there was, every now and then, something like a gleam of good sense. 'A man isn't everything in life,' he reflected. 'When a man begins to think he's the whole show because he knows how to manage things it turns out that there's something in life even stronger: woman.' These reflections were cut short by the engineer, who said in a loud voice:

'Margarito got all the people down to the wharf.'

'Who told him to?'

The engineer looked apologetic.

'I don't know, chief; I don't know anything about it.'

Trinidad was angry, but the bride's presence restrained him. In the capital he was homesick for the island. Now that they were nearing it and somebody mentioned that gutter-snipe Margarito, he thought of the capital, where people spoke with refinement and wore handsome ties.

'Margarito, hey?'

The engineer apologised for him:

'They say it's a special occasion.'

There was a stir in the water beside the boat, and near the

41

waterline appeared the head of a man who smiled, showing two rows of strong teeth. He hoisted his shoulders and made an effort to grab the gunwale. The muscles stood out on his sunburned shoulders; the head had the dignity of an unearthed statue.

'A little something, chief, for the fisherman from Virrey.'

The thought of the girl's seeing the man naked was unbearable. There was a bull whip on board. Black Trinidad snatched it and brought it down full force on the fisherman's face. The hands loosened, and the boat went on. The girl Lucha had cried out and was now looking at Trinidad with such amazement that he felt obliged to explain:

'These fellows are sharks at sea and poisonous snakes on land.'

'The city seems to have put you in a temper,' said the engineer.

The girl turned her head timidly to watch the swimmer who was forging ahead with long strokes. Realising that her interest annoyed Trinidad, she looked away and stared at a lock of the engineer's hair which fluttered in the wind. On the horizon appeared the grey line of the island. A green beacon flared and went out like a star.

'That's funny,' said Trinidad. 'It looks to me as if those swine had again broken the light while I was gone.' And he added: 'That's a game they love.'

The engineer opened the throttle, and a few minutes later they entered a little cove surrounded by palms and banana trees. At one point the shore was cleared and there was a kind of small breakwater. Two little boats with sails unfurled were bobbing in the distance. Trinidad asked for field-glasses, and the engineer handed him an ancient telescope. Trinidad looked at the pier and let out an oath, forgetting that the girl was there.

'Go to the pier on the right,' he ordered.

A restless crowd was swarming in the open place between the trees. Trinidad had expected something, but not this. As he helped Lucha over to the stone steps the engineer said that Margarito had prepared some rockets, and he couldn't understand why he didn't shoot them off. They landed, and Trinidad saw a mob gathered to the right of the landing. Barefoot, half naked, dirty, many of them drunk. Seeing Margarito, he asked:

'What's the meaning of all this?'

'In honour of the wedding, chief.' And in English: *'Congratulations, my boss.'*

A few people pressed forward from the crowd. Margarito yelled:

'Stand back! Keep away from the dock!'

Trinidad and Lucha stood still. He was thinking: 'They, too, want me to pay for their fun out of the worries and intimate things of my wedding day. Am I going to stand for it?'

A rickety fellow, barely covered with rags, came up dancing.

> *'I'm Gómez the Scamp,*
> *Trinidad is my boss,*
> *I'm Gómez the Scamp,*
> *and I'm going to do the rumba,*
> *going to do the rumba.'*

He moved back and forth, wriggling his hips. He was wheezing; the dance tired him. Trinidad clenched his teeth and gave Lucha a gentle shove in the direction of head-quarters, some two hundred yards away. In the city he had had to put up with this sort of insolence because it was the fashion among educated people. But on the island it was a different matter. The drunk followed them, sweating.

> *'I'm going to do the rumba,*
> *going to do the rumba.'*

Four others approached, one of them carrying a green

43

branch with an iguana tied to it. Just then a rocket burst in the air. The one with the iguana danced and sang:

> *'Look at the iguana,*
> *the ugly little mutt,*
> *she lays her little egg,*
> *and then she starts to strut——'*

Hot gusts struck Trinidad in the face; it may have been the wind or his own blood. Another convict, he too drunk, was wandering around all doubled up.

'Oh, oh, what a tumble it'll be, what a tumble!'

The mob came nearer. Trinidad heard vulgar comment on Lucha's beauty. She saw her husband reach for the pistol in his belt and laid a hand on his arm.

'Are you crazy?'

Trinidad tried to sound calm.

'Who told them they could go out of bounds?'

'After all, chief, it's a big day.' Margarito then turned to the bride and added in English:

'*Congratulations, lady.*'

Trinidad was keeping an eye on the people nearest to him. All the dregs of the island were there. An old woman was singing to the noisy accompaniment of a broken kettle and a stone:

> *'She is white as the snow,*
> *soon she will redden.'*

The people from the huts at the southern end had come, too, not convicts, but Indians who worked their little plots of land. They were shy and silent. The others wanted to roar out their good spirits but did not dare let themselves go. Margarito didn't know how to start the long string of congratulations he had prepared. Every time he worked himself up his words were drowned out. The dancer with the iguana, shook his body in front of the girl, this time dancing a conga:

44

> *'The bride said to him:*
> *"Untie my corset,*
> *untie my corset,*
> *untie my corset."'*

Trinidad was livid. Even Margarito thought these goings-on rather inappropriate for the beautiful lady in her white finery. Gómez the Scamp, seeing that he was not getting any attention, wriggled more and more frenetically, edging closer all the time:

> *'I'm going to do the rumba,*
> *going to do the rumba.'*

Trinidad raised his voice above the confusion. He still had his nerves under control.

'You have five minutes to get back where you belong.'

Margarito made an indiscreet remark:

'Can't we welcome the lady?'

Trinidad struck him with the back of his hand; when he withdrew it, it was spattered with blood from the man's nose. Behind Margarito an aggressive clamour of protest arose. The air was thick with threats. Trinidad was taken aback by their nerve. He drew his pistol.

'I don't want any of you sons of bitches near the house. To-morrow morning those who started all this are going to get the air.'

This meant that Margarito and the other leaders would be strung up by the feet for an hour. The uproar swelled stronger than ever, and some of them started for Trinidad.

'Oh, my wench! What a tumble it'll be, what a tumble!'

Trinidad fired two shots in the air. Some of the crowd pushed forward, and then he felt Gómez the Scamp touching his arm:

> *'I'm going to do the rumba,*
> *going to do the rumba.'*

45

Trinidad fired two shots. There were cries of pain; the people dashed for the trees, but two men were left lying on the ground. Trinidad, seeing them take flight, fired at their heels and shouted curses like a man possessed. He turned to the girl and said:

'I'll never forgive them for giving you such a shock.'

She tried to say something, but the words stuck in her throat. Stretching out her hand, she said:

'Those men . . .'

Trinidad turned, though he had already seen them, and, shrugging his shoulders, took her by the arm.

'One of them's a rumba dancer. He's passed out.'

He had fallen face down like a slaughtered calf. The other seemed to be only wounded. Lucha refused to move, so her husband gave her a gentle but determined push. As they left the landing stage they saw behind the mob, the dust and the shrieking, a long procession of little girls with white ribbons in their hair. In front of them, looking rather odd, marched their teacher, a correctly dressed old lady who carried a bunch of flowers and came diffidently up to Trinidad. He frowned. She trembled and dropped the flowers which she wanted to give him.

'My congratulations, señor commandante.'

At her signal the little girls began to sing. Lucha didn't even pick up the flowers. She turned her eyes in horror toward the men on the ground:

'Trinidad! What have you done?'

The little girls went on singing.

II

T HE TWO MEN STAYED THERE ON THE
ground, and every time the girl turned to look she thought
they were nearer. It was as though they were crawling backward on all fours and dropped, shamming death, just as she
turned her head. One of them showed half a naked leg,
covered with reddish fuzz, and no signs of wounds or blood.
The other was smeared with it. He lay face up, one hand
behind his shoulder, as if he were trying to scratch himself
in a difficult spot. His expression was that of someone on the
verge of physical satisfaction. Trinidad's composure affected
her like a threat. From the forest came a sound of music.
Someone was singing, and the voice came thinly through the
air still vibrant with the echo of the shots:

> *'Why do you get so mad, black man,*
> *if they call you trombone lips,*
> *when you've got that golden voice,*
> *to sing with black man, trombone lips?'*

'That's the Cuban,' Trinidad explained.

From the edge of the woods came a man in a mask, one of
a group of dancers who had not yet had a chance to perform.
He was dressed up as a skeleton, the ribs painted on black
cloth, the head dry and white, with a skull's grin. He made
leaps into the air, brandishing a pickaxe fastened to a six-foot
pole. Apparently he wanted to go near the bodies, but was
afraid of Trinidad, who turned to look at him and then let out
a friendly and spontaneous laugh.

'Look at him dressed up like Death!'

The ghosts of the crime flitted through Trinidad's
indifferent calm.

'The island goes on down that way. Nothing but rock. Good crabs, good lobsters, but all the Indians do is poke the ground with a machete and sit in the shade.'

The girl felt dropped on the island as into the bottom of a well.

'The sea is very rough here, the real Caribbean. Up that way you begin to get the waters of another country, our neighbour, Mexico. A good country; I was there once.'

The moon rose swiftly like a balloon filled with blood. Beside it the beacon was hardly visible and looked like a children's joke. But the two fallen and bleeding men were still following behind them. And this was the beginning of the wedding night!

'The real Caribbean, full of sharks. But sharks are better than these dirty convicts, my dear.'

It was a kind of apology, but the girl did not hear.

'There's buried treasure along the coast. Gimpy said he knew where it was, and they gave him the works to make him tell, but he was lying, and it cost him a hoof. That's why he limps, the bastard.'

The girl did not know what to make of his talk. As soon as he set foot on the island Trinidad reverted to his true self and didn't care about appearances. He paused, making a sweeping gesture.

'It's all yours, my princess.'

For the girl the wedding night turned into a frightening dream. She had seen red blood. It belonged to bridal nights, too, but she recoiled from the thought of that blood, now that she had seen the other. They reached the steps of headquarters. The sentries apparently had not heard the news. The officer was pretty well lit up and came forward, saluting. He was a tall, skinny man with cynical eyes.

'Nothing to report, chief.'

The girl saw the open door of the guardroom under the stone staircase. Trinidad said to her:

48

'This is Lefty. He's the one that swallowed a ramrod.' He was referring to the man's stiffness of manner.

Lucha pressed her husband's arm and turned once more to look at the two men on the ground. She didn't want to go in. Trinidad, realising that it would be too drastic to force her, begged her to come, but she let go of his arm and drew away.

'No, I'm not going with you unless you do something about those poor men.'

Trinidad turned indolently to the guard.

'A couple of those brutes passed out down on the wharf. Go and see if they've notified the first-aid station.'

But he knew very well that the station was closed and the doctor away on leave in the capital. There was another doctor on the island, but he was just one of the convicts. At regular intervals the green beacon flashed for a second over the woods; it played weirdly, in silence, on the darker green of the trees. Finally Trinidad gave another order:

'I want three pairs of sentries posted around here.'

As they were about to go in they heard behind them the song of the iguana. A barefooted fellow appeared on the landing. He was carrying the crown of an old straw hat which served as a receptacle for cigarette-butts, an empty bottle, and an incredible number of beer and lemonade bottle tops. He rattled these around, humming and wagging his head stupidly in time with the rhythm:

> 'I'll sing the conga
> for the newlyweds
> if you can tell me
> where I've got my tail.'

He gestured with a wantonness such as the girl had never imagined. They went in. Various people were waiting to greet them in the patio. The girl was introduced:

'This is Mother Leonor, the teacher.'

It was she who had met them with the bouquet. Trinidad explained that she had been a nun. Everybody thought it was queer for a nun not to wear a veil and to stay there with the prisoners. Still, they called her Mother Leonor, and Trinidad allowed her to live at headquarters, where she acted as a kind of housekeeper. Niña Lucha heard all this in a daze. There was also a thin and rather gloomy cook. Trinidad said he would end up on the gallows, but he didn't mean it seriously. Then he introduced the two maids who were to wait on Niña Lucha.

'This is my wife. She's used to the best, so watch how you behave, my girls.'

Niña Lucha looked around the big patio with its almost palatial wooden stairs and a high skylight covered with dust and cobwebs. As they started for the upper floor Trinidad suddenly slapped his forehead and turned back.

'Somebody's missing. You have to meet Gimpy.'

She didn't want to meet anyone. She listened strainedly, thinking the wounded men were groaning outside. Behind a pillar hovered a shadow, between shyness and curiosity.

He seemed to shrink away from Trinidad.

'What are you up to, Gimpy?'

Sighing behind the column was a rather small man, with the long face and sunken chest of a Gothic Christ, his legs lost in a pair of baggy white pants.

'I've already congratulated you, chief.'

Trinidad went up to the lame man and took him by the ear. Gimpy let out a comical howl. Trinidad laughed and tried in vain to get a laugh out of the girl, who was thinking:

'This Gimpy must be the court fool.'

'Come on, Gimpy, come over here and tell the lady where the island came from.'

It cost the lame man a great effort to lift his eyes. He seemed to have broken into a sweat, though he had obviously told the story a thousand times:

'When the Spaniards came,' he began, 'there was a storm, and the boat was wrecked and tossed helplessly on the waves. Three sailors managed to get this far. One of them sat down and started to smoke a cigar. Every now and then he put the cigar down beside him, and when the fire burned through to the stone the whole rock gave a leap into the water, because it wasn't really a rock but the back of a great serpent. The Spaniards fought with it for more than a week, and finally they spiked it in the eye and threw out the anchor. They sailed until the anchor caught on the bottom, and this is where it stayed. Great scales and hair grew on the serpent's back, and they are the rocks, the trees, and the corn.'

The girl didn't hear him. Trinidad said to Gimpy:

'You told it very badly, but I forgive you because this is a special occasion.'

The newlyweds' quarters were enormous, with bright curtains and windows and double balconies all around. The girl opened the windows and the metal screens and looked out. She searched the shadows of the square for the bodies of the two convicts. Trinidad gently pulled her aside.

'That's no business for a young lady.'

The island fused with the sea, little by little the darkening water ate it away from all sides. There were bonfires in the distance and the muffled sound of a drum beating wearily far away. From the trees came the voice of the man with the hatful of trash:

> 'Tell me, tell me, tell me
> where I will find it,
> at midnight, and at dawn. . . .'

When Trinidad went out the officer of the guard was yelling at somebody who stood at attention before him.

'To you,' he said, 'I am not *Lefty*. What makes you think you can be so familiar? I'm Mister Lefty to you.'

The green beacon kept turning. The light passed at regular intervals across the window where the girl was standing. She was thinking that the relationship between Trinidad and his people was angry and bloody, and that this system founded on curses seemed too strong to be changed by anything.

51

She turned to watch the beacon, the distant landscape. But those men were still bleeding on the stones.

Trinidad noted with a smile that the turmoil was still going on in the woods. The distant noises sounded well in the intimacy and silence of the house prepared for the nuptials.

'They haven't seen a day like this on the island for years.'

'Then why did you shoot down there on the wharf, Trinidad?'

She spoke again of the two men on the ground because he was ignoring them. He answered with some reluctance:

'Gómez was a scamp, and the guard would have bumped him off sooner or later anyway, just for that, because he's a scamp. The other has had his coming to him for a long time too. They had no business doing filthy things in front of you.'

The girl didn't understand. The men had danced and sung in their own way, and it had been quite funny. Trinidad, watching her, was equally baffled. For the first time he had an idea that seemed to him philosophy: *Man and woman do not easily understand each other. Perhaps never.* Beneath their conversation Trinidad was conscious of the wide bed weighed down by the night. He went to the balcony and, once more calling the officer of the guard, he repeated his orders and asked if they had notified the first-aid station. He told the girl that her wishes were being carried out, closed the shutters, lit the light, and with an absent look went out to order the supper, so as to leave Lucha alone. Outside he was aware of a furtive shadow silently crossing the hall.

'Gimpy. Where are you Gimpy?'

He added in a lower voice, taking out his whip and brushing it across his knees:

'Gimpy, if you come near this room I'll break your skull.'

Calmly and cautiously he searched for the shadow of the lame man but didn't find it. This was not surprising as the cripple was slippery and ran all over the house like a rat.

52

He gave orders in the kitchen, took a bottle of whisky, and went back to the room. Before entering he knocked softly. Lucha asked him to wait a moment, and then he asked if she was hungry and what she wanted to eat, because he was not satisfied with the orders he had given. The girl suggested tea, lemon, and a couple of sandwiches. Very pleased by this simplification of the supper ceremony (everything still seemed to him a ceremony), Trinidad ran back to the kitchen. Just then Gimpy appeared.

'There's a dance on, chief.'

It amused Trinidad to assume a note of affection.

'Hey, you little son of a bitch. What were you doing upstairs?'

'Why, I just came in, chief.'

'If it wasn't you, then, who was it?'

Gimpy looked so obviously puzzled that Trinidad believed him. He repeated the question:

'If it wasn't you, then who could it have been?'

'I couldn't say, señor.'

He ordered him to go and talk to the sentry, if he had not yet left to notify the first-aid station—he dwelt on this, though he knew there was no doctor—and to come back and tell him exactly who were the ringleaders and what they were after. Gimpy put on an expression of servility and left. Trinidad returned to the kitchen, got the supper on a tray, and went slowly upstairs. The wooden steps creaked under his weight.

Lucha had unpacked her toilet set, also the camera which her uncle had given to her and which was her most treasured wedding present. She opened it, closed it, sighed with satisfaction, ran her hand over the case, and laid it on the dressing table.

She began to do her hair. It was short and made a chestnut halo around her head. She had put on a strange garment that reached to the floor. Trinidad had never seen anything like it. She was a vestal virgin, tall and slim, even her slippers covered by the stiff folds of her skirt. The material was very thick, but it was plain that she had nothing on underneath. He smiled broadly and wanted to embrace her but didn't know how to begin. Lucha did nothing to encourage him. She had changed; she seemed like another person. Her eyes had been seductive before, now they were cold. There was neither shyness nor coquetry in her movements. This was so blatant that Trinidad had to speak up:

'You make me very sad, my darling.'

'Why?'

'You act as if your husband meant nothing to you.'

She tried to speak but could not, holding back her tears. Trinidad was troubled but didn't give in.

'Over two lousy bastards you make all this fuss!'

His lack of respect for the wounded men, who might already be dead, and his manner of speech in front of her were too much.

'Say something, Trinidad. Say you were out of your mind. Say something to comfort me. Tell me they had guns and were threatening you.'

Trinidad said nothing of the kind.

'You are my wife, and I'm your husband. You've got to approve of whatever I do, especially on a night like this. Or did I marry a bloody magistrate?'

But the girl did not laugh. Trinidad chose to take her hand in silence and lift it to his lips. She realised that he was not taking her protests seriously.

'I'm going to see if the guards carried out my orders. When I come back I'll give you supper in bed, and then I'll join you.'

When he had gone out she locked the door behind him, gave a deep sigh, and burst into tears. She was angry at everybody, including herself. 'I won't open the door,' she thought. 'Even if it is the wedding night and I ought to let him in, I won't.'

Trinidad went down to the guardroom and found only the

regular sentries on duty. The reserve squad had gone out with the officer. A far-off murmur of protest rose from the trees, mingling with the sound of the rollers breaking over the jetty. It quieted Trinidad to know that the officer was making the rounds with the patrol. As he turned to go in he noticed a shadow crossing the bottom of the stairway. Could it be Gimpy? He called three or four times without getting a reply and tried to give chase, but the figure vanished about ten yards ahead of him. He went back to the sentry, genuinely perplexed this time.

'What's going on here?'

The soldier looked around without answering and clicked his tongue against the roof of his mouth, shaking his head. There was a threat in the air, but the sentry could not explain it. Trinidad poked him lightly in the ribs with the butt of the whip.

'What's going on here?'

The soldier again looked uneasily toward the trees and went on clicking his tongue.

Trinidad told him to fix the bayonet and keep five cartridges in the magazine. Then he went back in, took a gulp of whisky, tugged at his moustache, and started slowly for Lucha's room. On the stairs he went even more slowly, stroking his moustache. The creaking of the steps got on his nerves. He walked on, hesitated a moment in front of the door, and at last knocked. No one answered. He tried to open the door and found it locked. As he was about to call a shot sounded at his back. Trinidad pulled himself erect, drew his pistol, tried to reach the balcony off the landing, and had just time to see the screen door of the balcony slowly closing by itself. He did not reach the balcony but fell by the stair railing and tumbled down five or six steps, head first. Lucha came out and stood in the doorway, her body rigid. She did not know whether to cry out for help, whether Trinidad had killed himself; she did not even know whether the boots sprawling on the steps, the black suit hardly distinguishable on the

55

grey stairs, were Trinidad's. The cook, Mother Leonor, and the servant girls came rushing upstairs and screamed. The girl paced back and forth in a daze. It was Trinidad. The victim was Trinidad. And she thought and felt nothing, because the deafening shot was still ringing in her ears. She went to Trinidad's side, but there was nothing she could do. The wounded man was holding his two hands over his belly. He groaned. Other servants came to the rescue, and Trinidad was carried to the great matrimonial bed.

'Bastards! I'll hang the lot of you,' he muttered between his teeth, his eyes bulging. It sounded like an attack on the very people who tried to help him.

The girl paced back and forth, not knowing what to do. The island doctor, the real one, was away on leave in the capital. They went to look for the convict doctor, while the girl and Mother Leonor tried to staunch the flow of blood with towels. He seemed to be wounded in the belly, or perhaps a little below it. The girl didn't dare to look. One of the soldiers of the guard tried to come into the room, but Trinidad told them to let nobody in. Lucha thought: 'If I had opened the door when he first knocked nothing might have happened.' This reflection on top of her already chaotic feelings—those two dead men abandoned outside!—was almost more than she could bear. Mother Leonor wiped away a tear, sighed, and kept saying with a priest-like air:

'Soften his heart, O Lord! Soften his heart in his last moments!'

'Shut up, you old witch!' Trinidad said.

After a while he seemed to fall asleep. His expression became more gentle, but now and then he awoke and glowered by way of insisting that no one was to come in. Later he thought that another armed guard was needed to make sure of this, but though he racked his brain he couldn't think of two reliable men to post at the door, and this, even more than the wound, made him feel utterly lost. It was a feeling he had had from the beginning, not so much in his wound, but at the back of his head, where the spinal column turns into consciousness.

The doctor arrived drunk, with Margarito in his wake as a bustling assistant. Apparently he had forgotten Trinidad's abuse—his nostrils were still caked with dried blood—or perhaps he was there because he remembered it only too well. He had two hypodermic needles stuck in his lapel.

Along with Margarito came a poodle, who cheerfully examined the room and then put his front paws up on the bed to sniff what was there. The doctor gave him a kick and said to the girl with an undefinable look:

'Beg pardon, ma'am. That's Whiskers.'

The girl, her eyes fixed on Trinidad, didn't hear him, but the doctor went on: it wasn't exactly his dog but it sometimes followed him around. The dog was ridiculously unkempt. The doctor himself, they said, had trimmed him with a pair of scissors, leaving great uneven patches. At the end of his tail was a tuft which he wagged continually. The girl heard the doctor talk, without listening. He completely forgot the patient, but at last he chased the dog out and approached the bed.

Margarito moved the hypodermic needles from the right lapel to the left and addressed the girl, saying over and over in English:

'So sorry, lady.'

He, too, had been drinking, and consequently he was making a great show of decorum and fine manners. From time to time he turned to look at Lucha, for no reason except to see her. He was glad of the accident which permitted him to come in and nose around just when everybody was talking about Niña Lucha. He made furtive gestures to tell her that he didn't think much of the doctor and asked in a tone of well-bred indifference:

'Is the assailant known?'

Trinidad closed his eyes. But he could not close his ears,

57

and there came to him from far off the sound of the accordion and the drum beating out a conga. He asked:

'What's that?'

The doctor, speaking more to the bride than to the patient, replied:

'The mob at play.'

Trinidad looked at him out of the corner of his eye.

'What kind of mob?'

'My contemporaries.'

The doctor began a fumbling examination—it was in his hands that Trinidad observed his drunkenness—and uncovered the wounds. One in the back, three fingers above the kidneys, and another, much larger, where the bullet had come out, lower down, above the sexual organs. He assured the girl with much delicacy that it was not serious but that it complicated matters for him to have been wounded *in that particular place on that particular night,* because the lower abdomen was congested with blood. Then he left. Lucha went with him to the head of the stairs, where the doctor concluded, very proud of the weight of his words:

'You must reconcile yourself, señora, to the sorrowful state of widowhood.'

Margarito put in:

'Maybe something can be done.'

'To stop the bleeding, of course. I'm going now to get ergotin injections.'

Both the doctor and his assistant spoke casually. In the doorway the dog came up to his master. The doctor said solemnly to Margarito:

'Do me one favour. When I go back inside you stay out here with Whiskers.'

'What for?'

Margarito didn't like the idea. The doctor looked him up and down, smiling sadly.

'Just as I thought. Nothing but lousy egoism everywhere you look.'

Lucha, instead of returning to Trinidad's side, went into the next room and gave herself up to tears. She had thought she was alone, but she heard a noise in the shadows, as if someone were getting up from the ground. She hurried back to Trinidad's room.

'Send Mother Leonor away and come here a minute,' whispered her husband.

When the old woman had left Lucha drew a chair up to the bed and sat down.

'What did the doctor say? Am I going to die? I'll have him strung up too.'

'He said that with a little luck you'll be all right.'

Trinidad took in her youth, her fragrance. 'And I am going away.' The white of the bedclothes—those nuptial sheets—hurt him, and he closed his eyes. Lucha stroked his temples and put a shade in front of the candles so that the light shouldn't bother him. She was going to open the balcony door to cool the room, but Trinidad called her back.

'Come here. Don't leave me.'

She sat down again beside the bed. Trinidad breathed:

'Closer.'

She kissed his forehead and cheeks but avoided his lips. It made Trinidad angry, and she thought she saw one of his hands try to reach under the pillow.

'Kiss me or I'll end it all right now.'

Niña Lucha kissed him on the lips. Trinidad, on his pillow, panted like a bull. The kiss had given him the strength to pull himself up, with his hair matted and his eyes fixed on the opposite wall. The girl was afraid. As he pulled himself up he cried:

'My whole life has been only a preparation for this moment.'

It was not clear whether he meant his marriage or his death. He listened with an effort:

'Who's outside there?'

Lucha rose, a little anxious, and went to open the door. For a moment she thought she heard the Morse-code whistling of her aunt. Trinidad took the pistol from under the pillow.

'Who's there?'

There was no one. The girl wanted to look on the balcony because on that side of the house, too, there seemed to be a strange noise.

'Quiet. Don't open it,' Trinidad said.

The girl was afraid, but what alarmed her most was her own incomprehensible calm. She had heard Mother Leonor mutter: *It is God's will.* A little earlier two men had fallen dead on the jetty. Now Trinidad fell. She had thought she was going into a marriage, and so she was, but in a place where men were at war. They killed or died for reasons known only to themselves. Trinidad looked at the half-closed shutters and thought of the recent past, his letters to the girl, the wedding, his boyhood friend, now Director of Penal Settlements, and even the old mulatto woman who sold ladies' hair and leeches. The girl was also remembering little irrelevant things. And both were silent, sunk in their recollections. Niña Lucha repented many things: having deceived him once by going to the pictures with her aunt, *without his knowledge,* saying *Sweetheart* to the cat, censoring him when he shot at *the rabble.* And, above all, not having opened the door when he knocked the first time. Everything accused her. The blame was hers, hers alone, and at the thought her eyes went dry; she didn't cry; she couldn't. A sergeant entered.

'I don't want any arms in here,' cried Trinidad. 'Get out; leave the gun in the hall and ask permission before you come in.'

The sergeant did as he was told, went out, and came in again, his eyes fixed on the girl with a lewdness that Trinidad took as a threat.

'With your permission,' the sergeant repeated for the third time.

He launched into a senseless conversation, staring at Lucha. Trinidad, in a rage, took the pistol from under the pillow.

'You like my wife?'

The sergeant made the stairs in one bound.

'The next time I catch you looking like that I'll put a bullet in your head.'

The girl realised that she was involved, but she was beyond hearing or feeling. Blood and hair. The wedding night was sunk in an abyss of blood and hair. And it was her fault for having locked the door. She tried to think of something else, but she could not. She stood there in silence, looking at the arrow-head pattern of the parquet floor.

Mother Leonor ran into the young schoolteacher, Darío Gonzáles, who was on his way up the stairs and looked very concerned. She took him into an adjoining room.

'The finger of God! The finger of God was upon him!'

Darío looked at her in inquiry. 'It's very serious,' Mother Leonor replied. 'It looks as if he couldn't be saved.' The teacher nervously flicked the ash from his cigarette. He had no confidence in Mother Leonor, who was apt to exaggerate misfortunes; he asked where the wound was, if he was losing much blood, and so on. And after a pause:

'Do they know who it was?'

Mother Leonor shook her head. She invited him to come in, but the teacher declined.

'I? What for?'

The old woman was offended. She was rather proud to have such a serious case in her care, and the teacher only shrugged his shoulders. Amid all that anxiety Darío appeared to be saying to himself: 'Yes, they live; they kill each other, but it doesn't affect me, because I am made of different stuff.' It annoyed her. 'Just because he's young and strong and clever he thinks the others are no better than worms. He doesn't even care enough to go and look.' There was a long silence between them. Mother Leonor was thinking about Darío who had no religion. 'Worse than Trinidad.' For she had seen the chief pray once in a while. This Darío was a well-educated reprobate who had the urge to be an apostle. He had been in

61

other tough places before coming to the island. He sought them out, the old woman was thinking, to fill them with his poison; he considered it a privilege to be in such places. When any of those who had shared his life in the mining towns or the agricultural colonies prepared to leave for the capital the teacher would become indignant.

'Back to the rut! Back to the same old filthy rut! That's what ruins us all.'

In face of this crime all he did was to shake his head and flick the ash nervously from his cigarette. Mother Leonor repeated:

'Nobody knows who it was. And I don't think they'll ever find out.'

The teacher thought that the children would tell him some-day of their own accord. The old lady narrated for the second time everything that had happened since she went to the wharf. Darío appeared to share her horror, but actually he was thinking of something else. Of the convicts, of the widowed bride.

'Who is she?'

'An innocent soul.'

'She must be half out of her mind.'

'It doesn't seem so,' said the old woman. 'I don't believe she realises yet. She goes around as if nothing had happened. As a matter of fact, the chief wasn't yet what you would call her husband.'

'Poor girl!'

Mother Leonor was in a flutter.

'Do you know that Lefty ran off, pretending to look for the culprits?'

The teacher looked more interested. 'Did he go to the mainland?'

No. He had just disappeared. But probably it was only a guess. The old lady disliked Lefty because he cracked dirty jokes about her virginity. The teacher asked if they had the proper medicine for the patient and offered to take the launch to the mainland and get whatever was needed. Mother Leonor shook her head.

'Only one thing will be any good to Trinidad now: the Holy Unction.'

She was glad that God had shown Himself fierce and vengeful, because that way He was harder to deny. But she promised to mention Darío's offer of his services to the bride, and the teacher left, telling her where he would be during the next few hours in case he was needed.

Trinidad's bedroom was dark. Niña Lucha went about, her arms soft, her eyes full of terror, and silence on her lips.

'Come closer, Niña Lucha. Come closer, unless you're afraid.'

Lowering his voice, as if he were plotting a crime, Trinidad said: 'Lock the door from the inside.'

The bed was soaked in blood.

'Go, Niña Lucha, lock the door.'

At the door she ran into Margarito.

'Chief, they want to know how to make out a death certificate for those two who got shot.'

Margarito was very pleased to be there again.

'Who sent for you?'

Margarito bowed, feigning a genteel respect for Lucha.

'*I am sorry.*'

He left. Lucha locked the door behind him. Trinidad strained his ears.

'Do you think he really went away? He's there, listening.'

He tried to sit up but couldn't.

'Come closer.'

Niña Lucha returned to the head of the bed. Trinidad begged:

'Closer.'

Lucha petted him like a nurse. The green light of the beacon flashed at intervals through the window-panes.

'Put out the light; it's nicer that way,' he told her. But really he wanted to blot out the blood on the sheets.

63

The girl laid her hand on Trinidad's forehead; it was burning. That greed in his eyes was fever. On the pretence of putting out the light she rose and went to the dresser. Trinidad called her in anguish, trying to sound tender:

'Niña Lucha, come here. You're my wife. I'm your husband.'

He raised his voice, shaking with fever.

'I won't get blood on you. Look in what state you keep me, Niña Lucha!'

The girl wanted to talk about something else, but it was useless. Hair and blood. She wanted to look, but she couldn't look without seeing. And far away the accordion played the same tune over and over. The sound brought Trinidad out of his attack of madness:

'They're happy. The whole island is happy because we're married. But I'll get Lefty!'

But after a pause he relapsed:

'Come here, Niña Lucha. Let me touch your wedding dress.'

She drew away.

'Closer, my darling.'

'Trinidad!'

He caressed her clumsily. She felt a mixture of repugnance and pity.

'Let me alone, Trinidad.'

'You're my wife, Niña Lucha.'

He felt a sharp pain in the back of his neck and had to drop back on to the pillow. He groaned in despair.

'God is punishing me. I'm a good man. I'm not a criminal, like Gómez and Gimpy and Margarito. But God is punishing me just the same.'

The girl put handkerchiefs sprinkled with eau-de-cologne on his forehead. Trinidad thanked her with a gentle look, but as soon as he felt relieved he returned to his obsession.

'Come closer, sweetheart.'

Seeing her recoil, he snatched at her clothes with both

64

hands and talked in a kind of rage against himself. There was so much he wanted to say, but he couldn't disentangle his thoughts. The girl heard only meaningless words: '*Toyse . . . gelbo . . . hitma . . . night . . . moon . . . if they . . . sonsa . . . till morning.*' He watched her in the shadow. Whenever the green light of the beacon swept the room she saw in Trinidad's eyes a threat wrapped in tenderness. She knew that if he felt his death near he would try to kill her first. It didn't matter. She was to blame, and it was right that she should share his fate. If Trinidad made a move to shoot her she would stand still to make it easier for him. But perhaps it was hard to die at her age, and probably the idea was sinful anyway. She felt guilty, but not of any wilful intent. How could she have known what would happen? Thinking of this, the girl glanced toward where Trinidad had hidden the pistol, under the pillow. The night seemed endless. Trinidad was beginning to like the sound of the accordion and the distant drum. Rockets rose into the air, and Trinidad saw them through the panes, bursting in the sky and tracing lovely red sunbursts. The doctor had not come back. Lucha gave Trinidad iced water. The heat was suffocating. And he was still bleeding. The doctor had insisted on his going to get ergotin injections. Toward morning he showed up at last. He said he had broken into the first-aid station with an axe and had found a box of ampoules. They happened to be cacodylate and had nothing to do with the patient's condition, but the doctor wanted to do something and gave him two injections, one in each arm. In the daylight the girl saw Trinidad's face and was horrified. 'It is the face of a dying man.' Worn out, she went to the window. Opposite the stairs of the headquarters a corpse lay face up, the naked feet together, arms crossed over the belly, the mouth half open, the skin yellow. Seated at the head was a man with his hand stretched out in the gesture of one seeking alms. His other hand held a burning candle-end; the flicker of the little flame was hardly visible in the morning light. The girl thought it some macabre joke, but the doctor explained:

'No, señora. That's Gómez the Scamp, who died yesterday. The one beside him is his brother Spitball.'

'And what is he doing?'

'Asking for alms to bury him. The other one died, too, but he has no relatives on the island, so they'll just bury him in his skin.'

Hearing a loud rattle from Trinidad, the girl returned to his side in alarm, but the doctor went on pompously:

'Primitive customs, thoroughly unhygienic. That's the way they are.'

'Who?' Trinidad stammered.

'My contemporaries.'

The door opened, and Margarito came in. Also the dog, who went straight to the doctor, wagging his tuft of tail. 'That dog!' grunted his master, giving him a kick. The animal, not quite sure whether or not this was a joke, decided to chew his shoelaces.

'What a pest! Whose dog is it, Margarito?'

Margarito shrugged his shoulders and, knowing there was some trickery in it, said to the doctor:

'It's your dog.' And in English: *'Don't try to tell me he is not.'*

The doctor flushed slightly.

At eight o'clock the sergeant came in to report. Gimpy had arrived a little earlier, and Trinidad ordered him to stay in the hall to receive messages. The fresh morning air had cleared Trinidad's brain of the spectres of the night. Out in the hall Gimpy was making the most of his authority by giving great shouts. But he, too, wanted to see the girl and kept inventing excuses to come into the room.

At noon Trinidad lost consciousness and his death agony began. When he looked at the girl his hand shook and at times groped clumsily beneath the pillow. She knew what he was looking for, and this need to take her with him gratified

66

her woman's instincts. But his movements were futile; the pistol was not under the pillow, for the girl had been unable to resist the temptation to remove it and put it under the mattress, out of his reach. And poor Trinidad died, a burning candle on either side. He alone died.

The accordion and the drum, which had never stopped once, began to strike up louder than ever. Niña Lucha wandered sobbing through the house. She thought that perhaps if she went to bed she would sleep and wake up to find herself in her own room in her uncle's house. It was hard for her to grasp that in so few hours so much had happened. But surely it was over now; nothing more could happen after this. She was afraid of the dead man now— *hair and blood*—and this made her doubt her own feelings. But if what she had felt was not love, then what was love, really? Once she had left the room she didn't dare go back. She thought the dead man was going to stretch out his hand to touch her wedding dress. And yet she felt very tenderly toward him. Left to herself, her thoughts kept turning to the two who had died on the wharf. To Gómez the Scamp, whose body still lay across from the steps waiting for alms for a coffin. She was sorry for them and felt her pity a cruelty to the other dead man, to Trinidad. She didn't want to think.

The house was very still. Occasionally the wooden stairs creaked, but no one came up. Niña Lucha went again to Trinidad's room, her aunt's telegraphic whistle in her ears. Mother Leonor was there, seated in a low armchair, with her face buried in a handkerchief. Trinidad was laid out in his formal wedding suit. The bedclothes had been changed, and everything was clean and in order. Mother Leonor rose and came to the girl and wept more shrilly, crying:

'Oh, my poor girl! What a wedding night!'

The girl wanted to stand by the window, to look at the trees and the sky, but Gómez' corpse made her turn away. One dead man by the steps, another in the bridal bed. She was afraid. She went into the next room and lay down. She didn't cry. In the dark, her eyes wide open, she thought of her aunt, of the wedding that had been so beautiful, and of the shot that had deafened her as she opened the door. And of her guilt. The guilt that was hers alone. Still she didn't cry. Her head sank on her naked shoulder. The shoulder was round and cool and lush. Feeling her cheek against it, a great tenderness awoke in her. She loved herself, pitied herself, loved herself as if she were somebody else. She kissed her own shoulder, her curving arm, and again her shoulder. And so she fell asleep.

III

THE BODY OF GÓMEZ THE SCAMP WAS
still opposite the entrance. His brother Spitball brushed the
flies away and called out at regular intervals:

'Through a bridegroom's anger he has gone to the Lord's
mansions.'

Toward noon Careto arrived. He was a man of European
type—some said Spanish, others Italian—who had been on the
island only a short time. He had been given that nickname
because of the dark spot on his forehead. He had on an old
jacket and no shirt, and through the hair on his chest showed
half-healed scars from scratching. Careto was on his way to
the harbour where he went every two or three days to beg the
engineer for a newspaper, even an old one. He had come to
the country as a political refugee; no one knew exactly what
his crimes had been because he hardly ever talked.

He paused now to inquire:

'Is the chief dead? Is it really true?'

'Yes, but the only respectable corpse on the island is my
poor brother's. Give me something for his coffin.'

'Chuck him into the sea.'

Careto went on toward the landing, and Spitball jumped
up in astonishment.

'Refugee! Profaner of corpses!'

Careto walked on in silence.

'Refugee! Beggar!'

Careto stopped and came back slowly. Spitball got scared;
everybody was in awe of Careto's self-possession, and Spitball
was no fighting man. While the others spent their time
getting drunk Spitball worked to get ahead by his own merits.
He had just decided to learn to play the accordion.

Careto was beside him now, looking at the corpse with loathing.

'What was that you said?'

Spitball retreated and planted himself prudently on the other side of the body.

'The truth. Refugee. That's what you are.'

At headquarters Mother Leonor was trimming the candles, kneeling, murmuring the prayers for the dead. Now and then she would go to the window and repeat the prayer for the other one. The girl, watching her weeping, praying, covering and uncovering the dead man's face, had a strange idea. She figured it out, in relation to Mother Leonor's age . . . No, it couldn't be. When Trinidad came to the island Mother Leonor was already pretty old. 'Where do I get these ideas?' she asked herself. She had never before thought of anything so *ugly*.

On the ground floor, near the kitchen, a woman was weeping and crying out like a wounded animal:

'Ay, my Trinidad! My chief, my darling! Ay, my poor Trinidad!'

The girl questioned Mother Leonor, but the latter put her off:

'Men!'

The girl found implications everywhere. Mother Leonor changed the subject.

'We'll have to wait for Margarito before we can get down to business.'

Margarito knew a little about everything. He, too, wanted to get ahead, though not by playing the accordion like Spitball. He took correspondence courses from two universities. When they realised he was not paying the course was stopped, but he subscribed immediately to a new one. Though he had not exactly *got educated* his studies qualified him to sort the mail on the island, and that gave him a certain prestige.

'He must be downstairs,' Mother Leonor said every few minutes.

At every mention of *downstairs* or *outside* the girl had an image of poor dead Gómez. Mother Leonor turned toward Trinidad's room with a sigh, inviting her to go first, as if that were a great courtesy. The girl, with utter indifference, said: 'All right.' They went in and kneeled at his feet, murmuring prayers. Lucha looked at Trinidad's feet, with their huge boots, and was afraid. As Mother Leonor said, 'Take to Thy bosom, O Lord, the soul of Thy servant Trinidad, the sheep returned to the fold,' she heard something fall to the floor by the head of the bed. Mother Leonor went to investigate and found Trinidad's pistol. She kept it and looked at the girl with curiosity, baffled by the terror that had come over her. 'Of course, actually,' she said once more, 'you were never really his wife.'

Margarito arrived. Behind him were two dishevelled women, one of them dragging a three-year-old child.

'Ay, light of my life!'

She was barefoot and rather pretty. The other had on huaraches, and her hair flowed black and gleaming as if soaked with oil. The barefoot one was sobbing.

'What have you got to weep about, you whore?' said the other. 'He wasn't fooled by you.'

'I knew you were just waiting for this moment to spit your poison.'

'They can't keep me out, nor my son either, my poor master's son! Come to your home, child of my womb, come and gaze at your adored father for the last time.'

A little boy, almost naked, crawled up the stairs on all fours, and the women calmed down.

'I had two of them,' cried the one with the gleaming hair, 'but they died.'

The girl went with perfect ease toward the dead man's room. Mother Leonor couldn't understand it, but she said to Margarito:

'It's only natural that she's so cool. Actually she isn't really his widow.'

71

There was a certain exultation in her voice that hurt the girl, though she couldn't have said why. These were feelings that she had never known before. Margarito suggested that they get hold of the schoolteacher, but Mother Leonor hesitated. She didn't want Niña Lucha and the teacher to meet.

The two women came in and stood mute before the corpse. Finally the younger burst into tears. 'This child of my womb would have lacked nothing if you had lived, my chief!'

'Nor mine, if they'd lived,' said the other.

Niña Lucha left the women there and on her way out ran into the doctor. He was all dressed up. When he saw the girl, he raised his voice to impress her.

'I can perform an autopsy if you wish. I have a hammer and can get a chisel for the cranium.'

He stepped forward, trying to accompany her into the next room, but the girl shut the door.

'Pardon me.'

She dropped on to a sofa. She heard the women weeping furiously and the doctor and Margarito each trying to make the other ridiculous. All their voices were raised so that the girl should hear.

She remembered the doctor's eyes that bulged whenever he spoke. What crimes had those men committed? Mother Leonor had told her that the doctor had killed his mistress and then *profaned* the body. *Profaned*? What did that mean? She didn't know, exactly, but got something like a glimpse into another world, where men killed their mistresses and then went on making love to them. It seemed weird. That, too, was an ugly, filthy thought. 'Where do I get these ideas?'

When the women had stopped howling the girl went back to Trinidad's room. Strands of the deceased's hair lay on the pillow and beside the bed; the women had been cutting off locks for souvenirs. A metal-framed picture of Trinidad that had been on the dresser had disappeared. The girl was very pleased to see that they hadn't taken her camera, and she moved it to a safe place. Mother Leonor was going through the office for the dead again, reading from a little book that had lost its binding and was stitched together with thread. The leaves were curled, and she blew on them to turn the page when she found them stuck together. At the end she said, clasping the book to her bosom: 'These offices give plenary indulgence.' Then she went to the window and crossed herself, looking out at the other body. But this time she went through the motions in a greater hurry and somewhat disdainfully. Then she sighed contentedly, pressing her chin down into the folds of her ageing neck.

On the way out Margarito found Careto having a discussion with Spitball beside the body of Gómez the Scamp.

'I told you to get it away from here.'

'He's a poor dead man, señor.'

'Take him away.'

'Have respect for the dead, señor.'

'Take him away.'

Spitball refused, so Careto bent over and grabbed the dead man's ankles. Spitball leaped to the head.

'Drop him! You're dragging his head on the ground.'

He took the body under the arms and lifted it gently.

Careto had got hold of a newspaper. The folded front page showed a headline: *London Last* . . . The paper was his treasure; it might be a month before he acquired another. Margarito joined him, and they walked off together. Careto was none too pleased; Margarito saw his scorn in the way he shoved the paper into his pocket.

They went to the teacher's house. The sun was high and it stung. School was held outdoors in a place marked off by a picket fence. There were boxes of live insects around, seed boxes, pieces of wood to build things with, and not a single book. The teacher was holding a glass lined with blotting paper. Between the paper and the glass he had put seeds, and the moisture he kept in the blotting paper made them burst

73

open in a few days, send out a white shoot and then a new stalk.

'We came to tell you that Black Trinidad is dead.'

The boys had already told him. He was surprised to see Careto, who hastened to explain:

'I didn't come to tell you anything. He did.'

Careto was interested in what the children were doing. Darío offered him cigarettes—Careto never had any—and then one of the boys came up, making a lot of noise. He had a little box in his hand and was singing:

> *'The fly, the fly*
> *was where he was.'*

It was a little glass case in which there were six live flies and one dead one. There was also a spider with white feelers which he moved nervously like pincers and beside him two others the same size with black feelers. Three more, of a dark earthen colour, were busy sucking the thorax of a dead fly over in a corner. None of them was more than a quarter of an inch across, including their long legs. Lying on its back in the middle of the box was the *king spider*—the boy had found the name in an American manual—apparently dead. This was of the same species as the small ones, but black all over, with thick legs, a whole inch across. All these data—size, date of capture, and case history of each one— the boy had recorded on a little paper fastened to the outside of the box.

The child said excitedly:

'They've killed him.'

Darío went to get a magnifying glass and made an examination.

'You see?' He let them look in turn. 'The king spider has two large wounds in the middle. Two more in his head. And the right feeler and part of his jaw are broken. That means there has been a fight.'

Careto bent for a moment over the box, and Darío ex-

74

plained about the spiders, careful of how he spoke because he had an idea that Careto took him for a little pedant. He gave the lens to Careto, who looked, turned, and then said to one of the youngsters:

'He looks like Trinidad.'

Careto had spoken. All the teacher knew about him was that he had recently come from Europe after living in the thick of recent events. Nobody knew his crime, but the teacher didn't care about that. 'Everybody is a potential criminal,' he used to say to himself. It was an idea that Careto would have thought pedantic, and Darío didn't say it aloud. Actually there is no pedantry more insulting than silence, but Careto's came naturally to him, and his eyes expressed only a confident ease.

'The king spider looks like Trinidad,' he repeated.

The wide, bulging mouth, the hairs, even the gestures both had made in life! The boy who had brought the box left the group, hopping and singing:

> *The fly, the fly*
> *was where he was.*

The king spider had been slain and they were glad. Careto looked at the teacher, thinking: 'It's strange to find here a normal man getting pleasure out of his work.' The teacher wanted at all costs to make him talk, but he didn't show it. Careto had been on the island for three months, and up till now no one had drawn the slightest confidence out of him.

'Did you see it?' asked Darío, referring to the murder of Trinidad.

Careto let out a nasal grunt and lit one cigarette from another. His look was insolent, and Darío kept quiet. Careto vigorously scratched his chest. The teacher, seeing the raw spots on his skin, offered him alcohol and went to get the bottle. He came out followed by a servant girl who looked at Careto with hostility. Careto rubbed his chest and blew on

75

the alcohol on his skin. Darío decided that the best he could do was to start talking himself and began explaining the system of the school. Careto seemed to listen. The boys had been classified into three groups but didn't know that, and apparently it was not noticeable, though Darío based their work on it. The first group consisted of fourteen boys *who were proud of their fathers' crimes.* In the second group were twenty who never talked about the sentences their fathers were serving and mentioned them timidly, if at all. The last group was the largest. In this were twenty-six boys absolutely indifferent to their background, who considered their parents as men and women who wanted their children to have a decent life in the future. They were fond of their parents but without sentimentality. The teacher was trying, little by little and without ever mentioning it, to have the third group grow at the expense of the other two. It was just as wrong for them to be proud of their parents as to be ashamed, whatever their crimes. A son's indifference to his father's guilt showed the impotence of moral ideas before the laws of nature. At this remark Careto woke up and looked at him with new attention; then he smiled without saying a word. Darío had been working with the children for two years.

'And what is it you want to do?'

'To educate them.'

'Educate them for what?'

'So that some day they will be socially useful.'

'And do you know whether in fifteen years society will value those qualities?'

'Anyway, they will be happier.'

'They'll be just as miserable. All you will have done is to complicate their misery.'

'So you think I'm wasting my time?'

'All people waste their time.'

Tired of having talked so much, Careto rose, excused himself with a gesture, and left. But he came back.

'Let me have a little of that alcohol.'

Darío gave him the whole bottle. Just then a group of convicts passed the school. They were all as well dressed as possible. The poorest ones had on the official striped jacket and dungarees which, as a rule, nobody wore. In the lead, on horseback, armed with pistol and cartridge belt, came Sixfingers.

'No work to-day,' they said cheerfully. 'We're going to headquarters to offer condolence.'

Careto and Darío stared at Sixfingers, wondering how he could ride a horse, let alone carry a pistol. But they were interrupted by the owner of the glass case, who apparently had decided to celebrate the death of the king spider and now arrived leaping and singing as before:

> *The fly, the fly*
> *was where he was.*

'Now we know who killed the king spider.'

'All of them together, or just one?'

'Just one. Peak.'

Peak was an insignificant little reddish spider.

'And how do you know it was Peak?'

'Because he's doing the same thing the king spider used to. He waits for the others to catch flies, and when they catch one he chases them away and begins to eat it.'

'Didn't he do that before?'

'Which one?'

'Peak.'

'No sir. He did not. Before, Peak used to eat the flies he caught himself. But he learned from the other one.'

Their attention was diverted by a boy standing nearby in the woods. He was ten or twelve years old, in rags, and of appallingly wretched physique. The little fellow stood watching the school. Some of the Indians from the south settlement said they had known his father on the mainland and that he had been a tribal chief of a little village far in the interior.

He had been killed in a revolt. The boy wandered around with delirious eyes. The teacher had often tried to persuade him to come in but with no success. Other boys, usually those of the first group, threw stones at him when they met him in the woods. The teacher went out and Careto after him. Darío went up to the boy, with a friendly smile. Rusty-Pants —that was what they called him; no one knew why—didn't smile. He had never been seen to smile.

'Why don't you come in?'

He drew back, growling:

'I'm going to my people.'

'Where are your people?'

'My father is over there.'

He pointed to the sea. He went on:

'He wasn't a man. He was a wolf and he wore a hemp collar. And they killed him. And when they killed him they had a dance.'

Careto seemed interested.

'Yes, he was a wolf,' he said in a hoarse, almost sinister voice.

'This man knew him.'

Careto walked up to the boy and patted him on the head. Rusty-Pants didn't run away.

'Your father was a wolf. I knew him. And they killed him.'

The boy took his hand. The teacher came closer and offered him chewing gum. Rusty-Pants took it, looked at it thoughtfully, then threw it away.

He looked at the teacher with his sombre eyes and said:

'Now they've taken it from me. They take everything from me.'

'No. Here's some more.'

He put it in his trousers pocket, which bulged terribly, and took out a piece of glass from a broken bottle.

'You're going to hurt yourself with that. Why do you carry it?'

'It's sugar for my people.'

'But where are your people?'

'Here.' He stamped the ground with his naked foot.

'Your father too?'

'Yes. But my father was a wolf.'

The teacher saw that he had thrown away the other piece of chewing gum, too. He handed him a coin.

'Here. But come see me to-morrow.'

The boy threw the money away among the trees. He was clutching Careto with the other hand.

'They've taken it from me again.'

'Don't you want to be my friend?'

The boy seemed on the point of laughing but quickly moved back without letting go of Careto's hand. When he was out of the teacher's reach he flung a coarse gibe at him and disappeared among the trees, still with Careto.

The teacher went back to the pupils, who were still fascinated by the box of spiders. Everybody thought of Trinidad, looking at the king spider, motionless, belly up.

Darío walked slowly to headquarters, where he found a great crowd waiting on the staircase, by the guardroom. There was no noise; the people going in and coming out moved indolently, as though tired. In what had been the guardroom Sixfingers, the Twin, and Lefty were having an argument, apparently over who should go first and be the spokesman. The Twin yelled:

'Let each one go up on his own!'

The teacher kept thinking about Careto. He didn't believe he was either Spanish or Italian. His accent sounded rather German.

The crowd gathered against the walls in silence. Gimpy, who didn't dare go upstairs, glided among the shadows as usual. When he saw the teacher he went up to him. Gimpy had been sentenced as a result of the marijuana traffic; he had a whole network of accomplices, and one night two of them had been found dead. He cultivated marijuana on the island

and sold it among the convicts. No one had been able to make him confess where he raised it.

His limp was more noticeable on the steps. The teacher looked around hesitantly, and Gimpy pointed to the room on the left.

'She's there.'

He rapped on the door. Mother Leonor answered, and the cripple, after introducing the teacher, pushed the door shut and sat down outside. Mother Leonor was indignant at the people thronging to headquarters. The teacher said it was only natural. Mother Leonor was embarrassed because she had not introduced him to the girl. The teacher gave his name and put out his hand. The girl saw him smile and thought: 'This is the first man I have seen smile on the island.' Darío spoke of the people, how they had stopped work for the day, and of the regret that everyone felt. 'All except you,' thought Mother Leonor, seeing him in such good humour. One sentence of Darío's impressed the girl. Speaking of the promptness of the convicts in coming to headquarters, he said:

'They are coming to offer condolences, because by being polite like city people they feel more respectable.'

'Yes, after murdering him,' grumbled Mother Leonor.

Darío smiled. Mother Leonor fretted. 'He hasn't offered his own condolences yet.'

'The island,' Darío said, 'is under the jurisdiction of a judge on the mainland.'

He thought the air smelled of the corpse and lit a cigarette. He looked at the widow in silence, and in his eyes there was a sympathy that seemed to the girl a trifle ironical. For the first time she had a glimpse of her tragedy from the outside. 'He thinks I'm a fool to have made such a mistake.' Darío saw that she was worried and spoke at random:

'This is no paradise, but it's not much worse than any other place.'

Mother Leonor kept thinking: 'He still hasn't offered his condolences.' Darío added that as soon as the judicial and legal formalities were over she could leave. He told her when the buses left, also the plane from the mainland to the capital, though there he hesitated, thinking perhaps the girl would not travel by plane. If she wanted to send a telegram to her family he would take it to the launch. The girl said yes to everything and wrote the message on a sheet of paper.

The convicts were filing into the patio of headquarters. Mother Leonor asked if they had to receive all these people, and the teacher nodded. 'All you have to do,' he said, 'is give them your hand as they come past.' The best place for it would be the patio.

The girl asked Darío to stay beside her. Gimpy stood elegantly in the position of chief mourner as the three lined up at the bottom of the stairway. The teacher asked that the ceremony be brief, in view of the widow's grief and fatigue.

The crowd filled the patio, and now that the three were there, like a tribunal, there was some criticism. The Pimp came first. He always liked to be first. The teacher whispered to the girl:

'He's abnormal, the poor fellow.'

The Pimp wore a shirt with no buttons, exposing his naked chest. Dust and sweat had made curious patterns on his skin. He stank.

'May you have many years of happiness.'

He kissed her hand. The girl felt the moisture on her skin but didn't rub it off, though it was rather more distasteful than being licked by a dog. The Pimp dropped his battered hat on the ground and in picking it up looked at her legs, trying to get a glimpse above the knees. The girl felt his look run up her thigh like a cold lizard and was disturbed. She wanted to wipe off her hand but didn't dare. The Pimp retired, bowing grotesquely. The girl looked over the crown of heads without focussing on any. She felt all their eyes running over her body and was afraid to look at anyone. The teacher did not usually dwell on the crimes of the convicts, but now they came to his mind. The Pimp had spent his youth in a brothel, helping the servants with the domestic chores, like a woman, though he boasted of being a male. His contact with professional killers had led him to sample the strange glamour of the dagger and pistol.

He was always trying to lecture and reform the women on the island, whom he considered prostitutes, and had been beaten up for it several times. He did not remember now that Trinidad was dead, though he had heard every one speak of it. He couldn't remember it and thought he was supposed to give congratulations at the wedding.

Sixfingers came up, a thickset fellow, standing very solidly on his feet. They said he had one shark's eye and one human one, and when he spoke he winked one or the other, according to his mood.

'First, my congratulations on the wedding.'

His hairy hand gripped the girl's cruelly, and she saw that he had two thumbs linked at the base and apparently without power of motion, like a vegetable growth. The teacher said, smiling: 'This is Sixfingers, a simple and loyal fellow.' But he looked more like a bandit.

And he didn't mince his words:

'In my opinion the chief didn't act right towards Gómez the Scamp, because——'

The teacher interrupted:

'This is not the moment to be talking like that, Sixfingers.'

Sixfingers shut his human eye and looked at him with the eye of the shark.

'What I say is that somebody here has a buzzard waiting for him.'

Darío was silent. How could he answer? Observing this, Sixfingers opened his human eye.

'I'm in prison, but prisons are made for men. Now I, Six-fingers, tell you in the name of all here present——'

Several voices arose in protest. 'I haven't given authority to anybody. . . .' Or, 'I can do my own talking; that's what

I have a mouth for.' The teacher silenced them with a gesture and said:

'The widow is very tired and would appreciate it if a group, four or five of you, would speak for all.'

There was a murmur of agreement. No more than four or five wanted to talk, anyway.

'I, Sixfingers, tell you,' he said, frowning, 'that we are all very sorry for what has happened and you have our deepest sympathy.'

Darío looked at the crowd, thinking, 'The murderer is among them.' But it was all the same; nobody really cared. In the silence that followed Sixfingers moved back, still holding the girl's hand, and said pointedly:

'I tell you, the buzzard is already after some of those who have been protesting.'

The pistol dangling at his side made the words more ominous. The girl trembled. The man was like a boulder rolling down on her, with those thumbs like twin acorns growing out of the rock. And yet something about him reminded her of Trinidad. The teacher, seeing his over-ardent look into the girl's eyes as he released her hand, thought of the man's crimes. He wasn't subtle enough to beat his enemies by making them recognise his superiority and had had to kill them. Sixfingers retired very pleased with himself. Again he turned to the crowd to say that those who wanted to see the deceased could do so, if they used the service stairway. Mother Leonor had a fit at his making so free with the house, but didn't dare to protest. The girl, hearing that they were going to go up, asked Gimpy to fetch the camera which she had left in the adjoining room. He came back proudly with it slung over his shoulder. Sweat, eyes burning with sexual hunger and desperation! Darío recalled Sixfingers' story, watching him talk to Lefty. Years back he had been jailed for matters of village politics. One day he was set free. He had a brother who was a businessman and who gave him money to set himself up. He acquired some land through a foreclosure.

Sixfingers worked hard and thought everything was going to be all right. But his enemies put the screws on the brother who had helped him and ruined his business. The brother blew his brains out. When Sixfingers heard about it he chewed his moustache and said with resignation:

'He must be given a proper burial.'

Two days later the funeral was held. At the ceremony were all those, or nearly all, who had brought his brother to ruin. They were high-class people who kept up appearances. From beneath his serape Sixfingers took out a Tommy-gun and began to spray the assemblage with bullets. He killed eight and wounded ten. The gun had to be wrested from his hands because he was determined to finish them off.

When the federal troops came to arrest him Sixfingers gave himself up quietly, saying:

'You can kill me right now; I've already done my job in this life.'

He was sentenced in December. The execution was set for June, allowing for an appeal by the defence.

In that little city there was a curious custom. Men under sentence of death were given a rifle and cartridges and made guardians and public watchmen, at the orders of the mayor. Sixfingers went through the streets, along the roads, and of their own accord people ran to offer him food and drink. Sixfingers had a good time waiting for the execution.

The teacher, mechanically receiving the file of guests, thought:

'That is a custom followed by many tribes, and it is rooted in the sacrifice whereby men are reminded that the glories and fortunes and happiness of this world are ephemeral. They selected a strong and handsome man, crowned him with roses, and gave him a flute. He wandered among the people for a year, being received and fêted by every one. If he entered a house they brought him quails, legs of chicken, puppies cooked in pulque, cocoa. The women went to his house, dressed and undressed him, bathed him in scented water. And

84

at the end of the year the victim was sacrificed before thousands of people who watched the spectacle with the utmost grief.'

Something similar was done now with condemned criminals. The judges made the selection. If they had not, in Sixfingers, chosen the most handsome candidate, at least he had had the satanic happiness of killing all his enemies. The day his sentence was commuted they took him to a crossroads where he joined a group of prisoners on their way to Faro Island. 'But I will have foam in my mouth always,' he had said. No one knew what he meant by that.

He became acquainted with a woman who had murdered her mistress in the house where she was a servant. The world looked ugly to Sixfingers' shark eye and kindly to the human one. He had foam on his lips, and it was bitter foam.

'Why did you kill her?' he asked the woman.

'She wouldn't let me talk to my man.'

Sixfingers reflected: 'That's how a real woman loves her man. You will be the mother of my sons.' And he married her on the island.

They kept filing past. Sixfingers was talking to Lefty and looking threateningly at the Twin, another convict who was now approaching the girl. When his eyes rested on the girl she felt the look in her breasts, especially the left one, and remembered the Pimp's lizard eyes and the saliva on her hand. But her aunt had told her about the social duties that rested on a married woman, and she kept her poise and dignity. Dignity. That was what her aunt had said. The dignity of a married woman. Some of the convicts stood paralysed before the girl, not knowing whether to go forward or back, and Darío had to push them gently on. All left something behind: a look fastened to her throat like a snake, the echo of a last spasmodic word, a gesture made in a grotesque attempt at good manners. All left something, and when they went away they looked as if they had lost a pint of blood. The girl watched the Twin approach. He was a man of about

85

fifty, broad-shouldered, vigorous, with a delicate mouth hidden by a thin moustache. A lock of hair flopped over his forehead, and in the flabby skin of his throat the tendons and Adam's apple stood out. Before the girl he felt very much bewildered but he still looked like an old lion stalking his prey. Before speaking the Twin kissed her hand, not with his lips, but with the end of his nose, in which there were two or three hairs, and his beard. Hair everywhere. The girl, who had been making a great effort to maintain her dignity, put on a look of kindly scorn. The Twin stammered:

'With your permission.'

He was totally at a loss. The teacher offered him a friendly hand. The Twin took it, grateful for the rescue, and said to the teacher, for he felt incapable of addressing the girl:

'You know that I regret what has happened to the young lady and that like all the others I am at her gracious disposal.'

A laugh broke out behind him. Sixfingers was making fun of him. Although the Twin had hurried through his last remarks, feeling he had hit on the right thing to say, something was gnawing at him inside. The teacher noticed that he was not carrying his pistol. That was all.

Watching him walk away, Darío recalled his case history, which was even more deplorable. He had broken loose, not as revolutionary, but as highwayman. The teacher insisted on the distinction because he thought of himself as a revolutionary. The leaders shoved him aside. Then in a little village something happened that finished his downfall. They arrived hungry and no one had any food for them. In some of the Indian huts he saw some strips of dried meat and a pile of tortillas still warm and soft. He tested the meat. Chicken? Before he noticed he had eaten more than half, and the tortillas also vanished down his throat. He finished and lay down for a nap alongside the hut, but an old man appeared, and the Twin, his hat tilted over his eyes, asked him:

'Did you say you had nothing to eat?'

'Nothing, chief.'

'Go to hell, you old bastard; it was damn good.'

In the previous village he had made a nice discovery, which was to use a wire instead of a rope for hanging. The advantage of the wire was that within five minutes the victim came down by himself, head on one side, body on the other.

The old man was amazed.

'I didn't think you'd eat that stuff.'

'Why? Wasn't it chicken?'

'No, señor: iguana.'

The Twin felt queasy and would have vomited if he hadn't had a strong stomach. He had the old man flogged. One of the soldiers strung him up just to show again how well the wire worked. Then a twelve-year-old girl appeared, weeping. The Twin raped her and, being ashamed of himself, took her by the ankles, swung her through the air, and dashed out her brains against a tree.

Two towns farther down they came after him. Half of his men deserted. The others were brave, but they were shot one after the other. The Twin took refuge in a rocky gorge and kept firing, bringing down a man with every shot. He held out all day. Toward evening four of his enemies advanced under protection of a waggonload of stones, a mobile entrenchment against which the Twin could do nothing. But he left his hiding place, climbed a tree, and stayed there quietly, playing possum, until they arrived. When they thought they had him in their power and were getting ready to dislodge him with dynamite the Twin, from above, killed all four. By night he was able to escape. He knew they would get him, but he planned to reach a neighbouring state where he had relatives and friends and had a chance of being taken to the judge instead of being bumped off on the spot. So it turned out. He had spent eight days in the municipal jail when the federal police told him:

'You have to go before the judge.'

The courthouse was an hour and a half's journey. They gave him the summons, and the Twin put the papers inside his shirt and set out. He went alone, unguarded. He walked all morning and arrived in the early afternoon.

He introduced himself:

'I am the Twin and here are my papers.'

The judge, who came from the capital, did not understand this procedure at all but told him that if he was really the man he ought to go to the municipal building and give himself up. He did, and it helped him later to obtain a reprieve.

He thought often of the little girl whom he had raped and killed, and in his repentant state she stayed in his mind as an ideal of purity. He would have liked to find her and rape her again. But this time he would not have killed her. The distinction made him feel like an exemplary character.

This was the Twin who had now taken up a position in the doorway, feeling that he had made a very bad impression on the girl. Across the patio Sixfingers, on the contrary, was puffed with pride.

Lefty drew himself erect. His shirt was dirty and his belt crooked. He spoke with insolent ease:

'I was the best friend of the chief of the island, and in my grief as a friend I offer myself to you as a loyal friend.'

He used the word *friend* three times to emphasise the fact that he was not a convict. The girl usually murmured, 'Thank you.' To Lefty she said nothing. She could not. It seemed to her that every time he bent from the hips he was going to bite her neck. In his eyes she saw her frustrated wedding night. That was what Lefty was thinking about. They all were. Now it was the doctor's and Margarito's turn. Both had offered condolences several times already, so Margarito said pompously and with interpolations in English:

'I do not offer you condolences. I repeat it. *I say: I repeat it*, what the rest of them say,' and he squeezed her hand in his own damp fist, so tightly that the air was forced out from between the two palms, making an embarrassing little noise.

The doctor had come, looking most impressive in his new suit. Whiskers followed him like a shadow, looking even more out of place now that his master was dressed up like a city bourgeois. The doctor had offered a small boy ten cents to keep him outside, but made the mistake of paying him in advance. The boy soon forgot the dog and went off to spend the money. And Whiskers attached himself to the doctor's leg just as he was addressing Niña Lucha.

The doctor gave him another kick, but Whiskers misunderstood and started gnawing his shoe. 'And he profaned her after death,' the girl was thinking, not knowing exactly what it meant. She looked at Whiskers, while the doctor turned pale and distorted his mouth in a grin. Then he felt obliged to straighten his necktie.

'Science has done all that could be done. I am sorry.'

The others went past without speaking. Once in a while someone would stammer a few meaningless words. The girl kept saying 'Thank you' and holding out her hand. One man had a split nose and a harelip. The girl felt something like her old childish terror of men who go along the roads with sacks on their shoulders. He was looking at her insolently. And the dark inside of his skull showed through the cleft nostrils. The servant girls and the cook were crowded in the kitchen door. One of the girls was weeping, wanting to remind everybody of her intimacy with Trinidad. 'So it gave them social position to be his mistress,' the girl thought.

A well-dressed man forced his way through the crowd. He hastened to identify himself:

'I am the lighthouse keeper. An official.'

He didn't look at Mother Leonor. They had been on bad terms ever since she said she had known an uncle of his and that his family were 'a bunch of tramps who never knew where their next meal was coming from.' The lighthouse keeper wanted to stay beside the teacher as one of the reception committee. As there were already four people on the step and there was no room for him, he stayed at the side, leaning against the railing. Some of the Indians shook his hand along with the rest.

Overhead sounded the footsteps of those who had gone on upstairs to view the body. Mother Leonor was very displeased by that. Women with nursing babies came past slowly, shaking hands with all four, including Gimpy, and went on. The girl watched the children sucking at the mother's breast, letting go now and then to stare at her. When they let go the breast shrank like rubber and the nipple stood up dark and swollen. The girl blinked nervously.

The teacher, who had had enough of it, asked her:

'What's the time now?'

A thought sneaked through her mind: 'What hour does he want it to be?' She would have liked to tell him something pleasant, if only the time. Darío took a paper from his pocket, adding:

'I must take the telegram to the launch.'

The bar-keepers were there too. Eminencias was the more respectable, that is, the richer; after offering condolences with his cap in his hand (a shiny black alpaca cap that he took off at the last moment), he handed her a price list. They went over and joined the lighthouse keeper. The reception committee was growing, to Mother Leonor's annoyance; only people really connected with headquarters belonged there.

'I'm sorry to say I'm known as Nosy-Posy,' a man said, shaking hands with the girl.

He was an effeminate fellow, with a smooth and affable face and an affectation of boredom. There were rolls of fat on his belly and jowls. He smiled, repeating his introduction:

'I'm sorry to say I'm called Nosy-Posy.'

He shook her hand and left. He was round, without a profile, like a caterpillar. His affected grace of movement struck the girl as somehow lascivious. Mother Leonor remarked in an undertone, 'He's not a man like the rest.' Nosy-Posy knew they were talking about him and looked back, smiling. An old half-naked Indian came up, his skin dry as paper. The teacher took him by the hand:

'The chief of the south settlement.'

The chief shook hands all around and said that there were two musicians with him who would like permission to play. The teacher gave his consent after consulting the girl. One of the musicians had a clay flute and the other a heavy drum which he beat with two sticks tied to his second and third fingers. The two sat down in a corner and began their funereal music. The flute whistled shrilly, and the drum beat out a queer rhythm. The funereal quality of the music filled the air, not with sorrow or mourning, but with a kind of cold madness.

Every one was sweating. The place reeked of sweat. The girl remembered childhood crises when there had also been a smell of sweat. She still felt the Pimp's eyes on her leg. The music continued. The combination of smell and music seemed to open every pore of her skin.

'What's the matter?' asked Mother Leonor, taking her by the arm.

'Nothing. I'm all right now.'

The girl continued to hold out her hand. There was a drowsy animal look on the faces that passed. Gimpy had taken the teacher's place as master of ceremonies and hustled them on despotically when they paused in fascination. But Gimpy, too, had an animal expression. The teacher was talking with the lighthouse keeper, who was protesting against Sixfingers' carrying a pistol. The girl didn't know where to look. Every face left its own distinct impression, but all were dirty in their hope or menacing in their lack of it. Some reminded her of the cries that rise from the abyss of a nightmare, others of the senseless delight of young animals biting and injuring without a thought. 'It's as if they all had horrible dreams,' she thought, 'and couldn't get rid of them when they woke up.'

Mother Leonor said that they looked at her in an indecent

way but that she must forgive them, because they were the dregs of humanity.

'I forgive them?'

She was thinking that every one of the prisoners' expressions reminded her of one of Trinidad's. Each one was like a fraction of Trinidad's look. The music went on, the flute sounding cool and fresh as if from the bottom of a pool.

The teacher went out to take the telegram to the launch. It was hot. In the sun the light of the beacon was even more dazzling than at night. He went to the dock. He had to notify the judge, not only of Trinidad's death, but of the two others' as well, Gómez and the anonymous convict. He had been thinking about it all morning. With three deaths the situation was confused, but the first two were already paid for by the third. Darío, the teacher, in notifying the judge, was making an accusation. A moral problem was involved. He could not approve of the murder of Trinidad, but he understood the murderers' reactions just as he understood the schoolboys' pleasure over the king spider. And now in sending in a report he would seem to be making an accusation, and it troubled him.

On the dock he found the engineer with two convicts. The teacher said he was going to write out a report for the judge, for the legal proceedings, and asked him meanwhile to take the telegram for the girl's relatives. The engineer read the paper, his lips moving silently.

'I'm sorry, but they won't let me leave the island, or take or send messages.'

He looked at the two others. One took out a pistol and showed it to the teacher. The other lifted his shirt, which was bulging, and exhibited another pistol stuck in his belt.

'Who's the chief now?' Darío asked.

Silence. They looked at him with animal indifference, without answering. Darío retraced his steps. He couldn't take this seriously; nevertheless, the island was really incomunicado. He saw Careto go by. He looked drunk, which was odd, because Careto never drank. It must be the noonday sun. Careto went past sunk in thought. Darío walked slowly on. There had been a *coup d'état*. Who could be the leader? Necessarily there must be a leader. He no longer felt the sun on his head, at the back of his neck. What a situation! A *coup d'état* on the island, and it had begun on the European pattern, with the lines of communication. The island was cut off. By whose order? He realised when he reached headquarters that it would be unwise to tell the girl.

As he went in he heard Mother Leonor talking excitedly, and thought: 'They have found out.' The two Indians were still playing, seated on the ground. Darío went up the stairs two at a time. The girl came out to meet him, wide-eyed.

'Trinidad's body has disappeared.'

'What!'

'Yes. They took it away.'

There were marks of bare feet around the bed. The covers were in perfect order, but the dead man was gone. The drum and the flute still sounded below. All sorts of possibilities occurred to the teacher, but he didn't want to say anything for fear of alarming the women even more. Mother Leonor went into the next room and found Gimpy with his face buried in a white cloth.

'Are you crying?' she asked him.

Gimpy looked at her like a guilty dog. He was not crying. He dropped the cloth and went away in silence. It was the nightgown that Lucha had taken off that morning. The bridal nightgown. Mother Leonor stood holding it pensively, then, remembering that she had left the girl alone with the teacher, she rushed back. She wanted to tell the girl about the nightgown but realised that it would be embarrassing. Darío was still absorbed in wild conjectures.

'Did you send the telegram?'

To avoid an answer he pretended to be deafened by the music:

'I'm going to chase those poor fellows away.'

He went out and paused on the stairs; then he walked down slowly, stood in the door, and gave a careful look around. Far off, the accordion and the drum were playing a conga. He came back into the house and went slowly upstairs, not knowing what to think. As he reached the top the two Indians again struck up their funeral music. Mother Leonor was saying to the girl:

'I'm not saying anything, but there have been cases where a dead man has gone to hell in both soul and body.'

She gazed at the empty bed.

IV

CARETO WAS THE ONLY ONE WHO HAD
not gone to headquarters to offer condolences. He walked
toward his hut in the sunlight, lifting his boots with care
because they had no laces and sometimes his naked heels
came out.

'Fooling with a corpse is a sport that has its possibilities,'
he said aloud, thinking of Trinidad.

At the door of the hut he squatted on his heels. He straight-
ened up to test his suppleness and again lowered on to his
thighs. Straggling groups were still coming from headquarters.
He settled himself on the ground but again rose and let
himself down slowly. The work on the roads kept his
muscles loosened up. But to-day no one was going to work.
The shovels were piled under the trees, the little wheelbarrows
resting with their legs in the air. He would have gone to work
by himself, but they would have taken it as a provocation and
killed him. 'And after killing me,' he added, 'they would
play with my corpse.' But how does one play with a corpse?
He looked up at the trees. Half hidden among them was
Eminencias' house. At the door a group of four or five
were discussing the girl. 'And then she said to me . . . And
I said to her . . .' Careto smiled. The lower part of the
building was of cement and brick, the upper part of wood.
There was only one little balcony with red shutters. A zinc
gutter pipe jutted out from the balcony floor. Sometimes,
when they poured out dishwater, it ran down with a noise that
reminded Careto of urinating cows. He had a side view of the
back part of the house. There was an open window through
which now and then appeared a hand holding a little paper
the size of a small bill. The paper would flutter away and the

hand draw back. If the wind carried it up into the air a woman would put her head out and solemnly watch its flight. It was Eminencias' wife. They said she was a leper. Careto looked at his own naked chest, opening his jacket on both sides. Why complain? He had never complained. But he had a feeling of having seen everything in life a long time ago and being condemned to go on watching nevertheless.

He entered the hut and, taking a tin bucket for which he had made a handle out of wire, he went out to dump it in the sea. Coming back, he put the receptacle carefully in a corner and sat down again in the same place. The newspaper lay at his feet. He was about to pick it up when Rusty-Pants came along and stopped, watching him in silence. Careto returned the look without speaking.

'Did you bring one?' he asked finally.

Rusty-Pants came forward and held out a bird clutched in his fist. Careto took it. It was a beautiful goldfinch.

Rusty-Pants said nothing.

'Go over there and get her,' Careto ordered. 'She's in a box by the fireplace.'

'Won't she get away?'

'No.'

Careto began to pull off the bird's wing and tail feathers. The little thing squawked pitifully. The feathers fell to the ground.

The boy came back with a cardboard box and put it on the ground. With a low, tremulous whistle Careto took off the lid, and when Ruana, as he called her, started gliding out of the box he released the bird in front of her. It was a large non-poisonous snake, white with brown markings. Her head began to sway, her eyes fixed on the bird, which hadn't yet seen her. When it did it stood with its wings half spread, contracting its claws as if about to jump. But it couldn't move. Rusty-Pants watched the snake as fixedly as the snake watched the bird. Ruana pulled enough of her length out of the box to make the attack, and in a split second bird and snake vanished in a puff of dust, reappearing beside Careto's boot. The snake had coiled around the bird, which was slowly choked, its beak wide open. Finally it died and Ruana swallowed it; it made a bulge in her throat, then in her belly. Careto whistled softly, thinking it helped her to digest. Rusty-Pants stared at her a long time and tried to whistle, too, but he didn't know how.

'They're all scared of Ruana,' he said.

Careto reflected. He was very fond of setting problems for himself and solving them. It seemed cruel to pluck the bird alive and give it to the snake to eat. But the snake had to live. And which of these feelings was stronger? It was easier to identify oneself with the bird, because the bird had feet and used them to walk with, as men do. The snake moved without feet; it walked without feet, and that was harder to understand. But he was a man of imagination.

Rusty-Pants said absently:

'We have to put her back in the box.'

'Let her alone. She'll go in when she gets cold.'

The boy started to go, then stopped.

'To-morrow I'll bring another one.'

He vanished among the trees. The man, watching him go, said to himself:

'His father was a wolf.'

He sighed and picked up the paper. It frightened the snake, and he tried to calm her again with the low, tremulous whistle. Reading the paper, he forgot Ruana. War, war. People killing one another on three continents. What for? Such a thing must be more than mere stupidity. Careto identified himself with the Nazis. He had to. His blood was Aryan. (The thought made him laugh, because that blood of his, Aryan or Jewish, had given him a lot of trouble.)

An Indian appeared. He stopped and pointed at the cardboard box, looking at the snake coiled inside. Ruana raised her head in alarm. 'Perhaps,' thought Careto, 'they are as sensitive to Indians' eyes as birds are to theirs.' But soon he was back at his cogitations. To one side of the cliff, near the sea, four women were emptying buckets. On the whole island there were neither cesspools nor latrines. Only at headquarters, and maybe at Eminencias' house and the lighthouse. He tried to remember what the convicts called those buckets but couldn't get it.

Oh yes! The 'stool'.

Darío came out from headquarters. He was worried. Near the guardroom an Indian was looking covetously at a rifle resting against the wall; finally he took it and slung it over his shoulder.

'Where are you going?'

Before looking to see who had spoken the Indian put the weapon back. Then he saw the teacher.

'It was left there.'

'What do you want a gun for?'

'Well, I really haven't any use for it. But it makes you feel more like a man.'

The teacher went on. That was unusual in an Indian. At his left, between the rises in the shore line, he saw patches of blue sea, sometimes topped with white spray, sometimes calm and smooth. He wondered who was leading the revolt. Six-fingers? The Twin? They all had a craving for power, and the death of the chief had made it more acute.

He arrived at his house. The boys had gone. La Chole, the half-breed servant girl, was setting the table. In the distance the accordion was playing the same little tune. La Chole observed:

'That's Spitball. Three months he's been at it and he can't get beyond *Shoot, Pepe!*'

Darío went on mulling things over. Niña Lucha, the corpse, the dance. Why had they stolen the body? If it were only a matter of burying it they needn't have done it in that fashion, making Mother Leonor suspect the intervention of the devil. She was always quick to see the devil. But sometimes she met

98

God and didn't know Him. She had been three months in the south settlement as a missionary. That was in the beginning. She taught the young Indians to pray. They were good people. But to Mother Leonor 'good people' were the humble ones who looked up to her. She taught the Hail Mary to a fifteen-year-old Indian lad who went into ecstasy reciting the part about 'full of grace, the Lord is with Thee, and blessèd art Thou among women'. Mother Leonor cherished the illusion that the boy understood the sacred words. But one day she caught him on the ground at the foot of a tree, his arms clasped around a girl his own age, to whom he was reciting the Hail Mary in a voice trembling with emotion. The nun fled in horror. The teacher used to say to her:

'That's as good a way as any of getting close to God.'

Mother Leonor was indignant that a revolutionary should use the name of God. She was always being indignant. But actually the old woman enjoyed herself amid the harsh life of the island. If everything was so gloomy and awful why didn't she leave? But life there was warm and enticing. And Darío thought: 'The old lady, like everyone else, has a touch of the swine in her heart.'

After the afternoon class Darío went to Tortola's canteen. The building was set on a shaky wooden support near the dock. For Tortola, a short, chubby man with red-rimmed eyes, it was an honour to have Darío there. Neither the Twin nor Sixfingers was about, but the proprietor was expecting them. The teacher went out to the porch, where a few convicts were drinking, seated on the ground. One of them declared:

'I saw Trinidad in a cloud. He held his hand out and made like this with his fingers.'

He opened and closed his hand slowly. Another put in:

'I saw him, too, but he went more like this.'

He made an obscene gesture with finger and hand and caused an uproar.

'Well, where is he?' said the cloud seer, feeling they were

making a fool of him. 'If you can tell me where Trinidad is I might agree with you.'

The Oriole's eyes formed an arrowhead above the bridge of his nose, and the sides of his mouth fell in the same angle. He was old and his skin looked dry and dead. With him was his son, the Slicker. They were both smoking marijuana.

The proprietor came out, wiping his hands on his apron, and said to the teacher:

'Very few of us on the island really have, as they say, clean hands. Do you think it's a good idea to let Eminencias run the food supplies?'

'They say he's a good manager.'

'Oh, I'm not accusing him. I'm not saying a word. Don't think I said anything.'

'You want them to give you the commissariat?'

'Me or anybody else in the business who not only has clean hands but can touch beans or rice with them without endangering the community.'

Darío sat down on the railing of the shed. The wall and the wooden underpinnings creaked under his weight.

Behind him old Oriole was yelling at his son:

'Say it! Is your father a dog that you can't talk to him?'

Someone got up from another group on the ground.

'And then she said to me, *Thank you so much!* And then, *I appreciated your condolences the most of all.*'

Bocachula let out a loud nasal snort, which meant that a laugh was coming. Then her guffaw came:

'Niña Lucha knows very well how to behave. She never told you any such thing. And if she had said it, it wouldn't mean anything, because respectable people don't act like us. Among respectable people you have to pretend.'

Chapopote swore:

'Strike me dead!'

Bocachula had a reputation for fine talk and a lot of it. A woman convict from Puebla who had come to the island with a buccaneer, seeing Bocachula in the circle with Chapopote, the Slat, and Congo, gave a great sigh and screamed:

'I've just found out she left her crystal palace to come here!'

'A real man, Trinidad!'

'Then she said to me,' Chapopote went on.

'You're dreaming. She said the same thing to everybody: *Thank you,* and shook hands.'

Bocachula was indulging in daydreams:

'If I hadn't had the misfortune to kill my man and come to the island I'd be just as respectable as she is. And if all that hadn't happened they'd be serving me at the table with silver and gold.'

'That's a lie. Nobody with silver and gold has got to come here.'

Bocachula, beside herself, yelled in a voice that sounded to Darío like a knife drawn across a pane of glass:

'I have just one thing to say to you—*mierda!*'

The sky was turning crimson. The teacher accepted Tortola's token of esteem—a bottle of beer. He opened it and drank in little sips. He heard slaps resounding now and then behind him. It was the time of day when the mosquitoes came out. Old man Oriole had malaria, and he liked them to bite him and then go and infect others with his blood. Everyone despised him, and he clung to his son, on whom he tried to 'impose his authority', as he put it. They called the young one the Slicker because he looked like a sophisticated city boy; his expression was that of a man who has never had any youth, though he was only twenty-three. He felt bound to his father as by a curse. The father said over and over:

'It was all because of that date. Why did I go?'

He was speaking of his own wife, whom he had killed with the assistance of his son. The bar was sinking into shadow. Tortola came out and hung an acetylene lantern on a nail. It threw crude shadows. The flame made a rapid hissing noise and fluttered in the wind. Congo came up to the teacher. He was almost naked, but he wore a dirty rag, the remnants of a serape, around his neck, covering the scars where his ears used to be. The teacher recalled his story: once he refused to take part in a murder, and his companions cut off his ears and made him eat them. After that he lost his will power and said yes to everything. He had two or three diseases.

'Cardinals would be serving me with napkins,' howled Bocachula.

Congo scorned these vanities. He laughed and put on an air of familiarity with the teacher. In spite of his muffler, one could tell that he was laughing by the slight crinkling of his eyes. He spoke from behind the serape:

'Life is very funny. I was thinking about it this morning at headquarters. Life is like a lovely girl looking for a husband.'

Just then the Lawyer arrived. Darío saw that he was looking for trouble with Congo.

'Get out of here,' he said, 'before I give you a present.'

'What do you mean?'

'You earless bastard, get out of here, quick!'

Bocachula got up.

'These days dogs look like wolves and wolves like men, and between dogs, wolves, and men it's hard to tell the difference. You're tired and drunk. Lawyer dearie, go to Eminencias' house and shoot your face off to his wife.'

Congo began to unwind the ragged muffler which covered his nostrils and the scars of his ears. Bocachula stood between them.

'He's drunk. A man doesn't fight over what a drunk says.'

'Get out of here, you scum!' the Lawyer insisted.

Chapopote dragged the drunken man into his group and made him sit down on the ground.

The teacher watched. By the end of the day the Lawyer was loaded with liquor—he drank pulque—and the storm burst.

'And her little breasts are like Saint Joseph's nard.'

The Lawyer asked whom they were talking about and, hearing the name of Niña Lucha, clapped his hand to his mouth as if he had a toothache. Then he burst into tears. Bocachula enfolded him like a mother amid general laughter.

'Weep, my boy, weep.'

The uproar increased. Bocachula managed to dominate it.

'Shut up! If people squeal like pigs it is because they are not brave enough to weep.'

Some became serious, but the rest began shrieking again. Bocachula sighed.

'The world is as ugly as a monkey's armpit.'

Old Oriole groaned again.

'Why did I keep that date that day? That date was the ruin of me.'

The son looked at his father with rancour. 'Always talking about that date. As if I had no feelings at all.' But he didn't dare talk back. The teacher, watching the pair from a distance, thought: 'They're all in the same state as the Lawyer.' He ordered a beer for Congo.

'The good life,' mused Congo after taking a swallow. 'Life is as lovely as a smart little virgin.'

A fresh breeze came from the sea. No one knew why that afternoon breeze, rustling a paper on the ground, gave them a feeling of remoteness.

Everyone was thinking of Trinidad's body, and they wanted to speak of him, but since the man had made that obscene gesture with his hand the subject seemed vulgar. From the woods came a little group, one carrying a resin torch. There were three men whom Darío recognised when the torchlight fell on their faces. 'There,' he thought, 'is the general staff.' Sixfingers, the Twin, Lefty. The Twin had now acquired a pistol and ammunition belt like Sixfingers, and this seemed to give him great assurance. Lefty was very drunk and was being meek and servile toward Sixfingers and highhanded with everybody else.

Someone got up from the ground. It was a man called Squinty, because his eyes were always half closed; he had the reputation of being a holy terror.

'The gang's all here,' he said, presenting himself to Six-fingers.

The teacher went out to meet the 'general staff', but the three ignored him. The rebuff hurt Darío; it stopped the words in his mouth. 'Power, power,' he thought. 'With a pistol at their belt, the first thing they learn is a subtle, feminine contempt.' He went over and mixed with the group, not wanting to be conspicuous. Sixfingers, in a burst of enthusiasm, said to Lefty:

'Give Squinty a gun. He's a good fellow.'

The teacher came up. Sixfingers turned on him insolently.

'Are you going to explain that business this morning?'

The teacher finally caught on.

'What do you want me to explain, Sixfingers? You mean my taking those messages to the boat? You must realise that I wanted to try to make arrangements so the widow could go back to her family.'

Sixfingers looked at him ironically.

'How kind of you!'

Darío began to feel uncomfortable. Sixfingers went on:

'Some men are so kind they wouldn't hurt a tiger. Aren't they, Mr. Schoolteacher?'

Sixfingers continued the attack:

'You couldn't bring yourself to cut off a tiger's tail.'

He opened his shark's eye wider, while the human one squinted. But Dario was not intimidated.

'I couldn't bring myself to cut off a dog's tail, either.'

He said it deliberately, but Sixfingers didn't notice, and the teacher fell back to a plane of familiarity, interceding for Niña Lucha. They had better let her leave the island. Sixfingers looked at him squarely without answering. Then he took the glass and drank. The others seemed not to be paying attention, but they were listening. There was a long pause; then Darío pressed his point, pretending to be casual.

'What's your answer, Sixfingers?'

'You're so smart, don't you know that silence is an answer?'

Lefty exclaimed:

'A good point!'

Darío became alarmed. From the other side of the grove a rocket rose into the black sky, showering the treetops with sparks when it burst. A few people started to make an outcry, but Sixfingers cut it short:

'Quiet there, boys. I'm going, too, and you come along behind.'

He signalled the torchbearer to get going, and they went out. But not all of them. Seated in a corner of the shed was old Oriole, dry as a mummy, and his son. The old man sighed.

'That date was the ruin of me!'

'Why did you go?'

'What could I do? My blood ran hot in those days.'

The old man became maudlin.

'That was the day you were conceived, son.'

'Why did you go? What got into you?'

'I wasn't made of stone.'

The son sighed too. 'That woman ruined us.' Both were smoking marijuana. The Oriole grabbed his son by the arm.

'Is that the way I brought you up? To call your mother *that woman*? Is that a way to talk about your mother?'

'Well, you killed her.'

'You dare to call her *that woman*?'

'You killed her.'

'Let me hear you say *that woman* again!'

The Oriole raised his arm to hit him, the son tried to grab at it, but the old man dodged, and the Slicker's fist came down on his father's head. The father replied with a blow in the face. They were still sitting on the ground, drunk, pummeling each other.

The teacher broke it up. He could handle them like puppets, but he had to be careful not to let them grab his arm, because once they got their fingers dug in they were terribly strong. When they saw it was the teacher they seemed to calm down. The son explained:

'He's always talking about the day he had a date with my mother. He says I was conceived then, and that's where all our troubles started.'

The father took up the theme.

'Where were you this morning, when all the respectable people were offering condolences to the poor afflicted widow? There! You see what kind of manners he has! And now he calls his poor dear mother *that woman*.'

'But you killed her,' the son repeated.

'Who?'

'My mother.'

The old man struck him at the back of the neck, reaching around the teacher who was between them:

'Say *my dear mother!* Go on, say it!'

Darío left them and went to headquarters. But he stopped for a moment to listen outside. From the dark he heard shouts, scuffling, blows. The family quarrel was beginning again.

The night was pitch-black. The beacon was not working. Darío took out his torch. At headquarters he tried to find Lucha and met Gimpy slipping by like a cat.

'Gimpy!'

'At your service!'

He was holding a white cloth. He had come back to take the girl's nightgown. The teacher saw that his eyes were bloodshot and uneasy.

'They're going to have a celebration in the woods.'

'Yes sir. It's the wedding celebration that got postponed because Trinidad was shot.'

The teacher decided to go home. In the woods someone was drumming on a hollow log to call the convicts together.

'Take your eyes off the girl; she's way out of your class.'

106

Bocachula was speaking, hanging on to the Lawyer's arm. Behind them came Careto, in silence. By the light of an oil lantern three old women were pouring out pulque. A little farther away men were turning strips of meats fastened to ramrods over hot embers. Bocachula, taking advantage of the fact that the beacon was dark (someone had broken the light), leaned on the Lawyer's arm and profited by her stumbling on the uneven ground to press against him. The man was anxious to get rid of her before they came to the clearing. In the glare of the acetylene lamps set up in the woods for the celebration he thought: 'I haven't yet fallen low enough to appear in public with this woman.' She mistook his look.

'I like you; you're so romantic.'

A great cauldron was boiling over a log fire. The cooks were hurrying, because the clearing was already full of people. The laughter and babel of voices drove the Lawyer to prise himself away from Bocachula.

They joined the crowd, he nervous and she in a huff. Careto was wandering around with his hands in his pockets, his sweating chest exposed, looking for a place to sit down. Along the sides a platform, supposedly in the shape of a horseshoe, had been rigged up out of tree trunks, worm-eaten timbers, mounds of stone, and anything else that came in handy.

Resin torches fastened to the trees threw out a leaping light. Baskets of tortillas, skins full of pulque, and flour and corn-meal titbits were brought in. The hubbub increased as new groups arrived. Around that circle the night breathed, harsh and black. There was hardly room for people to move. From far off came the sound of the sea. The light of the lanterns was blue, that of the torches red. The lanterns cast on the faces the spell of a water-front brothel. In one corner Spitball was making his public debut with the polka, *Shoot Pepe*, on the accordion.

They had hardly begun to settle down when a voice called for silence:

'Everybody stand up!'

Sixfingers arrived with his retinue and took the chair. He stared sternly at the assembly until every one was seated. Also in the presidency were the Twin and Lefty; other notables, including Margarito and the doctor, dressed in his Sunday best, were trying to gatecrash. Whiskers let out contralto howls at the doctor's side. Sixfingers struck the table with his whip and shouted something which only those nearest to him could hear. Most of them caught only the tag end of a threat:

'. . . his mother!'

Hardly anyone knew what he was talking about, but all gave their approval. The women patted their hair, murmuring:

'That's what Squinty said. Sixfingers has them in the palm of his hand.'

A drunk, with his shirt tail hanging out, began to sing the Cuban's favourite song, trying to imitate his dancing:

> *'Why do you get so mad, black man,*
> *if they call you trombone lips?'*

Spitball tried without much success to accompany him on the accordion. People were beating the tables with their hands or with sticks, and if they couldn't find anything to beat they cupped their hands into a trumpet and howled. They thought with emotion of Gómez. Some of the women wept. One said through her tears:

'On my old man's saint's day, he went on the booze for three days. And the poor old boy—he always did such funny things—he went to Rufa's house and pissed right in the baby's cradle.'

Squinty yelled out from a group of men who had arrived drunk:

'Hey you, singer! Make it hotter!'

Congo unwound his serape from the holes of his ears so

as not to miss anything. The Oriole said to his son, who hadn't opened his mouth:

'Show respect for your father's grey hairs, you scorpion!'

The singer changed his tune to a sly, insinuating conga; Spitball tried to keep up on the accordion:

> *'She's a fine girl*
> *Trinidad*
> *Where did you find her*
> *Trinidad?*
> *What will become of her*
> *Trinidad?*
> *You didn't get a try at her*
> *Trinidad.*
> *Not even one*
> *Trinidad.'*

Whenever the dancer was about to say *Trinidad* the whole assembly shouted it out in time to the conga, and now when the dancer said it he signalled the full chorus to come in.

The jugs of pulque went from hand to hand, fifteen or twenty people drinking from the same one.

Sixfingers rose to speak, and a reverent silence fell. All the same it was hard to hear what he was saying:

'... the chief ... for the present ... an ugly business ...'

Scattered voices expressed general admiration for Sixfingers as he stood there, erect and defiant. Six or seven half-drunken men had crowded up behind him.

'When we went to the dock to congratulate the bride and groom he received us not with thanks and cigars but with bullets.'

A murmur arose, but Sixfingers, with a smart blow on the table, demanded silence.

'And that was an insult to the good people of this community who had turned out to welcome him. His lady wife, on the contrary, has shown us the most delicate and exquisite courtesy. The distinguished lady, his wife——' He wanted to get off a lot of handsome compliments, but he was too worked up; they all ran together, so before his confusion was noticed he decided to give up the attempt. 'Black Trinidad didn't want to let you pay your respects, but in the end Black Trinidad had to be our host whether he wanted to or not. And, what's more, he has had to preside at the wedding feast. We present him in person!'

He turned with a gesture of the arms. The group opened behind him, and there, seated in the presidential chair, between Sixfingers and Lefty, was the body of Black Trinidad.

The coat was buttoned around the back of the chair and held the body in a fairly normal position. They were holding his head up from behind to keep it erect, and the eyes were open so that he looked alive. Careto shuddered.

'So that's where he was,' he thought.

A breath of chill air passed over. The blue flame of the lanterns wavered. Little by little, timidly at first, then louder, the noise broke out again. Every one was struggling against that dead man's chill which ruffled the silence as a breeze breaks up the surface of a lake. In a corner two old women began to pray, those around them joining in: 'Give rest to his spirit, O Lord, as we give rest to his body.' But they changed that part to: 'As we are going to give rest to his body.' The doctor struck a professional pose. 'If he stays like that much longer he'll get too stiff to handle.'

Since the chair was wobbly the body tilted over as though in weariness. This gesture of fatigue aroused pious feelings in a few of the onlookers:

'A great chief!'

'What a man he was!'

Those who were singing Trinidad's praises now had more than once been strung up by the feet by him. The woman who had come with her little boy to see him at headquarters approached the corpse, leaned over the table, overturning a jug, and kissed it. Then she came back, tearing at her hair.

On all sides there were convulsions and voices rising in hysteria; it seemed that all the women there had passed through his arms. Squinty watched his own woman, who was also crying out with a great show of grief, and became furious with jealousy.

'He was a dog, the chief!'

'He was no dog! He was a wolf!'

'A wolf!'

Rusty-Pants dangled his yellow mask from the low branch of a tree.

'A wolf, like my father.'

The ones in front were spellbound by the dead man, whose eyes seemed to have engulfed the night.

'Drink the ocean and then see this!' cried Bocachula.

Whiskers, as if conscious of the situation, howled pitifully.

The Pimp went around begging matches.

'Once I made a little fire,' he said, 'and the fire was my friend till it went out. If we burned the chief he would be my friend too. . . .'

The chill of the corpse was enough to freeze the flames of the candles. Again people began to howl as though possessed, but this time in acclamation. Then the dead man bowed. They grabbed his hair from behind to make him move his head.

Congo rubbed his nose:

'What a stunt! It's Trinidad to the life!'

The Pimp forced his way up to the corpse. His nose and chin were red and bloated from pulque. He was trying to get close to the body.

'When did he die?'

'What difference does it make? The dead have no yesterday and no to-morrow.'

The Pimp was always telling stories about beautiful women who had kept him. But now he couldn't take his eyes off Trinidad. When he had convinced himself that Trinidad was really dead he exclaimed:

'He rests in the Lord.'

And added:

'And the bridal night? No bridal night?'

Gimpy felt his marrow on fire like the candles. He took a jar of pulque that someone offered him and stood staring at it.

'I see the tree; I see the dark; I see the night; I see the pulque, and all I see is ruins and more ruins.'

He tried to go away and couldn't. It seemed as if the dead man was pulling him by the jacket. Men came up and asked him for marijuana. Gimpy took some out of his blouse and gave it away free. If anyone gave him something in return he kept it. A little old woman over in the corner with the others (who were praying) sang a song that she made up as she went along:

> *'The cock scratches his comb*
> *and the man asks the ghosts,*
> *"Where is the girl with the broken heart,*
> *the broken heart of silver?"'*

She went on with a thousand variations: *'The broken heart of corn, the broken heart of ivory.'* Then she went back to the cock scratching his comb. All those people, earth to earth, gave themselves up, unresisting, to the mystery of the night that was pressing on the woods. From somewhere Gimpy heard:

> *'Night will not last forever,*
> *an hour passes and another,*
> *every one drinking but the chief,*
> *every one happy but me.'*

He turned to see who was speaking but couldn't make sure. He asked the man beside him:

'Do you want to see the moon?'

'Yes.'

Gimpy left the woods, with the drunkard on his heels. Just then there rose a new burst of acclaim for Trinidad, who bowed like a puppet, his eyebrows raised because they were

pulling his hair too hard. As they left the woods the drunkard
pointed to the sky.

'Look, there's the moon.'

'That's not for you. Yours is the beggars' moon.'

'And where is the beggars' moon?'

Gimpy kneeled, parted the grass with both hands, and
showed the earth underneath lit by the moon.

'There, that's your moon.'

In the clearing the uproar swelled again. Coming into the
circle at a new point, everything looked different. The green
crowns of the trees were clustered above; between the tables
their roots showed like snakes.

The Pimp shook his head, drawing away.

'If they killed him I say it's not fair. Even the wolf is one
of God's creatures.'

A man raised his fist at him, and he retreated to his seat in
a fright. Jugs of pulque flew through the air, aimed at the
dead man. The Lawyer, with the help of the pulque, had overcome his depression of the afternoon and was in a gay mood.
He danced on one spot and, seeing Careto nearby, sang the
charm against the snake:

> 'And I will get you drunk
> Snake
> And you won't hurt me
> Snake
> And then I'll hurt you
> Snake
> And you won't hurt me
> Snake'

Suddenly he interrupted himself, crying:

'Ay, what a wench to tumble, what a wench!'

As if they were all contradicting him, he turned belligerently
to the ones nearest.

'Yes sir. That's what I say and I'll stick to it!'

H   113

But nobody paid any attention. The Lawyer went back to his charm against the snake:

> *'And then I'll scold you*
> *Snake*
> *And you won't hurt me*
> *Snake'*

The Pimp looked around and, meeting Gimpy's eyes, remarked:

'They call me a fool, but everybody's a fool.'

Gimpy reflected: 'That's true. Me too. When I was born I was a fool, and now years later I'm many fools. When I laid my first woman I was two fools, then three, four, five, six, seven, and now I'm an even hundred. To this very day I don't know myself.'

The Pimp rose, swelling his chest.

'Who can match me?'

The Pimp said to himself, very wide-eyed: 'Punch and Judy went to bed, and next day they gave birth to one hundred and twenty thousand-peso bills. Black Trinidad scratched at the ground and shoved it out beween his hind feet. Rap-rap-rap-rap. And I was watching from behind a tree. One and another and twenty and a hundred and twenty and all thousand-peso bills like little green crabs; when I counted them they crawled down my fly; they ran up my sleeves. But there they are.' And, looking around, he said:

'Look at me well; I am not the Pimp any more. I am a gentleman. I can fish treasure out of my pants. A gentleman. I will have an automobile and sweet-smelling whores.'

Careto listened to him, creeping up behind to hear better. Seeing him, the Pimp stopped talking and scratched his buttock. Careto watched him with an avid eye, but the Pimp was afraid of this man who never spoke. Beside him the woman who had kissed the dead man began howling again:

'That's enough of your cracks. What I say is——'

She was going to the centre of the ring so that all might

see her but fainted on the way. They picked her up and lifted her in the air. The young women made remarks; the old ones prayed. Spitball was picking out a conga on the accordion, accompanied by two white-bearded old men with *maracas*. Two or three convicts got up and began to wriggle around the old servant woman from the lighthouse. The rumba dancer performed again in front of the corpse. The conga whipped the drunken crowd like a whirlwind. Trinidad, staring out of the cavities of his eyes, his body slumped to the right, was listening.

The Pimp tottered to the centre.

'Take notice! Here you see the pants of a true gentleman, including the fly.'

He shook his hips to the conga. Banana peels were thrown at him. He stepped on one and almost went down. Nobody cared what he was doing, so he went back to his place.

Congo tore a strip of dried fish with his teeth, looking stoical. In his hand he had a pepper, which he bit right through. It was very hot; he stuffed a fistful of salt into his mouth, then cleared his throat, while two big tears ran down his cheeks. He still had the rag wrapped about his neck, but his sparse moustache showed above it as he chewed his fish with gusto. Then he went back to the pepper.

The rumba dancer sweated out the conga:

> *'Who do you leave the girl to,*
> *Trinidad?*
> *Tell us before you go,*
> *Trinidad!*
> *Who do you leave the girl to,*
> *Trinidad?*
> *Are you leaving her to the Twin,*
> *Trinidad,*
> *or to Sixfingers, maybe,*
> *Trinidad?'*

Lefty felt slighted at not hearing his name. The din grew

so loud that the singer had to stop because nobody heard him. Pito the Yute yelled for silence at the top of his lungs, but to no effect.

'Some whistle, that Pito!'

'Your mother!'

'You're going to listen to me, because this is a democracy.' At this Careto laughed without moving his lips, a laugh that seemed more like a death rattle. The Twin called for order. Two of the men who were manipulating the dead man stopped, and the corpse leaned to one side and fell, dragging the chair with it. It was hard to say whether the protests of the crowd were directed against those who had let the body fall or against Pito the Yute, who went on shouting and gesticulating all by himself. Black Trinidad had rolled under the table and stayed there. The Pimp was chaffing him, but without much conviction.

'Get up, chief. If you're drunk just say so, because I'm going out of my mind with this bloody uncertainty.'

The Twin went to the centre of the circle. He gesticulated angrily, trying to say something to Sixfingers, but all that could be heard were fragments of disjointed words, the end of one word joined to the beginning of another: '. . . nighter . . . linate . . . intono . . . forly . . . to-night . . .'

That went on quite a while. Then Sixfingers stood up, feigning the stony indifference of a conqueror. 'Everything has been decided, and to-night Black Trinidad's bed will be occupied by the man who now has the honour of addressing you. That's all I've to say, and enough!'

But the Twin conceded no such easy victory.

'I asked . . . esq . . . comra . . . ideal . . . cor . . . use of the word . . . ded widow . . . this evening . . . Lucha . . . ato . . . yesdela . . . for the duration of the present act . . .'

He seemed to be claiming Niña Lucha. Bocachula looked around. The naked trees in the night made her feel ashamed, she who had so often stood naked before men. Gimpy was imagining Niña Lucha in the middle of all these arguments;

Bocachula was seeing her among the wanton trees; the Pimp saw her, too, awaiting the bridal night. Gimpy pondered, listening to the discussion in silence, his mouth open. He felt a hand on his shoulder; it was Darío. Gimpy exclaimed in horror:

'They've all gone wild.'

Darío looked tired. He felt as if he were guilty of something. He had managed to slip through unnoticed. The doctor asked for the floor; it was granted, and he started out very well, though his voice trembled. Hearing his master, Whiskers barked, and people began to laugh.

'My esteemed contemporaries! Think of your situation. That is to say, of our situation.'

Sixfingers was becoming infuriated. The Lawyer cried out at a somewhat untimely moment:

'Hear, hear!'

People looked at him in surprise, and the Lawyer stared back challengingly. There was a certain nobility in his eyes, but his mouth was obscene and spoiled the effect. The Twin approached with a mixture of curiosity and contempt, intrigued by this man who had been shaved and well dressed ever since the girl arrived.

'We are too near the mainland. As soon as they find out——'

A voice cried out behind the doctor:

'Who's going to tell them?'

Sixfingers put down this idea with a sweeping gesture.

'Dispatches will be sent just the way Black Trinidad sent them, and there are plenty of people here smart enough to forge his signature.'

The doctor with much decorum again asked for the floor. He hadn't yet made his main point.

'I propose that the widow be brought before those here assembled and politely requested to make her choice.'

That brought the matter to a point; the doctor had confidence in his new suit and his well-shaved face. Darío shuddered. The words *be brought here* caused a mild riot. Margarito thought it was a wonderful idea and said so, smoothing his hair.

'Let the bastard talk,' Sixfingers ordered.

'I think,' Margarito said, 'that the doctor's idea would be a very fair solution.' And added, in English, '*That is my opinion.*'

'Explain that gringo talk, if you dare!'

Sixfingers accepted the suggestion. So did the rest. But in a simple and natural voice Careto began to talk:

'I haven't been in this. And here I am, Careto, who hasn't seen Niña Lucha, hasn't spoken to her, is not dreaming about her. I, the only one of you'—he raised his voice in a kind of chant—'who can be the father, your father, with no woman trouble in my head or heart. I, Careto, come to speak for the first time among you, and I speak to you now and raise my voice among you and tell you to repeat with me: "Chief Trinidad is dead!" '

A heavy measured rumble answered:

'The wolf father is dead. . . .'

The voice rose and fell arbitrarily with a sinister gravity. Darío thought: 'He's either a mountebank or he's crazy.'

'The wo-o-o-o-lf is dead! he is no mo-o-ore.'

'. . . more.'

'The wo-o-o-lf is gone.'

'. . . gone.'

'The fa-a-a-a-ther wolf, the murderer——'

'The murderer——'

'. . . is no mo-o-re, no more.'

Careto, sweating and trembling, went on surrounded by awed silence:

'Killed by you, his sons and his rivals——'

At this Squinty felt sure that his woman had lain in the arms of Trinidad and changed the trend of the litany, interrupting with a hoarse outcry:

'The wo-o-o-lf is dead, dead and gone.'

Careto continued:

'The flesh of the wolf stinks under the table. Virgins, wives, and widows sway before the reek of the wolf.'

'The wo-o-o-lf is no mo-o-re,' howled Squinty.

'. . . more.'

'And on Faro Island the flesh of the wolf's virgin also smells. I am your father, without phallus and without fangs. . . . I am no rival and have no rivals . . . because . . . the wo-o-o-lf is dead, dead and go-one!'

'. . . gone.'

Some, open-mouthed, struck their lips lightly with their hands. Others writhed, sweating. The Pimp came up to Careto and in the pauses mumbled: 'A real gentleman's fly.' Careto continued:

'To the gelded wolf, the gelded father, the gelded chief, come near, come near.'

'Come near.'

'To me, me, me, higher than woman and man.'

'The wo-o-o-lf is no mo-o-re.'

'. . . more.'

He wiped off the sweat, took a deep breath, and in a natural voice proposed:

'Let them bring her here!'

The leaders seemed to disagree. Seeing them arguing with each other, Careto resumed the religious refrain:

'The wo-o-o-lf is dead and go-o-o-ne.'

All joined again in the response, but the Twin waved his arms for silence. When he got it he enlarged upon Careto's proposal, his eyes burning with rage: after the widow had made her choice, if any of those present cared to dispute the issue, they would fight it out with knives and the winner keep the girl, unless somebody else came forward to fight.

'That's better,' cried the woman from Puebla, 'because that way the final winner can say the Holy Virgin herself gave her to him.'

Sixfingers tried to ridicule the Twin and became involved in a labyrinth of phrases from which he never emerged. He finished his speech by saying that some of those who had the nerve to argue ought to look behind them to see whether a black bird was after them. He meant the buzzard. This made no impression on the Twin.

'There are some,' he said, 'who have him on their shoulders and still can't see him.'

At last it was agreed that Careto should choose the weapons and act as referee. Then they resumed the litany:

'The o-o-o-ld wo-o-o-lf is no mo-o-o-re.'

The teacher waited no longer. He called Gimpy.

'We've got to rush to headquarters.'

Sixfingers had risen from his place and was approaching Margarito and the doctor. They were obviously discussing how to get the girl there. Watching them, the Twin thought: 'Sixfingers wants to go himself.' Sixfingers had an inspiration.

'Where's the teacher?'

They started calling him. Sixfingers ordered them to search and bring him back, dead or alive. Darío was considered a disruptive element. Two gangs set out, Sixfingers' and the Twin's.

Both started for headquarters.

The doctor joined first Sixfingers' band, then the Twin's. But Whiskers stuck to his heels, and the doctor didn't want the girl to see him again with that vulgar animal with its 'hand-sheared coat', as he put it.

So instead of going to headquarters, he headed for Tortola's bar, which was still open. He didn't like it there because some drunks were hanging around and his elegant suit attracted attention, though he would have been even more embarrassed anywhere else, except at headquarters.

From the woods came the murmur:

'The wo-o-olf is go-o-one.'

The doctor brushed the dust from the step of the shed and sat down. Whiskers curled up at his feet. The doctor looked at him. The 'hand-sheared' dog was contented and happy wherever he was. He was not sensitive to ridicule. 'This business of being sensitive to ridicule, is it a sign of superiority or inferiority?' This problem, stupid as it sounded, troubled the doctor a little. He sighed.

'The mysteries of nature.'

The dog, under his master's gaze, began to thump the ground with the tuft of his tail. The doctor, dreading the remarks of some of the marijuana smokers, went off, followed by Whiskers. When they were in the woods the doctor wanted to revenge himself on the beast, but his heart softened.

'When you come right down to it,' he said, 'he's the only real companion I have in the world.'

From the woods came the Cuban's song.

> *'When you've got that golden throat*
> *to sing with, black man.'*

V

DARÍO RAN AMONG THE TREES, AND WHEN
they opened enough so that the starlight fell on the ground it
seemed to him that he was stepping on crystals. The night
smelled of the body of the chief, the violent male, the jealous
father. 'Death, the stars, the night, my own blood burning
with impatience are all a single mystery.'

He confronted Mother Leonor and the girl. 'It's not proper
for a girl to go out alone with a man at night,' the old woman
said. The girl realised that she had no choice but to go with
Darío, but she held back. They argued heatedly. She felt
sucked into Trinidad's empty room. Mother Leonor, her
wrinkled old face full of objections, lashed out at Darío and
the girl and the convicts who were pursuing her. They were
startled by a noise in the patio, but it was only Gimpy. Darío,
irritated by the false alarm, grabbed the girl's arm, but as he
was about to speak Gimpy interrupted, his face radiant:

'I always said so!'

'What?' asked Mother Leonor.

The girl still held back, and Darío dragged her violently.

'Come on, or we'll pay for your folly with a disaster.'

'But why?'

'Come on! People aren't the way you think.'

Trinidad had said the same thing. Perhaps they were right.
Or perhaps they were both crazy. Or perhaps life was crazy
and swept people along in its madness. Mother Leonor, seeing
she had lost the battle, burst into tears.

'So young and forsaken by the hand of God!'

Gimpy was saying on the way downstairs that if the gangs
hadn't arrived it was because they were arguing over which
had the most right.

'Nobody has any right,' Mother Leonor screamed hysterically from upstairs. The girl stopped and clutched the railing, refusing to go on.

'Don't be an idiot,' Darío said.

Her feelings were hurt, she explained that she wanted to go back to the room for her uncle's wedding present. She went up and came back with the camera. Mother Leonor followed her with an acid look. Darío thought: 'The idea of a man and woman alone at night infuriates her.' Outside he felt the stars over his head. 'Love, too,' he thought, 'is part of this single mystery.'

'Where is Trinidad's body?' the girl asked.

'What an inopportune remark,' thought Darío; still, it was a perfectly natural question. They went on in silence, heading away from the dock.

Gimpy liked scrambling over the crags, clinging to the rocks like a crab. For him the island held no secrets.

Darío told him where to take the girl. She was still annoyed.

'Why are you ordering me about?'

Darío managed to warn Gimpy not to tell her what was happening and also advised him not to smoke marijuana while he was with her. Gimpy assured him that for a week he had been trying to stop. He had had an unpleasant dream. He dreamed that a tumour formed in his left side, then a dry wound without blood, and out of it came handfuls of hair, grains of corn, bits of glass, and dirty rags, all wet but not with blood. The thought of it made him want to lay off the weed.

Darío clasped the girl's hands and went away, leaving her disappointed and submissive. He was bold enough to wonder: 'Is it perhaps because I'm not going?'

He was beginning to realise that he had done all this—going to find her, dragging her out by force, insulting her, leaving her with Gimpy—with a strange voluptuousness. He paused a moment to see what road they were taking and then rushed back to headquarters. The gangs were not there yet. He went up to Trinidad's old room, having seen on the dresser the mail that had piled up while Trinidad was away. He stuffed it in his pockets and went out again. Mother Leonor had not only ceased weeping but was gently snoring, stretched on a couch. Recalling her tears, Darío thought: 'What an actress!' As he was about to go out he heard the voices of the gangs below. He was frightened and slipped out the back door.

He imagined that the best thing to do was to confuse the leaders by pretending to search for them himself. He went toward Tortola's bar. Congo was there, the scars of his ears covered with the serape, leaning against the door. He was singing in a low voice:

> 'My godchild is so fine,
> why should I baptise her?'

Darío asked for Sixfingers or the Twin. Then he returned to the clearing. In spite of the absence of the leaders, the revelling was still going on. The people had left the tables and gathered around a circle where two men were fighting with knives. One was using a dirty rag as a shield, a serape wrapped around his left forearm. The other held an open knife in his teeth and a broken huarache in his hand; he was holding his left hand behind him, a piece of bravura that aroused everyone's enthusiasm and made his opponent ridiculous. But Nosy-Posy shouted at the one with the knife in his hand: 'Carve him up! It's because you're so brave that I love you!'

They went forward and back. The man with the huarache had a torn shirt sleeve, and his arm was bleeding, but the fight went on. At the sight of the blood Nosy-Posy went into a frenzy, and his yelling threw the man with the knife into a frenzy too. But the other, now that he was wounded, finally took his in his hand. 'He's going for him!' screamed the woman from Puebla. The excitement grew. The wounded man tried to get his opponent in the ribs or belly, holding the knife halfway down, near the hilt. 'He's mad now,' people were saying here and there. And gradually in the heat of the battle they divided into two camps. The ones backing Nosy-Posy's favourite were partisans of Sixfingers, the others of the Twin. Some of them insulted the opposing leader, and arguments arose.

'Go tell him so to his face if you're a man.'

'I'll tell him and I'll give you yours too!'

'Hold me up, boys; I'm seeing black!'

They had to be separated. In these arguments the two groups took shape. Lefty had no followers. The hope and illusion of winning Niña Lucha dominated and polarised the struggle. They began to take notice of Darío, and the teacher decided to get away. And what about Sixfingers? And the Twin? Certainly they would soon find out that he had been looking for them and so was not running away. Darío went back to his house. Near the stockade of the enclosure a man and woman were blended into one shadow. 'Could it be La Chole?' Darío wondered. In his room, with his pocket flashlight set between two books, he took out Trinidad's mail and opened the official letters addressed to the officer in command of the penitentiary. Two official communications acknowledging receipt of the previous month's accounts. A trade journal. A notice from the Health Department saying that on the eighth—two days from then—a committee would come to make a survey of the sanitary conditions on the island. They would come in a little boat fitted up by the department as a laboratory. This was good news. Darío thought: 'If that boat is coming, then the island really isn't cut off,' and in his mind the girl's fate was bound up with that expedition. No matter what happened, the girl could go to the mainland with the sanitation inspectors. The weird cry still echoed in his ears: 'The wolf is no more!' And, watching the shadows beyond the window, he thought: 'Strange. That cry of Careto's makes the night darker.' Again he heard the accordion playing a conga in the distance and thought of Trinidad. When the accordion stopped he could hear a nocturnal bird, whose song gave the shadows a kind of damp solidity: *Bambu, bambu-le-lè.* Darío sat down and with his elbows on the table and his head in his hands thought that perhaps, after all, what Careto offered and what they all seemed to crave was natural. He knew that the idea was a desperate one, of a poisonous scepticism, but he went on. Beauty was a miracle, and they had to conquer it 'in their fashion'. Perhaps she herself didn't care if they fought over her with knives. Darío thought: 'The angel and the demon are always waiting their turn in the hearts of virgins.' He knew this was unfair, but the girl had scented all the sordidness of the island and still hadn't wanted to hide. He had to drag her away by force. Men seemed to go into battle over the girl as if it were a normal undertaking, with bleeding arms and a knife in their teeth. How sinister the night was and how full of magic! The magic came from the image of the girl. She was so beautiful that whatever the others did, however vile or stupid, had a kind of dignity if they did it for her.

Careto had known how to seize the right moment. Darío wondered what the man was driving at. Anything, really? He shrugged his shoulders and went out. 'The night is so soft and mild.' The island breathed with the murmur of waves against the shore. Darío decided to go to Eminencias' bar, being sure that if he went to bed they would come and drag him out. Night thickened, heavy-sweet and sensual.

Bambu, bambu-le-le.

Eminencias' bar differed from Tortola's in many respects, in addition to its well-lit counter, the alcove with a safe in it— the supply depot of the island—and the blue netting to keep flies off the hams. Eminencias' mother, a very old woman, stayed with him on the island. A devoted son, a model of virtue. His wife was no adventuress but really his wife, married by bell, book, and candle, whereas the woman who lived with Tortola was a convict and they were not married. Lately Eminencias' wife hadn't been seen around the place.

Darío felt a certain sympathy for her, in spite of everything they said, or perhaps just for that reason. Her name was Enriqueta. They said she had an incurable disease, perhaps leprosy, but it was all conjecture.

It was very late, but the bar was open. Various convicts were talking out on the porch.

'One of her feet fell off. That's why she doesn't come out to the shop.'

Eminencias was wearing his black alpaca cap and at his waist the pistol that he took out every day at nightfall. Near the counter Lefty was drinking. He greeted Darío.

'Fed up, hey?'

The teacher didn't want to commit himself. Lefty went on:

'I respect you because you're a gentleman.'

He lifted his jacket to see if he was unarmed. The teacher reminded him of the fact that Trinidad's place was vacant.

'I'm not after that place for the time being,' said Lefty. 'Let the others break their horns over it.'

'Trinidad's place,' thought Darío, 'means the chair the corpse is in, and Lefty is afraid of *that place* where the dead man is still sitting.' Lefty realised he had said too much and looked around suspiciously.

'I respect you more than anybody on the island. You go without a pistol, but mine is at your disposal, and my life, too, if necessary. And I know what you're thinking about: where I stand in all this. You have keen eyes. When the two of them have broken their horns that's when I come in. To-night I went to headquarters; I went slowly upstairs. When I put my foot on the steps they went *creak, creak, creak*. I got to the top and found the bird had flown. I ran into the Twin's gang and told them where to get off. When Mr. Superintendent Lefty went up he was very steady on his feet, but, seeing that the cage was empty, there was nothing for it but to come here and drink a couple of bottles.'

'Three,' said the man at the counter.

'You'll get your money. "Pay as you go" is my motto.'

He took the teacher's arm and spoke into his ear, but at the top of his voice:

'Tell me something. You're the only man on the island I respect. There don't have to be any secrets between us. You know where Niña Lucha is?'

'I saw her this morning, and that's the last I've heard.'

Lefty gave him a wink and sang:

> *By the seashore*
> *lies my love*
> *by the seashore.*

It sounded as if the superintendent knew where the girl was. 'I look up to you and not to anybody else. You're the only one. If anybody thinks different he can go to hell. And his mother too.'

Lefty went out to the porch and kicked a bunch of people out of their snooze.

'Where's the girl?'

'To-night she gave me her body, and I gave her mine. But I don't know where she is now.'

The teacher had gone out too.

'Maybe Sixfingers knows.'

The superintendent dismissed the idea.

'He doesn't know anything, nor the Twin either.'

The Pimp came in talking to himself.

'The deceased put her in my keeping because I have a treasure. The fly of my pants is a gentleman's fly.'

'I gave her my body; she gave me hers.'

'In your dreams.'

Lefty threatened them.

'Shut up, you swine.'

Then he came close to the teacher again.

'Señor, you are a respectable person. And so am I.'

The Pimp interrupted:

'She is lying in a golden bed.'

Eminencias stood stiff as a statue beside the door, his jacket flapping in the warm breezes that played whirling through the night.

'I have an agreement with Careto,' said the Pimp, 'a gentleman's agreement.'

'He's a real person, Careto. It's a pity he's a refugee; it spoils him.'

'He used to call the Holy Father by his first name in his own country. And I have an agreement with him. In the morning I have to bring him sixty thousand pesos.'

Sixty thousand pesos! The Pimp went out amid a gale of laughter. The teacher wanted more information.

'And Sixfingers?'

'He's looking for her. The Twin's looking for her. And everybody else running along behind. If you want to say I'm in love, then you'll have to say the same thing of the whole island. Sixfingers said to me, "Come with me and you'll be my chief of staff." Do you know what I answered?'

Lefty tapped out on the wall the rhythm of the island's most solemn and ritual insult:

'Ta-ta-tara-ta—tata.'

He drew away a little and with his head on one side looked at the teacher.

'That's what I said. What you just heard. With a respectable man like you I'd go anywhere, but not with this riff-raff escaped from the gallows.'

'What if Sixfingers beats you to it?'

'I'll get him,' Lefty said, 'him and the Twin and the whole damned outfit. There's nobody else like me. My mother bore me and broke the mould. There isn't another like me and never will be.'

The teacher recalled that he had been escorting Sixfingers a few hours before and mentioned it. Lefty proclaimed:

'I'm bodyguard for nobody. Only for you, if you want.'

Darío prepared to leave, but Lefty grabbed his arm and made him come back.

'Here, professor; this bottle was for you.'

The teacher drank half a gulp, gave him a slap on the back, and went out. People were waiting for him outside. There was a great hubbub, confused voices, laughter, a pistol shot. The only window-pane in the bar, at the level of Lefty's head, was smashed to smithereens. Then the sound of horses' hoofs receding. No one inside stirred. Lefty reached for his revolver but, seeing that the precaution was superfluous, slid his hand with a natural motion to his hip. A moment later he went out and came in again, kicking the door open. He was roaring and coughing with laughter.

'Ay, mama!'

'What's going on?'

'Nice going! They've kidnapped the teacher.'

The barman, wrinkling his forehead, asked:

'Did he get shot?'

'No. Somebody just fired to corner him.'

Some wine was dripping off the bottom shelf.

'Look,' said the superintendent. 'The poor little bottle's bleeding.'

The waiter dipped his fingers in the trickle of wine and put them to his lips. Lefty, his mouth full of tequila, burst out laughing again. The tequila slopped down his chest. A few drops hung from his week's growth of beard.

'Man, it was gorgeous! They fired and a minute later they carried him off.'

The shadows brought the echo of the crowd, still celebrating in the woods. At times in the silence the damp heat of the forest opened and let through that strange song with its taste of mint:

Bambu, bambu-le-le.

Gimpy led the way, sometimes giving the girl his hand. She took it fearfully, because his fingers seemed to twist in every direction, and she kept pausing, protesting inwardly:

'Who is this man, to take charge of me like this?'

'This happens in life. Sometimes I ask questions and

130

nobody answers. Why are the stars so cold? Because they are made of splinters of ice.'

Gimpy thought that only such subjects as the stars, or the sea, or the sky were worthy of the girl. There in the darkness, knowing that she could not see his limp, his oversized ears, his jagged teeth, he became talkative. He drew very close to her, and every time he touched her the hairs on his skin were electrified.

The girl hurt her finger; it was only a scratch, but it bled and she couldn't prevent Gimpy from putting his mouth to the wound, looking through the dark like a cat as he stood there. The girl managed to withdraw her hand and they walked on. Gimpy knew of a more efficient treatment; spider's webs were very good for stopping blood, but the method seemed beneath her. The only medicine for her would be made of star dust and butterfly spittle. Especially butterfly spittle.

'Why are they chasing me, Gimpy?' she asked.

He snorted his opinion of Sixfingers and the Twin, sounding as if he had a split reed in his throat.

'You are too beautiful. They would kill you.'

If they wanted to kill her for that, she thought, then she must be so very beautiful that she almost didn't mind. The idea appalled her. It was a new and incomprehensible idea (like others she had had against her will the day before), but though she repelled it, the sweetness of the thought, of that 'dying for her beauty', stayed with her. Gimpy continued:

'You must trust me.'

Lucha remembered the teacher in his anger calling her stupid. He dared to call her stupid because Trinidad was not there. Trinidad would have killed him. And the combination was somehow sweet, the idea of Trinidad protecting her to the point of killing another, and Darío's insult. But the thought of the teacher lying dead—if Trinidad had killed him—awoke in her a vast tenderness. If she thought about it too hard she felt like crying, and she couldn't understand that either. Perhaps life was like that. She concentrated on the sea, frightened by her thoughts. When a wave receded it left little holes scattered everywhere. Gimpy said:

'Isn't it lovely, walking like this in the night?'

The girl didn't answer.

'In every one of those holes there's one of God's little creatures,' Gimpy said with a horrible smile.

Only the fringe of the surf was distinguishable. The night was cool there beside the sea. He asked if she was cold.

'Do you know a lot of stories, Gimpy?'

So she wanted stories and quaint sayings, maybe to make fun of him, like Trinidad.

He replied with another question:

'Think of the sea. Where do the waves come from? They come from the place where the waters and the clouds and the winds mix, away out there. God sends them.'

But Gimpy's mind was on something else. He talked about the waves and wind, but he was thinking of the girl's danger. From among the girl's enemies, whom he was beginning to consider his own, he singled out Careto. Careto baffled and troubled him. Some time back, Gimpy had tried to introduce him to marijuana, but this stranger would act only on *his own idea*.

The wind changed, bringing the distant beat of the conga. The girl asked what it was, but Gimpy evaded the question.

'The beautiful little waves come from God. The mob says there is no God. But there is. Sometimes the things we can't see are the greatest.'

He drew behind a rock and crouched down as if to hide.

'Come here. Now do you see the sea? You don't because it's hidden by the rock. One stone hides the whole enormous sea. But the sea is there just the same. It's the same with God.'

The girl wondered what crimes Gimpy had committed, and he seemed to guess her thought. 'I traffic in marijuana. Some say the weed kills, and some say it's healing. They're both right, and what I say is that God put that weed in the ground so we can get a little relief from the filth and sorrow of mankind.' He added:

'Do you like walking with me?'

She was silent, and Gimpy couldn't bear her silence.

'Night is the other side of day. I like the other side of things.'

He asked her if her finger was still bleeding, but the girl was afraid he would suck the wound again and said no. 'Ah!' he thought. 'She doesn't want me to drink her blood.' It made him terribly sad. Her blood was precious, and she knew it and didn't want him to drink it.

The girl wanted to talk about Trinidad and find out what had happened to his body.

'I saw them lower it to the grave,' said Gimpy, 'in a casket lined with black velvet, and cover it with the blessed earth and place on it a fine wreath of flowers with a ribbon that said in gold letters: *To Black Trinidad, from the grateful penal colony.*'

His own fib made him very melancholy. He stopped talking. The girl realised he was keeping something back and, being afraid to hear anything more about Trinidad, she fell silent and set to thinking about herself. Two days after the wedding she was walking through the night looking for a hole in the rocks, like a little animal. Perhaps the nuns who used to tell her in school about the dangers of the world had been right, though at the moment the greatest danger was that those convicts wanted to kill her, and in this there was a spark of glory. Besides, no nun had spoken to her of God as convincingly as this poor man. Gimpy offered her a hand. They had to go close to the water and clamber over the rocks, waiting for the surf to recede. A turn brought them to a chasm where they stopped. Gimpy pointed to a cave opening off it.

'It's under water at high tide. We have to go another way.'

They went on, but the girl didn't want to go in there at night, which Gimpy understood. 'I lied to her about the chief's body, and now she doesn't trust me.' He led her to a higher place and sat down beside her halfway up the slope.

'It will begin to get light soon.' And after a pause he added unexpectedly, 'I'm happy enough. And I'd be happier, only now and then I tell a lie and then I feel bad.'

'Why? Why should you tell lies?'

From the distance there came still the beat of the conga and that other sound that Gimpy identified:

'*The wolf is dead; he is no more.*'

Yes, he was dead, but the convicts were there drinking, Bocachula spilling tears of pulque. Trinidad's corpse under the table, in his wedding suit. And the Pimp poking his head under the table, saying to the corpse: 'Get up, chief, if you're only drunk.' But he, Gimpy, was in charge of the legacy.

'I lie because there are people like that'—and he pointed in the direction of the conga—'who don't deserve to be told the truth.'

'And what about me? Would you lie to me?'

It seemed the waves of the sea were troubling his mind.

'Think what you like. It's all the same to me. I can't lie to you. I saw Chief Trinidad. A little while ago I saw him as plain as I see you. He had on his wedding suit; he was sitting at the head of the table, and he was bowing this way and that to the crowd.'

'But Trinidad is dead,' she said.

'Dead he was, but they had put him in a chair and were holding him from behind, to make him preside at the party. And Sixfingers made a face like an ox when he eats grass. The Twin like a goat. Lefty kept scratching himself down there, through his trousers. And everybody was singing: *Not even once, Trinidad.* And the whole mob yelled *Tri-ni-dad. Tri-ni-dad. Tri-ni-dad.* And finally Careto got up, a man who never talks, and said a lot of stuff about the gelded father and the wolf. So they all shut up, and then they all yelled together: *The wolf is dead and go-o-ne.* Over and over. Trinidad passed out again and fell under the table.'

He sighed deeply, looked away, and said:

'Now you know the whole story.'

He was expecting her to say, 'Why did you lie to me before?' but she remained cold and silent. He looked at her in surprise. She didn't believe him! With a great effort he had told her the whole truth and she didn't believe him. Night didn't bring them together. Nor the sea. Nor the little wound on her finger. Nor his merciful lie, nor the truth, nor the pure truth.

'I don't like your making up stories about such sad things,' she said.

Gimpy asked her permission to go away and sleep a little while. But immediately she begged: 'Please don't sleep.' If he went to sleep she would feel so alone. Gimpy had said it to see if she noticed his presence. The night wheeled on. He told her the story of his life, a base and scurvy tale. He had no crimes to tell; there had been none, but there were things worse. At the end, just before dawn, he wanted to tell her how he got his limp, but something told him: 'It's getting light; you won't be able to finish; leave it for another day.' Because he knew he hadn't the courage to talk to her except in the dark.

In the first rays of dawn he could see the girl's eyes, those eyes that were on him, and he felt ashamed. He made an excuse of going to inspect the cave and disappeared in an inlet. He sat down, took a white cloth from under his shirt— the girl's nightgown—and buried his face in it. Everything had been all right until then. Now daybreak had so come between them that he was embarrassed to go back, but he had to because she was calling:

'Gimpy!'

He went to her, bringing sea shells. There was a very big one that she held to her ear.

'It doesn't make a sound,' she said.

Gimpy swore he had heard the sea in it.

'Oh!' said the girl. 'It must be the Dead Sea.'

It was her first joke since Trinidad's death. She could say it because she was there in the sunlight, between the sea and the sky. But suddenly, with horror, she remembered her guilt. How could she have forgotten? She hadn't opened the door, and later, to save her own life, she had removed the pistol. She had tiptoed to the other side of the bed, holding her breath as she pushed her hand under the pillow and put the weapon—it was very heavy—under the mattress out of Trinidad's reach. And now she was making jokes. It was too much. She didn't even want to understand it. She contemplated an enormous open mollusc shell. The morning light was reflected by it in shades of the pale blue that plays over burnished steel.

'The wrecks of sailing boats,' Gimpy said, 'drift ashore here.'

He had made a torch; he said the cave was very deep and they could go in if she wasn't afraid. Whenever he added 'if she wasn't afraid' he was referring more to himself than to unknown dangers, and the girl understood and looked at him with friendliness. The look made him squirm. She started into the cave. When they came to a place that was totally dark Gimpy lit the torch, then went on a few more yards and said:

'They call this part the mouth of the whale.'

They had come to a small level place that opened to the sky a few yards farther on. 'It makes you feel like praying,' the girl said. After two open spaces the cave narrowed again to a neck three or four yards long. Each step gave them heart to take the next. There was a cold moisture in the air, and they could hear running water. The rocks jutted out hard as cast iron, and they had to be careful not to hurt their hands. Through the girl's mind ran a phrase from the office for the dead that Mother Leonor had been reciting: 'The depths of Avernus, where eternal evil reigns.' These were 'the depths of Avernus'. She thought of Trinidad and felt again his dying grip on her thigh.

'Where is Trinidad's body?'

Gimpy offered his hand to help her on.

'I just told you.'

She didn't believe him. The stalactites looked like inverted Gothic spires, and two or three rang out musically when Gimpy tapped them with his finger. The cave narrowed toward another barrier. There was a very short corridor, opening into a much larger part where the cave seemed to end. The ground gave way there to the mouth of a chasm some six feet wide and impossible to cross. Gimpy held up the torch so the girl could see it all. From the chasm there rose a current of warm air that made a distant rumbling noise. The noise was becoming louder all the time and the current of air more violent. The girl looked at Gimpy, who was staring down into the hole but for several minutes could see nothing. The rumble rose and fell almost with regularity, like the breathing of a monster. When Gimpy leaned closer the torch was nearly blown out. The girl's hair streamed forward; her blouse clung to her back and fluttered lightly against her breasts. Gimpy tried to light up the inside with the torch.

'It's a very deep crevice, and the water rises and falls in it with the tide.'

Sometimes before a wave had broken another rolled in, and the two fused in the depths, turning the peaceful breathing to a raucous sound, like a snore.

'Nature is terrible,' the girl said.

Trinidad was probably there, in the bottom of the abyss; he must be the monster who was breathing. The air rising from below, bitter with salt and dead fish, smelled like the room with the bloodstained bed. The smell of blood was the smell of the sea. The mystery of his death was surely there.

Gimpy was still holding the light down. Great white masses of foam rose, suddenly fell all in one second into the dark, and crept slowly up again. Gimpy discovered a place where the opening was narrower and they could cross to the other side. They jumped it and tried to find another path. When the girl jumped she felt the warm air on her thighs. 'It's

Trinidad,' she thought again. Gimpy suggested they go back, but the girl shook her head and went on staring into the abyss, where the breathing was becoming more violent. She sat down on the rock and Gimpy, finding a niche for the torch, lit a cigarette. The girl asked for one. She was thinking of Trinidad. 'If I hadn't locked the door nothing would have happened to him.' The cigarettes were of marijuana. The girl had seen women smoking in the city. She had wanted to smoke, too, before she was married, but her aunt said:

'When you're married, if your husband allows it.'

Gimpy rolled a cigarette for her very carefully in a corn-husk, then moistened it and lit it. The girl looked at his eyes. He had a diabolical expression, but it dissolved to honey under the girl's look. The girl smoked and thought, watching the foam that was now overflowing the crevice: 'Would Trinidad let me?' She studied the cigarette, the way it burned, and wrinkled her forehead when she drew on it.

'Did they throw the body in the sea?'

She screamed and pointed to a corner that was seething with white froth spilled from the chasm. They both saw a crab with greenish claws, making a little rhythmic noise as it moved. It was nearly two feet wide, and its claws and shell glinted like metal under the torchlight. A sea spider that had been flung up by the waves, or perhaps had its haunt in those rocks. It seemed to be moving toward the light. The girl drew closer to Gimpy, her mouth dry, the cigarette in her hand. The animal, hearing strange noises, tried to escape the light and get back, apparently, to its den; it seemed to be trying to bore through the wall. The girl, seeing the creature move, got up and wanted to leave, but Gimpy seemed very interested in the apparition. 'Be quiet and don't be afraid,' he said, advancing cautiously. He held the torch in front of him, perhaps to hide behind the light. It was not such a bad idea, because the crab was probably dazzled by the glare. Gimpy drew closer. The crab was motionless. The girl couldn't look at it. It was not an animal but a thing. Things that moved like animals, or animals that lay still like things made chills run down her spine. Gimpy shoved it with his naked foot, and the crab struck the wall and fell on the other side of the crevice. It fell on its back, its claws in the air and its pincers waving and snapping in a futile search for something to fasten on. The girl screamed and jumped back over the narrow part of the chasm to where it couldn't get at her.

'If I had a stick,' Gimpy said, 'I could kill him and we'd make a fire and cook him.'

The girl wanted to go. 'On his back like that,' Gimpy said without taking his eyes off the crab, 'he's harmless.' But the girl only wanted to get away. She was still smoking and could feel the contours of her head from her forehead to the nape of her neck, as if she were made of wood. They went out, she in front because she was afraid of the shadows behind. Before long they came to the open place where there was daylight, then the narrow corridor, more darkness, and finally the huge vault that formed the mouth. Gimpy walked slowly, shunning the crude light.

'If you had to, Niña Lucha, you could live here for years without being found.'

The girl thought: 'Yes, but what for? Just to live like the crab with the green claws?' Trinidad was still speaking in her ears but with the voice of the cave. She didn't know what he was saying, but it was something very specific, maybe that sentence: 'I am your husband; you are my wife.' And perhaps something about the pistol. But the girl was scared of these recollections.

Gimpy was reckoning the time by the sun.

'I must go and get food.'

During the day she was not afraid of being left alone. She picked a comfortable place in the rocks and, covering her head with a handkerchief, gave herself up to the sun and tried to sleep. In the distance the sea was of deepest blue. In the path of the sun was a brilliant wake that faded away a hundred yards from the rocks, as in the post cards that Trinidad used to send her. The girl heard little stones skipping from the top of the cliff and saw Gimpy clambering along like a crab. After a while she slept and had a wild dream which she remembered perfectly afterward. The cigarette must have had something to do with it.

She was in the cave. In the bottom of the abyss there was not water but fire: the fire of hell. The chasm snored, and the crab crawled over the rocks. Instead of Gimpy it was Darío who was with her. They talked of strange new things, and Darío said, sitting beside her:

'How little we matter to nature! The fire spreads out from there; it burns us up, and then what?'

He had on a very white shirt and was shaved. She was badly dressed, and that depressed her. She was making keener remarks than she usually did when awake. In real life she sometimes said to herself, 'I often think of intelligent things, but I can't say them.' In the dream she was saying exactly what she thought.

'I think that's silly,' she said to Darío, 'because we have all of nature inside ourselves. And to the nature we have inside we matter very much.'

'That's true. But come and look down.'

Below, Trinidad stood naked. Blood and hair. 'I would have to burn myself to touch him,' she thought, drawing back, 'and if he touches me he will burn me.' The breathing of the sea was gentler now. Trinidad rose and fell with the fire like a floating doll. They left the chasm and went through a place so dark she was sure the shadows had mingled with the water. They had metallic tones, green and olive, under the light. The edge of the sea was there. A subterranean sea with black boats.

'Why are the boats black?'

Darío laughed at his own joke.

'They're in mourning for a little whale that died.'

Oh. She had thought he was going to say: *Because Trinidad died*. Darío was painfully casual toward her in the dream, as in life. When she hesitated he said again, 'Don't be stupid,' and he said it gently. But now once more she was thinking things that she couldn't say. The crab seemed full of grace and beauty now; what was unbearable about the beast was that it seemed to be of wood. The most terrible thing she could conceive of in the world was not a man murdered by another or a tiger devouring a man, but a piece of wood suddenly starting to walk or eat. She wanted to look brave and said, pointing to the crab:

'Isn't it beautiful!'

'Yes, everything that lives is beautiful, if we know how to look at it. Beauty is not in things but in our hearts.'

Then it seemed that Darío was trying to take out her heart, but it tickled. And when he managed to catch her heart she felt a dull ache that might have been either pain or pleasure. Darío asked:

'What time is it?'

But he didn't give her back her heart, and she was suffocating. Darío said:

'I won't give it back unless the time you tell me is nice.'

She didn't dare because Trinidad was there, in the chasm. Darío spoke to her so haughtily that she became offended.

'Inside you there are beautiful monsters, and inside me there are fiercer ones, talking and howling.'

'What do they say?'

'They say that you must be mine and I must be yours.'

Just then she heard Trinidad's voice asking:

'Why did you move the pistol?'

The girl was afraid. 'Now that he's dead,' she thought, 'he knows everything.' She drew farther away with Darío. She went as far away as the cave allowed.

'Would you go out over the sea with me?' she asked Darío, to test him.

'I don't know. I'm not planning to go anywhere.'

141

At that point a doubt crossed Lucha's mind. 'Am I dreaming?' Darío put his jacket around her. She shuddered at the coarse touch of the cloth, not putting her arms in the sleeves. The fire leaped out from the chasm, and Trinidad's voice said: 'It's good here in the fire. I am fire. And you. And Darío.' Darío pressed her in his arms, and she threw her head back.

'What is happening,' he said, 'is real, not a dream. If it were a dream your mouth would taste of ashes.'

'And what does it taste of?'

'Currants.'

'Currants?'

'Yes. But wild currants from the high mountains.'

'The highest ones?'

'The ones that are covered with golden snow at midday and blue snow in the afternoon.'

Darío heard a noise behind him, as of someone slipping cautiously away.

'Who's there?'

They heard something skid and fall. Darío fired twice. Then Gimpy appeared with his head pierced by two bullets and light shining through the holes. Blue flashes played here and there in the cave.

'That,' Gimpy said, 'is phosphorus from dead fish.'

In the dark the wind from the chasm shook slender laurel trees where the crab was wriggling his clumsy claws. Darío said, pointing to it: 'You didn't see it. Say you didn't see it.'

They jumped to the other side of the chasm; the crab fled, and they went down the path without talking. Before they came to the narrow strip Darío said:

'When you become a real woman, then I will be a real man.'

As they left the cave she woke up. She was alone. 'I knew it was a dream,' she thought. She was very tired and she had left her little looking-glass at headquarters; she would have liked to examine her face, to see whether it showed traces of the dream and whether they were sweet or otherwise. How long had she slept? The sun had passed the peaks of the rocks. In a moment Gimpy was back at her side; he had been sitting nearby, waiting for her to wake up. He had brought bundles and bananas. He had gone directly to the teacher's house. The children were in the yard, but not Darío. La Chole told him a strange tale which he didn't believe, so he went to Eminencias to find out what had happened. There he learned that they had shot at the teacher but missed him.

'Shot? What for?'

If he told her they were after him because of her, the girl might rush off and give herself up to save him. And Gimpy didn't want her to leave him. As for the teacher, it wouldn't matter much to Gimpy if he were killed. He walked slowly to headquarters, but nobody there could give him any information. On his way to Sixfingers' house he heard the hum of a suspended log struck by a great mallet, the call to assembly. He saw Lefty heading for the woods. Lefty came up to Gimpy, grabbed his ear, and gave it a twist, just to show off, *treating me the way Trinidad used to.* When he let go Gimpy was scared and decided to go back to the cave. He found eight or ten bananas and used up his credit to buy corn meal. He took all the stuff back to the girl. He found her asleep and, not wanting to wake her, took himself off a little way, but he did allow himself to contemplate her. 'There are some beings who are really pure.'

'Why do you say that?'

Gimpy blushed and reddened even more trying to hide it. Then he tried to tell her stories about his life, but she kept interrupting him with questions. 'She doesn't want to hear about me but about Darío, and it's only natural.' After some beating about the bush he told her that the teacher had been kidnapped. The girl asked why, and Gimpy looked at her, thinking: 'I shouldn't have told her. After all, I don't really know that he's been kidnapped. I don't know it.' He made casual conversation to distract her:

143

'Once a girl told me I had such beautiful eyes she'd like to steal them. So you see, Niña Lucha.'

He realised at once that he had said something very silly and didn't know what to do with his eyes and hands. He got up and, taking something out of one of the packages, made a little cloth rabbit which he began to manipulate, one hand in his pocket and the other resting on his shoulder, so that the rabbit jumped from one shoulder to the other or peeked out from behind his enormous head, apparently all by itself. The rabbit skipped merrily, Gimpy producing a little shrill call with his lips closed so that it seemed as if the squeak came from the rabbit. The girl laughed, and Gimpy sighed in gratification. He went on to take advantage of his own deformities to make her laugh. He crouched down and his huge head rolled almost on the level of the ground, seeming to find its own way over the rocks. The girl laughed, but there was a shadow of fear in her eyes. The exaggeration of the deformity frightened her. Gimpy noticed it and went back to talking about his life. When the afternoon was well along and night drawing near he hauled to the mouth of the cave some dry cornhusks, a blanket that he had got from headquarters, a stump of candle, and a box of matches.

At sunset they heard a persistent humming sound, as if someone were beating a kind of tambourine. The sound was weak but penetrating. Gimpy thought it was coming from above and climbed up the rock. The sound seemed sometimes very close, but there was no one in sight. When he came back he made a little mound of corncobs and set it on fire.

'To keep off the evil spirits,' he explained.

Careto, standing beside his hut, recalled the celebration in the clearing. From far away there the strange words he had spoken had come to him. But all in all he had a feeling of failure. He had meant to take their minds off the girl, but he was aware that in every one of his cries, in his wild eyes, and in the sweat pouring over his chest she was there, the young the *heritage* of the father wolf. The wolf had no existence without her, nor she without the wolf. All the people that he, Careto, wanted to hold had gone out afterward in search of the girl. When he tried to put himself in the foreground and pulled that stunt of the *great gelding* the girl ruined his schemes. They all rushed off to look for her. And Careto himself was inclined to follow; he didn't know why or for what purpose. He must think it all out slowly.

He sat down on the ground beside the door and, hearing the water splash from the gutter of Eminencias' kitchen, tried to retrace his course. He was Aryan. It was rather funny, an Aryan in such a situation. He had fled Germany as a Jew. He reached Spain before the war and with the help of false papers had to pass as a Nazi and fight with the rebels in order not to be killed. He left the country and boarded a ship, still a fugitive. In America he found that he was an Aryan and that his relatives had been released from the concentration camps in Germany. He lived with two prostitutes whom he exploited. Some friends of his robbed and killed a Spanish businessman, and Careto was condemned without having had any hand in the matter. That amused him; it made him laugh.

But now the island posed a problem: power. He, too, wanted it. They were all grasping for power, in Trinidad's chair, in Trinidad's bed. In him the thirst had been aroused by the sight of the corpse in the presidential chair, the contenders surrounding the body, and the living eyes of the convicts on the eyes of the dead. But if in his craving for power he desired neither Trinidad's office nor his bed, nor even a better life, was he acting on what was called an *ideal?* He spat scornfully. It was nothing but a practical ambition, and he already had a method of realising it. 'I have the same method,' he thought with amusement, 'as the gelding of my clan, the Germanic clan.' Smiling with assurance, Careto was perplexed by how much of this was a cynical game and how much a natural fascination. 'It doesn't matter,' he concluded. 'I don't know what I'm doing. It's an atavism that's sweeping me along.' He would have been doing the same thing if he had spoken to the convicts of progress and the future. The only difference lay in having dragged them backward; he was urging them not toward a vague Utopia but back to the security of their animal origin. What was he after in all this? The same thing, perhaps, but in different fashion. It was curious that the ambition for power should have shown him the way. But what form of power? Careto shrugged his shoulders and went back to the newspaper, but before unfolding it he was reminded of two creatures, Rusty-Pants and the Pimp. He couldn't understand what impulse led him to take an interest in people to whom nobody gave a second thought. Neither of them was a real person; they were hardly more than two unresisting clots of blood. And because they were unresisting the truth sought them out and dwelt in them. And sometimes the miraculous came to lodge in them too. Rusty-Pants, with his talk of the *father wolf*, had suggested to him the possibilities of that idea. Then when the Pimp sang out his delight over the hidden treasure, amid jokes and incredulous laughter, Careto went up to him, treated him as an equal, and invited him to his cabin. Automatically the Pimp offered him sixty thousand pesos, which was something of a disappointment to Careto. Still, he was waiting for him. He didn't expect to get anywhere by waiting for the Pimp, though talking to him was absurd, and absurdities sometimes give inspiration.

But he was on his way to power, and this was his means: not people but clots of blood. He had come to see that there on the island he was hampered in this purpose by the ideal of the superwoman for which they were all falling. As long as they were smitten by that dream it would be hard going. He had to kill it, kill it by lust. The best would be if they could all achieve their hearts' desire, not only the leaders, but the lowest and most wretched as well. And leave the girl alive and sound.

What did you do to the girl,
Trinidad?
Nothing at all,
Trinidad.

He would kill it with the power of a truth that had been revealed to him by the unresisting clots of blood; the idiocy of the Pimp, the child's primitive mystery. All by itself a plan was forming in his mind. They would all have the girl. She would lose her beauty, would ooze misery from every pore. Quickly, in a few days, a few weeks. Once this was accomplished the stage was set for him. The gelded father—above the lusts of man and woman—would impose himself on the untenanted will of the convicts. It wouldn't matter if another sat in Trinidad's chair or slept in his bed. Careto would stay in his hut with a jug of water, three tortillas, his chest naked, and Ruana coiled in her cardboard box. Virtuous, ascetic. And perhaps he could go farther. If he held the sacerdotal leadership of the island, what greater heights might not be open to him? He might discover new expedients, more effective because of the fear and disorientation on the mainland. There were colonies of Nazi emigrants who wanted to have a *great gelding* nearby. Careto's mind was made up. He fell back to scratching his chest, and without quite managing to make fun of himself he laughed a little at the whole scheme that had been born of the Pimp, Rusty-Pants, the snake. More than any other people the Germans made use of old tooth-paste tubes, burned matches, and garbage to further their plans of aggression. Nobody on the island before Careto had thought of exploiting the murky atavistic images in the mind of Rusty-Pants, or the confidences of the Pimp.

The night bird sang on into the first flush of morning.

Bambu, bambu-le-le.

The Pimp appeared. He was skinny, rachitic, but his cheeks and belly sagged. His feet were not parallel: the heels were

147

close together, the toes out. He was in a great hurry. He stopped a little way off, cautiously.

'Where's the snake?'

He advanced slowly, muttering the spell: '*And then I'll hurt you, snake; and you won't hurt me, snake; and then I'll curse you, snake, and you won't hurt me, snake.*' Careto watched him closely, keeping his eye on his hands and his pockets. He didn't believe this poor creature could perform miracles. The first thing the Pimp said was:

'The girl isn't there any more.'

'What happened?'

'She's gone.'

'To the mainland? Did she leave the island?'

'She's gone.'

'But where?'

'Nobody knows where she is. What good does it do me to have a treasure? Gentleman's pants, sure, but I have to live like a monk.'

Careto, with no confidence, inquired:

'Have you brought the money?'

'If she's gone I won't give it to you.'

'Don't lie. Have you brought the money?'

'Here it is, right here.'

He revealed a wad of thousand-peso bills. Money, good money from the National Bank, backed by gold ingots buried in a vault, guarded by sentries with fixed bayonets. The money burned Careto's fingers. There was not sixty thousand, but sixty-three. The miracle. The clots of blood moving without will over the earth work miracles. But the Pimp, whining beside him, wanted the money back. Careto was sure that with enough pressure he would find out where the rest was hidden.

'We'll take it back where it was, but not now. At night, so no one can see us. If you tell them they'll kill you and take it all. How much have you got?'

'Another handful like this. And more.'

Careto pretended to be uncertain.

'Is it safe there?'

The Pimp assumed a pompous air of caution.

'Who knows?'

Careto told him that to find the girl and then win her over would take all the money.

'And if I bring it all to you when do I get the girl?'

'To-morrow.'

'No. This afternoon.'

'All right, this afternoon. But I also——'

The Pimp tried to grab the money back.

'No, no, you don't.'

Careto laughed, observing him. He was a frustrated male on heat. The Pimp added:

'You're supposed to be like a Holy Father.'

'Of course. You misunderstood me. I mean I need a little money for myself.'

'Fifty pesos,' the idiot suggested.

'Only fifty?'

Careto was trying to sound convincing, because idiots sometimes have flashes of common sense. The Pimp went to get the rest of the money, and Careto was left alone again. He hid the bills in the cabin and came out. 'As much again,' he kept thinking. This was power. 'To get gold or destroy it.' To destroy it meant desperation, and he was not desperate. He smiled. 'I always knew I wouldn't get at money by ordinary ways. I am too intelligent to waste my time accumulating profits. Some people haven't enough brains for that game, and some have too much. Money had to come my way by irregular means.' And there it was; an idiot gave it to him. What a twist in his destiny as a wanderer through a world where every one played at being either judges or thieves! But this created problems. First, how to keep the money. Would that be possible without getting rid of the Pimp? And if he had to be put out of the way could it be done 'correctly'? The sea was near. He looked to the right. He saw the leper's hand scattering bits of paper from the back window of

Eminencias' house. The wind tossed them playfully. Careto reflected: 'If I put him out of the way I must remember that from that house they see him come here and that the leper woman is at the window all day, taking in even the tiniest things.' But in order to see him she would have to put her head out the window, and this she almost never did. He calmed down. To get rid of the Pimp was simply to throw a clot of blood to the fish. From the zinc drainpipe next door splashed the dirty water that usually fell around nine o'clock. The night bird sang, reminding him of something very specific, but he didn't know what.

Bambu, bambu-le-le.

It was an hour before the Pimp came back. Pulque and lack of sleep gave him a deathly look. Careto tried to persuade him to go inside, but the idiot held back. Careto looked around cautiously. They went in. Seeing fifty-five thousand pesos more in his hands, Careto thought: 'There's no alternative.' He watched the Pimp avidly. The idiot was sleepy, and Careto urged him to take a nap in the hut, but he was afraid of Ruana. He went out into the open and at Careto's suggestion lay down on the side away from the Eminencias' windows. Careto returned to his place after hiding the money.

This was power. He went to wake up the Pimp, who was startled by his impatience, so that Careto had to smile and apologise. He had the money now. To keep it and guard it by whatever means were necessary was not so difficult. By whatever means. Though he was not a 'criminal'. His thoughts turned again to his 'case'. He was not a criminal. Months ago he had suggested a crime to others, and when he found out that they had taken him seriously he withdrew in disgust.

Even when he knew it had turned out all right he refused to look at the money they offered him. Then the others, fearing that he would 'betray' them, denounced him anonymously, and in the end he had to take the rap. The strangest of all was that he could have denounced the real authors of the crime, but he didn't want to. Why? He laughed as he thought of it. He had felt guilty. And when he felt guilty he smiled. And, smiling, sometimes he hummed in an undertone:

> '*Maria told me,*
> *Maria will tell me*——'

That was all he remembered, but he heard the rest in his imagination. He rose again and went back to the Pimp, who was sleeping curled up like a cat. A trickle of saliva drooled from his half-open mouth. Now and then he muttered words which Careto, by listening intently, was able to catch: 'A real gentleman's fly.' His decision was ripe. What did it mean, exactly, to make such a decision? According to conventional morality, it was scandalous, but he was beneath morality (*the wolf is dead and gone*), or above it, in the world of the Great Gelding, the new world that despised money and set a new goal in its place: unity and work. Though properly speaking, at the moment it was not a question of unity and work but of love of money. This confusion bothered him. He got up and went to look again at the Pimp. It made him angry that he should be there. It was as if he were seeing a stranger's hand poking into the place where the money was hidden. The arm that went with the hand was elastic, and though the Pimp was nowhere near, his arm had stretched and his hand was there on the bills. Careto, troubled, went back and sat down in his old place. He must cut off that arm. For the love of money? For a future in which money must disappear?

'To hell with it,' he thought. 'It's a minor problem.'

VI

IT WAS THE TWIN WHO HAD CAPTURED
Darío as he left the canteen. They took him to the leader's
cabin. The Twin, with his belt full of lead and his enormous
pistol, was beaming.

'Talk to me without formalities. You can leave off the
title.'

'What title?'

The Twin gave him a furious look, then went on:

'Last night you left headquarters with the girl. Mother
Leonor told us so, and a nun doesn't lie. Don't think ill of her.
She is a generous and tender-hearted lady. "If you shoot
him," she said, "promise not to torture him; don't make him
suffer." Those were her very words.'

Darío tried to enter into the spirit of the occasion.

'I appreciate her kindness.'

As Darío had never committed murder, nor even so much
as a petty swindle, they were surprised at his composure.

'You left headquarters with the girl. You went toward the
harbour. Nobody has seen her since. Some say Gimpy went
too.'

'Certainly.'

'Where did you go?'

'To take her to the mainland.'

'Gimpy too?'

'Where?' The teacher was stalling.

'In the boat. I suppose you used a boat.'

'Gimpy stayed ashore. Then he disappeared. Maybe he
went to headquarters.'

The Twin didn't believe a word of this but pretended to
take it seriously.

'So the girl is on the other side? She's already in respectable territory?'

'I think so, and I'm glad of it. That girl isn't meant to live here.'

The Twin's woman interrupted:

'I'm made of the same stuff, and I've been on the island eight years.'

The Twin, who always began with the word *so* when in doubt, returned to the cross-examination.

'So you mean that she's not on the island.'

He didn't believe it, as Darío could tell from the expressions of his followers. The Twin made a grand gesture of releasing him.

'I won't stand in your way. Go in peace, and if Sixfingers bothers you all you have to do is send me word. For me this business of the girl is finished. I have a high regard for her, and not just recently, because I've known her for thirty-eight years. If she has gone to her people God grant she may find someone who will bring her a better fate.'

Darío took a courteous leave of the Twin's woman and went away, thinking:

'Was that all they shot at me for?'

But that was not the only incongruity. '*I have known her for thirty-eight years.* How can that be, if she is only eighteen?' And then: 'They will follow me; they will watch me; that's why they are letting me go, and that only means that I can't go see the girl for the present.' He noticed that two of the Twin's followers were heading for the harbour. 'They are trying to find out whether I told the truth.' He was not much worried about their investigations at the wharf.

Darío had had no sense of danger. He knew that it was easy to fire a shot and that one dead man more or less was not going to keep anybody awake, but he had not been afraid. The Twin was hunting for the girl. Perhaps, as he pursued her, his whole body re-lived the memories of the little village where he had eaten iguana meat.

One of those who had gone to the harbour to check his story was Chapopote. He was a character. He had religious ideas, after his fashion, and Mother Leonor saw eye to eye with him. His crime had been one of those crimes of passion, so common among the convicts. He had killed his wife; he killed her because she had insulted his mistress. Before that he had never committed a crime. His wife was 'a saint' and his mistress a prostitute. That was the truth; nobody denied it, but his wife said it to him one day in the street—they were separated and met by chance—and Chapopote was angry. They started a dispute, which finally became so complicated that when Chapopote's wife said, 'You had to take up with that tart because that's all you're good for. You're just made to be robbed and fooled'—when she said that, Chapopote had to prove it wasn't true. And he killed her, right there. Instead of running away, he knelt in the blood, the knife still in his hand, and prayed for her soul until the police grabbed him. He accepted the sentence and lived 'honourably' on the island. If he wore a pistol at his belt and went around with the others it was just so as not to be a wet blanket, as he put it. His joining in the persecution of the girl struck Darío simply as rather odd and stupid.

'If they get baulked they'll be after me again.'

In the woods he met the doctor wearing a fancy necktie and a pin with an imitation pearl. The doctor, also obsessed with the idea of the girl, thought an explanation was in order: 'I dressed up because I am going to headquarters.' Whiskers was tagging along. 'The girl has gone back there.' This piece of nonsense gave Darío a start, and he asked who had told him.

'The Pimp.'

The doctor was so anxious for it to be true that, on hearing the idiot say it, he had rushed to his place, shaved, and changed his clothes. But he had the same old handicap: Whiskers was following him. There was no way of locking him up, because his hut had no doors. He threatened him until finally, ears drooping, Whiskers took two or three steps backward, but before the doctor could get around the corner he saw the dog coming after him. He threw stones at him. One of them struck and, hearing the dog's yelps, he felt quite proud of himself. 'What did he expect, the little tramp?' The dog went off, but fifty steps further he caught up again by a short cut. The doctor sat down on a tree trunk, with a feeling of doom, and clutched his jaw. 'Sometimes he looks at me as if he were my son. But, Whiskers, you make a gentleman conspicuous. I can dispense with you, because though you do console me in my solitude, the fact is that I really can live without consolation. Didn't I give up my mistress? Didn't I stop smoking? Really, Whiskers, you're no necessity, like tobacco or a mistress.'

The dog settled happily at his feet and started to go to sleep. The doctor hesitated a moment, then rose, his mind made up. He called Whiskers in a fond voice. The two, turning off a little, went toward the sea.

'I would like to behave better, but you make a gentleman conspicuous.'

He grabbed the dog by the scruff of the neck, held him out over the water, and let him fall. At that point the shore formed a bluff about six feet high. Whiskers thrust out his snout and barked three times. 'The poor devil thinks I'm playing.' To get him under water he wrapped a wad of paper around a stone and flung it far out. The dog swam after it and came back with the paper in his mouth. Close to shore, he realised that his master couldn't get down there, so he went farther along. The doctor watched him, at a loss what to do. 'By the time he realises it's not a game he'll be worn out.' The animal clawed vainly at the rocks. The paper fell out of his mouth, and he hurried to fetch it again. And he kept calling his master with short barks of anguish that nevertheless expressed a desire to please. He managed to raise himself with his front paws over the rocks, and the doctor came near the edge and leaned over. Whiskers still had the paper ball in his teeth. Seeing his master reach out an arm, his eyes lit up. The doctor thought: 'He looks at me just like a little human being.' He took the dog by the neck and flung him farther out. The animal sank and reappeared again, swimming with difficulty in another direction. His strength was failing. The doctor climbed a rock. 'He wants to land on the beach, but he won't last that far.'

Whiskers thought he was dying, but the surf was strong, and now and then a wave lifted him and threw him several yards farther. When his master realised that he might be saved he began to snap his fingers and whistle to coax him to a harder place. The dog didn't respond. Just as he was about to sink a wave enveloped him and set him down gently on the sand. Whiskers came up, leaving the track of his drooping tail on the sand. The doctor took a few steps toward him without realising what he was doing.

'Whiskers, you tramp.'

The animal shook his ears. He wanted to run away, but he couldn't. The doctor came nearer. After all, Whiskers was his oné companion in solitude. But the dog walked away, turning his head with a look full of that sadness of dogs that is so hard to dispel because it is more human than our own. He was taking an oblique course, as though idly.

'He looks at me like a little person.'

He followed him a few steps, but Whiskers broke into a lively trot. The doctor shrugged his shoulders and set out for headquarters. He was trying to think about Niña Lucha, but the thought of Whiskers kept intruding. The dog's last look ('like a little person') bothered him. He rubbed his nose with the back of his hand. When he was nearly at head- quarters he burst out laughing. It was incredible that Whiskers should fill his mind like that.

He asked for the girl, but she was not there.

The waves slowly lapped the escarpment. A little farther up, in the direction of the cave, the rocks stood out boldly against the waves. In the cave all was quiet. Gimpy had gone back there after roving around in search of news. Before he got there he had seen something that made him stop, shrivel, kneel devoutly, and finally throw himself down on the ground. As he lay prone, there before him, less than twenty feet away, was the ghost of Black Trinidad. The ghost. Tall, pale, naked. The ghost itself. In the evening light it seemed to be floating in the wind. Gimpy, eyes tight shut, pronounced the spell:

> '*Pious soul,*
> *in sorrow pale*
> *the Holy Face,*
> *the rose and the veil.*
> *Repose, my soul,*
> *sleep without fear,*
> *no evil thing*
> *will come near.*'

He opened his eyes and shut them again. He dug his nails into the ground. The ants crawling on his neck divided into two streams and advanced rapidly towards his forehead. He had heard it said that feeling pins and needles on your neck in an abandoned house is a sign of evil spirits. Was Trinidad's spirit good or evil? He continued the incantation at the top of his voice:

> '*On four posters*
> *my bed is slung:*
> *Saint Joseph, the Virgin,*
> *Saint Joachim, Saint Anne.*
> *I deny you*
> *if God denies,*
> *and if you are blessed*
> *give me some sign.*'

He repeated the verse three times for the three persons of the Trinity, the Trinity whose name the ghost bore, hoping in vain that the apparition might give him some sign that it was not a messenger from hell. But Trinidad stayed there, silent, naked, erect, gently swaying in the breeze. Gimpy, repeating the charms, crawled backward with his eyes shut. When he thought he was far enough away he opened his eyes, got up, and began to run. The cave was near. He looked back to see if the ghost was pursuing him but saw nothing. He heard the buzzing sound he had heard before—like someone beating a drum capriciously, irregularly—but there was no more ghost. Perhaps it was he who made the sound, but Gimpy hadn't been able to solve the mystery because he hadn't dared to keep his eyes open.

He made his way down over the rocks recklessly, not caring where he trod. His crippled foot performed miracles, and soon he was standing before the girl. He wanted to tell her about the ghost, but she didn't give him a chance. He could tell from her eyes that she had been crying.

'The Indians from the south settlement have been here all afternoon. A hundred, two, three hundred Indians. They brought me fruit and tortillas and water.'

Gimpy had a thousand things to tell her, but she wouldn't listen.

'What am I doing here? Why? If all the island knows, why do I need to hide? Why doesn't Darío come?'

'The Indians can keep a secret. They know, but nobody else does. And about Darío, he can't come.'

'Why?'

He had heard strange stories and he didn't want to repeat them. All he could talk about was the ghost. He told what he had just seen. He held his breath; so did the girl.

'Do you hear it?'

Every now and then the humming was audible. Gimpy pointed in that direction and said:

'That's him,' and he kept talking, talking, in a kind of drunkenness:

'I was near that ridge when I stopped and began to listen.

Boom-boom, boom-boom. I'd heard the same thing before in the same place, but this time I said to myself, "There's somebody here, and it's not the time or place for anybody." I went closer. Boom-boom, boom-boom... The buzz came closer too. I climbed on top of a rock. I was shivering to my marrow. I couldn't move. I had to see it and I flopped down on the ground. I moved a shoulder forward, then a knee, and then there it was. If the ghost had had a grudge against me he could have hit me with a stone or even his spit. My eyes were falling out of my face, and my feet were running off by themselves. There I was in front of him and couldn't move a finger. It was Trinidad to the life, standing up, stark naked. His belly white and swollen and his chest black. Boom-boom, boom-boom . . . He didn't say a word. Ghosts only talk at the change of the moon, so it didn't surprise me. I felt my breath on my hands like red-hot coals. I'm quite a man, Niña Lucha; that is, in a manner of speaking, but my blood froze in my veins, and my heart was hitting the ground.'

Niña Lucha was inattentive. She didn't believe a word of it. Gimpy thought: 'That's because the first time I met her I told her the story of the sea serpent.' But the humming was there, still there. The girl thought: 'How obsessed he is by Trinidad's body!'

'Why did you say Darío couldn't come?'

Since she wouldn't believe in the ghost, he decided to tell her about the danger that Darío was in. He said he had to be very careful because they were watching him and at the least slip would seize him and even kill him. Kill him? The girl was afraid of Gimpy. He sighed. She didn't believe that either. She seemed to be thinking: 'Gimpy is crazy.' He didn't dare go near her. Lucha thought of Trinidad. Then she saw herself in that situation, and, imagining Trinidad's feelings for her, if he had been alive, she became so sorry for herself that she burst into tears. She had to make a great effort to avoid thinking of Trinidad. All day she had been absorbed in her own solitude, thinking that Trinidad's memory was no longer pleasant, as it had been, but threatening. The lines of the rocks at the entrance to the cave formed a human face not unlike his. And all day long it had seemed to be saying to her: 'Did you want to come with me or not? I, your husband; you, my wife. To the other side of the grave. You had told me that. If it was true why did you take away the pistol?' Just when the shadows were erasing the image, Gimpy turned up with his ghost story. She didn't want to believe it, but perhaps it was true, and if Trinidad was there he was going to want an explanation. She was afraid, but at times, and in spite of her fear, she was moved by the tender memories of her wedding. Gimpy, sitting on a rock some distance away, held his head in his hands, thinking: 'I am nothing to her.' But now the girl was thinking of Trinidad's ghost, finding it not in the intermittent throbbing of the drums but in the mystery of a cloud with shining edges. A cloud that looked like the Scandinavian countries on a map. She was still Trinidad's wife. And Trinidad was pursuing her. All that day he had been crying in her ears:

'Why did you take the pistol?'

She remembered the clumsy motions of his hand groping for the weapon. So strong, so brave, his huge hand searching a way to take her along with him. And not finding it. And she knowing why he couldn't find it. And all of him, so seasoned, *so much a man*, groaning and making clumsy gestures like an animal.

The girl wept, but the tears brought no relief from her fear. 'I am paying for it. I am alone, abandoned, forgotten, living in a cave.' And Trinidad watching her from the cloud on high.

But she had one consolation: 'If the dead know everything he must know what I am feeling now.' But perhaps he also knew that she had kissed Darío in her dreams.

She heard a groan. It was Gimpy. The girl went up to him. 'Are you sick?'

The cripple was trembling. His eyes rolled wildly. He had a white cloth in his hands.

160

'Yes.'

It was lovely to be sick and have the girl pay attention to him.

'This morning you wouldn't eat, nor yesterday either. Your stomach must be upset.'

He hadn't eaten because there was not much food, and he didn't want the girl to go without. She misunderstood.

'Go to the sea and get a little water.'

He obeyed, and the girl advised him to drink. He hesitated, though he enjoyed her solicitude. Finally he drank. And Gimpy thought: 'It's always been that way in my life; whenever I do something fine nobody understands.' The girl was speaking to him kindly, as one speaks to the sick. She spoke that way because she was thinking: 'I am so wicked I don't deserve even Gimpy's friendship,' and she tried to wait on him and take care of him.

Gimpy was touched; he stopped talking, and the girl put her hand on his shoulder. On his shoulder. He would have liked to be really sick. And die. But her mind turned easily to other things.

'Did I tell you the Indians said they would come back tonight?'

Now it was Gimpy who wouldn't talk. The girl was easily distracted from his suffering. She repeated the question, and others, but he still made no answer. The girl misunderstood his silence.

'If I believed the things you tell me I'd have to throw myself into the sea.'

After a while she went off and stared at the clouds, remembering her old home. Her aunt said to her one day: 'When you see a man looking at you and his look makes you feel naked, and then he takes your arm and you feel safe and as if you owned the world, then you'll know that's your man. And you must go with him and live and die with him, if necessary.' And die. Oh! She had felt that with Trinidad, but the second time Darío looked at her she had also been ashamed of her moral and physical nakedness, and when he took her arm and called her *stupid* she felt protected. And now . . . Trinidad knew it. Trinidad knew everything. What should she do with her life? 'My life,' she thought, 'was Trinidad.' Her aunt had said it long ago: 'That's all life is, for a woman—a man.' She got up, wanting to walk, to go far away. Perhaps to the cloud shaped like Norway. Life was a man, a man, and she hadn't opened the door for him, and then she had tricked him, and now . . . Trinidad loomed up like a giant, filling the entrance of the cave, the whole cave, and he seemed to be saying in her ear: 'I died alone, I alone. Why didn't you come with me?' In the dusk she saw Gimpy, who was apparently weeping again with his face in the white cloth. She was glad that Gimpy was crying. She dared not think about Darío. Darío was a tool of destiny, designed for her punishment. Pretending to save her, he was burying her there among the rocks. But later, remembering what Gimpy had said about Darío's danger, she was overcome by a new tenderness and desire to cry. At the height of this feeling she remembered Trinidad and thought she saw his face in the lines and shadows on the rocky wall. And then she felt neither love nor hatred, but fear. Fear of Trinidad, of Darío, of Gimpy, of life —*or perhaps life was like that.* Even so, she still had some strength, and a recent happening gave her even more: they wanted to kill her for her beauty. It gave her courage, but underneath she felt a great despair.

She didn't believe in Darío's danger, but she was waiting for the Indians to come so she could ask them. There was not a sound from Gimpy, who was still off in the shadows. But the humming of the ghost was plainly audible. The girl was afraid. At her cry Gimpy ran to her side.

'Do you hear it?'

Perhaps he had been telling the truth after all.

'Do you hear it? Think of it. Every sound is like a word. Not only that sound, but all of them. Our feet walking on the ground say, "Yes, no, yes, no," and when they stop they say, "Well, maybe." Now the ghost is saying he wants company: *alone, no, no, no. Alone, no, no.*'

'What can we do?'

'Suppose we went away from here,' Gimpy suggested.

'Where?'

The Indians wanted to take her to their huts. Gimpy seemed to guess her thought:

'We'll go. All the Indians know where you are, but Six-fingers hasn't found out, nor the Twin, nor Lefty.'

'Why do they want to know?'

Gimpy wanted to tell her but didn't know how. 'You ask questions that nobody can answer, Niña Lucha. Life is like that. And it's not bad. Everybody likes it.'

Gimpy climbed the rocks to see where the wind was coming from. Finally, sniffing like a dog, he said:

'There's nothing. It must have been in my own head.'

The girl was also intent on the wind and Gimpy on the place where the ghost had appeared.

'The breeze is coming from the harbour.'

Gimpy held his breath, listening.

'No, it's not my imagination.'

'What?'

'Don't you hear it? The ghost. But somewhere else now.'

Gimpy was sweating at the thought of the ghost moving from one place to another. The girl held her breath, too, and heard the humming sound. It came not from outside but from the cave, from the inside of the cave. They looked toward it uneasily:

> '*On four posters*
> *my bed*——'

'Why do you say that?'

'Because that protects all four sides.'

The girl repeated the charm. The moon rose from the sea, huge and red, as it had been the day she arrived on the island. The Indians from the south settlement appeared on the top of the cliff. There were more than fifty of them, and they swarmed down all over the ravine. It looked as if the rocks there had started dancing, but it was only the Indians with their white trousers and coppery faces and their straw sombreros.

In front came old Voice of the River of Stars, who bowed gravely. Gimpy pointed to the cave and asked him to listen to the ghost. The old man was convinced.

'It's because the girl didn't close his eyes when he died. The one most loved by the dead man must close his eyes, because otherwise the spirit goes out through them and follows her through life.'

'Forever?' the girl asked in terror.

'No, only until God lets him into heaven. The best thing for that is to say masses and prayers.'

It seemed to the girl that the wind had died down when the Indians came. With Trinidad's spirit at her back she was afraid of being left alone. Voice of the River of Stars repeated that she should leave the cave. She looked at Gimpy. He seemed to have made up his mind, though the huts of the south settlement were far away. But perhaps just for that reason she would be safer with the Indians. Their presence was comforting, and, being afraid of the cave, she decided to go. They waited for the night to grow darker before they started the journey.

Once the girl had decided, nobody mentioned it again. The Indians sat on the ground, most of them in the cave so as not to be seen from outside. They didn't seem to care about the ghost. After a long silence the old Indian spoke to Gimpy:

'We can get in touch with the teacher and have the launch meet the girl on the south beach.'

The ghost was still humming inside. Now that there were so many of them, Gimpy suggested they should go in and investigate.

'Leave him alone,' said the old Indian. 'If he sees you he'll follow you wherever you go.'

The Indians were getting ready for the trip. The girl, tired

from lack of sleep and eating only cold food, from her isolation with Gimpy, and her own remorse, thought she heard her
aunt's Morse-code whistling. They set out, the Indians posting an advance guard and two flanking parties. They walked
in dead silence. Their feet never stumbled or broke a twig.
Now and then they heard the hoot of an owl from one side,
and the procession paused. It was a signal from their scouts.
They would wait for another signal and then hurry on in
silence. Gimpy, all cheered up, returned to his obsession
with the stars. He considered that the only subject good
enough for the girl, especially when they were walking,
and at night.

'I have seen some,' he whispered, 'as big as the palm of my
hand, and some nights they come down to bathe in the sea.'

At first the girl was lively and vigorous, but after a while
she began to flag. Six or eight Indians came up with an
improvised litter. She protested but finally gave in and before
long, lulled by the measured rhythm of the footsteps, fell
asleep. An Indian covered her with a serape. Gimpy asked
how they knew she was asleep.

'When a person passes from waking to sleep,' they told
him, 'the body grows heavier. It's the mind that was flying
around before and then settles down in the heart.' The noise
of the march died down, leaving total silence. They were all
careful not to scrape their feet on the ground. And so they
walked all night.

Voice of the River of Stars saw the moon through the trees.

'The day after to-morrow,' he said, 'it will wane, and
the rain will come.'

Gimpy would have liked to put his shoulder under the
stretcher, to feel the girl's weight like the rest, but they
wouldn't let him because his limp would make the march
uneven. For some time he had been feeling the effects of the
sea water he had drunk, but he hadn't dared leave the line
for fear the girl would notice. Now that she was asleep he
left the path and disappeared among the trees. A little later

165

the girl cried out. They stopped and lowered the litter. She looked around in terror.

'They've shot him!' she cried.

'No, they haven't shot him. God is protecting him.'

She asked for Gimpy, who came back very embarrassed. The girl hadn't mentioned Darío's name, but they all knew she was referring to him. The Indians were like the light in the daytime and the dark at night. They went everywhere, found out everything, and never talked.

'She dreamed it. God wanted her to dream it so He could reassure her.' The girl was crying, and the knowledge that she was crying *for Dario* made her look around fearfully for the ghost. But if she thought of Darío it was God's will, and perhaps God could keep the vengeful ghost away. She prayed for Trinidad's soul, remembering what the Indians had said. She wanted Trinidad to get to heaven as soon as possible so he would stop persecuting her. The train started on again. The old man took one of the girl's hands in his. His hand was rough and dry like cardboard, but the girl was pleased. She stayed awake, not wanting to go back to her dream.

Voice of the River of Stars looked at the sky again.

'Once,' said the old man in a far-off tone, 'the storm clouds came down full of water the colour of gold, and the corn and beans grew better than any other year, and the women were fruitful, and the pigs and the goats.'

Another Indian said:

'There are people who go on living after they die. Then the evil spirits go and live in them.'

Hearing this, Gimpy thought of Careto, thought of him so hard that he had to talk about him. The girl tried to place him from the day of mourning but couldn't remember him.

'No, señora,' said Gimpy, 'that man doesn't go to funerals or christenings. Nor weddings, either.'

In the morning the Pimp had been seen asleep behind Careto's cabin. Nobody paid much attention. They didn't know what the idiot was doing there, nor could they have guessed what would happen afterwards. When he woke up the Pimp went over to Careto, who was still sitting beside the door.

Careto thought: 'It's broad daylight, and they can see us from Eminencias' house.'

He told the Pimp he had left his fishing-pole on the ledge by the sea, and they walked that way. Careto was carrying a little basket 'of accessories'. The Pimp said:

'Now you've gone and spent all the money. While I was asleep you spent it all.'

Careto showed his naked chest in witness: 'Wouldn't I have bought myself a shirt?'

They reached the shore and climbed around among the crags, looking for a place to sit down. Careto, making sure that they were hidden from prying eyes, sat down on a rock. The Pimp stood in front of him. Careto wanted to know if he had any more money.

'Sure. Two thousand more. Right here in my pocket.'

'Show me.'

'No. You'd rob me.'

He was gloomy and disappointed. This sadness irritated Careto. 'Can idiots be sad?' Yes, they could be idiotically sad. Careto fell into a kind of melancholy he had never known before. But the Pimp kept saying, hopping about on one foot:

'You spent it all and I need it!'

'What for?'

'Lefty will get me the girl if I give him the money.'

'Does Lefty know we have it?'

'No, not yet.'

The Pimp was weak, Careto strong. And there was nothing in life but matter, manifest always in the compulsion of its weight and mass: in violence. In energy, the energy of aggression. In man it showed itself in what the weak call

167

egoism. The weak call their own frailty magnanimity, another's strength egoism.

The Pimp believed in good faith that Careto's fishing-pole was there and was surprised not to find it. He looked all over for it and said finally, shrugging his shoulders:

'A fish got it, a big, fat fish.'

Careto was still pondering the obligation of mankind to exert force.

'So you still have two thousand?'

'You want to steal it from me!'

'And you have it on you?'

'The mark on your forehead is laughing because I have them in my pocket. But you won't get them from me. Lefty has a forty-five on his hip and a lot of ammunition in his belt.'

The Pimp realised he had gone too far and backed down a little.

'Are you afraid of me?' Careto asked.

'Not of you, but there's that snake in the box.'

His hair was plastered to his forehead with sweat. He went on:

'If Lefty gets the money everything will be fixed up to-night.' He held out his hand. The palm was pudgy and the fingers soft; he stretched out his arm with a trembling of his forefinger.

'Give me the money!'

Careto looked around carefully. They were alone. He held his breath and listened. Not a sound. The Pimp came up to him, trustingly. Careto showed him the roll of bills.

'Open your mouth and shut your eyes.'

It was a children's game. When they wanted to give somebody a surprise they said that. If the other did it they popped a caramel in his mouth or a cooky or, for a joke, a pebble. The Pimp obeyed, but, hearing Careto fumbling in the basket, he opened his eyes again.

'Don't let Ruana out! Give me just half the money, but don't let Ruana out.'

The basket was empty; there was no snake there, which greatly reassured the Pimp. Careto took from the basket a dirty cloth and a rope. Not a muscle of his face moved. His eyes looked past the idiot, at the sea. Perhaps the sea had eyes, too, and was watching them.

'Here is the money. All of it,' Careto said.

At the same time, with his left hand, he wadded the dirty rag into a ball. But the Pimp was watching the mark on his forehead and the grim mouth. Careto was not laughing. If he had laughed, as one was supposed to in that game, he would have believed him.

'Open your mouth and shut your eyes.'

Careto smiled. The game was getting serious. The idiot drew near, shut his eyes, and, tossing his head back, held up his open mouth. Careto could see way down to the tonsils. And there he stuffed the wad of dirty rag. At the same time he doubled the idiot up and squashed his face against the rock, holding him with his knees. He heard the soft crunch of the nose against the stone. Calmly he tied his hands with the rope, threw him on the ground, tied his feet, and rolled up a stone that was nearby. He wound the other end of the rope five times around the stone, tied it in a triple knot, and the Pimp, the stone, and the rope went flying through the air. Careto noticed that his right hand was wet. The victim, realising in Careto's arms what kind of safety he was in for, had urinated. At that place the sea formed a quiet backwater, and the stone and the body sank with a hollow noise. Careto stared at the water, wiping his hand on his trousers. He held his breath, and calculated the length of time the Pimp would be able to struggle. When he was about to suffocate he breathed again and shrugged his shoulders.

'That's that!'

But suddenly he clenched his hands, his eyes wild. 'Idiot!' The Pimp still had two thousand-peso bills in his pockets. 'I've always been like that; I always forget the practical side of things.' He picked up the basket, went slowly back to his cabin, and sat down as usual beside the door. 'Perhaps Rusty-Pants will come along,' he thought, forgetting that he had already been there with the bird. He would have liked him to come. Now that the Pimp was drowned he seemed neither so worthless nor such an idiot. Death dignified him. But in a moment Careto's thoughts turned from the Pimp to a child-hood companion of his who had also drowned one day in a lake near Berlin. That was his secret. His secret. How strange that he should remember it now! Berlin. Childhood. The country on Sundays grew picturesque and exciting. And that was the setting of his secret. Bicycles wheeled along the paths. The boy who drowned had a very fine one. There were girls with bare legs—those lovely German legs—who used to ramble not only on the roads but along the paths and under the trees, over the lawns of the Grunewald. Green and white. In those days Careto had no nickname. His name was Oscar and he went with his parents. His mother made apple tarts and wrapped them in warm napkins; he didn't like the first part of the excursion because they had to take care of all that stuff. One day Karl—that's right; his name was Karl—fell into the water and was drowned. Fell? Did somebody push him? Did he push him? At that asexual age they were romantically attached to one another. Yes, he had pushed him. And that was his secret. In the beginning it didn't make any difference. He hid it like any other prank. Later it grew and grew, and at the age of twenty sometimes he couldn't sleep. He remembered especially the bicycle with its wheels painted red inside. At that time Careto and his people were Jews, but now they had turned out to be Aryans. And his parents had recovered their property; they might even have become rich. And Karl? If he had pushed Karl it was in the confusion of childish passion and he didn't exactly remember doing it. That is, yes, he had pushed him, wishing him to fall in and drown. Why deny it? All he remembered about it was Karl's blue eyes and the red wheels polished by the rub of the brakes.

Again water ran down Eminencias' gutter. He got up. He was not in the Grunewald but on Faro Island. He wanted to go to the bar not to drink but to see people and be seen. This was the most important, that he should be seen. He was about to go when he realised suddenly that he was not a convict but a hero, and a hero ought not to display himself too readily. He would eat in his cabin. That day, at least. He began to make lunch. He had three eggs and five or six tortillas. Chilli too. He would eat as usual. For drink there was stagnant rain water full of dysentery germs. But—why should he eat so badly? He had money. He had it; he had won it by violence. He had behaved like the father wolf, not like the gelding, and the father wolf had a right to celebrate his triumph. He left the eggs where they were, looked with distaste at the tortillas and the jug of water, and went out. Not to see people or to be seen, but simply to buy things for a decent meal, a bottle of wine and some canned goods. He found Eminencias in the canteen, his manner so unmistakably cool that for a moment Careto was upset. Perhaps he had seen him with the Pimp. If he'd been on the shore he'd have chucked him in the water too.

'Are you alone here?'

'Yes,' the proprietor said. 'They're all chasing after the widow.'

Careto inspected the canned goods, fruit, meat, jam. Bottles of Spanish and American wine. He had already picked out his purchases when it occurred to him that he had nothing but thousand-peso bills. Eminencias was observing him.

'Do you want something?'

Careto asked for the things he always bought on credit and paid for with the few cents' wages he received for working on the road: cigarettes, matches, dry chillies. He went back to his cabin. The nearer he got to it, the more uneasily he looked at

171

the shadows over the sea, but he didn't want to admit that he was afraid and walked more sturdily than usual.

He started preparing his lunch again, without the wine and the other delicacies. When he had eaten he came to the door, sat down, and lit a cigarette. The Pimp had been there a few hours before. Where did people go when they stopped living? The question amused him and he laughed. It was always like that. He had let himself be condemned by the judge, smiling. He had rich relatives and yet went about the island without a shirt, smiling. It had been going on for twenty years. Smiling, smiling for no reason at all. Karl, drowned in the lake, pursued him and touched everything he did, his loves, his business affairs. 'If I were a Catholic I would confess, and that would be the end of it,' he thought, but he was not one. There were times when he thought everybody was coming to ask him about Karl's death, to dig it out of him. Everywhere he was followed by Karl's blue eyes which had darkened as he fell into the water. Somewhat later, before he was thirty, Oscar, who was still not Careto, went half crazy. They said he was really crazy and took him to a sanatorium. He was there a year. When he left, cured, he could not remember what had been said to him or what he had said during that time. He was afraid that he might have confessed his crime, revealing his secret. He began to make inquiries about his own talk and finally became convinced that he had not given himself away, but with this assurance remorse set in again. He decided to shout out his crime at the top of his lungs, but at the last minute he couldn't go through with it. And then he thought: 'Why didn't I tell it when I was crazy? If I had confessed then, the memory would not burden me, and the doctors would have blamed it on my madness.' He could have confessed without shame or risk. But perhaps the virtue of confession lay precisely in risk and punishment. He smiled, mocking and arrogant. And now he bade a cynical good-bye to those blue eyes and to that secret. He had drowned Karl and drowned the secret, too, with a new one. He had killed the Pimp and wondered, smiling: 'Where do people go when they stop living?' In this case, to the bottom of the sea. But he felt calmer since giving up the idea of wasting money in the shop. He didn't know why, but for some reason the fact of not spending the money gave him heart again. Perhaps with that money things could be done for society.

'I am not a criminal,' he told himself emphatically. 'The Karl affair was only a childhood lapse.'

He no longer felt depressed. Nor did he have to smile. 'I am a soldier.' He had killed only to fulfil *a mission*. He had not bought wine or canned goods. On the contrary, he would put his strength, his austerity, and his money at the service of the cause. And someday, perhaps, the cause would consecrate him among the great. A soldier. And, since the other soldiers of the clan were triumphant in Europe, a conqueror. The presentiment he had had on the night of the celebration would come true: he would be the sexless father, the religious leader. Once he had torn down the myth of the girl it would be easy even if another commander came with other troops. He had enough money for the first steps; perhaps he could get hold of materials for a secret radio station. Later he would have whatever funds were needed. The soldiers of the Great Gelding were already in America, and he, though isolated, was one of their outposts. The secret? What secret? It no longer existed. He had surmounted that old secret by means of a new one. It was possible that he had an enemy in Darío, but he was not to be taken seriously. They had come near to killing him the night before. In the end they would get rid of him as a dangerous rival for the girl.

The teacher was at the harbour. He wanted to see if the boat from the Health Department was coming and had gone there after finishing his teaching duties in the afternoon. The sky was rapidly clouding over. A storm was coming on. Darío, happy with his recollections of the girl, tried to find her essence in the delight and miracle of things. And he did.

Flashes of distant lightning furrowed the sky in all direction and were so frequent that the clouds seemed to be throbbing incessantly. The light was a metallic mauve, with streaks o rose in the distance, in the direction of the sea. From such mysteries magical beings like the girl were born. There was still light from the last reflection of the sun. The storm broke. Darío found shelter in an old limestone quarry and had scarcely taken cover when a peal of thunder rumbled through the valley.

He decided to try to reach his house before the rain became too heavy. He thought of the girl. If she were alone she might be afraid of the storm, as children were. Beneath the tense clouds he thought of the Twin, Lefty, Gimpy. 'Among such men and in such places everything is, or seems, puny, and Nature looks monstrous and immense. The storms are more terrifying, the rain more torrential. Nature lures us to tropical lands and when we are here it besieges us with little poisonous insects and swamps and putrid water.' What Darío loved was the nature that smiles in brooks and mountain snows, friendly, without treachery.

Outside of the tropics it was pleasant to watch a spider in the heart of the woods flinging its young into the air on a slender thread—he was amused to find himself thinking of spiders because they had spent the last week studying them in school—or to hear the birds and even the beasts roaring at night. From these things also came miracles no less wonderful. And he thought of Niña Lucha.

Another clap of thunder sent an enormous reverberation over the island, as if fifty tree trunks were being split. For several seconds the echo rolled over the sea, passed over Darío, and died out in the depths of the woods. Darío stood still, breathing in the damp air and hearing the furious beat of the rain on the leaves, in fields where rain was not fecundation but an orgy. He was waiting for it to increase, knowing that some bolts would strike, and not until he had felt them nearby would the storm abate. But it seemed to pass on, leaving rain still dripping from a few rearguard clouds. He had another remembrance of his childhood.

'Will the frogs come out the way they used to in my village?'

He would have liked to play with the rain frogs with the girl, make a game of the ferocity and evil of the storm, perhaps even reduce the whole ignoble torrent of passion on the island to a children's game.

He went on toward his house. When he had gone a few steps his eye was caught by a shiny object in the bottom of a little ravine. He climbed down and found a kind of toad with luminous skin which jumped on the nearest rock and kept jumping until it disappeared. Darío remembered seeing a similar phenomenon in his village. There had been a violent rainstorm. He was in the open patio of the house and suddenly noticed a toad staring at him with round eyes. Just as Darío saw him there came a flash of lightning, and from the belly of the toad issued a sphere of light as strong as a magnesium flare. For several minutes after it had vanished he could still see a circle of light on the toad. When he had made himself invisible the animal hopped away. The peasants had told him that toads were very useful because they ate harmful insects, but he had heard the same peasants praise other animals that ate toads. He walked faster now, the sun having already sunk behind the clouds. He decided not to think about the situation on the island, about the Twin, but the passionate currents of the soul cannot be soothed by reflection or by wishing it, but only by giving them up. Darío couldn't do it and walked home thinking that the Twin or Sixfingers, whom he did not take seriously, might nevertheless change the goals of his life, those goals that seemed to be connected with the idea of the girl. He tried to think of other things, but it was no use. Trinidad dead, Gómez and his companion dead too. Without indictments, without trial. And all so simple, so *without ritual*. Trinidad's corpse presiding at the feast. Then its second disappearance (no one knew where it was). The Twin threatening, shooting at the feet of those who hesitated. And the girl, the girl, the girl, in her hiding-place that only he knew. The rain increased and slackened intermittently. The last pale light, scarcely filtering through the clouds, was reflected in the rain, and every drop was a thread of platinum. The storm was over before Darío got home. The rain had stopped, but the sky was still overcast. Everything looked newer after the storm; everything carried a suggestion of its own. The roots of the trees showing above ground were those roots in old engravings that had so impressed Darío as a child. The dampness of the forest was luxuriant, almost indecent, and the earth crunching under his feet was wildly voluptuous. Far off, among shreds of clouds on the sea or in the sky, was a star. Only one. Darío thought: 'It's going to clear up, and the night will be hot.'

Two glow-worms lit up in the dusk. The green light kept changing in intensity. The first spectres of night swung from the branches, and in the distance the yellow strip of shore seemed luminous, too. Far out on the seaward horizon there was a light. Could it be the sanitation boat? A little later another light appeared some distance from the first. 'A couple of fishing boats.' He looked around, enervated by the spectacle. He reached his house, dropped into the rocking-chair under the porch, and sighed. Why didn't he go to see Niña Lucha? He knew he couldn't do anything but what he was doing, but he felt foolish. He couldn't go to see her because they were on guard and would inevitably trail him and catch her. Darío realised that he was conjuring her up, was seeing her, and at the thought of her everything—shapes, sounds—dissolved around him. There remained only the pure image, in pure recollection. And her essence in things, in the rain and the luminous toad. He remembered her during the condolence ceremony at headquarters. Morning shone in the patio. Through the glass roof the light fell softly on her head, and in the midst of her grief her chin showed bright and polished as marble, veined with red at the mouth. In spite of everything there was a coquettish lift to that chin, and Darío was moved by its youthfulness. He tried to distract his imagination but could not.

'Gimpy will be here early to-morrow. I ought to write the girl a letter.' He got out paper, started a stupid phrase: *Dear señora*. He threw the paper away, rose, sat down again. In the darkness drawing over the starry night—the clouds were parting; the storm had petered out—Darío tried to forget the girl. He observed the tranquillity of the trees, the waters, the clouds, thinking: 'Here you see everything changing, alive and active even in repose. And you have here the birth of two obsessions: beauty and truth. And here am I, held fast between beauty and truth.' The sense of it intoxicated him. Over the trees, over the sea, under the arch of the sky, he felt drawn into an ineffable harmony—but the image of the girl returned. All this—truth, beauty, the ineffable harmony —was nothing but *the girl*. He leaned back, closing his eyes. He heard La Chole talking to herself inside, thinking that Darío was not home. The teacher felt himself saturated with the hidden truths of nature. And feeling that he had penetrated the heart of it all—the secret of the glow-worms, the luminous toad, the voracious spiders, the waters defending themselves against the land in their slow counter-attack of surf, the star casting its trembling light across torn clouds —he thought:

'Now'—as if he had found the proof—'now I know what life is.'

He added:

'Life is an ideal in progress.'

An ideal unfolding, never to be fulfilled and yet fulfilling itself every instant. He understood it, but perhaps he could not express it. It all fused in him into one vast feeling. The great task was to *discover states of consciousness for which there were still no words*. But to express it all was utterly impossible. The absolute was only an illusion. But at the core of this illusion there might be something terribly concrete: a person. A woman. The woman. And this most concrete illusion made him aware of the absolute in the firefly and in the toad. He needed that absolute. There was mysticism in those ideas.

'I call myself a revolutionary, but I'm only a religious man who has lost God.'

He lingered, bringing the shadows of the woods close to his eyes through the field-glasses. A bird flung out sharp intermittent cries. The rifts in the clouds widened. Darío raised the glasses and focussed on one star, then another. 'There's Saturn. Saturn's year—its revolution around the sun—takes nine of ours. And maybe its revolution on its own axis is slower, too, and its days longer. For the inhabitants there, if there are any, our days, our years, our life must seem as ephemeral as the life of insects, butterflies, for instance, seem to us.' And again he posed the question:

'What is all this? What is life?'

And again he answered: '*Life is an ideal in progress*. We can sleep or wake, walk or lie on the beach, laugh or cry, consider ourselves the happiest or the most unfortunate beings on earth. It makes no difference. The ideal goes on unfolding, without pause, without haste, and it contains us all. I feel far away. Far from what? However far away I seem to myself, however isolated and remote, I am always in the centre of the ideal that is in progress. But in the centre of this ideal lies an abstract nucleus, and in the centre of this nucleus the girl. And man cannot wait, like a thing—stone or sea water—to be caught up and carried along in the unfolding of this ideal.' And if the girl was in the centre, then he was outside the play of those elemental forces of which the ideal made use, while he was not with her. But what could he do? How to integrate himself with it? Must he pursue her like the others, desire her, take her? Darío desired her, but that was an ideal. And it was— he now realised—outside him; he could not attain it. To realise an ideal, Darío thought, was monstrous. The ideal was in itself a reality, and there it was: 'This is the whole problem of revolutions,' thought Darío; 'an ideal becoming realised; that is, destroyed.' The whole universe was agitated at the spectacle. Darío was amused by his own thoughts. In the presence of a woman like Lucha he had almost delirious associations of ideas. But the ideal that he had felt before, that had risen in his path and given him so violent a shock— he now was obliged to admit it—was one which was still there, alive, climbing the rocks of the cave of Virrey, endowed with cool lips and viscera and sex. And perhaps she was thinking of him too. But above all, it was an ideal not to be possessed and destroyed—that was what they were all after— but to be won over and joined to the rhythm of one's own ideal being. To become integrated with it. There, there was the problem. To become integrated with it.

A cry came from the woods, a bird's cry, that left the whole forest quivering when it stopped. 'Why, when I felt her presence, did I think of the revolution?' The truth was that Darío could think of nothing, not even the revolution, without her intervening. The other bird, foolish and stubborn, answered the first one:

Bambu, bambu-le-le.

Darío told himself candidly:

'When we fall in love we feel as if our passion had absorbed all the forces ever mobilised in that direction since the beginning of the species. For me, the possession of a woman is not the realisation of an ideal but the miraculous working of that ideal in progress of which our species consists. When man feels that the miracle is denied him he suffers a shock even worse than death. And in that case, what does a crime mean to him, or a hundred? Shouldn't I, then, join in the mob that wants to "fight for the girl"? Isn't it they who have hold of the truth?'

Darío let himself sink to the level of the Twin, Sixfingers,

Lefty. Were they perhaps right? More than once that afternoon there had passed like a cloud over his mind the desire to realise the ideal and then tumble into some moral abyss. If he had her no abyss was possible. 'That is the truth,' he said; 'it must be. What happens is that in civilisation we lose sight of it.' Perhaps she would have to be obtained by all the methods of force, all the 'aggressive matter'. Perhaps all his wisdom was only a perversion. Weakness. Everything was matter, and matter was everything. Agreed, but there was no need to be fooled by words. Some weeks ago, reading books on physics, Darío had made a discovery which it interested him to connect with his thoughts on love. An isolated atom weighed, for instance, $0·00035$ units. Broken up, all its parts together weighed $0·00029$ units. That is to say, it had lost, in the form of energy, a quantity of matter. The matter 'radiated'. These radiations became invisible energy which acted on the material and reconditioned it. And if this were so—apparently it was irrefutable—all matter was active and animate fluid; all matter was thought. Everything in life, in the world, was matter, but matter was spirit. There was nothing in the world more realistic than idealism. Nothing more practical, solid, and material than a living ideal. All physical life, all chemical life (and social, economic, and political forms) were only thoughts in development, related ideals in progress. And if this were true, was not his attitude in all this perfectly just and right?

Night was lowering. Darío thought of the girl and wanted to savour, one by one, the words he had heard her say and feel himself alone and strong with that echo. He decided to write a few lines in case Gimpy showed up in the morning. All he could think of, sitting by the oil lamp at the table where La Chole had spread the cloth, was: 'Niña Lucha: We are thinking of you every moment and are sure that in not more than three days you will be able to return to your family.' He thought about the boat from the Health Department. But he didn't want her to 'return to her family'. His fingers turned to iron as he wrote, and his spirit felt dry and arid. In this arid state he gave in to protest. It was natural: he had exchanged nothing but meaningless small talk with the girl, and nevertheless he was in love. He tore up the paper and began anew, with equally inane results. How hard it was to write! He gave it up. 'To-morrow, maybe,' he thought and went to his room, carrying the oil lamp. He returned to his earlier reflections. Everything is matter. There is only matter, but all matter craves to become abstraction. And energy is also tangible and visible. It changes with light; it combines with air and water. There are no frontiers between matter and energy, thought, spirit. Reality, for gods or poets, is only a fiction. A gamma ray, projected with a determined intensity upon an atom, disappears as a ray and becomes an electron. There is only matter, but all matter is arbitrary, an image, an abstraction. 'My position is sound.' There was only *the ideal in progress*, and he was placed solidly at its centre. His idealism was an active material force. He lay down on his bed and smoked without undressing. It was hot, and he got up again to open the windows and let in some air. He left the metal screens partly closed to keep out the mosquitoes. The bird's song—*Bambu, bambu-le-le*—was a-quiver with the sultry shadows of the storm. The real world gave him joy, but he wondered:

'What should one do in the midst of all this?'

By way of answer familiar voices sounded in the doorway. La Chole went out and came back in a flurry.

'There are two men with guns.'

They were the Twin's men.

'You're in for it now,' one said, coming in. 'Anyone who fools the chief has to pay for it.'

Chapopote, showing his pistol, added:

'For better or worse.'

Darío let them take him to headquarters. They halted at the guardroom under the outside stairs. There he was locked up, with sentries in sight. Should he descend to the 'other level'? Fight with their weapons? Seeing the thick bars of the grating, he thought:

'I have a slight disadvantage. *A handicap*, as Margarito would say.'

VII

'THIS MAN WILL BE THE TOOL, THE AGENT. The first agent always should be blind and foolish. In war the less the soldiers know, the better they fight, and I must be careful not to let Lefty know what my errand is about.' Lefty, somewhat piqued, quietly took his foot from the step of the bar.

'What do you want?'

He looked with distaste at the other's hairy chest. Careto began:

'Well, you see, when they took me from the capital I had a little money put away, and I brought it with me. Not much, a thousand pesos. The trouble is, it's just one bill. I need to buy something and I don't like to go there like this without a shirt and with a thousand-peso bill. If you go nobody will be surprised.'

'You may not have a shirt on, but you're a gentleman!'

'You can buy something, a good bottle of wine, for instance.'

'Whatever you like. I wouldn't do it for anybody else, but you're a gentleman.'

Lefty took the bill and went out perplexed. Careto watched him put the money in his pocket and go into Eminencias' house, reappearing shortly with a bottle in his arms. He carried himself as a man should with that much money on him.

'Here. He asked me if it was mine. Of course I didn't answer. And he gave me the change: nine hundred and eighty-four.'

Careto told him the bottle was a present. He had decided not to use a single penny for his own advantage. Watching

183

him pocket the money, Lefty became terribly melancholy. He hinted that he was without funds, at which Careto played deaf, so he ended up asking for a loan of a couple of hundred.

'All my life,' Careto said, 'I've made it a rule never to lend a penny. Loans bring nothing but resentment and enmities.'

Lefty launched a speech about loyalty and being a gentleman and concluded by lowering his figure from two hundred to fifty. Careto softened his refusal with a smile. In desperation Lefty asked for one peso. Then fifty centavos 'for cigarettes'. When he was about to go off in a huff Careto dazzled him with a promise:

'I don't lend money, but perhaps something could be fixed up for you.'

Lefty stammered:

'I always said——'

'But in return for a service. I'm not crazy.'

'Oh no, sir, no.'

'I still know what I'm doing.'

'Oh yes, sir, yes.'

'Are you agreeable?'

Lefty put his hand on his heart. 'Lefty,' he said, 'doesn't need to know what it's about. With no questions asked I say yes.'

'Do you know where the girl is?'

'Yes sir. I'll bring her to you to-night.'

It was a lie. He knew nothing.

'That's not exactly it. But I have to find out where she is.'

'What for?'

'To take some people there and get her.'

Lefty didn't understand.

'You don't want me to bring her?'

'No.'

Careto smiled mysteriously.

'I knew the girl in the city, in a fancy house. She used to cost a hundred pesos.'

'Cheap at the price.'

184

The readiness with which Lefty accepted the idea made Careto suspicious. Lefty had not believed him.

'Recently she was an inmate in a house for minors. A scandalous thing happened. One night they took her to the jail because they were going to hang the Ape, that famous criminal, and as his last wish the good man had the idea of having some fun with her. His lawyer managed to get him permission at a price. After that they called her the "Hanged Man's Widow" in the house. Some clients wouldn't touch her, but some paid even higher.'

Lefty, listening with open mouth, didn't doubt it for a minute. He burst out laughing.

'When I think of Sixfingers and the Twin going out of their heads over her!'

'The whole lot of them. I wouldn't have said a word. But I can't bear to see everybody falling for these ridiculous ideas about the girl. I can't let people go on killing each other because they think she is an angel.'

Lefty was delighted, because two days ago he had had the sad idea of giving up the girl.

'You're going to help me, Lefty.'

'You can count on me. What should I do?'

Careto came straight to the point:

'You catch her and let a gang have her, whether she likes it or not. One right after the other. Get the wildest ones, the worst you can find.'

'How many?'

'Thirty at least.'

'Me too?'

Careto shrugged his shoulders.

'That's for you to decide.'

He gave him five hundred pesos and pointed to the door. Lefty backed out, making wild promises. Careto warned him:

'What we've been talking about is nobody else's business. And when it's over you get another five hundred.'

When he was alone he thought: 'Lefty will be discreet,

because he won't want to tell where he got the money. He'd rather have people think it's his own.'

Beside the empty barrel where Lefty had been sitting was the bottle of wine. He must have been completely dazed to forget it. It was a fine brand. Careto pulled the cork, smelled it, and was about to tip the bottle to his lips, but he refrained. He wanted to be a hero, not a criminal. He was not even planning to buy a shirt and still went around with his chest bare under his coat. If they did not pay him the wages owing to him for his work on the road he would try to get something on credit. But that money was going to be kept for 'the cause'. Was it possible that he should be governed by a moral idea? He had killed Karl. Killed him. Child's play. He had killed the Pimp, too, because he had to. Nature had blundered there, had made a monster but with puny arms and legs. And beside that monstrosity Nature had set Careto.

He eyed the newspaper again. Bombs on Unter den Linden. The aeroplane allowed the weak to threaten the strong in their own homes. But the weapon of the weak was not the aeroplane but 'the ideal'. And the weak gave up quickly, returning to their corner with 'the ideal' intact and material positions lost. Unfortunately 'the ideal' was the individual's relation to the eternal and not to ammunition; at the very sight of ammunition the idealist had a fit. Careto's impulse toward conspiracy—his thoughts of the future permitted him to use the word—sprang from no ideal. Maybe, maybe a gauleiter-ship on the continent? But remote ideas, ideal incentives: what for? Strong arms and a stout heart. These were what carried weight in the world, as was natural. They were changing the world. At the end, when the conquest was finished, there were two possibilities: the strong might have the gold, or they might have destroyed it. In either case it would be they, the ones who were free of morals and ideals, who would dominate. This dominion was not an ideal but a natural tendency of the fittest, a phenomenon of great animal purity. That was the direction Careto was going in, and he had taken it unconsciously, which was the only sure way. The same impulse, the night of the celebration, had led him back to primeval animality: 'The wolf is dead; he is no more.' He thought of his victims. What were Karl and the Pimp in the midst of the struggle of eternal forces? Two clots of blood. One pretty little red one, the other repulsive. Two among millions of blood clots that happened to have sprouted arms and legs.

Careto laughed aloud. He had new victims: first, the Pimp —stupidity. Next, the girl—the sublime. The two disrupted the order of the strong, the killers, the assailers, the destroyers, with their statistical charts tacked up beside the engine. Stupidity, the Pimp, happened to represent money, the false spirit that moved all things without giving life, that moved corpses. The sublime was the dream, the ideal. Oriental races, especially the Jews, embedded in the civilisation of the strong. Careto's people, those of Unter den Linden, would use the stupid as he himself had used the Pimp. And as for the sublime, how could any power of dreams hold out against bombers? The call to reality is matter taking divine revenge. No abstraction is possible under the impact of a thousand-pound bomb. Five years before people might have had doubts, but now, after the war in Spain and the conquest of Europe, no one could deny it. Careto built up his reflections without taking his eyes from the paper. There was an editorial: 'The Road to Chaos.' He didn't need to read it to know what it was about. His eyes lit on two or three names. Cultural allusions. The usual quotations in Latin-American journals: Plato, Epaminondas, Bernard Shaw, and Count Keyserling. He laughed and muttered between his teeth:

'The Great Gelding will teach you to write German, the language that allows for no digressions.'

He went to the door and sat between shade and sunlight. Several Indians went by, one of them carrying a great load of brushwood. The rest were empty-handed, but they seemed to know where they were going. They all had that indifference that comes from engaging in lowly occupations. 'For them,' he thought, 'there is no revolt, no celebration in the woods, no leader, no Niña Lucha.' They went their way like ants, dumb and blind. But without looking at him the Indians had seen him. They had seen him; they knew that he was sitting down, that he had no shirt on, that the sole of one of his shoes was flapping, and there was no shoelace in the other. They saw everything without looking, and they didn't look because they didn't want to provoke the answer that is always called for by a glance. But they were always there, with their muffled presence. Good slaves for the master race. Good beasts of burden someday for the Great Gelding. Good blood clots for the fishes. He got up, went to the shore, and looked for the place where he had been with the Pimp. There were deep footprints near the rock and traces of dry blood on the rock itself. Blood from the nose. If it came to that perhaps those stains could be analysed. He started scraping them off with a rock. When they were gone he sat down again and, taking the same position as on the day before, seeing the same things, and at a time when the light was almost identical, he had a sense of 'recurrence'. If the Pimp had been there he would have thrown him into the sea again. That was no crime.

Something was moving at his left, on the rock, near the water. It was white, like the rock, brown and copper-coloured, like the rock, with greenish stains on the trousers, like the stains on the rock. It was a man. If he had stayed still no eyes could have discovered him. But he had moved. Careto looked more intently but lost him again. He had become still and was one with the rock. The lines and colours blended with the cliff. Careto rose and moved closer. Whoever it was might have been there the day before and seen what happened. In that case it must be an Indian. Only an Indian could hold still so long and see such a thing without coming nearer or running away. When he got there the Indian was gone. But the shape of the rocks was not the same as before. Something about them was changed, but as he walked off and looked back from a distance they resumed their normal shape. A man.

He returned to his place, to the 'scene of his crime', and sat down again. Eyes on the water, he waited, motionless. Finally he got up and started back to his hut. Perhaps he had failed to take into account all the elements of reality. He had succeeded in having secrecy, solitude, silence on the part of the victim, the complicity of the bottom of the sea. But now he saw that mystery might be an element he had left out of account. He went to headquarters. He needed to see people. There were guards posted beside the outer stairs.

Darío was in the guard lock-up. He had been put in at midnight. Being alone there gave him a feeling of being deaf, and he could understand why prisoners sometimes cried out at night. They needed to hear their own voices. 'They've got me all right.' The bolts and bars were evidence. The first thing he felt in the jail, along with the sense of being deaf, was the bodily presence of idleness. Bodily as a gas. Any moment the girl's trail would be discovered.

Two men were talking on the other side of the door. A casual conversation, but Darío listened attentively.

'I couldn't help it, because she betrayed me with Chief Trinidad.'

'Did you see it? Did you catch them together?'

'No. I didn't see anything.'

'Did they tell you?'

'No. Things like that don't count. I found out in a better way.'

'How?'

'I had a dream. Clear as daylight. And when I understood it all I could do was go to my wife and let her have it, right in the throat. I didn't kill her, but she's been hoarse ever since.'

'What was the dream?'

'There was a turkey and beside it a strip of dried meat covered with flies. My wife was selling it and yelling: *The turkey is twenty pesos and the meat sixty centavos*. Don't you understand it yet?'

'No.'

'Twenty pesos is what Black Trinidad earned every day, and sixty cents is what I earned after I got malaria and went on half time.'

'And you stabbed her just for that?'

'Right in the throat with a knife, but all it did was make her hoarse.'

Darío thought: 'So that's it. He wanted to be a turkey and be worth twenty pesos.' He was in love and felt dramatically inferior to Trinidad. He couldn't stand it and wanted to kill his beloved. But he hadn't succeeded, and now he was waiting at the door with a gun to kill Darío if he tried to escape. If one knew how to see and hear, life had a wearisome consistency. That sentry was imprisoned in a passion that formed the boundaries of his world. Darío's passion was the opposite, extending his horizon. The girl had not said a single word to lead him on; he had no idea what impression he had made on her. 'I would give half my life,' he thought, 'to know what she thinks when she thinks of me.' Still there was something rather cheerful, like a sense of freedom, in this idea. 'It must be,' he thought, 'because for me her love is only an aspiration, and I am surprised and dazzled by the ideal of love. An ideal is a religious emotion and therefore gives us a deep feeling of freedom.' There was nothing in the world but love. Every passion, hate, rancour, envy, ill will, was only a form of love. The sentry's knife at his poor wife's throat was also a sorry form of love. He forgot the jail. But since it was already growing light he went to the window and pulled himself up to look out through the high grating. He wanted to see the new day in which the girl was living. In the distance, the landing, the blue strip of the sea, the trees in their green morning lacquer. Nearby, two hens at the foot of the steps. One was scratching its comb; the claw sounded like dry leather against its beak. Still nearer, the sentry picking his nose and thinking about the turkey.

The day was like crystal. Yellow crystal. The reflection of the sky was yellow, and the mole in the harbour. The motionless leaves of the trees threw a yellow glint. And in the yellow air a hollow the size of the girl opened, and there, also of crystal, she stood encased. It stirred another memory of his childhood, something that lay perhaps at the root of that idealism of his which would have been stupid in a man who could not surrender, body and soul, to the discipline of the ideal. His childhood memory had to do only with 'idealism in love'. Darío was seven. One of his brothers had been in the United States and reported that the girls in Massachusetts were made 'of crystal'. And from then on, all through Darío's childhood, his feminine ideal was 'the girl of crystal'. He was well aware that the girls he liked (in the larval sexuality of a boy of seven) had faces, arms, and legs of the same stuff as his own, but the parts covered by their dresses were made of crystal. And sometimes a shadow of that fancy was projected into his adult dreams. The girl was not blonde, nor did she come from Massachusetts, but her covered parts were surely crystal. To fuse with that crystal seemed possible and even imminent to him, though in practice his way seemed more than ever blocked.

'Beauty is difficult.'

He added, almost aloud:

'A problem in magic.'

To be having such thoughts in a cell was somewhat grotesque. While he theorised the others were lining up. He heard the door being unlocked, and Mother Leonor appeared with her hands folded across her stomach and the contrite air of someone visiting a death cell. She asked Darío if they had maltreated him.

'What for?' he asked, smiling.

His smile was a disappointment to Mother Leonor.

'You are very calm about it.'

The teacher paid no attention.

'Where is Gimpy?' he asked.

'If he's the one who's in charge of the girl, I don't approve.'

'They're all in love with her,' Darío thought, 'even Mother Leonor, in her way.'

Perhaps even the old nun's nose scented the ideal. She looked at him with curiosity.

'I wouldn't be so calm if I were in your place. The chief has a grudge against you.'

'The chief? Who appointed him chief?'

'Be careful,' said Mother Leonor, looking around cautiously. 'You might get capital punishment for that.'

So for Mother Leonor his murder would be 'capital punishment'! The woman accepted facts blindly. As long as the Twin didn't pester her everything was in order. Like the Church, thought Darío. But the old woman had come to tell him that the Twin was waiting to question him and he had better tell the truth. The truth? The truth, for him, was that he was against everything that was happening. What good would the truth be to the Twin? And Mother Leonor's only interest in it was that she wanted to listen at the keyhole and find out the girl's whereabouts. He went out, escorted by Mother Leonor and two armed men.

The Twin had installed himself in the biggest armchair he could find.

'Let him appear!' he cried.

That *appear*, which they had all heard in the courts, was impressive. The teacher was brought before him.

'I am the chief,' the Twin said. 'I am in command of the island and I have to straighten out all matters pertaining to persons, animals, and provisions. I have to know at once where Niña Lucha is.'

The teacher shrugged his shoulders. He had never responded to coercion.

'I have to know,' the Twin insisted, 'not for myself, but

to straighten out matters pertaining to persons, animals, and provisions.'

As he said 'not for myself', there was in his voice—who would have suspected it!—a curious melancholy, a heavy sexual melancholy. Observing him, Darío thought: 'It's old age.' Old age that comes without having been earned and seems, therefore, strange and meaningless. But the Twin, noticing the teacher's glance, fell back on violence. He was always at his ease when he could be violent.

'Where's the girl?'

'I don't know, and even if I did I wouldn't tell you.'

'Why?'

'For various reasons. The first one is that I don't feel like it.'

Mother Leonor's eyes were popping out. The Twin, with a facetious expression, asked:

'Don't you know what's done with people who won't talk?'

The teacher didn't answer, and the Twin, raising his hairy finger, repeated:

'Don't you know what's done with people who won't talk?'

He settled back in the chair.

'Have you forgotten that a chief can do what he likes? Beat, kill, expropriate? Especially,' he said weakly and irrelevantly, 'since I don't want the girl for myself.'

Darío was surprised to hear him repeat that; it was somehow convincing. 'It may be,' he thought, 'that he's protecting himself against the imagination of the others who remember the village where he ate iguana meat and raped and killed a little girl.'

'We're going to pull your tongue out.'

A man went out and brought back two others with whip-lashes. The Twin took them and began to snap them in the air, testing their flexibility. The leather thongs whistled merrily.

From far off came the din of rioting people and one or two shots. The Twin listened sharply. He ordered them to tie up the teacher, who held out both hands, knowing that if the other faction attacked headquarters it would be better for him to be found with his hands tied. The Twin drew his revolver, ready for the fight, and reared up like an old cock.

'Now he's in his element; he feels young again,' thought the teacher, trying to loosen the cords which were hurting him. He was terrified for the girl, now that violence had broken out openly.

The Twin paced back and forth.

'Shut the doors. Everybody at the windows!'

Sixfingers' gang approached the building and, meeting preparations for defence, took up their positions. It was they who fired the first shots. The bullets spattered against the window frames. Some went through, causing a shower of glass and splintered wood. One broke a lamp chain, and the lamp fell with a crash. The Twin was firing his revolver and posting his men in strategic positions. In his corner, hands bound, the teacher thought: 'Fighting for beauty, dying for beauty.' The Twin moved clumsily with a peasant's stiffness; Darío always saw him in the attitude of rape, with his coil of wire looped over one arm. He was waiting expectantly for Sixfingers' bullet that would come in the window and hole his head.

After a half-hour's fighting without casualties the Twin gave orders to raise the white flag. There was nothing else at hand, so they shoved the girl's wedding dress through the window. Then he gave orders to open the main door. Sixfingers had three times as many men as the Twin. When the attackers realised that the door was open they came in without firing, just as the Twin fled out the back door with all his men but one who hadn't heard the order and was taken prisoner. Sixfingers' men looked around in great surprise and excitement.

'Did they carry off the dead?' they asked.

The teacher didn't see Lefty in the attacking party. 'Lefty

must have a faction of his own,' he thought. Sixfingers asked Darío, fixing him with his shark's eye:

'Where's the girl?'

'I don't know.'

'No jokes. If you don't tell me you'll be stood against a wall. I must have that girl.' He added, thumping his chest: 'For myself.'

He called for Mother Leonor, to whom he repeated the question. Not being able to find out anything put him in a frenzy. He snatched the bridal dress from the window and crumpled it in his hands.

Sixfingers gave orders for sentries to be posted everywhere. His followers swarmed through the building, pillaging what their predecessors had left. The sack over, they seemed more anxious to set out again than to perform their monotonous duties as guards. The teacher, when they began shoving him downstairs, looked out for familiar faces. Every one near him was apparently his friend, but that was no guarantee. He remembered the girl and wondered disinterestedly who would save her if he were wiped out. And if someone did save her, who could give her what he had to give? Sixfingers rushed down after them like a hurricane. Word had just come that Lefty was at the edge of the woods. They set out after him, exulting in their recent victory and full of assurance. The teacher was left alone by the main stairway. He shrugged his shoulders and sat down on the steps. His position as scapegoat in the centre of all this violence was extremely awkward. That crazed mob would only be goaded further if he walked off. And he was unarmed. Sixfingers' men disappeared among the trees, and presently the shooting began. Just then four Indians from the south settlement appeared around the corner of the building. One of them came up to the teacher and whispered:

'The girl is safe and well.'

Then he went away. Was it possible that the Indians knew where the girl was? They were still shooting in the woods, but apparently not to much effect, for Sixfingers' men came back looking rather dejected. Lefty had managed to escape.

Sixfingers went up to the teacher.

'You'd better tell me where that little girl is, unless you want to be blown to hell.'

Darío heard Mother Leonor in the hall, praying for his soul. To make it all perfectly clear she was using his full name, surname and all. Just at that moment Careto went by, very calmly, coat open to expose his naked chest. He saw Darío out of the corner of his eye and smiled without moving his lips. His very manner of walking was a smile. Careto was on his way to the harbour to get an old newspaper.

Sixfingers went into the guard quarters. Once more Darío was left alone. But they were watching him. He remembered Sixfingers crumpling the wedding dress, his human eye closed, his shark's eye open. The man was all fire and urge. And in this fever lay his danger and his weakness. He attacked like a bull and had a good chance of breaking his head against the wall. He would probably go for Darío, and it was going to be hard to get out of his way. Mother Leonor was still praying for his soul, standing at the window while she said his full name, so that he should be sure to hear. It made him smile to hear her in the midst of his predicament. He looked at little objects near him. A stone chipped off one of the steps, an old tin can. The sun drew a white spark from its side. The can must be hot. He remembered that as a child he had once burned himself trying to pick up a can like that. Near the tin a half-squashed grasshopper.

Perhaps they were going to shoot him, but he no more hated Sixfingers than one hates the bus that runs over one in the street. Every one travelled his own road. The roads had crossed, and Darío stood at the intersection, wondering if he would be able to go on. Perhaps the shadow of death that hung over him at that crossroads would turn out to be the real thing.

He saw Gimpy approaching warily, his enormous head

sweating in the sun. And the day was yellow. He seemed uncertain whether to come closer or not. 'He looks as if he hadn't slept for two or three days,' Darío thought, 'and against his chest, under his armpit, he's carrying the girl's nightgown.' The sentry kept Gimpy at a distance. Sixfingers arrived, accompanied by Squinty. The teacher had never thought much about him but had noticed that Squinty looked at him with hostility. Very brave, Squinty, but he had developed his courage, his swagger, after his conviction. He was a peasant. There was a birthday party at his house; they lived outside the capital. And he had a niece. The guests danced to music from the radio: a barber, a couple of dyers, a few peasants and servant girls from neighbouring families. The barber tried to show off doing modern dances with Squinty's niece, and all of a sudden Squinty came up, separated the couple, and hustled the barber into the street.

'I am very sorry,' he said, 'but I have to kill you.'

'What for?' asked the other, seeing the knife in his hand.

'Because you've been dancing indecently in my house and with my own niece.'

And he killed him. The dance went on till dawn, when the police came. After his conviction Squinty tried to get what compensation he could by playing the bully. Now he had chosen the teacher for his enemy. The others were only too glad to deflect his need for aggression into that channel. But the Indian had told Darío that the girl was all right. And he was on the new plane of a love that has found its object. He looked at the sea and saw no sign of his last resource, the inspection boat. Sixfingers was talking:

'You can't fool me; I don't waste time in threats.'

He ordered the guard to form a firing squad opposite the side wall. Then he came back to Darío, who saw what was up. 'He is going to shoot me,' he thought, but the idea left him impassive.

Sixfingers half opened his human eye:

'You know my story, don't you?'

He was proud of the Tommy-gun and his outburst of revenge in the cemetery. He had no use for self-possession.

'You aren't the only one who knows where the girl is. There are others. One, two, maybe ten. All I need is one. And when he hears I've shot you he'll come out with it, meek as a lamb. If you let yourself be killed you will be doing something very manly but completely useless, because two hours afterwards I'll know where the girl is.'

'How brave!' Darío exclaimed. 'Take me by surprise, unarmed, and have me killed.'

Sixfingers acknowledged the blow. The teacher saw him fumble with his holster, but instead of the pistol he drew out a pair of knives, which he threw on the stairs.

'Sixfingers doesn't need lessons from any dirty bastard.' He pointed to the weapons, whose blades glinted coldly. 'Take your choice.'

Darío was on the point of accepting, though he thought it futile. He went toward the knives, calm and assured. In the blue bay a trim little boat was in sight. The sanitary commission? The only way he could preserve his masculine pride was to make a game of the whole thing. He took a knife and hurled it against the guardroom door. It penetrated deep into the moulding and stuck there. He looked coolly at Sixfingers, took the other knife, and planted it beside the first one.

'A minute ago,' he said, 'I could have stabbed you in the heart before you knew what was happening.'

'Me? Stab me in the heart?'

Darío was afraid of having gone too far. Still, there was the boat. Since he couldn't retreat he went on:

'Yes, you.'

Sixfingers drew his pistol.

'And why didn't you?'

A woman of about forty appeared, dirty and dishevelled. It was Sixfingers' woman. He looked at her in silence with the shark's eye. She screamed at Darío:

'They say you know where the girl is! Don't tell this man, unless you want to put us all in mourning!'

She paused and, looking at Sixfingers, went on:

'Especially as she doesn't deserve a man like you. Lefty says she's a tart, and in the city they called her the "Hanged Man's Widow." '

'It is written,' said Sixfingers slowly. 'It is written. I am the hawk and she the dove. It is written.'

He went slowly up to his wife. She backed away, screaming:

'You're thirty years older than she is! How are you going to keep up with a woman like that?'

Sixfingers took another step forward, and the woman saw the two knives in the wood.

'She'll put her arms around you and stick a poisoned dagger in your back.'

Sixfingers kept coming, and the woman fled. He turned to the teacher:

'You have one minute to talk.'

But he saw, behind Darío, the trim little boat aiming for the dock. He thought it was federal troops arriving. Darío, after giving him time to become thoroughly alarmed, told him what it was about, gleefully relating the entire contents of the letter from the Health Department. Then he showed it to him. Sixfingers sent a message to the docks forbidding anybody to land without his express permission.

The firing squad was lining up.

The vessel was bigger than those generally used for such inspections and in too good condition for a government ship.

Sixfingers re-read the letter, turning it over in his hands.

'You mean they're coming on official business?'

'So it seems.'

His massive nose was sniffing around the mystery of the little boat. The Oriole came up to him.

'Chief, I wish you'd have my son bumped off too. He takes advantage of his youth and beats me.'

Groups of convicts arrived, discussing whether or not Niña

Lucha was a prostitute. Opinion was divided. Hearing them Darío thought he must be dreaming.

Bocachula had something in her hand for Sixfingers.

'We made a barbecue of wild rats. Right over there.' She pointed toward a group of convicts squatting around a little bonfire near the woods. 'Seven wild rats roasted in the embers. Here's the first one for you, chief.'

Sixfingers was appreciative of delicacies. The shape of the rat was unchanged. The chief took the front feet in one hand, the back feet in the other, and bit into the back. Out of the corner of his eye he looked at the sea and the little boat. Then he took a gulp of beer and turned toward the teacher.

'Before I kill you I'm going to make use of you, because you're a presentable bastard. You're to go there with this paper. With an escort, of course. I don't think the little doctors are very anxious to land. You're going to persuade them to leave. You'll answer to me with your life if they set foot on land. You're not going alone; don't fool yourself. Squinty's going along with a pistol. If you say a single word to get me in trouble or try to get on board, he'll put a bullet through your head.'

They went out. Darío's mind was working fast. He saw the firing squad lined up. 'For me. They were going to kill me.' It left him cold. 'I am in the absolute of love,' he thought, 'and the rest doesn't matter.' Careto passed in the other direction and again smiled without moving his lips. Darío, eyes fixed on the boat, was working out his plan. When they got there it turned out that the people on board had an English accent. It was not the boat from the Health Department, as Darío learned from the pilot, but a pleasure yacht. Sunburned young people in bathing suits. They were not planning to come ashore.

'We're cruising around the island and expect to be here two or three days.'

Two or three days. In that time he could surely get the girl aboard. But to do that he would somehow have to avoid returning to headquarters. He started back with Squinty. In a place screened from the harbour by trees Darío stopped, set his feet, and with all his strength hit him on the jaw. Squinty went down like a log. Darío took his pistol and ammunition, looked around, and turned to get out of sight of headquarters. On the pier a group of people were staring inquisitively at the yacht. He went off in the other direction, among the rocks by the shore. He didn't know where he was going, but he was sure he could hide. After dark he would go to the girl's cave.

He walked tensely, feeling the comforting weight of the pistol in his pocket. He had certainly thrown away his last chance with Sixfingers. If he caught him he was lost. He saw the doctor walking alone, talking to himself. Darío hid. The doctor was calling fondly to Whiskers, who trotted away from him distrustfully. He disappeared, and the doctor turned back the way he had come.

'Just like a person, he looks at me.'

Darío kept going for more than an hour until he reached the other side of the island. He scouted around the vicinity of the lighthouse and finally went up and knocked, hiding in a niche in the wall until the door was opened. The lighthouse keeper appeared:

'You?'

Darío went in without answering. No one would think of looking for him so close to headquarters. The old fellow was always in his tower. He didn't count; nobody ever gave him a thought. In his quarters were a worm-eaten table, an old clock with a noisy pendulum, and a washbasin on an iron stand. A winding staircase led to the upper part of the tower.

'Can you tell me who I'm supposed to report to now?'

'We've got to watch our step,' Darío warned him, looking around.

'Twelve years. I've seen a lot, but never an outrage like this. What's going to happen with you? I heard they wanted to kill you. What for? Of course,' he answered himself, 'because you're a good man. And they'll be after me too.'

'I don't think so.'

The old man shook his head and sighed.

'Thank God my poor girl's not on the island!'

His daughter was already grown up and strikingly ugly. Whenever he could her father sent her to the city. She didn't like going away because she was having a love affair on the island. But she didn't do badly in the city.

Darío told him not to worry and asked whether he had heard anything about the situation on the island.

'I don't know. The little girl said that federal troops had come this morning.'

'When does she come back?'

'Who?'

'The servant girl.'

'Any minute.'

Darío took him by the lapels and tried to make the words sink in.

'If the servant finds out I'm here they'll shoot both of us.'

'Sure, I understand. I'll take care of that.'

The lighthouse keeper began to talk about his daughter again.

'There's no reason why you shouldn't stay in her room upstairs. If they come looking for you, while I'm letting them in you'll have time to let yourself down into the inside; there's a little door. They wouldn't be likely to find you there.'

The teacher went up. The building had two windows on different sides. One looked out on a stretch of sparse woods, over which the roof of headquarters was visible. The other gave on the sea, and if worse came to worse, he could run in that direction and hide among the reefs. The lighthouse keeper had left him alone in the room, but before long he was back.

'The way to get those beasts would be to put poison in the places where they go to drink.'

He scratched his week-old beard in which the hair was grey and yellow and black. He led the teacher to a sinister-looking place under the stairs.

'This is the heart of the beacon. In a pinch you can hide here.'

The flashlight revealed a dead cat on the floor.

They went upstairs again to the living quarters. Beyond the trees, on the blue disk of the sea, Darío saw the trim little yacht which had left the bay and was proceeding along the coast. Its course was straight toward the cave. In the distance it looked like a child's toy. The clouds were high and lazy, and the gulls swooped screaming on to a little black spot on the sea. Darío thought: 'That stain might be a body, perhaps Gómez' or Trinidad's.'

He wanted to think of the girl but couldn't see her, couldn't imagine her. He felt her within himself. She called to him from there. But that was not enough. She was within him, but he was in danger and she was not his. Darío, noting his own composure in relation to all this, thought: 'There is a kind of terrifying calm in which one is transfixed by things.'

The day passed. By afternoon he was fed up; he could not bear to stay in the tower any longer. The old man said the same things over and over, and Darío, who had stopped listening, caught certain disconnected phrases: *impure half-breeds . . . the honesty of the old-time officials . . . corrupt democracy . . . filial virtues,* and one that he repeated a thousand times, with or without relevance: 'I don't say I'm a model father, but——'

Darío yawned. The old man noticed it and rose.

'May I give you a piece of advice? You ought to get married. Not some young thing, someone more on the mature side, with a good level head.'

'That's true, but where?'

'We find the best things in life without hunting for them. You only have to look around you.'

He went on talking on the way downstairs. 'He would like

me to marry his daughter,' Darío thought, his mind on something else. Again he looked out toward the sea.

'Furthermore——'

The old man was talking mechanically. 'If I go out and face the danger it will be less, and perhaps I can even eliminate it. As long as you're shut up, behind walls, the danger keeps growing.' The girl must be in the cave. The boat would be passing near. By night it would be easy to reach the cave without being seen. Besides, he had Squinty's pistol in his pocket.

But it was not yet night. The afternoon breeze stirred the branches. When one of them waved aside he caught a glimpse of the lower part of Careto's cabin. And the legs of Careto himself, who must be sitting down with his back to the house. He saw more, the cardboard box open at his feet and Ruana's head swaying over the box. Darío watched him put the snake inside and leave. Was he bound for Eminencias' bar? His guess was correct. Careto went in, came out, and sat on the porch with a bottle of vintage wine, two tins of food, and bread. A group of convicts gathered enviously around him.

Darío stayed at the window. Both of them, with different motives, were waiting for night. Darío, in order to go to the cave. Careto, to meet Lefty—whom he had forbidden to come to his hut—at a place in the woods. Meanwhile, Careto was finishing the bottle. He was a little disappointed. The effects of Lefty's work, so far, had not been favourable. In general, the convicts wouldn't stand for the girl's being slandered. Some of them took her part with too much enthusiasm, with a kind of furious delight, and went on hunting for her, waiting for their chance.

Congo stood near, watching him drink. Every time Careto put the bottle to his lips Congo raised his head slowly and licked his own. Then he pointed at the bottle and said to another convict, called Touchy Johnny:

'That's vintage wine, and it was brought from the other side of the sea.'

The ragged serape muffled his throat and covered the scars of his ears. The Lawyer came over from another group. He stood outside the shed and from there baited Congo as usual, calling him *scum* and *starveling*. He wanted to kill him, simply because he had no ears. Since somebody had started to destroy him the Lawyer felt impelled to finish the job. Congo looked around for Bocachula, who always stood up for him, but she was not there. Instead a round-faced man came up, with more hair in his beard than on his head. Congo thought he was going to take his side, but he spoke of something else.

'Lefty told me so, and he'll keep his promise. The girl is waiting, and I've drawn a number. I'm number seventeen, no more or less. Lefty promised, and he knows that if he lies to me he's as good as dead.'

'You'd better be satisfied with Mother Leonor.'

'That's right. Virgin and virgin.'

'A worn-out virgin!'

Everybody laughed. At the name of the girl the Lawyer forgot about Congo.

'I'll kill anybody who fools with her. I myself, with my own hands.'

They calmed him down, giving him pulque. The Lawyer, furious at first, finally gave in to talk and drinks. He enjoyed flirting with the terrible. Like Squinty, he would have liked to get a reputation for fearlessness, but he didn't succeed. His crime had been too stupid. He had gone to the pictures with two friends who worked in the same office, and on their way home they made the rounds and got drunk. They were arguing over the salaries of Hollywood stars, and pretty soon the Lawyer lost his temper. 'Be careful what you say.' The other man paid no attention, and then the Lawyer said to the third man: 'Get hold of him; we're going to kill him.' The other man grabbed him from behind for a joke, and the Lawyer twisted the victim's handkerchief into a noose and strangled him. They left him lying in the street, and the one who had held him phoned for an ambulance. The Lawyer walked off and continued drinking. In the morning he appeared at the Red Cross station. 'I've come to claim the body of my friend.' They told him there had to be an autopsy. 'All right,' the Lawyer remarked. 'See that you do it with the care and cleanliness that a decent person deserves, because you won't find a better man anywhere than my friend was.' He wanted to pay and walked away in a huff when they told him there was no charge. Next day they caught him. Having committed murder with a pocket handkerchief made him an undistinguished criminal, and his bravado with Congo did him no good.

Careto, satisfied by his bottle and his meal, got up, left the bar and went to the woods. He told himself that a soldier had to be well fed. At the same time Darío was leaving the lighthouse, telling the keeper that he might not be able to come back before dawn. The old man, with his usual irrelevance, said only: 'What you need is to get married.'

Careto went to the clearing in the woods where they had held the wedding celebration. Lefty was not there yet. He sat waiting on a stone for him and thought about Ruana. In the beginning people despised them both, but gradually they got used to them. He had said one day that the snake did his house cleaning because she kept away the rats, and the convicts, by now, were saying it was a magic snake that could do housework: it swept, washed, scrubbed, made the meals. Careto would have liked to take the snake with him everywhere, coiled on his shoulder—between shoulder and armpit—and he was sure that if someday he succeeded, and the attraction of the girl was eliminated, he would be an object of veneration. He and Ruana. It would be a good augury for the conspiracy. The word seemed over-ambitious. Conspiracy. Still, that was the crux of the problem. The forces were already in America. Agitation, conspiracy, organisation.

When he was least expecting him Lefty showed up, not as drunk as might have been feared.

'Look, chief.' He exhibited a bruise on his neck and two others on his face. 'Take a good look. It's tough going working for you.'

He was making a fool of himself, not to mention the cause. Careto pointed at his pistol:

'What are you carrying that for?'

'I can manage with men. But women are a bunch of whores. What can you do with them?'

Careto was disgusted.

'What you're supposed to do is catch the girl right now.'

'Where?'

'That's your business.'

'She's vanished on us, chief.'

'You have a nose to smell with.'

'Sixfingers won't let me do what I want. His boys keep shooting at us.'

'Don't be a damn fool. Track down Darío.'

'Where? He lit out just when they were going to shoot him.'

'That's your business. Catch the girl and let the gang have a toss with her. Keep my name out of it. If you do what I say you'll get another five hundred.'

'Many thanks.'

'Stick them up your arse.'

They went off in opposite directions.

'Weaklings,' Careto thought. 'Their guts run out of their mouths, like Eminencias' lemonades.' There was a bright moon. It was good to be in the woods. The ground between the branches was strewn with white mirages. At a turn in the path a man was sitting, in silence, looking at his own feet. His white trousers, with the bare feet sticking out, blended with a patch of moonlight. Chest naked, in the shadow. He went toward him, but before he reached him he saw that no one was there and that the blotches of colour had shifted. He went back to the clearing. With a bottle of good wine under his belt he could tackle any mystery. He strolled along, going no farther away, and when he looked again saw the same motion-less shadow. He shrugged his shoulders, but his flesh prickled. Could it be the man he had seen on the cliff in the morning? And if so, why was he following him? And if he was following him, why didn't he speak? Careto turned his back and walked away, changing his course when he felt that he was out of sight. He went farther inland. Now and then a loathsome whiff was brought in by the breeze from the sea. He soon recognised the smell, which he had been familiar with in 1918 and recognised again in Spain during the war. But he couldn't believe it came from the remains of a man. Perhaps a dead horse that had been killed in the recent skirmishes. A dog crossed his path on a scent and, seeing him, Careto was scared and went faster. Another dog arrived, slanting off on a tangent to follow the other's trail. Careto was intrigued. 'Where are they going?' He followed them, the smell becoming stronger as he went on. And the recollection keener. He found that his hands were shaking a little. 'A nervous Aryan,' he thought, 'but it's not so strange, considering that I had a good meal to-day for the first time in three months, and good food takes my whole body back to the old forgotten times.'

The woods gave way to a little open space, where eight or ten dogs had collected around an object stretched out on the ground. They barked and fought some of the time, but when they had snatched a morsel they ran off with it in their teeth, looking for a quiet spot. Careto was afraid the sea had dis-gorged the Pimp and could not bring himself to leave until he had made sure. Outside the group, not daring to take part because of the hardier veterans in the way, was Whiskers, the doctor's dog. He was the only one that didn't object to Careto; the others growled. He kicked them out of the way, bent over the corpse, and lit a match. A few birds were frightened away by the glare.

The dead man was much stouter than the Pimp. 'It's Trinidad.' He hadn't the courage to make sure, because the body was without skin, the face without features, the head

208

without a scalp. He had been stripped of his clothes and then of his skin. The dogs had partly torn up the rest. Careto burned himself with the match and lit another. He started a cigarette, determined to face the gruesome sight until his nerves were under control. 'I will not go away until I am calm,' he said. 'You heard the summons, Trinidad. You answered the sinister call. The sinister call of the ideal.'

His voice was unperturbed by the spectacle of death.

'Let yourself be eaten. I wish you peace. I truly do. My grudge doesn't carry to the other shore.'

He looked at the entrails, the bones exposed where the dogs had been at work.

'Your mother spent thirty years fashioning and strengthening those bones, making those eyes, those hands, those guts. But in making you your mother was also answering the sinister call. The call of the ideal.'

He wanted to leave but checked the impulse. He ought not to *disregard life*. Life had worked hard over that body, its nerves, its veins, its fluid, creating at last the larva of a chief. Life had done all that work, perhaps for the sole purpose of offering it to him, Careto, in the end, as an exercise in composure. And Careto wanted to take advantage of it. Behind him, in a semicircle among the trees, he saw the dogs waiting avidly.

'You set your eyes too low, Trinidad, and that wasn't the trouble so much as that all your being followed your look. The secret is to look down from above, not letting anything creep up from behind.'

Trinidad was silent. 'His skin has been taken off. Why? The skin was already gone when the dogs found him.' A dog came up, impatient. 'Wait till I leave. Have some respect for the proprieties.' The breeze from the sea was freshening. Trinidad lay there, exposed to the shadows. The wind swept over his blood, his naked blood. Careto suddenly left, slipped through between the trees, and walked toward the place where he had seen Lefty. In the centre of the clearing he sat down on a stone. The male, the sire of the clan, the fornicating father wolf, was being eaten by the dogs. Careto sighed and muttered at God:

'I would believe You and worship You if You accepted crime.'

Careto lit a cigar; cigarettes were not enough to gratify his senses, already inflamed by wine. 'If You accepted crime I would believe in You.' But God was too weak to accept it. Or perhaps—he was not sure—true strength was just that. God brought the dogs to the corpse of the man in whom God had himself one day put His trust. And, nevertheless, God kept talking about the ideal. Perhaps that was the true and only strength: a tranquil faith in ultimate ends, above all the misery brought about by oneself.

He was about to go back when he saw a shadow among the trees. The mysterious Indian? This one moved more solidly; it was not a shadow. He stopped; the other had stopped too. The breeze lifted a bough, and the moonlight streamed through. He saw Darío.

'So it's you!'

Darío looked past Careto, wondering if this curious character was walking by himself. Darío was desperate because he had found the Virrey cave empty, and directly opposite that reef lay the yacht, all lit up as if waiting for them. Their last chance seemed lost, and he had now only one concern: 'Where is the girl? Have I lost her forever?' Careto approached.

'I am glad to see you like this.'

'How do you mean?'

'Like this, free.'

Darío knew that Careto was not glad at all but simply surprised.

'Thank you.'

This affability from Careto, usually so glum and silent, made an unpleasant impression on Darío. He wanted to leave, but with an excess of courtesy Careto detained him.

'I'm sincerely glad. Believe me.'

'Thank you, but I'm in a hurry.'

He went on, leaving him behind. Before he disappeared Careto called out anxiously:

'Watch your step, Darío: everything's topsy-turvy.'

'The same to you.'

'For me it's different; I'm not in love.'

Darío, the echo of Careto's laugh in his ears, felt ridiculous. A few hours before he might have been shot. To survive only to fall victim to Careto seemed worse than being shot. There was no one in the woods. He could smell the stench from Trinidad's corpse when the wind shifted. Darío stopped and went back:

'Do they matter so much to you?'

'What?'

'My personal feelings.'

'Now listen. . . .' Careto was disconcerted. 'All in all, I think of you as a friend.'

'But do my personal feelings matter to you?'

Darío drew his pistol and held it against Careto's chest.

'Mind your own business, Careto. Make one move, say one word, and you're through.'

Darío was chafing under his disappointment in the cave. Even so he wouldn't have turned back if he hadn't been provoked by that laugh.

'Just answer me, that's all. There's a smell of putrid flesh, isn't there?'

'Yes sir. It comes from over there. It's a disgrace that——'

'It's Trinidad. Trinidad was not only a disgrace but a danger every minute, and I guess your shoulders know it.'

Darío laughed, and the other, noticing his hand shaking in anger, was afraid.

'I didn't mean to annoy you.'

'I am in love, and lovers have certain rights.'

Careto looked at him in surprise. The pistol was still at his chest. Darío continued:

'Not far from here there are some picks and shovels from the work on the road. That's where we're going. You're going to bury those remains. I'll watch you, and you're going to do a good job and a quick one. As a man in love, I have the right to demand this of you.'

As a man in love? Careto didn't understand. In his excitement Darío thought he had told him everything. But his words had a hard time keeping up with his mind. He meant to say that those foul emanations must be purged from the air, the air that the girl was breathing. Careto didn't understand, but he saw the pistol clearly enough. Darío shoved it in his back.

'Move along; hurry. Faster! And don't look around!'

Careto obeyed, blaming himself. As a matter of fact, the money in his pocket and that bottle of wine had made him go too far. When they got to where the work was being done on the road he took a pick. Darío commanded:

'That's not enough. A shovel too.'

Careto took one and, prodded along by Darío's pistol, went back to the body. Then with sublime scorn the teacher went over Careto's pockets and his belt. Still flabbergasted, Careto explained:

'I have no weapons on me. I never have.'

They reached the corpse. The dogs ran off and stayed howling among the trees. Darío stood with his back to the wind, where the stench was less noticeable. On the other side Careto began to dig. Darío could not understand why the body had been skinned. Night came down thick and evil-smelling through the trees. Darío watched Careto at work, remembering with pleasure his expression as he walked past headquarters that morning. Around the dead man the wind stirred in yellow lights, and murmurs from deep in the woods travelled through the shadows against the wind. Now and then Darío saw pairs of eyes burning like coals, almost always close to the ground—the dogs—but sometimes a little higher, which made him wonder whether it was men or dogs standing on their hind legs. He spoke to Careto:

'You want to find an outlet for your energy, but you're fooling yourself.'

Careto paused, leaning on his shovel to answer, but Darío pointed the pistol at him.

'Keep working. Don't answer me.'

Careto obeyed after looking through the trees.

'You want to be aggressive. The oldest way of fleeing from suffering is just that: causing it to others. You want to free yourself of pain by wounding others. Why? The power of aggression isn't everything.'

The shadows stirred in the woods, moaning, howling. The smell of the dead body incited the dogs and the night's beasts of prey to aggression. Sometimes Careto whirled around and waved the shovel to frighten them off. But soon they were back again.

Trinidad's head—the phosphorus was decomposing—began to radiate a blue halo whose fluorescence every now and then lit up Careto's face. And in that blue light his face also looked like a dead man's. One corpse burying another. Darío now was frightened. From the burning eyes in the forest came howls that wriggled and crept through the trees, or lay along the ground. Each cry turned into a snake with eyes, hissing tongue, and venom. They were going down to the sea but stopped on the way, crawled into Trinidad's belly, torn by the dogs, and went to sleep there. Where they moved they left a phosphorescent trail.

The cranial lumps of the skull seemed to burn dim blue. The half-open jaws revealed the teeth, behind which the cavity of the mouth extended inward in its old sensual greed. But now it could only kiss the earth, drink rain, and eat itself. At the bottom of the grave Trinidad's wide mouth would feed on itself.

'Strength is not aggression,' Darío calmly went on. 'We all rejoice in our own blood, but it isn't the joy of cutting our neighbour's veins. The greatest triumph of aggressive power is nothing but the beginning of a long hard road.'

213

In the woods, among the crawling cries, rose a new one. Darío started in alarm, but warned Careto:

'Go on. Go on or you'll be in the grave yourself.'

No one was there.

'For the last half-hour,' Careto thought, 'I've had water in my veins.'

The smell of the sea and the crash of the waves grew heavier. 'The living come into the world and go where they please. But God disposes of the dead,' thought Darío. 'One here, ten there, seven more somewhere else. God disposes of the dead, and so to bury a dead man is to put him where God wills. It is a sacred task.'

He rose and flung a stone in silence. It smashed through the branches, but he didn't hear it fall. The shadows on the ground, the roots heaving up around the grave, gave the body waving tentacles. Or hairy feet, like a spider's. The king spider that killed with its feelers and drank blood with the point of its belly. Trinidad had feet like a spider, and he was still dreaming the spider's nuptial dream.

'The girl's world,' thought Darío, 'was the green heaven of childish love, and in that heaven Trinidad was an impatient spider, with the point of the belly threatening.'

'All right,' he said to Careto. 'That's enough. Throw him in.'

The body fell in with a good honest sound as of potter's clay. Darío went up and with his foot shoved the first earth on to the body, thinking: 'It is a privilege to be a man. To bury a man. To sow man's life and death.'

'You finish it,' he ordered Careto.

He heard birds with featherless wings moving impatiently in the trees. They were birds that couldn't fly and that climbed up the tree trunks with their beaks and claws. Up there on the branches they looked less like birds than rotted fruit. They perched there. Darío felt the dead man's shadow still on the ground beside the closed grave.

The birds flapped their bare wings. They had green

plumage and seemed to have been born of seaweed. Darío saw them without looking.

'Are they chickens?'

There were chicken roosts in the ancient sepulchres of the sea; the hens were green and slept in the seaweed. But he could not prove it in the dark.

Careto was still stamping down the soil, dancing on one spot like the Indians, two steps forward, one back.

The shoes of professional gravediggers always wore out as if scorched.

'It's all done,' he said, halting.

Darío ordered him with a motion of the pistol:

'Go on.'

It had to be packed down more to keep the sea-hens and the dogs of the forest from digging up the body. Careto kept at it, breathing heavily. 'Strange,' Darío thought. 'I'm taking Trinidad's downfall, his death, and even this act of burying him as a personal triumph.' And he enjoyed watching Careto dance.

'I'm sorry,' he said, 'but you have to keep it up all night.'

Physical fatigue was the least of it, but there was no longer any sense in stamping the earth down, and so he was exhausting himself as stupidly as those beggars who go around crushed under a load of rubbish.

'Take your shoes off.'

'Me? What for?'

'Don't argue.'

He took them off, pressing one against the other. Darío took them and flung them into the sea. If he were barefoot he couldn't follow him or, in any case, he wouldn't be able to overtake him when he went away. He ordered him to get up and go on stamping the ground, which he did, and then said:

'Sing something. If you do it to a rhythm you won't get so tired.'

'I'm not tired.'

215

'Sing. But sing something I don't understand. Sing in some other language.'

In a toneless voice, dragging and broken, Careto began:

> *'J'ai cassé le Re*
> *de ma clarinette.*
> *J'ai cassé le Re——'*

'No, not that. Something else.'

He sang in German, keeping time with his feet:

> *'Das Wandern ist des Muellers Lust,*
> *das Wa-andern.*
> *Das muesst ein schlechter Mueller sein,*
> *dem niemals fiel das Wandern ein,*
> *das Wa-andern.'*

Darío started to leave, but as he turned toward the luminous eyes of the dogs he became afraid.

'Naked as a worm, poor fellow.'

Who said that?

Careto raised his head and looked at him stealthily. He had the same expression of surprise and dread. Darío thought, 'He doesn't know what to make of my not insulting him and not raising my voice. Perhaps that's what frightens him.' He wanted to go on but was baulked by the dogs' eyes. Finally he pulled himself together and went off at random, later setting his course for the lighthouse. Careto, barefoot, remained behind. He was not used to walking without shoes and couldn't follow.

Careto picked his way slowly toward his cabin, feeling himself the butt of his own ridicule as well as Darío's. But any fool could feel ridiculous. What mattered more was that he felt guilty. He had been indiscreet and he was paying for it.

It was not yet the moment to attack the 'pillars of society,' and still less to lay himself open. He must bide his time in the dark. But the rewards would come.

VIII

DAWN CAME WITHOUT FRESHNESS OR
fragrance, and the sea in the distance was weary. Everything
lay scorched by the sun, and now and then a dry branch
creaked in protest. The girl felt the silence in every pore of
her body. Two days before, when she went to the cave, she
had wondered: 'Would Trinidad approve?' and now, in the
Indian village, she was asking herself: 'What would Darío
say?' Darío had sent her to the cave and told her to wait there.
In the cave she had been afraid of Trinidad; he would not
have approved of that and perhaps would have killed Darío
rather than permit it. Now she was afraid of Darío, who also
might have killed the old Indian to prevent her being taken
away.

When Voice of the River of Stars came back the girl saw
that his trousers were fastened at the waist with a bottle-top
instead of a button, and this detail suddenly made her aware
that his protection, however well meaning, would nevertheless
be ineffectual. She looked around without fear, expecting
the unexpected.

Behind the old man came two convicts. They had both been
at headquarters on the day of condolence, but the girl did not
remember them. They were Spitball and Nosy-Posy. Gimpy
turned pale. Nosy-Posy was talking about Gómez:

'Some people think a lot of him, and some say he was no
good. All I say is, he was the best man on the island with a
knife.'

Spitball, the dead man's brother, listened modestly. They
all went out and when they were outside the village the old
man halted the girl in front of a cornfield.

'Now you must look hard at the corn. The leaves, the
217

stalk, the poor little dry ears. Look hard to make them grow.'

She stared at the corn, believing the old man. She was pleased that her look should be important enough to make the ears grow.

'Do you see the hidden parts now?'

'Yes.'

'The roots?'

'Yes.'

'The little worms in the ground?'

'Yes.'

He took her to other places, saying the same things, until he was sure her eyes had embraced the whole field, and then they went to the sea. He stood the girl on the beach, facing the waves that rolled in and spread their foam over the sand.

'Look at the clouds so the rain will come quickly.'

The girl looked at them. The morning shone on her forehead and throat. The old man seemed satisfied.

'Now,' he said, 'I must ask you to wade out into the sea.'

She drew back, smiling.

'Oh no!'

'The sea wishes it.'

The girl was still smiling. She looked at the waves rising wearily. She had to take off her shoes.

'It would be better, if you don't mind,' the old man said, 'it would be better without any clothes.'

She made no reply, pretending not to have heard. Spitball wanted to show her the cemetery where he had buried his brother a few days before. Having had a recent death in the family was his one source of vanity.

Before they got there he lifted his upper lip, showing a gold tooth.

'This little tooth used to be my brother's. He got it in the capital when he was a soldier. I don't need it, but I wear it just as a souvenir.'

He had carved on the stone the words in which he had begged alms for the burial:

'The wrath of a bridegroom took him to the truth of the Lord.' The girl remembered Gómez dancing at the harbour. And as she remembered she prayed. Seeing her pray, they took off their hats. Nosy-Posy, in a sentimental trance, wrinkled his nose to keep from crying. The girl asked:

'Is there another cemetery on the island?'

'Ah,' they all thought, 'she wants to know where Trinidad is, so that she can go like a good widow and burn candles for him.' They were all pleased by the idea, but they put off answering. She asked another question:

'Is there any news about Darío?'

'Yesterday they shot him for good,' said Nosy-Posy. The girl stopped. It was as if a light in her had gone out. Spitball noticed it.

'Nobody heard the shot. I saw him go to the harbour and then to his house.'

'But in the afternoon he went back and they shot him.'

'Did you see it?'

'You don't need to see a well-known thing like that,' Nosy-Posy insisted. 'Besides, Sixfingers has no secrets from me. I command and he obeys.'

They reached the hut. The old man went in with the girl, and the others stayed outside. He put a hand on her shoulder.

'I know where Darío is. He's all right. I won't tell you the place, because you'd want to send your cripple there.'

Outside, Nosy-Posy's mincing voice rose coyly: 'I'm the only one who gives him orders because I tell him to take off his shirt to have it washed, and he takes it off, and I tell him to let me take off his shoes, and he does it.'

Gimpy turned away sourly.

'Well, I've heard him call you a bloody pansy.'

'He's a real man, and naturally he has his moods.'

The girl was happy about Darío; she hadn't realised the depth of her feeling until she heard that nothing had happened to him. But when she was happy she always wanted to

219

share her joy with others, and the old man, perceiving this, pushed her gently.

'If you go into the sea there will be abundance and good fortune in every house.'

He seemed to attach no importance to the fact that she must undress. The girl would have liked to comply. She was happy because Darío was alive, and she wanted to please the Indians, but she had no bathing suit. She apologised:

'I can't. I have no bathing suit.'

'You don't need one. The sea loves people who are naked like the fish.'

The girl was torn. She was the widow who was supposed to wear black and mourn for her husband. Take off her clothes? Still, the Indians would not *kill her for her beauty*. And perhaps . . . Perhaps alone, at night, with no moon . . . Feeling herself yielding, she turned back in horror. The Indian went out without speaking. At the door he met Gimpy. Nosy-Posy joined them. Gimpy was raging but said nothing.

Rusty-Pants appeared. He asked the girl:

'Who are you?'

'A friend of yours.'

'You're no friend of mine. You're the "Hanged Man's Widow."'

Gimpy tried to hit him, but the boy bounded out of reach. The girl was unmoved. The boy's talk was like a bird's song or the grunting of a little animal. No one spoke; the boy looked at Gimpy.

'The goats were bewitched. They went *Ba-a-a* and brought forth human beings. *Ba-a-a*, and brought forth human beings.'

'It's the truth,' said Nosy-Posy. 'I can testify to it.'

Rusty-Pants walked off. When he was out of reach he pointed his finger at Gimpy.

'The cripple killed his father. The *gachupines* killed mine.'

He vanished among the huts. The girl saw him go up to three scrubby children, who stared at him in amazement. They were naked, with golden skin, gleaming in the shadow.

One of them had a bloated belly and spindly legs.

'He's weak,' his mother said without looking at the girl, 'because he won't eat earth. The other children always have their mouths full of muck. Before, when my cousin had goats, they had milk to drink.'

'Doesn't she have any now?'

'She had to kill them because they were bewitched.'

She added, still with her face turned away:

'Old Rat-Eyes, Rusty-Pants's uncle, used to take them to pasture. They would never bear, and my cousin asked Rat-Eyes about it, and the old man said: "It is not God's will." But the goats always had milk in their udders. The thing was that the old man was in the woods two or three moons in a row, and when the goats gave birth he made a hole in the ground and buried the newborn kids. So my cousin discharged Rat-Eyes and brought the goats here.'

'Of course,' said Niña Lucha.

'When the goats were on the ranch they had to be killed because they gave birth to little animals with human faces.'

Gimpy gave a start. He had tried to avoid it, failed, and then blushed violently. Nosy-Posy laughed. Lucha had felt a blow on her heart, but by something soft, such as cotton-wool. 'Oh!' she managed to say. 'That's what the boy was saying.' The unexpected and the incredible had their own consistency. But this was too much.

She felt a desire to cry and went back to her hut. Whenever she was shocked she had to cry. Gradually she calmed down and began to have thoughts so lofty that they seemed like someone else's. She was thinking: 'Perhaps life has nothing to do with people's dreams and desires. Perhaps life flows along in its own way, and monsters wander among us, and we should stop being afraid of them.' Life *seemed* very ugly and people abominable, but there was no one on whose shoulder one might not put a friendly hand. Life was not made up of goats or Rat-Eyes. And later, when she had recovered, she thought of *that* and wondered: 'Could I do it, after all?' She was appalled by her calm, remembering the old man's proposal: 'Go naked into the sea.' Perhaps at night if there was no moon . . . She liked the idea of being, in some miraculous way, useful. Perhaps if there was no moon . . . Or even if there was a moon and she could be seen from a distance. The only thing that horrified her was the idea of Darío's seeing her, but there was not the slightest chance of that. Now that she was back among people she was ashamed to think of Darío, but she could not help it. So many things had happened that the very memory of her husband was full of references to other people. It was as if Trinidad were leading her by the hand to Darío's side. This idea disturbed her all day.

When the heat of the day was over the Indians began to appear, their faces painted red, their chests naked. Some had leaves twined in their hair. From among the huts came the sound of a little drum. She heard their voices closer: cries always ending on a downward note. She thought it was wrong that they should express their joy in cries of anguish. She would have liked to spare them sadness by looking again at the roots and the little worms and watching the fulfilment of the miracle. But that of the sea was hard. Several Indians came dancing from the huts. One, who seemed to be the leader, shouted:

'The white father is dead, dead and gone.'

Trinidad rose again in the voices of the Indians. And the Indians called him the *white father*. The mestizos, *Black Trinidad*. But they didn't love him. They all seemed glad of his death. She had seen it in the patio at headquarters, then in the cave, and now here. 'And I am his widow.' She didn't know how to react to this rejoicing at his death.

'The sun dances before going down, before going down the cliff.'

'The sun goes down dressed in mirrors.'

'Under his mirrors he has the scab. He dances and scratches, and scratches and dances.'

Now the girl understood why they had brought her here.

The white father was dead, and she, his virgin widow, could work miracles. That was the last thing she would have expected. Wide-eyed, she looked at the Indians.

Each seemed obsessed by his own dance. They were gathering in the little square, barefooted, with white trousers and palmetto sombreros. Some sported coloured serapes thrown over one shoulder. It was strange to see them covering their chests and shoulders with those serapes in the broiling sun, but the Indians were apparently insensible. Others wore little figures made of baked corn meal around their necks. The eyes were black beans and the teeth pumpkin seeds.

'The sun dances before it goes down.'

'For the white father who passed away.'

The girl was afraid. Gimpy came back to her. The rumble of the drums that so fascinated the Indians and that had kept up for more than two hours was dull and tiring for her. The Indians' dance was so remote from her and sprang, too, from such habitual despair that in the end the girl saw nothing but misery and grief in it.

'The white father is no more.'

'. . . no more.'

'And the sun will come down among the Indians.'

'. . . the sun will come.'

'Like a man he will come.'

All of them were doubled over on their haunches to be closer to the earth. There was nothing sensual in it; it was as though they were responding to an atavistic call. Old Voice of the River of Stars explained:

'Every year, before the rains, we hold this celebration, but it was never so fine as to-day.'

He smiled. He smiled because Trinidad was dead, because the widow was there. And in spite of that smile she was helping them, and she wanted to help them more. By now most of the Indians were on the ground. The drumbeat was slower. And the dancers on the ground went into convulsions, face down, in the motions of fecundation. Niña Lucha looked on

223

in horror, not at what she saw, but what she felt. She wanted to leave but was ashamed; it would be a confession of her turmoil. The Indians rose, and the drums quickened again. When they were all standing the girl started to leave, but from the far corner of the square, accompanied by the old man, she went on watching.

All she saw in the Indians now was their remoteness. A certain resolution seized her heart and brought her lips together in a charming youthful line. If she let herself go everything would be ruined and all would turn against her. But she didn't let go. Now that the Indians were so far away she understood their asking her to undress and go into the sea. But it was not easy. Once, when she was changing her underwear in her room her aunt's canary watched her from his cage. She almost fainted on noting it.

It made her laugh to remember it now, but she did remember.

The Indians went on dancing. Voice of the River of Stars said that he had organised a supply column for Sixfingers. He was demanding food, and they would have to send it to him. They were already gathering up everything there was in the village, and it would leave them destitute. But perhaps she would help them by going into the sea. The old man accompanied her to the hut. She made casual conversation to keep her mind off the muffled drum that was still beating.

'The sun will go down the cliff.'

'He will go down with his black breeches and his hair like a corn cob's.'

At the hut the old man left her, saying he would soon be back. The girl wanted to flee; she didn't know from what. She groped for somebody or something to lean on, and unconsciously her eyes fell on her camera. She picked it up and stood examining its delicate mechanisms, not thinking about anything.

Gimpy drew aside the curtain of sacking which covered

224

the door, but she went out instead of letting him enter. The
old man was outside.

Niña Lucha realised again how little she could rely on the
Indians' protection. Sixfingers carried off their stores; it was
they who needed protection. Gimpy drew near, happy because
the shadows of evening were gradually enfolding him. The
girl wanted to go away, but where? And the dances went on
alluding to the *white father*. The funereal meaning of it all
stood out more clearly at night.

Gimpy went out, thinking he had heard cautious steps at
the side of the hut. He was confronted by an old man.

'I am Rat-Eyes.'

'What do you want?'

'God sent me a message. If I slept one night with the little
virgin my body would become young again.'

Gimpy drove him away. The girl had heard them. In
distress Gimpy started prattling about whatever came into his
head.

'There we lived, my mother and I. In a little house with a
green roof. The river went by and went *glug-glug* all day. At
night there was a pretty little spray of stars over the house.'
There always had to be stars in anything he said to the girl.
She was aware of it, and by sheer force of folly his insistence
became poetic.

Night came down, and the old leader timidly approached.
Finding them awake, he said the escort had left with all the
provisions for headquarters. But the Indians were still dancing.
Gimpy mentioned his suspicions of Nosy-Posy, and at the
thought of his having left before the supply convoy the two
looked at one another in silence.

'Do you think he might give us away?'

'Pansies are like that. Nobody knows what they'll do.'

The yacht, its lights burning, glittered on the rim of the
sea. The old Indian said to the girl:

'Sixfingers has taken everything.'

Voice of the River of Stars looked at the yacht. Gimpy

hated the old man for letting Nosy-Posy get away. The old chief seemed worried. 'If the girl wants to go, if it's really the right thing for her to go, the boat is right there. But first she must go naked into the sea. First go into the water and then leave.' They could signal the yacht with a torch and then go out to it in a canoe. She, too, was watching the little boat in a kind of ecstasy. The old man realised that her thought was the same as his own. After a long silence he said:

'The people have nothing left to eat. If you are willing, to-morrow we will be rich in fish and corn. You looked at the corn before, and it has grown a great deal already.'

The girl believed in the old man's superstitions.

'All right. I will go to the beach. Before the moon rises I will go to the beach.'

The drum continued, and now and then a cry rose in counterpoint to the ritual phrase:

'The sun will come, will come. With breeches and a red beard he will come.'

She looked at the boat in the distance, and both prospects, that of going naked into the sea and that of fleeing from the island, seemed equally improbable. Gimpy talked about the boat, and she agreed mechanically, but the idea remained vague in her mind. Her spirit was absent, suspended. And this was a burial feast. For Trinidad. Still for him.

'Now, Niña.'

They escorted her to the beach. Gimpy lingered behind. He was disturbed by the thought of the girl's nakedness, and the place where it would happen assumed for him a fabulous importance. But the Indian went calmly along with the girl and when they reached the wet sand said to her:

'I will be behind that little clump of banana trees. Don't go in very deep.'

The girl saw before her the beach, the phosphorescent water and the low sky sprinkled with stars. She was not thinking or feeling anything. The old man went away, leaving her

226

alone. He looked for Gimpy in the banana grove but could not find him. The old man sat down and waited.

Gimpy ran in great anxiety to tell the girl that there were sharks, that the beach was dangerous, that the water was very cold. All sorts of scruples had suddenly smitten him, but, coming around the rocks on to the open beach, he saw the girl naked. He turned back, trembling, and hid. He had seen her without meaning to do it. He dropped, unable to go on, fearful of being seen and seeing, in spite of everything, whether his eyes were open or shut, the naked girl before him. He pressed the gown she had worn to his chest and groaned. He heard a birdlike cry from the girl at the first touch of the water and, fearing she might be in danger, looked out. He would have liked to run to her aid, lift her in his arms. There was no moon, but the curves of her body gleamed like metal. Eyes were made to see light. But not only the sun gave light. It came also from a woman's skin, and it was a light as of clouds laden with snow.

'How bitter the water of the sea will seem to me now!'

It was the bitterness of nights of shipwreck on forsaken beaches. Nakedness he already knew in his imagination. But imagination was nothing. That is, yes; it was everything. Or rather, no; it was nothing. The body was everything. That body that was making the sea bitter. The body alone. He remembered an accident that had occurred on the island several years before. A relative of Sixfingers was seen every day by the sea, at the highest point of the cliff, with his girl, a young convict. And one day, clasped in each other's arms, they fell over the edge. They fell more than thirty yards through the air, struck the cliff, bounded off, and fell to the bottom beside the sea. Their heads were torn from their bodies and fell far away, one on each side, but the bodies remained entwined as they had been on the top of the cliff. And the bitter sea washed away their blood, cut their lives into pieces so tiny they could go into the mouths of the smallest fish. Here there was no cliff, no rocks, but the sea held out its avid green arms, and if they took hold of the girl he would run to her rescue, and if the sea cut both their lives into little pieces perhaps the fish would eat a little of her and a little of him, a little of her and a little of him. And so they would be united. Inside a dead fish, behind the bones of its head, he had once seen a naked woman. She was alone and very tiny. And the strange thing was, she was both there and not there.

Gimpy stayed there, wild-eyed, his mouth open, watching. Watching without seeing. The night bird sang near the rocks: *Bambu, bambu-le-le.* Gimpy saw so much in the dark, he thought he was going blind. 'To see all this and go blind,' he said several times, as if in prayer. The girl faced the waves, then the shore, she rolled in the sand, and Gimpy saw that she was trying to get up, but a wave knocked her down, and she lay as if violated by the sea. And she was that woman he had seen in the fish's head.

'But I will die in the bitter sea.'

Open-mouthed, hands shaking, his body flat against the rocks, he trembled. His love was like the crab's, the giant crab in the cave.

A wave covered him with spray. It came softly and silently but soaked him to the waist. He got up and ran. He fled away from the girl without watching where he was going, stumbling over bushes and rocks. He had run quite a way when he heard his name called. It was not the girl but the old Indian. Gimpy was terrified and ran faster than ever. He went into the girl's hut as if expecting to see her there, and, finding that neither the girl nor the old man was in the village, he cleared his brain as best he could and set out for the banana grove.

Behind the little hill the Indians were answering the summons of Voice of the River of Stars. One of them walked at the head with the drum.

'When the clouds cover the sky the sun goes down and rests beside the storm.'

'The sun goes down like a man.'

'The grey heifer and the white gown and the wet grass.

The wet grass that makes smoke.'

'When the sun goes down.'

After dancing a long time in silence, and without even the drum, they began again at a signal from the leader:

> *'The rain will come, will come,*
> *and put its fingers in the sands*
> *to take gold to the sea,*
> *to take worms to the sea,*
> *to take blood to the sea.*
> *The rain will come, will come,*
> *and take everything to the sea.'*

Others answered in chorus, and sometimes one voice rose and the rest stopped.

> *'The fish in the green seaweed*
> *giggles and giggles from cold,*
> *and rises and dives and drinks*
> *the bubble of sleep,*
> *but she has gone into the sea.*
> *The white virgin in the sea,*
> *she has gone into the sea,*
> *the white virgin in the sea.'*

The Indians swayed in the shadows. A dog followed the last one. There is always a dog behind the last Indian. Voice of the River of Stars cautioned them:

'Lower, lower, so she won't hear.'

The same singer began again:

> *'The rain will come, will come,*
> *it will come on the wings of white herons,*
> *and black goats and white goats are waiting*
> *under the ground,*
> *and the pregnant women are waiting,*
> *and the men with cracked lips and dry skin,*
> *and the cistern with a dead frog,*

229

> *and the serpents of evil desire*
> *and the sleeping butterfly.'*

They repeated the dance in a long file, weaving and un-weaving spirals. The old man nudged Gimpy.

'Go on. You say something.'

And Gimpy said:

> *'The sea is very bitter*
> *on her body, the sea, the sea*
> *fights to destroy her like sugar,*
> *like salt,*
> *like snow,*
> *and the sea fights,*
> *the sea fights with the girl;*
> *and the sea is no longer mild*
> *and the girl is no longer little.*
> *They fight for the sweet and the bitter*
> *and the man doesn't know what to do*
> *nor the crab where to go*
> *nor the moon when to rise.*
> *To the rhythm of the stars*
> *the crab waxes and waves.*
> *In the girl is the bitter breath*
> *of the black and the white of the sea,*
> *and the man sees it all*
> *and then he pauses and says:*
> *"An almond-stone is lying*
> *in my heart, bitter as the sea."'*

The old Indian wanted to ask Gimpy where he was going when he ran so fast, but he refrained.

And Gimpy went on:

> *'And I chew the stone of my heart*
> *but my teeth break*
> *and my gums split open*
> *and my hands are ground by my teeth,*

> *and the sea is daily greener*
> *and more bitter the foam;*
> *and my hands drop away by themselves*
> *and in my fingers I squeeze*
> *the unbreakable stone of my heart.'*

They were beginning the first song again when they heard the girl calling out; she was coming back. The old man sent Gimpy to tell the Indians to get the canoe ready. But she came up, asking:

'Who are those people in the boat?'

She said it stubbornly. She didn't want to go. She was not going. She wondered if it was because of Trinidad. Was Trinidad's death holding her back? She would have liked to pray at his grave, but it was not that. The island was a jumbled mass of crazy voices and frantic eyes, like a vast death struggle. She thought of Trinidad, but his image eluded her. So then she tried to erase it. In that chaos she couldn't grasp why she was staying.

While she was naked on the beach, hearing the men sing—the voices had made her feel that their eyes were on her—she had begun to have more faith in things. Before she went to sleep she thought a long time about herself. But she did not cry; this time she smiled. And she remembered Gimpy in the cave, saying: 'Life is like that. And it's not bad. Everybody likes it.' Now she was really beginning to see it. The Indians were singing and dancing for the death of the *white father*. They were glad of his death. And at the same time they were singing:

> *'The sun will come down like a man,*
> *like a man among men. . . .'*

And giving herself up to the images awakened in her mind by the Indian rites, seeing them with perfect clarity, she imagined that the sun had already come down among them. Not the Indians' sun, with black breeches and scratching his scab, but the sun, the good golden sun.

'Life is not bad,' she said aloud. 'Everybody likes it.'

She thought of her life as a married woman—the last five days—and concluded: 'It's queer, but it's true: I wouldn't want to be a different person or be in a different place.' She fell asleep.

Gimpy and the old man stayed outside. Gimpy was wheezing like an old bellows.

'I knew,' said Voice of the River of Stars, 'that she wouldn't go away.'

The old man smiled.

'No, it's not for the reason you think.'

He added, not wanting to talk any more:

'It's not good for every one to understand what an old man is thinking.'

'But what's going to happen?'

They both watched the yacht dwindling to the left, going on around the island. As it passed out of sight they became more aware of the girl's danger, but since there was nothing to do about it they went back to thinking about the convoy.

IX

AT DAYBREAK SIXFINGERS ARRIVED. HE had a magnificent escort, increased by some of the Twin's followers whom they had captured on the way. Shackled and tied to Sixfingers' saddle, the Twin dragged along after the horse as best he could.

'Let's be magnanimous, Sixfingers.'

No one answered him. Whenever the girl was mentioned the Twin sighed. 'I have known her for thirty-eight years.'

The little band occupied the village like troops. The Indians looked out from their huts in alarm. Sixfingers sought out the old chief, who was already surrounded by three armed men.

'Where have you hidden her?'

'She's not hidden.'

'Shut up!'

'You asked me, chief.'

Sixfingers raised his whip, and the old man was silent. An Indian woman said:

'Beautiful women are for men with horses and guns. It has always been that way.'

The Indian went to the girl's cabin and came out with her. Gimpy followed, yellow with fear and rage. The girl noticed that the Twin was bound. 'Why is that man tied up?' she asked.

'He knows why.'

She drew back.

'Untie him.'

Sixfingers looked at the Twin and at the girl, taken aback. Was it possible that a woman like that should defend a man who raped and murdered little girls?

233

Sixfingers refused.

'If you don't untie him I won't go with you.'

The Twin sighed.

'Let's be magnanimous.'

'Magnanimous?' said Sixfingers from his saddle. 'Were you magnanimous at headquarters day before yesterday?'

Sixfingers dismounted to get at the girl, but again she drew back.

'You will have to tear me to pieces.'

'What reason have you got to defend this wretch?'

'If the horse runs away,' the girl warned him, 'he will die a horrible death. Untie him.'

Sixfingers asked:

'Will you come of your own free will?'

The girl nodded. They untied the Twin, who murmured proudly: 'For thirty-eight years.'

The girl felt Sixfingers' hand on her arm. The thumb, split in two, trembled on her skin. Were they going to kill her now? She looked squarely at Sixfingers. Then she looked at Gimpy, but his face had become dry as cork. The girl pushed Sixfingers' hand away and walked, alone, to the litter. She was carrying the camera.

Sixfingers struck Gimpy with the whip.

'When you see how we cut out your guts and wind them on the reel of a fishing rod you'll tell us where the teacher is.'

The girl's mouth was pressed in a stern line; her eyes wandered without focussing on any face. Sixfingers thought: 'She won't talk to me. She doesn't want to talk.' He would have liked her to talk to him, to tell him, for instance, whether she used to dream about a man like him when she was in school.

The morning was cool, the sea fragrant. The girl knew that the Indians could not protect her, but the fact that she had been able to do them a favour simply by looking at the maize and the clouds and going into the sea had given her an entirely new idea of herself. And now in the scented morning

234

that idea seemed to be growing stronger in spite of everything.

Sixfingers barked out orders in an arrogant military voice. 'The rearguard's lagging; tell those bastards to snap to.' Or: 'Six men to relieve the patrol.' Hearing him, the girl was for some reason reminded of those letters of Trinidad's telling her that he had been obliged to beat up two sentries. 'Oh,' she thought, 'they think they can impress everybody that way.'

Some of the men began to sing, making sly references to the girl and Sixfingers. One of them tried to sing the song that went *untie my corset, untie my corset,* and without a word Sixfingers rode his horse over him, knocked him down, and dragged him along the ground. Then he let him get up. The poor man limped the rest of the way, Sixfingers swearing at him between his teeth.

At nightfall there was a crowd around headquarters. The convicts, most of them drunk, seeing the procession in the distance, thought it was Lefty bringing them the girl. Chapopote moved his long legs in a solemn dance, asking the men around him what number they had. The Cuban began to dance too. He didn't know the words of the conga:

> *Here's the tart, here's the girl,*
> *bomba, recus, maguey.*

But Nosy-Posy made up better words:

> '*The Hanged Man's Widow,*
> *The Little Widow,*
> *The Hanged Man's Widow got away.*
> *The Little Widow,*
> *Oh, she got away! Oh, she got away!*
> *Oh, she gets away from me!*'

When Nosy-Posy stopped others kept up the beat:

> *Bomba, recus, maguey.*

'Killed their fathers!' screamed the Slicker in tears. 'They

235

all killed their fathers and came here. But I didn't kill mine. And he beats me because I didn't kill him.'

Spitball, suspecting the girl was not all he had thought, gave himself up to cynicism:

'She's going to bitch us all.'

Watching him, Careto thought: 'He, too, has heard the sinister call.'

Nosy-Posy cried:

'I brought her. Give me your thanks, my boys.'

Sixfingers whispered an order to Squinty, who went up to the nearest man.

'What's your number?'

'Thirty-three.'

'You'll get them right where they belong, thirty-three right where they belong.'

Squinty grabbed another man, who protested:

'I haven't got a number. Nor him either.'

He pointed to Careto, who was sitting on the ground with a can of food between his legs and a bottle of wine beside him. He was waiting for news of Lefty from the woods. He had on a shirt and a new suit. The arrival of the girl and the fact that Lefty had not caught her changed his plans. Squinty came up.

'All dressed up! Congratulations on your prosperity.'

He felt the cloth of Careto's lapel. Careto had succeeded in bringing Ruana along under his coat, near his armpit, where it coiled, content, in the warmth. The snake stuck her head out, and Squinty drew back his hand as if it had been bitten and retreated. Ruana sniffed Careto's ear. He gave his low tremulous whistle, and she slid back under his coat. Squinty rubbed his hand on his trouser leg. Number thirty-three was still hanging around, panting:

'Chief, if you want, I can bring you the list right away with all the names and numbers. But have mercy on me.'

'All right. You have my word and Sixfingers', if you bring the list right away.'

236

Thirty-three left in delight. Careto spoke at last, spitefully:

'Was it Sixfingers who caught her? If it was he'd better look out. The same beggars that helped him catch her will try to kill him. It is the law.'

'What law?'

'The ancient law.'

Careto whistled to the snake, and Squinty thought: 'She sweeps his house; she washes his dishes.' But that warning intrigued him and he went to repeat it to Sixfingers, who frowned and said only:

'Who? Careto? What a far-seeing man!'

They went into headquarters. Mother Leonor, in tears, embraced the girl. There was still an ironic undertone in the old woman's weeping. 'Actually it can't be said that she is really his widow.' She looked at her eyes, her mouth, her eyes again.

'I don't understand why you're so calm.'

Gimpy was sitting with his back to the guardroom wall, Sixfingers not having allowed him to go in.

Careto watched him from a distance and murmured: 'He, too, has heard the sinister call. But the one who's head over heels in it now is Sixfingers.'

The officer of the guard told Sixfingers that Lefty must be prowling around somewhere. Sixfingers burst out laughing, looking down on Lefty from the pinnacle of his victory.

'Take him a good bottle of rum so he can drink to our health. The whole world has to be friendly to-night.'

He went up to the room, looking for the girl. He looked out of the window and, seeing the people below, smiled threateningly. Careto, who had prophesied his death, was still there, a little farther away, sitting on the ground. The thought of the prophecy sent Sixfingers into spasms of laughter. Niña Lucha watched him in surprise. Her old terrors were there, in this man's arms and legs, but she was no longer frightened by the terrible. It only surprised her.

The chief spoke:

237

'There are others after you and for no good end, but Six-fingers will give them what they deserve.'

He went out. Left alone, Lucha wandered around the room; she paused before the door, tempted to lock it from the inside, but she remembered with horror what had happened to Trinidad. 'If I lock it they will kill him too.' She stood before the mirror and tried to prink 'in reverse,' so as to be as unattractive as possible. Still, in spite of everything, she was not displeased to see that she was pretty. From inside the room, without going near the window, she watched the convicts moving around restlessly.

One went up to another.

'What number have you got?'

'Thirty-five.'

He made a note of it and went away. Gimpy, who had found out what Sixfingers had up his sleeve, was keeping mum. He wanted nothing more than for them all to be beaten up on the girl's account.

Sixfingers' voice boomed from the stairs. He came in carrying a huge tray with biscuits, tortillas, and several pounds of ham. Under his arm he had a bottle of syrup which he had found in the first-aid station.

'Here's a drink for you.' He opened the bottle and smelled it. 'It's no drink for the rabble either. It's for lovely young ladies when they feel low.'

His wife appeared, her eyes blazing.

'If you want to know what you are——' she stammered.

Sixfingers said in a low voice, enunciating slowly:

'It is written!'

The woman, before leaving, looked at the girl and screamed:

'His heart goes out to you because you're young. But if you fail him, if you deceive him with another man, I'll tear out your heart with my nails.'

The girl felt a certain flattery in this threat. 'I am a monster.' And she added timidly, 'Or perhaps everybody is one sometime and it doesn't matter.' The night throbbed with echoes. The people on the landing seemed to have dispersed, and from behind the house came cries of pain, at which Sixfingers smiled mysteriously.

'They're getting theirs, my Niña.'

'What for?'

'This time I can't allow your generosity, because it was you they sinned against.'

The night was thicker in the silence between the outcries. Some screamed like children, some like old men, and every now and then one bellowed like a bull. She was distressed to hear the sound of her name through the moaning.

'What's happening?'

The cries still rang out. Extreme grief and extreme happiness awaken the beast, and now the whole dismal concert was reminiscent of hungry wolves on winter nights, around farmyards where oxen are bellowing in terror.

'Why are they beating them?'

Sixfingers closed the door, muffling the sound. The girl didn't know what to think, but in front of the building Spitball's accordion struck up again, and that eased the situation. Gimpy wandered around, quite cheered up by the groans of the flogged men.

Sixfingers went to the window and looked at what was left of the crowd. He sent orders for the guard to be reinforced; he didn't know why.

The girl saw that his hands were trembling.

'You eat,' she said. 'I'm not hungry.'

'I'm not either,' Sixfingers replied. 'We'll eat between sins.'

He laughed, showing his yellow teeth. He was coming toward her.

'Even if you scream no one can keep me from showing you my affection.'

He was upon her. Feeling his breath on her cheek, the girl gave him a slap in the face. Then she opened her eyes, surprised at herself. The struggle had begun; she should not

239

have provoked it, because the male was sure to win. She had hit
him with all her strength, but Sixfingers put on a dulcet
expression.

'That's the way I like my women, with a little spirit. My
wife is like that, but the poor thing never had any upbringing.'

He noticed that the girl was wiping her hand clean on her
skirt. It humiliated him. He felt his beard and found that it
was damp.

'I'm not up to my usual appearance. Wait a minute.'

She remained motionless after he had gone. She started
toward the dressing table but stopped. She was afraid, because
near the carved wooden feet, between the wall and the curtain,
beside the shiny mahogany moulding, there was a little
man, less than a foot high, wearing a wedding suit. And if
she went too near she might step on him by mistake and kill
him. Or the dwarf might peek under her skirt, like the Pimp.
She went a little closer. He was making excursions after bits
of ham and tortilla. Greedy as a cat, he took all he could hold
in his hands and went back to his corner.

She thought that Sixfingers would probably not be back
for a while, so she ventured as far as the door in search of
Mother Leonor, but, seeing the dark hall and hearing strange
noises, she went back.

Mother Leonor was in the room, looking at her inquisitively. She asked:

'Do they know anything about the body?'

'What body?'

As soon as she had spoken the girl thought: 'What other
body could it be?' And what would Mother Leonor think of
her? There was no way of telling what the old woman thought,
but she said:

'It's only natural. The marriage was not consummated.'

Mother Leonor went to get her a drink of water, and the
girl was alone again. She walked back and forth; opposite the
dresser she thought she heard the same strange noise that had
heralded the ghost in the cave, but perhaps the humming was

only in her head. She was willing to believe it might be a real ghost, but in that case, if it was following her, it was perhaps trying to remind her of things that were in themselves unforgettable. And she began to feel a new sort of fear, an apathetic fear. She got up and went again to the window. On the ground, between the trees, she saw three green glow-worms, like three fallen stars. The night bird was singing its humid song:

Bambu, bambu-le-le.

She tried to remember the charm but could get only the beginning:

'*On four posters*
my bed is. . .'

She drew back, went to the window to close it, but was afraid of thrusting her arms into the night air. She sat down again, her hands in her lap, and waited. Mother Leonor came with a glass and pitcher. The old woman still looked at her with meddlesome curiosity.

'It was really not consummated.' With a look full of distrust she asked: 'Where did Darío take you?'

The humming sound came from the right wing of the building. Dim moonlight illumined the tree tops. She thought she could *feel* Trinidad there, as she had felt him before in the cloud shaped like Norway. But this time he had nothing to say to her. The moon made her feel more friendly toward the little man by the dresser. She was curious about him and wished he were big enough so she wouldn't step on him by mistake.

The ghost was humming. The girl told Mother Leonor what had happened in the cave.

'Ah! So you were in the cave!' she said, eyes alight at the discovery.

That was the only part of it she heard. The girl wanted to ask if she knew the charm, but the old woman was not listening. Her imagination had taken her off to the cave.

And only when the girl began to recite *On four posters* did
Mother Leonor speak—this was her province—going through
the words of the charm mechanically:

> '*Saint Joseph, the Virgin,*
> *Saint Joachim, Saint Anne.*
> *I deny you*
> *if God denies,*
> *and if you are blessed*
> *give me some sign.*'

They heard Sixfingers' steps again. He had shaved and
really looked like a different person. A different kind of
barbarian. In his haste he had cut himself two or three
times. He staunched the blood with his hand, then wiped
it on the bedspread. Mother Leonor fled when she saw him.

'Take a good look at me, Niña Lucha. Now I really look
like myself.'

The strange humming sounded outside. Sixfingers came
closer, and the girl, backing away, could not help glancing at
his holster with the pretty metal ring of the revolver-butt
sticking out.

'Are you afraid?'

'No.'

After a short pause the girl added:

'Though I was told they wanted to kill me.'

'Kill you?'

'Yes, me.'

'But what for?'

'I don't know. They said *for my beauty.*'

Sixfingers felt like answering her in fond phrases, but he
couldn't think of any. When he spoke again it was in a very
tired voice.

'All my life I've been cursed.'

'Why?'

'I've never succeeded in doing what I wanted to, good
things or bad.'

He swore and added, shaking his head:

'Ever since I was little. They must have put a skull in my cradle.'

The girl said nothing. Sixfingers went on:

'When I was fifteen I wanted to save you from danger. You weren't born yet, so what danger could I save you from? When I was thirty I said: *That girl is in the world somewhere, but where?* And you still weren't even born.'

Lucha didn't answer. Sixfingers added:

'What a thing life is! Me thinking of you, and you not even born!'

She was silent. 'It was the same with the other one,' she thought, 'the one who said he had known me for thirty-eight years.'

'Do you know why I rescued you from those lousy Indians?'

She looked at him, balanced between fear and curiosity. He shrugged his shoulders.

'I rescued you for myself. To be my wife, for better——'

He was going to say 'or worse,' but instead he put his hand on his hip and sighed.

'A man and a woman alone are a beautiful thing. The most beautiful thing in the world.'

The girl was afraid but set her mind on hiding it.

'We can do whatever we like with our bodies. Nobody can see us. Doesn't it sound wonderful?'

Sixfingers laughed, but the look in his eyes was not consistent with his mouth, nor his mouth with the tone of his voice.

'Are you afraid?'

'No. Even if they kill me I'm not afraid.'

'It's the first time you've been alone in a room with a man like this, and you're not afraid?'

'No.'

There was no telling whether Sixfingers was pleased by that or not. He shrugged his shoulders:

'Woman is woman, and man is man.'

243

He looked her over from head to heels. The girl felt naked, but her nakedness did not frighten her as it had before. He came closer.

'They put a skull in my cradle. And you aren't afraid of me?'

'No.'

She was, but since she had been on the beach and heard the songs of the Indians behind the banana grove (she had heard them very clearly) her fear was of a different kind. She was no longer sure they were going to kill her. It was all strangely fitting. Trinidad was dead, and the reactions of the people made her wonder: 'Did he die because he had to?' While the Indians were celebrating Trinidad's death they treated her in a way that made her feel, for the first time, as if she were beginning to be alive. Perhaps she had to live for the same reasons that Trinidad had to 'kick off' (the words, which came to her mind just because she had been hearing them so often, filled her with remorse). She was not afraid. And if she was it was a different kind of fear; she didn't know what kind because she had never felt it before.

Sixfingers came closer, clutched her hand, and put his arm around her waist. The girl, trying to break loose, stumbled over a wrinkle in the carpet but didn't fall because Sixfingers held her up and, feeling her at his mercy, slipped his hand under her knees and lifted her into the air. With her feet off the ground the girl's comfortable faith in things vanished.

'Look at me and you'll see I'm not a beast.'

He pressed her to him, kissing her cheek and throat. She avoided his lips, and Sixfingers took what he could.

'I for you, you for me.'

The girl heard the ghost humming and began to murmur between her teeth: '*I deny you—if God denies—and if you are blessed—give me some sign.*'

'What's that you're saying?'

The girl pointed to the window.

'It's Trinidad's ghost.'

244

Sixfingers burst out laughing. Squeezing her gently, he repeated:

'I for you, you for me.'

She shook her head, and Sixfingers frowned threateningly. He thrust his hand between her arm and her side and took hold of the left breast, which was pulsing like a little live bird. The girl reacted to the caress with no more than a look of surprise, and this upset him. He drew his hand back slightly but kissed her again on the cheek. The girl smiled. The smile made him feel ashamed; he didn't know why.

'It will be wonderful,' he said.

'No.'

'Why?'

The girl cried out in protest:

'You don't realise!'

She spoke to him there in his arms in a tone of familiarity, as if she had known him all her life.

'I?'

He looked impatiently at the bed. 'You for me and me for you.' The girl saw the pistol at his side, and his arms held her fast. In their grip she felt weak and helpless.

'Please!'

'I want only your happiness, Princess.'

'Then leave me alone.'

'Am I so loathsome?'

She made a gesture of annoyance, which was not lost on Sixfingers.

'No, no,' she said, seeing the butt of the pistol.

'Then you're going to be mine.'

'I can't.'

'Ha, ha, ha! You can't? Why?'

The girl put a hand on his chest.

'There are some things people can do and some they can't. This is the kind that's impossible.'

'Not for me.'

'For everybody.'

245

'But why can't you? You will be the queen of the island. All the other women would give anything to be in your place. You, the queen; I, the king.'

The girl shook her head. Sixfingers made for the large bed.

'You for me, me for you.'

'No.'

'But why?' he roared in a rage.

The girl gave fantastic reasons.

'You don't realise, but if I did a thing like that my aunt and uncle would die of grief. They have heart trouble and they'd die. You must understand that.'

Sixfingers was about to let out a bellowing laugh, but he heard noises on the stairs. He listened, his hand on his holster. The girl slipped to the floor and managed to wriggle free.

The alarm passed. Niña Lucha went to the window and pointed out the three fallen stars.

'What are those?'

'Glow-worms.'

'Are glow-worms animals?'

'Yes, little animals with their bellies on fire.'

The girl was trembling with fear, but she laughed.

'With their bellies on fire!'

'Yes.'

Sixfingers put his hand on his buttock. The girl thought: 'Next to the pistol.' He looked sullen now.

'I'm a real man.'

'Oh,' she said.

'Do you know why I brought you here? Do you know?'

'Yes. Because you thought about me before I was born and you think I'll be safer with you than with the Indians.'

'And for something else. I told you just now.'

'No, not that.'

'Don't you like me, Princess?'

The girl looked out the window and said absently: 'Glow-worms.'

'Don't you like me?'

'Do glow-worms have feet?'

'Don't you like me?'

She laid her hand on his arm.

'Oh yes!'

Sixfingers' face glowed with bliss. He became very loquacious, but he didn't know what to say. He was all gratitude. The girl looked at the glow-worms and said:

'Have they got feet? Have they really got feet?'

Sixfingers shook his head from side to side, baffled by the childishness of the question. Without speaking, still smiling, and wondering at his own tenderness toward the girl, he went to the door. He seemed hesitant. Was it worth the trouble? He went out to catch some glow-worms, saying:

'I am going to make you a bridal crown.'

On the outer stairs he heard the humming sound more plainly. He asked one of the guards:

'What is that? Is it really a ghost?'

The girl watched him go out of sight and reappear with the stars in the palm of his hand and a spectral green light on his chest and face. He was almost handsome, with the green light on his hands and the luminous bird, green, too, in the woods. But she felt the Pimp's look scratching at her knee.

Sixfingers came back almost running. His newly shaved face in the green reflections looked like jasper.

He shouted to the guard:

'Shoot him!'

'How can we kill him if he's dead?'

'By firing at him, you sons of bitches.'

In the darkness of the room the glow-worms gave off an unearthly light. With his palms held up Sixfingers might have been an ancient idol. The humming continued. The glow of the bird's song waxing and waning was ancient too:

Bambu, bambu-le-le.

Mother Leonor came in to say that 'Trinidad's actual ghost' could be seen in the moonlight through the bathroom window. Sixfingers wanted to drive her away, but the girl took Mother

247

Leonor's arm. Sixfingers realised that with that ghost around it was going to be difficult. He shouted again through the window:

'Shoot him, boys!'

'Give some other order. You can't shoot at a ghost; the breech will blow up.'

Sixfingers, tired of being so thwarted, finally got rid of Mother Leonor and fastened the window. But the girl was looking anxiously toward the bathroom, and Sixfingers grew impatient.

'Are you afraid, my sweet?'

The girl became indignant. Why did he call her that?

Sixfingers laughed:

'That's a funny question. You and I are not going to be two, but one.'

The girl looked at the bathroom.

> *. . . and if you are blessed,*
> *give me some sign. . . .*

The sea breeze brought the humming louder than ever. Sixfingers strode resolutely to the bathroom, but before reaching the window he scratched his jaw, picking a scab off from under his ear.

'As a matter of fact, I don't feel so easy with these things from the other world.'

His distress brought Sixfingers to a decision.

'Take off your clothes and get into bed. I'm going to send him to hell, and then I'll be right back.'

He drew his revolver and, cocking the trigger, went downstairs. As soon as he was gone the girl called to Mother Leonor, who came in, saying:

'One moment of contrition brings salvation to the soul.'

'Is it his ghost?'

'Don't you hear me praying, my dear?'

My dear. The girl couldn't understand why they all addressed her with such intimacy.

'What can we do?' asked Mother Leonor. 'The best thing would be to pray. Pray for his soul.'

Lucha called the servant girls, who were all terrified, lit two more candles, and placed all four below a picture of the Virgin. 'Yes, yes,' she kept saying, 'we must pray, but everybody must come.' She ordered the servants to their knees, dashed to the stairs to call the cook, came back, and knelt down. The old woman was thumbing hurriedly through the book of prayers for the dead, looking for the Trisagion: 'Prayer to invoke the aid of the heavenly powers against the Evil One.' Without pausing in her prayer she let out a sigh charged with infinite weariness. Since the girl had the star rôle in the affair Mother Leonor told her to lead the prayers and with heroic abnegation handed her the little book. The humming was louder. The girl read the service in a voice warm with feeling, accompanied by Mother Leonor and the servants, including the woman who had wept so shrilly at Trinidad's death. Soon the cook arrived and knelt beside the girls. He was paying court to the demonstrative mourner but got nothing for his pains but rebuffs. He looked at her now, but she had said to him a little while before: 'The girl isn't as much the chief's widow as I am,' and he was without hope. Gimpy came in, looking scared and surprised. He was trying to say something, but the girl, very pleased to see him there, motioned him to kneel, and he took his place beside the cook. He looked from the girl to the door, remembering Sixfingers' threat to wind his guts on a fishing rod.

'Appease, O Lord, Thy wrath, Thy justice, and Thy severity.'

'By Thy passion, dear Jesus, Thy mercy, O Lord.'

Sixfingers arrived and was stopped short by the lighted candles, the mystical eyes, the hushed voices. He had expected to find the girl naked in bed. Gimpy made ready to escape, drawing himself together like a cat. Sixfingers looked utterly disconcerted.

249

'Holy and just, holy and mighty, holy and immortal,' Lucha prayed, indicating a place for Sixfingers to kneel.

'Deliver us, O Lord, from all evil.'

'These prayers won't do you any good,' said Sixfingers angrily, and added, 'The ghost is as naked as the day he was born, and sometimes he pats his belly with his hand, like this.'

He patted his stomach.

Lucha pointed again to a place on the floor. Sixfingers finally bent one knee reluctantly, resting his elbow on his thigh. He gave Gimpy, who was beside him, a clap on the back, throwing him down on all fours.

'Pray for the dead, you bastard!'

Sixfingers turned his head slowly and one by one looked at the people praying. Gimpy felt those eyes on him, rough as a cat's tongue.

The girl filled in the blank spaces in the print with Trinidad's name.

'Pardon his pride, his covetousness, his sins against honesty. Thy servant Trinidad was the prey of the beast, living in sin, wallowing in filth, but Thy mercy, O Lord, is infinite. Our Father——'

Sixfingers growled:

'It's the truth.'

The people murmured the responses. Toward midnight they heard voices arguing on the stairs. Squinty came in.

'It's Lefty and some of his pals.'

'How many?'

'Four or five. But Lefty says he thanks you for your present and that he submits.'

Sixfingers felt that his victory was complete. He told Squinty to let them in and got up, so as not to be found in such a humble position. The guards tiptoed out, and presently Lefty appeared in the doorway. Seeing what was up, he took off his hat. He held out his hand and when Sixfingers reciprocated said:

'This is clean and above-board. I swear by the Holy Virgin that I am your loyal comrade.'

The girl hushed them and again motioned them impatiently to get down on the floor. Sixfingers remained standing hesitantly, until Lefty began to kneel. They looked at one another sideways, somewhat ashamed, but Lefty finally joined in the responses. Apologising for the interruption, he asked permission for his friends outside to come in. The girl nodded, and Sixfingers watched the two of them suspiciously. By now there was no room left, and the new people who were arriving had to station themselves on the stairs. They probably had no great faith in the efficacy of the prayers, but their souls were touched by the respectability of the lighted candles and all those people on their knees. Suddenly Sixfingers heard the Twin's voice boldly demanding a place: 'If Lefty can be there, then I can too.' Sixfingers didn't mean to allow it and drew his revolver, not that he cared if the Twin was there or not, but Lefty had made him nervous. The two got up, looking at each other out of the corners of their eyes. There was a shot on the stairs, and someone put out the candles on the dresser. Sixfingers also fired, but at the ceiling, because he was afraid of wounding the girl. An uproar broke out, over which Lefty and Sixfingers could be heard hurling insults at each other. Mother Leonor tumbled over on the floor and felt someone's foot in her ribs.

'Sacrilege!' she screeched, like a cat that has had its tail stepped on.

The servant girls dived for the corners of the room, shrieking. The humming of the ghost was drowned. Sixfingers commanded:

'Shut the doors! Sentries, if anyone goes out open fire!'

He stumbled over people in the dark. He fired at some and tried to shove some out of his way, but he was driven back. When he had managed to reach the door he turned and looked back. The tumult had spread to the stairs and the patio, where the girl was crying out in anguish. Sixfingers went down, cursing; when he got there they had all vanished. As he was attempting to go out, his own followers, in confusion, fired two or three shots at the door.

'They've got me,' Sixfingers cried, dropping the pistol and clutching his wounded arm.

He went up again and looked over the room. One candle had been relit. Blood gushed through his sleeve and between his fingers. Mother Leonor was there, the servant girls, and the cook. Gimpy had fled. Sixfingers, beside himself, growled threats at everybody.

'And I trusted the sanctity of prayer!'

The guards were saying that Lefty was behind it all.

'If you knew that why didn't you bump him off?'

But he had said that he didn't want to have any enemies on that night. And he had sent Lefty a bottle. They were all thinking about Sixfingers' wound. All but himself; he went on clutching his arm and hurling insults. Outside, night whispered through the treetops.

The bird poured into the shadows its damp, quivering note: *Bambu, bambu-le-le.*

Downstairs Sixfingers' wife was shouting:

'Ay! They have killed my man and I can't go up and comfort him!'

At the rumour that Sixfingers was wounded—fatally wounded, as they were all putting it—and that the girl had not only escaped but was in Lefty's hands, the 'rabble' gathered again. Not all of them, because some had been cruelly flogged, and many of those who did come were dragging an injured foot. 'I have a good number. Number three,' one whispered.

'The way I see her,' said the wheezing one with the split nose, 'the way I see her is cuddled up to me like a little bird on the highest twig of a tree.'

'Happy hunting!'

The Lawyer pricked up his ears.

'If you touch her I'll kill you.'

Two shots rang out at the left of the building among the trees. The din stopped for a second. The ghost was not humming any more.

'The chief has kicked off,' Careto shouted, 'because he dared to lay his hands on her.'

They all thought they were going to have the girl any minute. Spitball was dancing.

Kicked off, kicked off,
gone away from me. . . .

At this the Lawyer gave Spitball a smack on the mouth.
'Shut up!'
'Why?'
'Shut up!'
Spitball began dancing again:

gone away from me. . . .

The Lawyer went at him with his fists. Spitball shut up. A melancholy voice was sighing nearby.

'Ay, Holy Virgin! We're going to have the girl; it's almost too wonderful to bear.'

Number one yelled at the Lawyer:

'Did he kick off or not?'

'He's dead!' cried Careto, interrupting. 'Every one will die who breathes her breath.'

Gimpy was hanging around.

'I too. I too.'

He said it, longing to die. Every one seemed crazy.

They could hear Mother Leonor weeping at headquarters, and this supported the rumour of Sixfingers' death. Careto was electrified. He rose and, feeling the night warm on his temples, intoned in the darkness:

'You heard the call! You died! You died and they will peel off your skin and make it into a stinking ghost.'

Spitball stopped dancing and took up the accordion. The

253

only thing he really could play was the polka, *Shoot, Pepe!*
and he failed miserably trying to play the wedding conga.

And through the sultry night, the bird:

Bambu, bambu-le-le.

X

CARETO LIFTED HIS VOICE:

'The son of the wolf . . . is no more!'

They answered in chorus. Sixfingers went to the window. He ordered Squinty to go out in search of the girl, with the few guards left; then he dropped on the bed and began talking to himself with his eyes closed and an expression of ecstasy.

'I wasn't afraid at all, taking hold of the girl; she said they wanted to kill her for her beauty and that her aunt and uncle would die if she went to bed with me, and then she put her hand on my arm and told me she liked me. She liked me, but her aunt and uncle would die. And with the other hand she pointed out the window at the glow-worms. *Do they have feet?* I was thinking: "Sixfingers is a man of delicacy." And I went to get the glow-worms. And then God sent the ghost himself, as if to say: *This girl is as pure as the driven snow, and less than a week ago she was Trinidad's wife.* And there was the ghost, naked as the day he was born. And he patted his belly with his hands. I'm no coward, but my heart was in my boots. I came back with the glow-worms, and though my blood wasn't racing in my veins in the same way, I still wanted to have her. But I went up, and there she was, praying like a little saint, and everybody in headquarters around her. The room was like a real high-class chapel. And I said to myself: *Shut the shark's eye, Sixfingers,* and I shut it. And it's still shut.'

He was lying down, but he could still hear Careto outside.

'All will fall like Gómez the Scamp, like the iguana dancer, like Black Trinidad, like Sixfingers.'

He liked the idea of all the leaders dying, but he was waiting for the girl to be finished off first.

He had heard two shots. Probably the girl was no longer alive, and if she was it was not for long. Lefty had promised to get rid of her and had received four thousand pesos on account. And this time Lefty had taken his promise so seriously that he had gone after her right into the very lair of the beast. A real stroke of valour. He had taken her, and then came the shots. He had shot the girl. Careto didn't know it for sure, but Lefty knew that another four thousand were waiting. If he hadn't killed her yet he soon would. Careto scratched his chest through his open shirt front and rubbed his nose.

The convicts were beginning to be infected by Careto's cry of alarm:

'Everybody will die! There'll be only the fool Indians left to bury us.'

Careto laughed, knowing that if the girl was dead the evil spell was already broken.

But Sixfingers, hearing the convicts, felt that his wound had taken on a dark and deadly power.

There were still some people around. Gimpy went up to Careto.

'I drank her blood. Will I die?'

The sky was closed, without stars. Gimpy felt his intestines being wound on the reel. Dawn was breaking. Shreds of mist hid the sun on the rim of the sea. The convicts drifted away. Careto sat on the ground and observed the island becoming quiet again. Everything was going well, but there was perhaps one factor not under control. He tried to visualise this possibility more concretely but was distracted by a song running through his mind. The words and music took shape against his will:

> *'The leper woman bore a fish*
> *and the bishop of the fens*
> *christened it with sherry.'*

The blood rushed to his face, and an idea flared and faded

256

in his brain. He returned, however, to the unforeseen factor.
There was on the island a real miracle: the girl. The whole
convict population in love. And there was another miracle,
of the kind that deranges the senses: Trinidad's ghost
pursuing her. To all of them the girl was a miracle. In that
case, if she had died and if her death had been violent and
dramatic, would not the myth of her purity become even more
powerful? Careto would have called Lefty back, but it was too
late; he had heard two shots. The girl was probably dead. But
he was appalled to think how the myth of her purity might
grow. He would have to overcome it with a noble deed. Again
shots in the distance. 'Yes,' he thought, 'if I destroy Lefty
after the girl's death I will have added to my resources the
defence of the innate and elemental truths: beauty and goodness.' Could there be any doubt? He would kill Lefty with
his own hands, as he had killed the Pimp. He was bothered
by the thought that Lefty, when he saw that he was lost, might
also urinate on his hands. For such cases, as for surgical
operations, it was wise to wear gloves. The last time he had
had any was three years before in the war, when he wore them
as protection for charging the barrel of the machine-gun. A
pity he didn't have it here. He would kill Lefty. But why
hadn't he done it already? A man can be finished off well
enough without a machine-gun.

He got up and began to walk. The damp penetrated his
bones.

'Why haven't I killed him, that Lefty?'

He went quickly toward the woods but remembered that he
had left six thousand-peso notes in the hut on top of Ruana's
box. He went back for them, running as he had never known
he could run, in great leaps, full of energy. 'It's the Spanish
wine,' he thought, 'that makes me so strong.' He reached the
hut, grabbed the money, and stuffed it inside his shirt with
the rest of his fortune. Feeling it all there, between his shirt
and his skin, he went to the door and took counsel from the
early-morning light. He pressed the money to his chest as

feverishly as Gimpy had clutched the girl's nightgown. The world was beginning to look different. He raised his hand in the salute of his clan. He thought: 'Yes, all is well, but I must kill Lefty.' He listened for sounds from the woods, but there was nothing. Now and then the breeze made the leaves rustle like silk. Careto felt in his eyes, in his bones, a new inexplicable calm that might have come from the sea or from the sky or was perhaps the breath of the earth itself.

'But I was going somewhere. Where was I going?'

Oh, to kill Lefty. Again he rose and started for the woods without the least idea of where he would find him. But the sea breeze was stronger in that direction, and the smell was pleasant.

Pito the Yute was leaving Eminencias' bar dressed as a skeleton. The group of dancers who always celebrated when a new chief took over on the island had dressed up the night before to 'inaugurate the rule' of Sixfingers. But the events at headquarters had stopped them. Touchy Johnny was half dressed in a red tunic covered with spangles and copper foil. And Pito the Yute disguised as a skeleton. The dances consisted of mock sword fights between Indians and Spaniards. While various couples fought duels, the skeleton (yellow skull with bare jawbones, ribs painted on a black shirt, black elastic trousers, tibia and thighbones) jumped, swaying from side to side, carrying a long pole with a pick fastened to the end. The pole hovered over people's heads, choosing a victim, but Death danced without ever deciding, because that was the way the dance was. The skeleton was determined to dance now, whatever happened, and he pranced around Touchy Johnny, who was rolling a cigarette. They went on with an argument they had been having at the bar.

'You've got some nerve.'

'It's true! I knew the deputy.'

'So what? I've known a lot of them. And I don't talk about it.'

'That's a lie. A deputy isn't a man like us. He's the incarnation of the popular will. You never knew one.'

'I certainly did.'

'Tell me his name. I know all their names.'

'His name! Who cares about a name!'

'Go on, tell me his name.'

'What difference does the name make? It was Perez Barbosa, or something.'

Margarito went by, the man who was so distinguished that he sorted the mail. They called him in as umpire. Margarito was preoccupied. 'Where did Lefty get so much money?' he was wondering. He didn't know the name of Perez Barbosa and didn't think he was a deputy. He said he wanted to go to sleep, but Pito the Yute held him back.

'Isn't it true that you had an automobile?'

'That was my ruin. That automobile was my ruin.' He launched into his story:

'Nobody would have discovered our gang, but one night I ran over an old man and stepped on the gas to get away from the police. And the old man's coat caught in the crankshaft, between the back wheels. There he was rolled up like a dummy, and I didn't know it, and I was trailing blood all over town, and I went to my house with the car and the old man. And the next day I went to a wedding with the old man still wound around the crankshaft. And when they found him they investigated me, and my crimes rattled out like a string of beads. If it weren't for that old man I'd still be living in the city and I'd be married to a fine lady like the girl.' He went toward his hut. The skeleton yelled after him:

'It's a lie. You never knew a deputy either!'

Touchy Johnny went off, leaving only Death, who flopped beneath a tree. The birds woke up and began singing like mad. 'The one I had sang more,' thought Pito the Yute, 'but he died on me.' He had died singing. He had caught him and put out his eyes with a red-hot pin, and when he was blind the little bird burst into song. He sang day and night,

259

without eating or drinking or sleeping. Until he burst. He remembered him now. Among all the common daytime birds there rose now and then the voice of the other one, the night bird:

Bambu, bambu-le-le.

Below, the skeleton dozed. The sunless dawn wrapped everything in a grey silence. And the girl, the passions of the convicts, the fever of the night before seemed far off and forgotten. The skeleton listened to the birds. He thought he understood them. He had always wanted to know what they were saying. That was why he hunted them. Ever since he was a little boy he had been fond of them and hunted them, but when he really loved one he had to kill it. And seeing it small and mute in his hand, with its feathers bristling, he would burst into tears and sometimes kiss it and blubber: 'Poor little thing.'

But he would become attached to another and kill it and weep again. 'If they could talk to me,' he said to himself, 'I wouldn't kill them.' But if he came to love them he couldn't stand their not telling him what they felt. Inside they had feelings for him and he couldn't find out what they were. Only by killing the bird slowly could he see something in it: terror in its death throes, pain. A tiny little pain, but very deep. Some time ago he had felt that he was beginning to understand them. Whenever he caught one he blinded it so it would sing more, and when it was blind Pito the Yute would listen to it. That was how he learned. If the little thing died afterward—from singing so much—that was different. Pito would weep.

Now, lying face up, he counted six birds on one branch and two on another. At the very top of the tree was a finch with breast and belly the colour of fire. The bird opened and folded its wings, giving a little trill. The sun was behind the clouds, but the novelty of it—grey days were unusual on the island—gave him a perverse pleasure. The redbreast was watching the birds below.

Chrri . . . chrrri . . .

The ones below were watching too. One of them was an ash-grey turtledove, a bad omen for Pito. The turtledove spoke:

'I saw the owl yesterday. He was on the rock beside the lighthouse.'

'What was he doing?'

'He was lying in wait for a lizard. When the lizard came halfway out of his hole the owl swooped on him and snapped his head off with one stroke of his beak. Then the rest of the lizard went off by itself without any head.'

'He, he, he,' the redbreast interrupted. 'If the lizard went away he was looking for his head.'

'And the owl took him to his nest. First the head. Then he came back to look for the body. And he took the whole thing to his nest.'

'There are pebbles that burn at noontime.'

It was a humming-bird. There were some low bushes at Pito's left, and a little white butterfly fluttered above them. Behind her came another, chasing her. Pito watched them.

'Are they making love?'

They drifted up and down; they seemed to be flying awkwardly, in spurts, sometimes whirling like snippets of paper in the wind. One caught the other on the ground, near his feet. He watched them roll around, fly, and fall again.

'Love?'

But a little later one flew away, and the other stayed on the ground. Pito went closer to look. It had no head. One of its wings was quivering. The victor had vanished among the trees. The redbreast went on:

Chrri . . . chrrri . . .

The turtledove left the branch, wheeled over the skeleton, and disappeared. 'Something about me surprised him,' Pito said to himself. 'He came to take a look, cleared up whatever it was that bothered him, and then he went away.' But the butterfly's head and the lizard's reminded him of another

261

story. His father had been an Indian. An Indian from the neighbouring country. He was dead and he had died right in the penitentiary of his country. There had been a very famous man who spoke in verse. He couldn't speak in any other way. And not even in verse, because he could hardly talk at all. So he said everything in writing. But it was extraordinary. The whole country said so, and another country, too, like New York. And another, like Paris. And another, like Madrid. The whole world waited for what he wrote, and when he had written it everybody recited it. And his country sent him travelling because his head was a treasure and they wanted everybody to see it. And when they had seen it he went back to his own country. They welcomed him with music and floral wreaths and carpets in the streets and more flowers. And this man, whose head everybody had seen, was called Ruben, and pretty soon he died. Pito's father brought flowers, like all the others, to the great man's little cottage. And he heard them saying: 'His head, the head that all the world has seen, is worth millions.' And Pito's father waited till dark and climbed in a window and cut off the head of the great dead man and put it in a sack and went away. Day and night he walked along the roads with the sack over his shoulder till he crossed the frontier and came to another country. And there he poked around inside the head with his fingers and a stick and didn't find anything. And then he went to a bank and took the head out of the sack. It was swarthy, with a broad dark nose and great big sad eyes. And not only did they give him nothing for it, but they took it away from him and put him in jail. That was his father. Pito the Yute would never have done anything like that, for times were different, and he knew what a poet was and what was valuable about him. If his head had treasures inside, that was only a piece of foolishness, a way of speaking. But Pito also had had a head in a sack. That was a different problem. It was not a question of selling it but of preventing the police from identifying its real owner. But they caught him just the same. When he told the story on the island they told him that to keep from being discovered he should have cut a strip of flesh from his victim and eaten it raw. That way the police would never have got on his track. The only thing Pito had done, besides taking the head, was to take the victim's name as his own, which in the beginning confused the police very much. His victim's name was Pito the Yute, and it had stuck to him ever since. He rather liked it.

He lay looking at the tree. Birds went away and others came. One of them kept saying his name:

'Pito! Pitilyute!'

The skeleton felt very friendly toward him.

Whiskers came through the trees. He looked at Pito and began to bark ferociously. Pito called him, but Whiskers did not seem very pleased by his disguise. He went all around him, at a safe distance, barking like mad. But when he came to the windward side, and sniffed the air he recognised a smell that was, if not familiar, at least not unknown. Pito called him affectionately, and Whiskers came up and smelled one foot. 'Oh, now I know,' he seemed to be saying; 'you're a friend of my master's. I've smelled you before.' Behind Whiskers appeared the doctor, all dressed up.

'Good-for-nothing!'

Whiskers prepared to run away. The doctor came up to him slowly and gingerly.

'Whiskers, I'm your master. Don't run away, Whiskers. I gave up my mistress and my tobacco, but I can't get along without you. Come here, Whiskers; I'll tell you all about it.'

He managed to catch him and went running to the woods with the dog in his arms. Whiskers gave little yelps and licked his nose. The skeleton sat up and, seeing them disappear in the woods, clicked his tongue against the roof of his mouth.

'It's queer that nobody is talking about the girl,' he thought.

Morning drew on, and the square was still deserted. Under the grey clouds the earth seemed hotter than in the sun and was the colour of men's skin. Nobody went to Eminencias'

263

bar; nobody came from the harbour. And the clouds kept gathering, promising rain that never came.

The solitude weighed in his bones, his own and those of the skeleton he was wearing on top. He looked at the tree. Another grey turtledove. It came, beat its wings, perched on the branch, and puffed up its neck feathers that were the colour of the fluff one finds under a bed. He had held many turtledoves like that in his hands, and he remembered that his fingers would sink in through the feathers until they felt a tiny feeble body with a tremendous heart beating in it. 'They're all chasing Lefty to get the girl back.' If anybody went home to his hut it was because all the strength had been beaten out of him. He had seen one man with a broken leg dragging himself on his back like a crab. Others ran, limping.

'Lefty has her now!'

They believed in his promises.

It must have been around noon when he saw the teacher coming from the woods. The skeleton stood up. He couldn't believe it. They were after the teacher; they had tried twice to kill him, and now there he was, perfectly calm. He passed close by without speaking and went straight to headquarters. The skeleton followed him and, when he saw him go in, thought that something was going to happen. He waited but didn't hear anything and finally sat down on the outer stairs.

Darío had gone to the patio and run into Mother Leonor.

'They've gone.'

'All of them? Sixfingers too?'

The old woman put on a look of circumspection.

'I don't know, and I mustn't answer.'

So she was on Sixfingers' side or was pretending to be to annoy him. Darío went up. He opened the door and entered Sixfingers' room. He went in with his pistol cocked, and Sixfingers, lying on the bed, raised his sound hand in the air.

'Now I see,' said Sixfingers; 'now I see how wrong I was.'

Darío approached him slowly, keeping his eyes sharp.

'What were you wrong about?'

264

'Now I see that you're capable of cutting off a tiger's tail—when the tiger is tied and toothless.'

'Where's your revolver?'

Sixfingers reached out to take it from the shelf of the night table, but Darío took a step forward.

'Don't move. Keep your hand up if your life means anything to you!'

Darío kept his pistol forward, aimed at his chest. Sixfingers repeated sarcastically:

'Tied and toothless.'

Darío took his revolver. With both of them in his hands he went to the foot of his bed and sat down. He toyed with the guns and said:

'I'm not interested in the tiger's tail.'

'Then what are you after here?'

'First to make you shut your shark's eye.'

'I just shut it. And what else?'

Through the window, in a great silence, came the distant breath of the sea. Sixfingers asked again:

'And what else?'

'I want to see how you are.'

Sixfingers burst out laughing. Darío acted as if he hadn't heard.

'Who took care of you?'

'Little Mother Leonor. The blessed woman!'

Sixfingers was still suppressing a laugh. Since Darío was silent he spoke:

'Just the day before yesterday I was on the point of shooting you. You saved yourself by the skin of your teeth, but things have changed.'

'So it seems. Where's the girl?'

'Do you care very much?'

Darío replied genially:

'Who knows?'

'Then wait for her here. She is coming. Well escorted, to be sure.'

Someone was coming slowly upstairs. Darío turned to look but saw no one. Mother Leonor was screaming in the patio, apparently at the person who was coming up:

'Who gave you permission?'

The skeleton appeared in the doorway.

'Chief,' he said through the teeth of the skull, 'I came to be dismissed. We were going to celebrate your rule, but the others have gone after Lefty. So I've come to be dismissed.'

Sixfingers being wounded, it was a good omen for death to appear and be dismissed. Darío turned his head, and at that instant Sixfingers kicked his hand hard from under the sheet. The two pistols went flying through the air, and Darío managed to grab only one. He backed toward the door and stepped out into the hall just as Sixfingers, entrenched in the bed, fired. Darío fired too. The skeleton raced through the gallery around the patio, trying to get out of the line of fire. He found a spot under cover and stayed there, hopping up and down, jittery with fear. Mother Leonor was screaming outside.

Sixfingers kept firing, and Darío waited behind the door. Sixfingers, thinking he was safe, exposed himself. Darío fired twice, and Sixfingers retreated, cursing. Darío thought he must have hit him.

'Drop your gun!' he shouted.

'Your mother!'

Sixfingers went on firing at random, without taking aim, and Mother Leonor continued her clamour in the patio. But Darío heard the weapon fall to the floor. He darted in, picked up the pistol, and before looking at Sixfingers, who was standing doubled up, he saw fresh bloodstains on the floor. He called to Mother Leonor, who hurried in, pale and clenching her hands. The skeleton came with her, saying again:

'Chief, I want my dismissal. It makes more sense now. Let me go, chief.'

Sixfingers said nothing. Darío, knowing him to be disarmed and wounded, shoved him rudely toward the bathroom.

'I'll aim better next time.'

But he said it with no satisfaction. He was as pale as Mother Leonor. Sixfingers didn't answer.

'The boat from the Health Department is supposed to come to-day. The doctors can fix you up all right.'

Sixfingers opened his lips to say languidly that the boat had already come and he had made it turn around and leave, without letting anyone land. Darío shrugged his shoulders.

'So much the worse for you.'

But he felt rattled. The boat had gone away. That is, there was no use waiting for it, because it wouldn't come.

'My chief, let me go.'

When Sixfingers had lain down again he opened his eyes without looking at Darío. The teacher told him his wounds were nothing—a flesh wound in the leg—and that he would be well in a few days. He was surprised to have wounded him in the leg; he had aimed at the heart. The skeleton came in and went out with a pail, helping Mother Leonor. Darío added after a pause:

'You can count on me if you need help.'

Sixfingers said with his eyes shut:

'There are all kinds of men.'

After a long silence he began to relate, in a tone of indifference, what was happening to Niña Lucha. Darío already knew all about it, but he let him talk. Mother Leonor, who had gone out, came rushing back to listen. When Darío had gone Sixfingers said to her, pointing to the door:

'A gentleman!'

He asked her to look for his pistol on the floor, but the old woman could not find it. Sixfingers clenched his teeth in rage.

'He was afraid of me. He took it, the coward!'

He meant the teacher. Mother Leonor wanted to whet Sixfingers' anger and had a sentence on the tip of her tongue: 'And who is Darío to take it away from you?' But she kept quiet. Perhaps she was afraid of Darío.

The skeleton showed up again.

'Let me go, chief.'

Sixfingers flung an empty bottle at his head. It missed and broke with a crash against the wall. Pito went downstairs quite contented. Darío ran into him.

'The chief let me go!'

'What chief?'

'Not me. I never said Sixfingers was the chief, señor.'

'Go on. Get out of here.'

Pito didn't wait to be told twice. He fled like an arrow and went with his disguise to the foot of a tree. 'He let me go,' he said, laughing. He set to examining the tree, to see if the ill-omened turtledoves were there.

Darío stayed at headquarters. He avoided speaking to Sixfingers, knowing that he would get no answer.

The square outside was still deserted, and the sea breeze had become a restless wind, fitfully shifting. Pito was still flopped on the ground, looking at the tree. He looked at the harbour pressed against the sea behind a screen of trees and the distant horizon of the sea. And on the other side, beyond a long stretch of warm-coloured earth, the trees, the light-house with its broken light rising among them, grey and heavy.

Pito didn't take off his disguise. He liked it. The solitude, the silence, the peace woke cumbrous and stupid ideas in his mind. He was still absorbed in: *the chief let me go; he let me go*.

Sometime late in the afternoon Spitball appeared. He was dragging behind him a dirty elastic rag like a collapsed balloon.

'What's that?' Pito asked.

'The ghost. They fired at it, and the air went out of the holes.'

'The ghost? What ghost?'

'Sure. Trinidad's own skin.'

Spitball stretched it out on the ground. The arms, the legs, the head. That degraded skin, dried out and full of deep cracks, was Trinidad's. The Indians knew how to do that. It gave off a sweet and pungent smell. The hands were still whole —stuffed, Spitball said—and the feet too. Spitball pointed to the holes in the chest.

'That's where they shot him. That's where the air got out.'

He pulled out a knife and cut off the head at the neck. He folded it and tucked it under his shirt but took it out again because the hair tickled his skin and turned it inside out like a leather pouch, with the hair inside. He said everybody was chasing Lefty to recover the girl and they already had him surrounded, with his back to the sea and no means of escape. It was all so exciting that Pito was on the point of going there with him, but he changed his mind. At dusk the two turtle-doves might come. He said with an air of springing big news:

'Sixfingers isn't in command of the island any more.'

'What do you mean?'

'Darío shot him and made a fool of him.'

Spitball didn't believe it and went off scoffing at Pito.

At nightfall the shooting started again, scattered at first, and then more frequent. The skeleton had left. Darío was very uneasy; he went out to the square, feeling the need of some fresh air after his victory. Hearing the shots, Mother Leonor tried to pray again, but it got on Darío's nerves and he made her stop. Sixfingers was groaning from the bed:

'Haven't they come with the girl yet?'

Darío walked up and down in front of headquarters. Violence was easy; he had defeated Sixfingers, but he didn't want to defeat anyone. He would have preferred to talk to him and win him over. But Sixfingers was an element of nature, like wind or rain, and there was no sense in trying to influence him by talk alone.

Night closed in. The skirmishing increased, and two messengers arrived with reports. Darío went out to meet them. They were a little startled to see him, but they knew that Sixfingers had been wounded again, and they considered him done for. They brought news.

'Lefty has opened fire under cover of the trees, and he has

ammunition for a week. He's already picked off two of our men.'

'For the same price you could have caught him.'

'Exactly! That's what I said.'

'Who are they?'

'Congo and Chapopote.'

'Serious?'

'No, señor. Just grazes. They were lucky.'

The messengers started for headquarters, but Darío stopped them.

'Where are you going?'

'To report to the chief.'

'What chief?'

Again the convicts were thrown off by the question.

'Come on, let's go in,' said Darío, turning them back.

The three walked slowly in silence.

'Don't hear any more shooting.'

They stopped and listened to the sounds from the woods. There was shouting, as of hunters beating for game. They walked faster, but Darío suddenly halted.

'I smell smoke,' he said.

Before the words were out he saw a tongue of flame far off between the trees. Before long the fire was throwing a yellowish glow against the clouds. The clamour of the hunt grew livelier. Darío began to run, followed by the two others.

They lost no time in getting there. The branches crackled in the flames, and everything was shrouded in smoke. The wind was driving the fire toward the sea. The convicts were coughing and trying to stand clear of the smoke. Darío looked for an opening in the barricade of fire, but the convicts had made a semicircle beginning and ending at the sea. Lefty was trapped in the ring, which was closing in before the wind.

'And the girl?'

The Lawyer was leaping around with a burning faggot of cornstalks.

'The girl is dead.'

'That's a lie!' And after a pause: 'How much of a drop is there at the shore?'

'No danger,' said the Lawyer, still rushing about setting fire to the bushes. 'No danger. The brush goes right down to the sea, and it's forty feet deep.'

'How do you know the girl is dead?'

'Careto says so.'

Darío breathed again. The girl was alive, though in danger of a horrible death. 'And now fire,' he thought. 'How many more resources has Nature got?' The Lawyer and the others running around with their torches didn't know what they were doing. They were a blind force. Were there still other resources? He looked around and said: 'I am the only one here who has a right to be mad.' His will searched the chaos around him for any possibility of decision and action. The others seemed very pleased with the situation. Darío thought: 'It can't be more than two hundred yards from here to the sea. She must be smothering.' The smoke billowed up, glowing near the ground. Some birds rose, screeching, and managed to get away. Others fled like arrows and, dazzled by the fire, dashed against the trees and fell dead. Darío went around trying to talk to the convicts, but no one paid any attention, and the fire raged more furiously. He tried to talk to the Lawyer, but he didn't want to listen either. He snatched the burning cornstalks from his hands, and when the Lawyer resisted and tried to get them back he hit him in the stomach and again on the jaw. The Lawyer fell senseless into the brambles, getting his face all scratched up. Darío ran on and met the Twin, who was as crazed as the rest. 'I didn't do it; I didn't do it,' he insisted, referring to the fire, but there was a wild joy in his protest.

Darío started to go for the canoe to rescue the girl by sea, but when he had run twenty yards he realised that the fire was increasing and he would not have time. He went back as close as possible to the flames. What could be done? The convicts wanted to finish off Lefty and didn't care if the girl died on the same pyre. They were apparently making Lefty a scapegoat, but she was a woman, and that they did not see.

Congo, who was wounded, seemed to be raving while the flames crackled:

'Soft as thighs! All over she has skin soft as thighs.'

But others were shouting, imploring the heavens:

'The Virgin! The Holy Virgin!'

No one knew, not even themselves, whether they meant the mother of Jesus or the girl. Some were still wandering around saying:

'Number three.' Or: 'I had twelve, and now it's nine, because five has a broken leg, and eleven got shot, and seven says he doesn't want to outrage her.'

The skeleton had lifted the lower part of his mask and folded it back over his nose. He was trotting along beside Careto, who with some others was pacing the shore on the more accessible side, in case Lefty should try to swim to safety. Careto was preparing the people.

'Lefty killed her.'

This infuriated Darío again.

'That's a lie!'

'He's bumped her off, and I heard the shots. Lefty fed on dogs' hearts, and he's capable of that and much more.'

The convicts were gathering around. Touchy Johnny asked in a tone of polite and discreet curiosity:

'Did Congo kick off too?'

The Twin joined them and said that Congo had only fainted, and it was the Lawyer who had kicked off. Bocachula wailed:

'Ay! I was afraid of it! I knew it!'

She explained that just a minute ago a big black butterfly, with a skull painted on its wings, had brushed her face as it passed.

Careto yelled at the teacher—they were all yelling because it was hard to hear over the noise of the fire—reminding him that it was inside that ring that he had danced on Trinidad's grave, but in the same place the girl would probably be turned to ashes. As he had just finished saying that Lefty had murdered her when she left headquarters, Darío was sure that she was still alive. She was alive and inside the ring of fire.

The flames were thick between the trees. The branches crackled. The sap evaporated in them, and the trunks split open with a crash. Darío tried to see through the wall of fire but could not. It was more than fifteen yards deep. To try to cross it would be suicide. Like the rest, all he could do was to go along the length of the ring, which terminated at both ends in the rocky cliff over the sea. 'Is she going to die here? Is it possible that fate brought her to me only to end in this torture, with a ring of fire around her and another of madness beyond the flames? Can everything in life be so senseless? All reduced to a game played by monkeys crazy with hunger? Hunger for bread, or sex, or power?'

Careto came up and shouted with jovial sarcasm:

'Don't be impatient; you'll find the girl all right.'

'Where?'

'Where all roads meet.'

Oh, in death! Darío regretted having spoken to him. 'Everywhere I turn I am baulked,' he thought. 'So why is it given to me to perceive all this? To be more unhappy? And why have I the capacity for dreams? As an escape? Only to be able to escape from the filth and enormity of the real? And the thirst for purity? Just so I can laugh at it and at myself? And moral stature? So I can pity myself in my laughter?'

Gimpy had the girl's nightgown under his shirt.

'Look at it. The poor grass comes right out of the ground with the heat.'

He avoided talking because when he talked he could hardly keep from crying. Darío went on: 'What good does my love do me? What good does it do her? I know that God speaks to me through this feeling and that in it my naked foot touches the eternal, but between my dream and reality there are tongues of fire stronger than I am, clouds of smoke that can choke us, wickedness, infamy, lack of understanding, the misfortunes of others, their madness, their animal apathy. Everything is against me. Perhaps the only reason they're not trying to kill me now is because for the moment they have something more dramatic to think about.' He thought of all this mechanically, while his eyes tried to penetrate the flames and his ears the roar of the fire and his feet searched for a path. A path. The only one left was the one to 'where all roads meet'.

Careto, sure that Lefty was done for, gathered the people around him.

'The fire is cleaning the island of the passions of woman and man. I am above these passions. And above the fire. I am higher, higher.'

Gimpy came up. He felt neither anger nor grief but a sort of gentle dizziness which, however, did not throw him to the ground, but allowed him to remain on his feet.

'Higher, higher. What do you want to be higher for?'

He spoke calmly to Careto but seemed to spit on him with every word.

'Yes,' Careto went on, 'I am above the fire, and the sea, and man and woman.'

Gimpy twisted his mouth. Sweating and lit up by the fire, he looked like an alabaster devil.

Spitball asked him:

'Have you got a number?'

Gimpy didn't understand. He thought he was saying something about the fire because he had jerked his head in that direction. Holding back his tears, he said:

'God will see this fire from on high. And if He doesn't see it He's blind. And if He's blind——'

He clenched his fists and wept. Spitball, paying no attention, unslung his accordion and struck up the bridal conga, which he played a little better now. Bocachula arrived.

'They will all die,' she said, imitating Careto.

Darío looked everywhere, wondering: 'Where is Squinty?'

274

They told him he had gone to headquarters to get instructions from Sixfingers. Instantly Careto raised himself to his full height, shaking like an epileptic.

'Only the man who is above the passions of man and woman can avenge the infamy of the man who ate dogs' hearts, who ate dogs' hearts and followed the sinister call.'

A stone whizzed by his head. Gimpy had thrown it and was standing in the shadows with more stones in his hands. Careto took it as a warning and changed his tune. The branches crackled. Not far away a great tree fell in flames. Darío was still pacing the edge of the ring. He had heard Careto. 'Could the call of the ideal be a sinister call? Could it call us only to devour us, as the fire is devouring the insects?'

Just then the Indians from the south settlement arrived, each with a basketful of earth and a shovel over his shoulder. They had taken them from the road job. They went close to the fire and began shovelling soil on to its rim. This, of course, went unnoticed in the conflagration, but Darío ran to them and led them all to one place, where he had noticed that the fire made a narrower swath and where there were a few openings in the arch of burning gold overhead. There were less embers on the ground there, and the heat of the burning branches was not so intense. But even so it was impossible to get through. They would have to wait until the high branches had burned out. And meanwhile the fire was surging ahead in other places.

'The drums of the clouds will bring the water.'

Who said that? Oh, the old chief. Darío looked at the sky, but the rain was still far away. The old man, who was looking up, too, said:

'Someone saw the sun. The sun came down and is walking among men. That means that the rain will begin.'

Darío watched the flames devouring everything in their path and sweeping on. If the rain held off for two hours it would be too late. And it would have rained by now if it was going to before dawn. Darío told them all to keep shovelling in the same place. More than a hundred Indians were there, passing their baskets along in a line. Others were wielding the shovels to fill them again. The work went on steadily. The high boughs were burned out now, and as the blaze died down they were able to go farther in. Darío looked at the convicts who were gathered around Careto with no interest in the Indians' work; he was about to go toward them when he saw them break up and run toward the sea. Lefty was coming. He was swimming.

He came out of the water, his wet clothes clinging to his body. Careto advanced at the head of the convicts. Lefty was busy wringing out his clothes and taking four thousand-peso notes out of his mouth; before he had a chance to speak Careto grabbed a knife from the man nearest him and stabbed him in the belly. Lefty doubled up and fell face down. The bills slipped from his fingers. In the glow of the fire the convicts saw what they were and snatched them up. Someone turned Lefty over.

'I swear, I swear . . .' His voice faltered.

'What do you swear?'

'I didn't touch her.'

'He killed her!' Careto shouted. 'He killed her! He killed her and he dies! It's the old law!'

Darío came up at a run. None too confident, Careto, knife in hand, repeated: 'He killed her! Killed and dies.' He said it almost as if seeking Darío's approval. Lefty tried to make himself heard, but only Darío heard him. 'I didn't kill her. She's alive. She's in there, but she will die. She will die too. All will die.' He asked them to send the money they had taken from him, and the rest that Careto owed him, to his mother.

'The knife went in just right,' said Spitball, looking at the wound with the eyes of an expert.

The Indians, impassive, went on with their job. Darío, on hearing that the girl was alive, went back to his post with burning zeal. He went to the head of the file, next to the fire.

The Indians handed the baskets along in a steady rhythm.

Darío, at the end of the line, threw the earth into the blaze ahead. The Indians sang, monotonously repeating the phrase the old chief gave them:

'The scorpion of fire!'

'. . . of fire.'

'The turtle of fire!'

'. . . of fire.'

'The alligator of fire!'

'. . . of fire.'

'The swallow of fire!'

'. . . of fire.'

'The butterfly of fire!'

'. . . of fire.'

'God calls them. The Holy Virgin calls them. Let them go to the cliff without touching the girl. Let them go; let them go!'

'. . . let them go.'

'The gelded wolf of the twilight has turned them loose. All of them. The scorpion of fire!'

'. . . of fire.'

Lying on the ground, Lefty was making an effort to talk. He told the whole story. When he mentioned the sum Careto owed him—another four thousand—every one was dumbfounded. Careto, finding himself exposed, backed away with the knife in his hand. Lefty told everything. That Careto had money, that he wanted to kill the girl. But Careto was drawing the crowd, too, shouting:

'I have more. I have a fortune! Kneel down, sons of the wolf, kneel down!'

The Indians didn't hear him. They had no interest in anything that happened on that side.

'The gelded wolf of the twilight willed it, and the alligator of fire lies in our path. But they will all go away. The moth of fire!'

'. . . of fire.'

'The rat of fire!'

'. . . of fire.'

'The owl of fire!'

'. . . of fire.'

The Indians kept passing the baskets to Darío, and he threw the earth in. They were all sweating. The fire and their own feverish activity cut them off from the convicts.

Lefty died. The convicts searched his pockets. The ones who had failed to get anything, did not want to give up and kept looking, ripping the seams of his trousers and shirt and finally leaving him stripped. Then they all went after Careto, knocked him down, tore off his clothes, and searched through all the seams and creases. His entire fortune was dragged out; Ruana fled, writhing away in great loops. Afterwards the ones who were still without loot ran to Careto's hut, dug up the ground, and demolished in a second the walls of mud and branches. Then they went back to the fire. Lefty's corpse, near the flames, had the vague, luminous pallor of dead men in the dark. Careto, naked, too, fled inland. The convicts followed like frenzied monkeys, destroyed his clothes, ripped the seams, felt over every fold again and again. They looked at dead Lefty, and thought: 'It's true. He laid hands on her and he's kicked off.' Some, in their delight at having two or three thousand pesos in their pockets, went over toward the Indians. Spitball had been lucky, and now he was playing *Shoot, Pepe!* Gimpy, all eyes and silence, stood watching.

Darío went on working and sweating. The old chief said to him, looking at the sky:

'We spent all day yesterday making rain.'

But Darío, like the Indian, had little hope that it would rain in time. And the scorpion of fire darted here and there, and the turkey of fire fluttered, shedding his feathers everywhere. And the Indians implored the alligator of fire, the butterfly of fire, the turkey of fire, to go away. Finally the old man said:

'The gelded wolf of the twilight brought you, but the great Lord of the Dawn orders you to leave.'

Darío worked frantically, and without realising it he

278

thought: 'The wolf of the twilight is Careto. It must be Careto.' And in that case was he the Lord of the Dawn? It was an odd notion, in which he felt a certain glorious assurance. He went on taking the baskets and heaving the dirt. The wind was sweeping the fire toward the sea, not all along, but at the two flanks.

At the place where they were working the burning stretch didn't widen, and Darío, when they least expected it, darted through the breach and disappeared in clouds of ruddy smoke. The Indians raised their heads, pausing, but in a moment they were working again as if nothing had happened. Spitball said in great excitement:

'He dived right into the blaze.'

Darío passed through the fire; he was enveloped in smoke, but the heat was less intense there, and he could see enough by the light of the flames to keep from stumbling over fallen trees. He ran straight toward the sea, sure that the girl would have gone as far from the fire as possible. He went on, still holding his breath. But even at that distance from the fire the smoke was dark and opaque and he could see nothing; anyway, his eyes smarted painfully if he opened them. He remembered that as he plunged into the flames he had heard a familiar voice—Congo's—far away, saying, almost screaming:

'Ay, God, all over her little body she has skin like on her thighs!'

He reached the shore and took a deep breath. He shouted in one direction after another, but there was no answer. In the silence the crackle of the fire came closer. Black birds fled toward the sea. He shouted again; no answer. He tried to run to another section but stumbled into thick clouds that rolled up in his path. 'All right, but must I die alone?' He was caught by animal terror. 'I alone? The great Lord of the Dawn alone?' He shouted again and heard a voice: 'Help!' Darío ran that way but saw no one.

'Where? Where?' he kept calling.

Coughing and reeling, he went on searching for the voice.

And he found Niña Lucha. She was huddled beneath an over-hanging rock surrounded by vegetation. She was motionless. He saw her there beside him, and she did not move or speak.

'Niña Lucha!'

'Who is it?'

'Me.'

'Who?'

'Darío.'

'Why didn't you say so before?'

'Come out of there.'

'Why?'

'Any minute all this'—he pointed at the trees around them —'will be on fire. You, too, will be burned alive.'

The girl lifted her eyes now, and Darío saw that her expression was of indifference.

'Didn't you hear me shouting before?'

'Yes.'

But she was afraid of everything and was resigned to dying. Darío's presence had not made much impression on her. The smoke was again clinging to the ground and shrouded them. Darío coughed and said:

'Come on.'

'Where?' she asked in terror.

'Come on.'

Darío seemed to be heading straight for the fire.

'No.'

'In a few minutes we won't be able to get out.'

She resisted as she had at headquarters. Darío took her hand. 'I'm not Sixfingers,' he said, 'nor the Twin. Come on!' But she still held back. She stood up, looking all around in horror.

'Lefty,' she managed to say, 'went that way.'

She pointed to the sea. There was a twenty-yard drop from the rocks to the sea.

'Can you jump it?'

She drew back in fright and said something absolutely stupid: Trinidad hadn't allowed her to swim when they were engaged, and she had never really learned. Darío muttered: 'Trinidad! Trinidad!' He pulled her along by the hand, groping his way inland. The smoke thickened, and the breath of the furnace grew more violent as they went on. Darío was gripping her hand, but that was not firm enough, so he took her by the wrist. She resisted.

'No, I won't go in there.'

'Come on, don't be an idiot!'

After he had said this Darío noticed that her whole body followed along almost without compulsion.

'Breathe as little as possible and don't look at anything but the ground where you put your feet.'

They reached the area of the fire. The wind had slackened, and the smoke rose to the sky through the burning branches.

She began to resist again. 'We'll both die on account of your idiocy. Follow me.'

He seemed to be going straight into the flames. He had found the place where the Indians were throwing the earth. She was appalled at the thought of going in there; perhaps Darío wanted to kill her. She stopped; she pulled back with all her strength, but Darío managed to drag her along. The girl protested; she screamed; finally she bit his hand so it bled. He let out a sound of pain and she let go. But she was thinking: 'Oh, I never would have dreamed that it would be Darío who would kill me.'

'Quick!' he cried. 'Faster!'

They walked on the coals and when they reached the earth that the Indians were flinging down they were wrapped in flames. Darío, one hand over his eyes, kept pulling the girl after him. His shoes were on fire. She coughed and screamed. They reached the other side with only their hair and clothing singed and a strange fever in their heads. And there was the whole crowd, waiting for them. Number three came up eagerly.

'Señora . . . Señorita . . . '

Gimpy tripped him up, and he sprawled like a frog. 'Oh!' she said, wanting to help him. But Darío took her by the waist and màde her walk on as if they were still in the fire.

The girl did not know what she was doing. She still resisted, turning her head to look at the burning forest; she seemed half unconscious.

'How many nights without sleep?' Darío asked.

'I don't know.'

But her voice was hoarse with sleep, with a troubled sleep. Darío himself was in a semi-conscious state. 'I am the Great Lord of the Dawn.' He thought of it with delight and seemed to see all his ideas turn lucid and orderly in that phrase. He heard the Indians in the distance going away, singing something about the scorpion of fire and the gelded wolf of the twilight. Darío felt now that there were no more obstacles before him. Everything he had longed for on the island would happen; it was inevitable.

They reached headquarters, Darío still holding her, still pulling her by the arm. Fifteen or twenty convicts were gathered around the guardroom door, through which they were trying to shove Careto, stark naked. Squinty was in Sixfingers' room. Seeing Darío, he half drew his revolver. Darío looked at him undaunted, while Sixfingers pulled himself up, saying:

'None of that, Squinty.'

'But who's the chief here? If I can't pay off the fellow who insulted my mother, who's the chief here?'

'I tell you to lay off!' Sixfingers cried menacingly.

He had asked who was chief, and Sixfingers had not replied! Below, everyone was talking about the girl and Darío's heroism. They had never before seen a man cross fifteen yards of fire and come out alive.

Careto howled at the peephole of the cell:

'Sons of the wolf, kneel down!'

The doctor arrived with his grand airs and mincing steps.

Whiskers followed him. Seeing Careto, the doctor thought: 'The distinguishing mark of the gentleman. Knowing how to drink. His indecencies shame us all. He is the worst of my contemporaries.'

Careto pressed his face against the grille.

'Kneel and learn to adore the Great Gelding. He who leads the violent. He who sheds the blood of the violent male.'

'It's hard to believe,' the doctor murmured, going into headquarters. 'An intelligent man like you!'

Whiskers followed him, and the doctor no longer felt humiliated by his company. Darío watched Congo being brought along on a stretcher and felt dazed. 'More dead? Still more dead?' He asked for the doctor. Mother Leonor was looking for the prayer book.

Darío went down and spoke to the armed men:

'Two of you stay and guard Careto; the rest go and put out the fire.' As soon as he had gone in, a racket broke out. Every one was trying to explain the teacher's presence and, even more, his authority. Darío was startled at not finding the girl upstairs and went to look for Mother Leonor. She stared at him in stony silence. Her cold, inquisitive look troubled him. The old woman, hands crossed over her stomach, had a strength of her own which had nothing to do with risks and heroism. Before he had asked she said:

'I took her to my room to sleep.'

'Is she already in bed?' he said, making a move in that direction.

'It's no use. She doesn't want to see anybody. Least of all you.'

'Me?' he asked in astonishment.

'It's only natural.'

Darío thought: 'The old woman hasn't changed.' He didn't want to bother the girl. Mother Leonor repeated smugly:

'It's only natural.'

Gimpy appeared.

'Careto is down there in the jail.'

Careto, the gelded wolf of the twilight! Gimpy was happy, but one thing was still upsetting him.

'Out there'—and he gestured toward the fire that was casting a glow on the clouds—'hundreds of innocent little animals are burning up.'

Darío didn't answer.

'I know every single one on the island. Two *cachichinqui* fell in the fire, a male and a female. They're called that because they like to suck air. They suck it and suck it like a caramel, and they have a very ugly, stupid way of singing.'

Darío still said nothing, and Gimpy, thinking he had guessed his thoughts, said:

'I'll take charge of that if you want.'

Darío seemed to be coming out of a dream.

'Of what?'

'Finishing off Sixfingers.'

XI

OUTSIDE, THE STORM GATHERED NOISE-
lessly, with purple flashes in the distance. The rain began,
beating furiously against the window-panes. A dim vapour
seeped from the ground and from the trees. Black smoke rose
in the sky from the woods, the wind and the rain brought it
in wads over headquarters. Smelling the smoke, one still
seemed to hear:

'The scorpion of fire!'

'. . . fire.'

Gimpy scratched his head. His marijuana crop would be
ruined. It was going to be a real downpour. Gimpy knew a lot
about rain, and he could see that this was going to last all
night. And Lefty, by the sea, lay naked to the rain. Darío had
given orders for him to be brought back, but he was still there.

In the south settlement they were welcoming the water
joyfully. They had made little furrows to hold it and were
waiting for the heart of the storm. The water ran in reddish
rivulets over the hummocks, crossed the paths, and formed
great puddles, with luminous bubbles floating on the surface.
The sea seemed covered with a light green mist. Rat-Eyes, his
hands resting on a staff, swayed lightly, rising and falling back
on his heels.

> Take it all
> to the bottom of the sea,
> the gold, the saffron,
> and the marijuana.

The waters tore away dry leaves and chunks of clay.

'There will be more,' said Rat-Eyes.

A reddish mist hung above the storm. When the Indians

saw it was going to last all night, they retired to their huts.

But some stayed, many of them boys, glad of the mist and the waters. The branches of the trees were dripping, and the sky was still overcast. A grey sky was so rare there it made everything look new.

'I saw him. He had on black trousers. He has skin like corn and black trousers.'

'He sat down beside the storm.'

They meant the sun.

'And the turkey of fire is dead.'

The children amused themselves throwing stones and mud pies.

'I saw him.'

They pointed to a dark object, like a branch, which came floating down. It was a human body.

'Rusty-Pants!'

They looked at the body that floated slowly down and was now almost opposite them. They could see the face. Floating down to the sea he seemed to be saying, as always: *I'm going to my people*. The children forgot the sun. Even the one who *saw him*. And the turkey of fire.

The children shouted. One said to the Indians:

'Why don't we get him out?'

The Indians looked for a rope. They found one and went downstream. The body floated toward the other shore and caught in a small cove. They made a noose.

'It will be hard,' one said, calculating the distance, 'to throw the noose as far as that.'

A little boy suggested tying a stone to the end of the rope and throwing it over the body. The Indians threw the stone several times without success. Finally it struck Rusty-Pants' chest with a hollow thump and rolled off on the other side. The body, all by itself, came down and drifted toward the shore. When it was nearer they saw that it was just as they had seen it the last time, naked from the waist down.

They managed to pull it out. The boy, his hair plastered

with mud, stared indifferently at the clouds. Far off, over the sea, rumbled the last of the thunder.

'If we leave him here the buzzards will come.'

They looked for a hollow place. They found a little ditch, quite narrow, which could be covered with branches and stones. They went back for the body, picked it up by the shoulders and feet, and carried it there. Being able to bury it made them feel as if they had carried out a full ceremony.

The children took their eyes off it only when Rat-Eyes came along dancing:

The gold, the saffron,
and the marijuana.

The next day the island, the salty moisture from the sea intensified by the moisture of the rain, had a barbaric perfume. But the sun was still hidden behind bright clouds. Gimpy wandered in and out of headquarters, stepping over the bodies of some Indians who had spent the night in the hall. A lot more were squatting on the outer stairs. Careto was still naked in the cell.

Sixfingers, with his wound, was glad to be in bed. Mother Leonor changed his bandages.

The wounds had depressed him, and the depression abated his venom. He insulted the teacher, but without closing his human eye, and they were the same insults that marked his bursts of friendliness.

Darío had risen before sunrise. He wanted to feel the dawn, go out to meet it, welcome it. The Great Lord of the Dawn felt his blood fresh in his veins, and his feelings, which had not changed, were also new. In the first jumbled streaks of light he thought: 'Our joy is the joy of gods, our grief the grief of gods; our dreams are God's own. And yet we are doomed to live like swine.' He didn't try to explain it. He looked around and filled his lungs with the early morning air. He would have liked to be one of those little animals Gimpy had talked about, which sucked and sucked air like a caramel.

Niña Lucha was still asleep. Again Darío felt the air, purified by the storm, caressing his blood. While he was dressing he had made sure that his pistol was fully loaded. 'Will I have to go on using it?' In any case, violence was easy. When it was a way to a higher harmony it was natural and unimportant. 'But the others think they are after the same thing,' he thought. 'Actually, it seems there is no alternative but to shed others' blood or let them shed ours. And if we don't want to do either we have to give up living among men.' From the balcony he saw little shadows fluttering hesitantly at the edge of the woods. Darío wanted to prepare the girl's departure without consulting anybody, as if it were the natural outcome of what had happened the day before. When Mother Leonor told him that she was up he went to her room. He felt strong in that clean air beneath the cloudy sky, in the half-light of the lingering dawn. He felt so full of confidence, he didn't think about anything but simply gave himself up to the delight of the moment. And his senses dilated to unexpected depths and dimensions. His senses were reaching to the absolute; for them, too, there is an absolute.

He had not smoked since the night before, and when he went more than eight hours without smoking he would begin to recapture the sensations of his early youth, of the period before he started smoking. He went on without smoking, tasting the air like spring water. And his nerves, reconstructing the sensations he had known at fifteen, reawakened also his earliest ideal that was still there, sleeping within him. He knocked at the door and went in. The girl in her new day was as fragrant as the island.

'Am I disturbing you?'

He answered himself in silence: 'I must leave this room. I can't stay here. Your image is beating at my forehead.' But aloud he said:

'Get ready; we're going to the mainland.'

The girl remarked that she didn't know the schedule of the planes or buses or the train. She had no money for the trip.

288

And she wouldn't know what to do on the mainland. It seemed that she had no interest in leaving, and this idea baffled Darío.

'Just like the night of the celebration in the woods, just like yesterday in the midst of the flames.' She didn't want to go to *any other place*. It was always better where she was than where she was going to be.

'Ah!' he exclaimed in a way that seemed to her terribly grown up.

Looking at the girl's mouth, Darío felt a hunger as of early adolescence. She noticed it, and then suddenly both became aware that their feelings were known to the other. The silence was excruciating.

'It rained all night. Did it put out the fire in the woods?'

The smoke was still drifting over headquarters. The teacher was back at the age of fifteen, before he started smoking, and he felt himself floating without weight. The sea breeze, drowsy with a seaweed smell now that the night's madness was over, entered through all his pores. He stood silent at the window with his back to Niña Lucha. Her eyes were measuring his shoulders. Darío, back at the age before he started smoking, felt exactly as he had one day when he went with some other boys to see a palace lost in the middle of a distant valley. The light was the same as now. The stones were gilded by the years, and around the building was an immense park. There was the same cloudy sky, and it must have rained shortly before. Darío went into the park. The grandeur of the landscape was not that of the wild forests, and yet somehow it was.

He came to a dark place with a tunnel opening between the trees, which met above and kept the light from falling through. It was a wide avenue, strewn with yellow sand, and it extended a long way. That heavy darkness, in full daylight and in untamed surroundings, spoke to him in a strange language. At regular intervals along both sides were little iron posts with crossbeams and parrots perched on them, chained by the foot, and with a little feeding-trough in front of them. The parrots, like the trees, extended on both sides into the infinite. It seemed the owner of the palace was a Spaniard, crazed by the tasteless riches of the Indies, and he had built a sort of zoological garden. A park for its own sake. And Darío remembered walking slowly, very slowly, down the avenue, feeling the shining sand crunch under his feet. Ahead of him a parrot screamed. Another seemed to be answering, and that echo, under the arch of the trees, in the dim light, created an atmosphere as of an ancient temple. Darío, his mind empty, listened to the parrots' racket, in which there were occasional words:

'Marrrrrrrrrrrvelllllous!'

Or inexpressive cries:

'Enarkeeay!'

'Flicnto, filanto kaneya,' said another.

And now it was just the same: his youth, his blood, pure as the air, and the intoxication of the ideal standing there behind him. Niña Lucha spoke:

'When are we going?'

It startled him; he had said nothing so definite about it. Before he could answer she asked, quite determined now:

'What time will we get there?'

Darío still had his back to her, hearing the parrots along the avenue.

'Oclavinto gaya!'

'Scroopslee!'

'No, no, no!' cried one farther away, as if he were being murdered.

Darío turned around slowly.

'I won't be able to go to the capital with you.'

He still heard the *no* of the parrot that was being murdered, and the girl's expression was appropriate to its anguish. Darío looked at her and said:

'I can't go all the way to the capital. I will leave you in the motor-coach or the plane.'

The girl heard only *I will leave you*. The idea of his leaving her and his air of formality disheartened her. Darío noticed it and thought: 'What can I do?'

'Orlavinto gaya!' screamed the parrot.

The ahuehuete trees met overhead, their soft, spongy foliage muffling the parrot's cries, which sounded strangely toneless.

'Barbari-landa!'

Remembering it, Darío thought: 'Millions and millions of parrots, screaming syllables for millions of centuries, would finally hit on what I should say to her now. One of them would say it. And so to speak to her and say the right thing can only be a miracle.'

'Ekanillarible marrrrrrrvelous!'

Love was a mystery, and Darío thought again: 'One of those parrots would finally say it.' All the efforts of thousands of millions of parrots, of jungles, and of centuries were needed to save him at that moment.

The sand on the old avenue, damp with rain, and the green drops still dripping from the ahuehuete trees enfolded him. But if he went on like this he would turn to stone, or glass, or smoke. And she was the ideal. And he must speak to her.

'You must start right away,' said Darío.

'All right, but you don't have to come.'

She spoke so forcefully that Darío weakened. He drew closer, full of tenderness, and tried to explain, but she, feeling that she had given herself away, burst into tears. Her breast heaved, and her throat, and when Darío caressed her head and put his arm around her shoulders she sobbed more violently. Darío was radiant, but back there when he was fifteen, before he started smoking, the parrot was still shrieking:

'Anateya shoo alikely rakateeeeeeeeha!'

The parrot perched first on one claw and then the other, with a deep and meditative look. Darío remembered this, and the memory seemed fitting as a rite of dawn, a part of the new ritual of dawn in which he was officiating. He realised that someone was winding up a speech on the steps outside. Now he was hearing the mouthings, incongruous from a distance, of an orator. He suspected that they were in danger again. A mutiny, perhaps. The speaker was Sixfingers. They went to a window on to the hall, from where they could see the main entrance. The square was full of people. Sixfingers had one arm in a sling and was limping. Off to one side someone called out in a weak, malarial voice:

'We're with you there, chief!'

'Then why don't you applaud?'

There was scattered applause here and there. Sixfingers seemed satisfied.

'We have gathered to say farewell to Niña Lucha. Now that she is going away, let us be no less gracious than when she came. This time there is nobody to stop us. But I tell you that the girl and the honoured teacher who is going to escort her haven't the means to get to the capital. Anyone who has anything and wants to show his goodwill——'

Sixfingers was interrupted by a tumultuous outcry in which now and then a phrase was distinguishable. '. . . then . . . respectable place . . . *coming from where she comes from . . .*'

Sixfingers could think of nothing more to say, so he raised his voice and shouted:

'And then every one back to his work!'

Darío went down, leading the girl gently by the hand.

Congo, wounded, muttered to himself: 'All over, skin like her thighs.' Careto was howling through the peephole, but nobody listened. Nor were they surprised to hear him.

A sinister figure appeared. No one would have known who it was if he hadn't sung out his name:

> *'Gentlemen, I'm Spitball*
> *and I'm going to do the rumba,*
> *going to do the rumba.'*

Over his face he wore the skin of Trinidad's head, put on

like a glove. The thing was almost unrecognisable, but it made
the Indians laugh and the whites shudder.

> *'I'm going to do the rumba,*
> *going to do the rumba.'*

The girl looked at Spitball indifferently. He went on
dancing. She thought he had on a peculiar disguise of some
kind.

Sixfingers did not want to disturb the peace by kicking
Spitball, who was doing a very vulgar dance, and pretended
not to see him. Darío and the girl started for the harbour
without further ceremony. Careto howled from behind the
bars:

'The wolf is no more! No more!'

But the sentry gave him a punch in the nose. Darío was
afraid something might still happen to stand in their way. Two
Indians came up to give them fruit. Various convicts, Bocachula, the Lawyer, Congo, shoved their way through to the
girl and put something in her hand. Bocachula said to her:

'You use it; it's better for you to use it.'

And the two others, almost in the same breath:

'Send us a post card with your signature.'

The Lawyer added:

'Address me as *Dear. Dear friend,* I mean.'

The girl was surprised to see that they were giving her
money. Thousand-peso bills. Convicts came from all directions with more money. Among them was the Twin.

'And may you find your honourable family in the best of
health.'

His smile was still terrible. Another also put money in her
hand.

'A slight token of esteem. And pleasant memories when
you spend it.'

The Slicker reached out his hand to the girl with a bill.
Congo tried to intercept it, but the Slicker hung on, giving
him a threatening look.

'I'm the one who's giving it. Me, myself. You're just trying to steal my glory.'

When they had given her the money they all began to say in a loud voice, but as if they were only talking for their own benefit, what they would have done with the money. It pleased them to think they were giving the girl something more than a little piece of paper printed with pretty colours. The smoke from the woods, which were still burning, drifted out toward the sea. The Slicker reached out his hand again, but there were too many people between him and the girl. The woman from Puebla gave him a slap on the arm and said to the girl:

'Don't take it from him.'

She went on to explain without being asked:

'He killed his mother, and a criminal who kills his mother brings mourning.'

'It wasn't me; it was my father.'

'It was you.'

'But my father told me to. My mother forgave me.'

'You're a liar.'

'She forgave me. The blood spilled on my chest, and I repented and tried to help her, but she said, *Be careful, you have on your new suit; you're getting spots on it.* That's what she said to me.'

The woman from Puebla interrupted and shoved him back. The Slicker's father, his jaw trembling with anger, came up to him.

'Shut up, scorpion! That's all you know: compromising your father in front of gentlemen.'

The two bar keepers looked around in amazement; they could not understand where all that money came from and, much less, why it was being given to the girl. It was a frightful calamity for them to have the money leave the island.

'The Virgin help you!'

Congo, though wounded in the shoulder, uncovered the scars of his ears and showed them to the girl.

'Look, Niña. That's why I'm always wrapped up.'

Did he want her to see that so she would not be able to forget him?

The girl looked at him without blinking, and he went away content. The girl tried to refuse other gifts. Could the money really be legitimate? And if so, why, in their wretchedness, out of the depths of their misery, were they giving it to her? Every one around was looking at her and smiling proudly. Darío did not know what to make of it. And more were coming.

They could hardly make their way toward the sea. Mother Leonor showed up. The girl was in a daze. Darío pushed her forward to avoid the old woman. Spitball, still dancing, was trying to get close to the girl. When they were already at the harbour he managed to get through and, taking her hand, he said:

'Look at my face, Niña Lucha.'

The girl had noticed in his hair and moustache a certain resemblance to Trinidad. The reminder of the dead man was terribly untimely and struck the girl as a kind of shameful accusation. The hair growing up from the narrow forehead was really like Trinidad's. She walked on toward the dock. Tortola came up and gave them fifty pesos. He was still harping on the old theme:

'Lady, nobody can refuse you anything, and, besides, the Eminencias woman has leprosy.'

Darío promised to speak to the girl about the concession of food supplies, and Tortola retired with new hope. Before jumping into the launch the girl turned toward the crowd and waved her hand. Gimpy hadn't dared to come closer, because they were all giving her something and he had nothing to give. And because she was going with Darío. But it bothered him that he had not told her everything. He wanted to tell her how he became lame, which was very awkward and would cost him a great sacrifice. And now that he saw the girl again as he had seen her in the beginning,

pure as the stars—no one dared to remember Lefty's slanders
—he would have liked to make that sacrifice. But he hadn't
the courage. Spitball, waggling his hips, danced on ahead,
repeating the stanza that had cost his brother his life. The
Twin laid a hand on his shoulder.

'Go on, dance. Trinidad can't shoot you now.'

> 'No, I'm not Spitball—
> I'm Trinidad,
> No, I'm not Spitball—
> I'm the chief himself,
> and I'm going to do the rumba,
> going to do the rumba.'

His eyes looked out through the empty ones of his disguise.
The girl was horrified. The cripple tried to come nearer, but
he could not get through the mob. He gave up and drew
away with the crumpled silk in his bosom. The launch
shoved off, and the guards fired a salvo in the air. The girl
and the teacher saw the engineer tremble at the sound of
the volley.

'Don't be afraid,' said the girl. 'God has touched their
hearts.'

The engineer shrugged his shoulders.

'Not even God can help those people.'

They counted the money. Darío's pockets were full, and
so were the girl's hands. Ninety-two thousand pesos. Darío
turned them over and rubbed them between his fingers. He
shrugged his shoulders. The girl gave him her share to keep,
with the same bewilderment. They remained pensive and
silent.

They had left all their baggage on the island. Darío thought
of the king spider and the boys; the girl of the camera. Neither
had any sensation of having been in danger. And both had
several times been on the point of being murdered. But
together in the launch, their backs to the island, the girl was
thinking: 'I know about life. I know there are monsters, and

296

life consists, first of all, in being able to save ourselves from them.' Darío said nothing, but, thinking of what he would say to her later, he couldn't help laughing at himself. 'Señorita, I love you.' And he laughed again. She asked him what he was laughing at, and without answering her he looked at her and put his hand over hers on the seat.

'She is the great lady of the dawn, too.' And both of them being that, everything seemed wonderfully in place. He felt himself again, or rather for the first time, on a plane of true human dignity. A sad dignity. 'The only dignity permitted us is that of having squarely faced a truth. A truth that is unworthy of us.' He shrugged his shoulders. What had happened had been, after all, a truth. And truth and beauty were a magical combination. He looked at the girl. And she looked at him, too, smiling.

They had gone less than halfway when they saw another ship appearing over the waves under a cloud of thick smoke. Leaden grey on the light grey of the sea, beneath the dense grey of the smoke.

'That's the gunboat *Liberty*,' the engineer said.

They could already make out the gun in the bow. The boat pitched on the waves and was bearing directly toward the island.

'They're going to spray them with lead,' said the engineer approvingly.

After a pause he added:

'The whole mob is at the harbour, and the officers won't like the look of it. Maybe they'll begin to shoot right away.'

The breeze was blowing off the island, over the damp woods, the burning trees, the little golden beaches. They didn't hear the engineer. Darío wrinkled up his nose a little to tell the girl that the sea smelled good, and it was true that the smell was strong and sweet.

The gunboat came closer. The engineer observed again with satisfaction:

'They'll get what's coming to them.' The girl looked at the grey bulk of the ship and then at the metal glint of the waves. The teacher was surprised and upset.

'They can't do that,' he said in confusion.

Darío struggled with himself. The wind still brought them the aroma of the island.

'What?' the girl said.

'Perhaps we should go back and do something for those people.'

The girl agreed, perhaps to obey Darío, or perhaps because of the idea itself.

'Yes,' Darío said. 'Let's go back. If someone doesn't help them they're lost.'

She remembered the six fingers on the sweating hand, the Indians lying face down on the ground, Trinidad's ghost, the fire in the woods, Lefty dead, herself running away. Always running away. But she remembered, too, the corn under her eyes, the stars reflected on her naked skin beside the sea, Gimpy in love, and Voice of the River of Stars. Even Spitball, dancing and dancing with a weird mask. And in all this, life peopled by monsters, but with a little path between the monsters. For everybody, no matter whom, some little path.

Perhaps life is like that. She looked at Darío. His nostrils were quivering.

'Faster,' he said.

The engineer opened the throttle. Darío directed him:

'Pull in to the landing on the right.'

The teacher took the girl's arm. She was smiling, but when they stepped on to the dock her lips were solemn again. *The dignity of a married woman.*

The gunboat had not yet entered the bay. The crowd again hailed the girl and the teacher. Sixfingers came forward to meet them, perplexed. Darío, taking his arm, said:

'The sanitary commission reported you, but it doesn't matter. Every one to his job. Every one keep out of sight.'

'We're lost,' the Twin exclaimed.

'No, you're not. We'll see what happens.'

Each went his own way. Gimpy approached the girl very timidly, his whole being aglow from the surprise. She saw on the ground something like a strip of rubber from a punctured balloon with eyebrows and hair. She spread it out with the toe of her shoe. It looked like a human face.

'What is it?'